THE BLINDED MAN

Arne Dahl is an award-winning Swedish crime novelist and literary critic. *The Blinded Man* is the first book in the internationally acclaimed Intercrime series. The second book in the series, *Bad Blood*, will follow in Harvill Secker in 2013.

Tiina Nunnally has translated more than fifty books from Swedish, Danish and Norwegian.

ARNE DAHL

The Blinded Man

TRANSLATED FROM THE SWEDISH BY
Tiina Nunnally

VINTAGE BOOKS
London

Published by Vintage 2012

2 4 6 8 10 9 7 5 3 1

First published with the title *Misterioso* in 1999
by Albert Bonniers Förlag

First published in the United States in 2011 by Pantheon

First published in Great Britain in 2012 by
Vintage
Random House, 20 Vauxhall Bridge Road,
London SW1V 2SA

www.vintage-books.co.uk

Addresses for companies within The Random House Group Limited
can be found at: www.randomhouse.co.uk/offices.htm

The Random House Group Limited Reg. No. 954009

A CIP catalogue record for this book
is available from the British Library

The Random House Group Limited supports The Forest Stewardship
Council (FSC®), the leading international forest certification
organisation. Our books carrying the FSC label are printed on FSC®
certified paper. FSC is the only forest certification scheme endorsed
by the leading environmental organisations, including Greenpeace.
Our paper procurement policy can be found at
www.randomhouse.co.uk/environment

Typeset by Palimpsest Book Production Limited, Falkirk, Stirlingshire
Printed and bound by Clays Ltd, St Ives plc

THE BLINDED MAN

1

Something was forcing its way through the winter.

He couldn't put his finger on it, but there was something. Maybe a warming breeze, a flicker of light smack in the middle of the mass of grey clouds, or possibly just the fact that he heard a splash rather than a crunch when he stepped in the puddle that all winter long had encircled his personal parking space – the one that still bore his name.

He paused for a moment and squinted up at the morning cloud cover. It looked the same as usual, hovering there like a virtual ceiling of security above the bank, bidding him welcome.

The same silence as always.

A short distance away was the little town, undisturbed, sending up only one sign of life: fine tendrils of smoke from chimneys. He heard the repetitive cheeping of the marsh tit and saw it peek from its nest just under the eaves. Then he locked the car and strode the few yards to the small, modest door of the employees' entrance.

He took out his even more modest key ring and one by one opened the three deadbolts.

Inside the bank office it smelled like an ordinary Monday, a bit stuffy from the weekend, but Lisbet would soon air it out when she arrived second, as usual, bringing her flood of cheerful chatter.

He himself was always the first to arrive; that was the routine.

Everything was exactly the same as always.

That was what he told himself several times: *Everything is exactly the same as always.*

He may have said it once too often.

He stood at his teller's window and pulled out the drawer. He took out an oblong gilded case and cautiously weighed one of the long, bristled darts in his hand. His special weapon.

Not many people, even among the initiated, really knew how a dart was supposed to look. His darts were long – specially designed to four and three-quarter inches, almost two and three-quarters of which were a long point that always surprised his opponents, and very short, bristly flights.

He picked up the three darts and slipped around the dividing wall into the office interior. There was the board. Without looking down, he took up position with the tips of his toes on the little black throw line exactly seven feet nine-and-a-quarter inches from the dartboard and rhythmically flung the three darts. All three stuck in the large bed of the 1. He was just warming up.

Everything landed where it should.

Everything was as it should be.

He clasped his hands and stretched them outwards until they made a light cracking sound, then let his fingers flutter freely in the air for several seconds. Again he took the key ring out of his jacket pocket, swung back around the dividing wall to the public area of the bank, went over to the vault and unlocked it. The vault door opened slowly, ponderously, with a muted groan.

It sounded the way it always did.

He carried a box containing thick bundles of banknotes to his teller's station and spread them out over the work surface. He studied them for a moment, just as he always did.

Soon Lisbet would come drifting in through the employees' entrance and start babbling on about her family; then Albert would arrive, clearing his throat in a slightly superior way and nodding stiffly; and last would be Mia, dark, silent and reserved, peering out from under her fringe. Soon the smell of Lisbet's coffee would waft away any remaining stuffiness and fill the office with an air of quiet humanity.

Then the scattered knots of customers would appear: the farmers fumbling with ancient passbooks, housewives meticulously recording their meagre withdrawals, pensioners struggling to avoid resorting to cat food.

This was where he had been happy for so long. But the town was getting smaller and smaller, the customers fewer and fewer.

Everything is exactly the same as always, he thought.

He went back around the dividing wall to play a quick round of 501. From 501 down to zero. A couple of triple-20s and some single bulls sped up the countdown. Exactly as always. The darts landed where they were supposed to. The slightly unusual wavering flight, which was the trademark of his darts, made them hit the mark every time. He had 87 points to go when the alarm clock rang.

Nine-thirty.

Still engrossed in the strategy for the last round, he went over to the front door and unlocked it.

Everything was exactly the same as always.

Let's make it simple, he thought, a simple 15 and a simple 20 and then the one double bull of the morning for 50 points, as the perfect combination: 85. Then only the checkout left, the double ring of the 1. Eighty-seven. No problem. The hard part was putting the third dart in the little black centre of the bull's-eye. A good start to the day.

A good start to a completely ordinary day.

He hit 15 in the outer bed and 20 in the inner, just to make things interesting. The dart teetered at the wire next to the irksome 1, but it held. The wire trembled a bit from the contact. Then the bull's-eye was left, right in the centre. He focused his attention, raised the dart, lined up the ring with the long point and drew the dart back four inches, exactly at eye level.

The door slammed.

That couldn't be. It wasn't right. It was too early. Damn.

He lowered the dart and walked out to the bank office.

An enormous, ox-like man was pointing a big, long pistol at him.

He stood there petrified. Everything fell apart. This was wrong, this was so wrong. *Not now. Not now, please.* The floor seemed to fall away from under him.

The man came up to the teller's window and held out an empty suitcase.

He put down the dart, opened the hatch; stunned, he took the bag.

'Fill it up,' the ox-like man said in heavily accented English.

Quietly and methodically he placed one bundle of bank-notes after another into the suitcase. Next to the bag lay the dart with the long point. Thoughts were surging through his mind, helter-skelter. *Only the bull's-eye left*, he thought. He thought about Lisbet and about nine-thirty, and about a bank door he had unlocked out of old habit. He thought about checking out in the double ring.

The ox-like man lowered the pistol for a moment and looked around nervously.

He thought about his ability to perform his best under extreme pressure.

'Hurry up!' snarled the ox, casting nervous glances out the window. His eyes were very black inside reddish rings.

Bull's-eye, he thought and grabbed the dart.

Then all that remained was the checkout.

2

What struck Paul Hjelm first was how long it had been since he'd sat in a patrol car with flashing blue lights and a wailing siren. Now he was squeezed into the back seat between two uniformed cops and a plain-clothes detective who looked exactly like him. He leaned forward and placed his hand on the driver's shoulder just as the car burned rubber, pulling out abruptly onto Botkyrkaleden.

'I think it'd be best to turn off the siren,' Hjelm said.

The driver reached out his hand to push the button, but that didn't bring silence; the squealing tyres and the furiously accelerating engine kept the noise level high.

Hjelm studied his plain-clothes colleague. Svante Ernstsson was clinging to the little strap that hung from the roof. *Are there really straps hanging from the roof in modern police vehicles?* thought Hjelm, thinking that was probably not what he should be thinking about right now.

Then he thought about the fact that he often thought things that he shouldn't be thinking.

Which just made him think about them all the more.

It was only a month since Ernstsson had climbed unharmed out of a demolished police patrol car on Tegelängsvägen after an absurd high-speed chase down in the Fittja industrial area. Now Ernstsson laughed faintly as the car flew across the busy dual carriageway at Fittjamotet, careened to the left through the long curve towards Slagsta and passed the intersection. Tegelängsvägen stretched off to the right; Ernstsson kept his slightly rigid gaze fixed on the left. After that he relaxed just a bit.

Hjelm thought he was seeing exactly what his partner saw and feeling exactly what he felt. After almost seven years of working closely together in one of the country's toughest police districts, they knew each other inside out. And yet he realised that what they actually knew about each other was minuscule. Was that really all he had learned?

Hjelm felt completely empty. That was why he had stepped into his colleague's fleeting terror – to escape from himself for a moment.

The day had started in the worst imaginable way. The bedroom was utterly suffocating; the early spring sun had played over the blinds for a while, trapping the stuffiness. With a stiff, persistent morning erection, he had crept closer to Cilla, who as unobtrusively as possible had wriggled in the opposite direction. He didn't notice, refused to notice, crept closer with his stubborn, stifled urgency. And she slipped away, inch by inch, until she suddenly got too close to the edge of the bed and fell to the floor.

He bolted upright, sitting up in bed wide awake, his erection abruptly lost. She quietly got up off the floor, shaking her head, wordless with fury. She stuck her hand into her pants and fished out a pad soaked with blood, holding it out towards him. He gave a slight grimace that was both apologetic and filled with disgust. Then they noticed that Danne was standing in the doorway, a look of obvious horror on his pimply fourteen-year-old face. He ran off. They heard a key turn, and Public Enemy started rapping at full blast.

They exchanged looks. Suddenly they were reunited by a bewildered sense of guilt. Cilla dashed out of the room, but knocking on Danne's door was pointless.

Then they were sitting at the breakfast table.

Tova and Danne had left for school. Danne hadn't eaten any breakfast, hadn't uttered a word, hadn't exchanged a glance with any of them. With her back to Paul, Cilla said, looking at the sparrows on the bird feeder outside the window of their terraced house in Norsborg, 'You've witnessed two births. Why the hell are you still disgusted by a woman's bodily functions?'

He felt completely empty. The car passed the Slagsta allotment gardens on the right and the Brunna School on the left. It made a sharp left turn down towards Hallunda Square; for a moment he had Ernstsson in his lap. They exchanged tired glances and watched as the truncated but crowded stretches of Linvägen, Kornvägen, Hampvägen and Havrevägen flew past outside the window. The street names – *flax, grain, hemp, oats* – were like a textbook on

8

agronomy. Everywhere loomed the antithesis of the agrarian society, the brutally unimaginative facades of the identical tall apartment buildings from the Sixties and Seventies. *A breeding ground*, thought Hjelm without understanding what he meant. The extinct voices of a peasant society echoed through him like ghosts.

Over by the square three police cars were parked with their doors wide open. Behind a couple of the doors crouched uniformed officers with their weapons drawn. They were pointed in all different directions. The rest of the cops were running around, shooing away curious bystanders, baby buggies and dog owners.

Hjelm and Ernstsson pulled up alongside the others. The officers were helping with what would later be called 'the evacuation of the area'. Hjelm was still sitting halfway inside the vehicle while Ernstsson got out and went over to the next car. Squeezing out of it came the dishevelled figure of Johan Bringman, who stretched his creaky back.

'The immigration office,' he managed to say in the middle of his stretching. 'Three hostages.'

'Okay, what do we know?' asked Ernstsson, peering down from his towering height at Bringman's hunched form and unbuttoning his leather jacket in the late-winter sun.

'Shotgun, third floor. The majority of the building has been cleared. We're waiting for the hostage negotiators.'

'From headquarters at Kungsholmen?' said Hjelm from inside the car. 'That'll take a while. Have you seen the traffic on the E4?'

'Where's Bruun?' said Ernstsson.

Bringman shook his head. 'No idea. Maybe he's waiting for the top brass to arrive. In any case, it was a clerk from the office who managed to get out. Come on out, Johanna. Over here. This is Johanna Nilsson. She works inside the building.'

A blonde woman in her forties got out of the police car and went to stand next to Ernstsson. She held one hand on her forehead and the other to her lips, chewing on one fingernail, then another.

Ernstsson attempted to comfort her by placing his hand on her shoulder and said in his most reassuring voice, 'Try and take it easy. We're going to resolve this situation. Do you know who he is?'

'His name is Dritëro Frakulla,' said Johanna. Her voice broke, but her words were firm. 'A Kosovar Albanian. His family has been here a long time, and now they've been sucked into the general wave of deportation. They thought everything was fine and were just waiting for their citizenship. Then all of a sudden they were informed of the opposite. I assume that's when things went wrong. The rug was pulled out from under them. I've seen it so many times before.'

'Do you know him?'

'Know him? For God's sake, he's my friend! It was my case. I know his children, his wife, even his freaking cats. I'm probably the one he's after. He's a timid man – he'd never hurt a fly. But I lied to him.' She raised her voice. 'Without knowing it, I was lying to him the whole goddamned time! The rules kept changing and changing and changing. How the hell are we supposed to do our job when everything we say gets turned into lies?'

Hjelm got wearily to his feet. He took off his heavy denim jacket with the sheepskin collar, unfastened his shoulder holster and tossed it inside the car. He stuck his service revolver into his waistband behind his back and put his jacket on again.

He felt empty.

'What the hell are you doing?' said Svante Ernstsson and Johan Bringman in unison.

'I'm going in.'

'The hostage team will be here any minute, for fuck's sake!' Ernstsson shouted at Hjelm as he crossed Tomtbergavägen. He ran after him and grabbed his arm. 'Wait, Paul. Don't do anything stupid. It's not necessary. Leave it to the experts.'

He met Hjelm's gaze, saw the blank look of resolve and let go of his arm.

We know each other too well, he thought, and nodded.

Hjelm slowly made his way up the stairs to the immigration office. He saw nothing, heard nothing. The air was stifling in the dreary, deserted building. Everything was concrete. Concrete with thick, plastic-like paint that seemed grey-tinged no matter what colour it was. The walls were covered with chips of flecking paint like half-hearted decorations. A strange heat, shimmering as if in the desert, sucked up the stench of urine, sweat and alcohol. *This is how Sweden smells*, Hjelm thought as he reached the third floor.

It was the mid-1990s.

He made his way cautiously down the empty, dismal government corridor until he was standing outside the closed door. He took a deep breath and shouted, 'Frakulla!'

It was very, very quiet. Not wanting to give himself time to think, he went on.

'My name is Paul Hjelm, and I'm a police officer. I'm alone and unarmed. I just want to talk to you.'

A faint rustling sound could be heard behind the door. Then a husky, barely audible voice said, 'Come in.'

Hjelm took another deep breath and opened the door.

Sitting on the floor of the office were two women and a man with their hands on their heads. Standing very close to them, against the windowless wall, was a short, dark man in a brown suit, complete with waistcoat, tie and shotgun. The last was pointed straight at Hjelm's nose.

He closed the door behind him and raised his hands in the air.

'I know what's happened to you, Frakulla,' he said calmly. 'We need to resolve this situation so nobody gets hurt. If you surrender now, you can still appeal the decision; otherwise it's going to be prison and then deportation for you. Look, I'm unarmed.' He carefully shrugged out of his denim jacket and dropped it to the floor.

Dritëro Frakulla was blinking rapidly. He aimed the gun alternately at Hjelm and at the three civil servants on the floor.

Don't ask me to turn round, thought Hjelm. *Keep talking, keep talking. Focus on showing him sympathy. Use words that'll make him think. Distract his attention.*

'Think about your family,' he managed. 'What will your children do without you to support them? What about your wife – does she work? What kind of job will she be able to get, Frakulla? What sort of qualifications does she have?'

The shotgun was now aimed at him; that was what he wanted.

Frakulla suddenly spoke, almost as if he were reciting the words, in clear Swedish: 'The worse crimes I commit, the longer we'll be able to stay in this country. They won't send my family away without me. I'm sacrificing myself for their sake.'

'You're wrong, Frakulla. Your family will be deported immediately, forced to return to the Serbs without any means of defending themselves. What do you think the Serbs will do with a woman and a couple of pre-school kids that tried to flee from them? And what do you think will happen to you if you're charged with murdering a cop, an unarmed cop?'

For a second the man lowered the shotgun an inch or two, looking utterly confused. That was enough for Hjelm. He reached back to fumble at his waistband, pulled out his service revolver and fired one shot.

A voice was silenced inside him: *'Why the hell are you still disgusted by a woman's bodily functions?'*

For a moment that seemed lifted out of time everything was absolutely still. Frakulla held the shotgun in a tight grip. His inscrutable eyes bored straight into Hjelm's. Anything could happen.

'Ai,' said Dritëro Frakulla, dropped the gun and toppled forward.

For every action there is an equal and opposite reaction, thought Hjelm, and felt sick.

The male civil servant grabbed the shotgun and pressed the muzzle hard against Frakulla's head. A patch of blood was growing larger under the man's right shoulder.

'Drop the weapon, you fuck!' yelled Hjelm, and vomited.

3

At first it's only the piano's bizarre little strolls up and down the keys, accompanied by a hi-hat and maybe the faint clash of a cymbal, possibly the sweep of the brushes on the snare drum as well. Occasionally the fingers digress a bit from the marked path of their climb, into a light, bluesy feeling, but without breaking the choppy rhythm of the strutting two-four beat. Then a slight pause, the saxophone joins the same riff and everything changes. Now the bass comes in, calmly walking up and down. The sax takes over, and the piano scatters sporadic comping chords in the background, broken by a few ramblings behind the apparently indolent improvisations of the sax.

He presses the tweezers into the hole, tugging and tugging.

The saxophone chirps with slight dissonance, then instantly falls back into the melodic theme. The piano goes silent; it's so quiet that the audience can be heard in the background.

The tweezers pull out what they've been looking for.

The sax man says 'Yeah' a couple of times, in between a couple of rambles. The audience says 'Yeah'. Long drawn-out notes. The piano is still absent. Scattered applause.

Then the piano returns and takes over. It meanders as before, making successive detours, rumbles, ever freer trills. Just the piano, bass and drums.

He presses the tweezers into the second hole. This time it's easier. He drops both lumps into his pocket. He sits down on the sofa.

The wanderings of the piano have returned to their starting point. Now the bass is gone. Then it comes back in, along with the sax. All four now, in a veiled promenade. Then the applause. Yeah.

He presses the remote. A vast silence ensues.

He gets up cautiously. Stands for a moment in the big room. High over his head dust motes circulate in the non-existent draught around the crystal chandelier. The dull metal on the streamlined shape of the stereo reflects nothing of the faint light: Bang & Olufsen.

Bang, bang, he thinks. *Olufsen*, he thinks. Then he stops thinking.

He runs his gloved hand lightly over the shiny leather surface of the sofa before he allows himself to tread tentatively across the pleasantly creaking parquet floor. He avoids the huge Pakistani carpet, hand-knotted over a month's time by the slave labour of Pakistani children, and goes out into the corridor. He opens the door and steps out onto the terrace, stopping for a moment, close to the hammock.

He fills his lungs with the tranquil, chilly air of the spring night, letting his eyes rest on the rows of apple trees: Astrakhans and Åkerös, Ingrid Maries and Lobos, White Transparents and Kanikers. Each tree is labelled with a little sign; he noticed that on his way in. So far the apples can be found only on the signs, showy, brilliantly hued, long before any blossoms have even appeared. Flat, surrogate apples.

He would like to believe that it's crickets that he hears; otherwise it's inside his head. *Sonic bang*, he thinks. *And Olufsen*, he thinks.

Although it wasn't a real bang, of course.

Leaving the terrace, he closes the door behind him, goes back down the long corridor and returns to the enormous living room. Once again he avoids the red-flamed frescos of the hand-knotted carpet, goes over to the stereo and presses the eject button. In a vaguely elliptical trajectory, the cassette tape gently rises out of the tape deck. He plucks it out and puts it in his pocket. He turns off the stereo.

He looks around the room. *What an atmosphere*, he thinks. Even the dust motes seem custom-made to complement the crystal chandelier, as they elegantly swirl around it.

In his mind's eye he sees a list. In his mind he ticks off each item.

Kuno, he thinks, laughing. *Isn't that the name of a party game?*

He leaves the living room by a slightly different route.

A teak table and four matching, high-backed chairs stand on another hand-knotted rug; he imagines that it's Persian. It is predominantly beige, in contrast to the red Pakistani carpet.

Although right now they're very similar.

Close to the table he has to step over what is colouring the Persian rug red. Then he lifts his legs to step over someone else's.

Out in the garden a drowsy full moon peeks from behind its fluffy cloud cover, as a veiled fairylike dance skims the bare apple trees.

4

Detective Superintendent Erik Bruun must have pressed a green button somewhere on his desk, because accompanied by a buzzing sound a green light lit up his nameplate on the doorframe out in the hallway. Paul Hjelm, in turn, pressed down on the handle to the perpetually locked door and went in.

This was the police station, whose peculiar geographic coordinates were something like this: located in Fittja, with mailing address in Norsborg, in Botkyrka municipality, Huddinge police authority. If you wanted to avoid using the name Fittja, because of its obscene and derogatory association with the Swedish word for *pussy*, you could always say Botkyrka, which, in addition to providing the location for the church, encompassed quite lovely areas such as Vårsta and Grödinge; or you could say Norsborg, the hometown of the table-tennis genius J. O. Waldner and the Balrog floorball team; or you could use the name Huddinge, even if it sounded like a bedroom suburb. Hjelm lived in a terraced house in Norsborg, just a few doors from Waldner's birthplace. But he could never really specify which district he lived in, least of all now.

The place that God forgot, he thought fatefully as he stepped into Bruun's room. The wallpaper was changed at least once a year, nevertheless it would turn brown within a matter of days. Erik Bruun always inaugurated his new wallpaper by allowing his black cigars and equally black lungs to puff clouds of smoke over the walls. Hjelm had never visited Bruun in his bachelor apartment in Eriksberg; the place had acquired a reputation of mythic proportions, but he could imagine how the walls must look. Hjelm was a non-smoker, although he did inhale an occasional cigarette to avoid becoming a slave to virtue, as a wise man once expressed it.

Today Hjelm had already smoked six, and he knew that there would be more. The nicotine was swirling around in his head, and for once he sensed no immediate shock upon stepping into Bruun's inner sanctum, which the authorities had designated a serious health hazard. An overly zealous official had once taped a skull and crossbones to the door, and Hjelm and Ernstsson had spent three hours of valuable work time scraping it off.

Erik Bruun was not alone in the room. He was sitting behind his cluttered desk, puffing on an enormous Russian cigar. On the sofa below the row of windows sat two well-dressed gentlemen. They were about Hjelm's age, somewhere in their forties. But no one would ever think of calling Hjelm a gentleman; in their case, it seemed natural. He didn't know these gentlemen, but he recognised the stern set of their expressions.

Oh well. This was pretty much what he'd been expecting.

Bruun raised his substantial body to a standing position and came forward to meet him; such an attempt at a jogging workout was rare for him. He shook hands with Hjelm and scratched his greyish-red beard.

'My congratulations,' he said, putting obvious stress on the word *my*. 'Excellent job. How do you feel? Have you talked to Cecilia?'

'Thanks,' said Hjelm, glancing at the gentlemen on the sofa. 'I haven't been able to get hold of her yet. I assume she'll probably hear about it some other way.'

Bruun nodded several times and returned to his favourite chair.

'As I said, you have the congratulations and support of everyone here at the station. But you didn't answer my question about how you're feeling.'

'No, I didn't,' said Hjelm, and sat down on the chair in front of the desk.

Bruun nodded several times again, in the same knowing manner.

'I understand,' he said, sucking on his cigar. 'This is Niklas Grundström and Ulf Mårtensson, from Internal Affairs. Whether they intend to offer you their congratulations is an open question at the moment.'

Since Bruun's little tirade sounded as if he was on the verge of leaving, both gentlemen got up from the sofa.

Then came a moment of doubt as the superintendent remained where he was and continued puffing on his black cigar. This display of a hint of uncertainty was what both of them would have given anything to avoid. Hjelm thanked Bruun with a seemingly neutral expression and received the same look in return.

The superintendent took one last puff and sluggishly got to his feet. 'The ombudsman for department safety has determined that I'm not allowed to leave my office holding a cigar,' he apologised, stubbing the butt into an ashtray. Then he left the office swathed in a cloud of cigar fumes.

The crushed butt continued to emit brown smoke. Grundström pushed aside the ashtray as if it were a month-old latrine bucket and sat, with some reluctance, in Bruun's smoke-saturated executive desk chair. Mårtensson sat back down on the sofa. Grundström set his briefcase on the desk and pulled out a pair of glasses with almost perfectly round lenses, which he ceremoniously placed on the bridge of his nose. Then he took out a large brown envelope and an evening newspaper. He set the briefcase on the floor and held up the front page of *Expressen*. In big letters the headline screamed: EXTRA. HERO IN FITTJA. POLICE HERO IN HOSTAGE DRAMA. Under the headline was a photograph, almost ten years old, of Paul Hjelm, who had been a police sergeant when it was taken.

'The media have assigned the roles,' Niklas Grundström said in a clear, educated voice, tossing the newspaper aside. He fixed his gaze on Hjelm. 'Things certainly move fast these days, don't they? Imagine, they got the story into the evening edition. The pen moves faster than the brain.'

'An old proverb,' Hjelm said without thinking. He bit his tongue.

Grundström regarded him without expression. He leaned down and pulled a little tape recorder from his briefcase. 'I was hoping to avoid this,' he said, pressing the start button. 'Interrogation with Detective Inspector Paul Hjelm, born 18 February 1957, conducted by Grundström and Mårtensson at the Huddinge police station on March the thirtieth at seventeen-o-six hours.'

'Interrogation?' said Hjelm.

'Interrogation,' said Grundström. 'It was your choice.'

Hjelm bit his tongue again. *Don't give them anything.*

Then it came. 'Are you now, or have you ever been, a member of any anti-immigrant organisation?'

'No,' replied Hjelm, trying to stay perfectly calm.

'What is your attitude towards immigrants?'

'Neither good nor bad.'

Grundström rummaged through the big brown envelope, took out something that looked like a report and began reading. 'Of all your arrests made during your time in this district, forty-two per cent were of individuals of foreign origin. And in the past year that figure increased to fifty-seven per cent.'

Hjelm cleared his throat and paused to gather his thoughts. 'According to the latest figures, in all of Botkyrka municipality, thirty-two per cent of the population are of foreign origin, and twenty per cent are foreign-born citizens. Up here in the north, in Alby, Fittja, Hallunda and Norsborg, the figures are even higher, well over fifty per cent and fifty-seven per cent. A forty-two per cent arrest rate of immigrants actually indicates that there is a greater propensity to commit a crime among Swedish-born individuals in the area. The figures demonstrate no basis whatsoever for racism, if that's what you're getting at.' Hjelm was quite pleased with his reply.

Grundström was not. 'Why the hell did you think you could go in there like some sort of Dirty Harry and shoot that man?'

'That man, as you call him, is named Dritëro Frakulla, and he belongs to the Albanian minority in the province of Kosovo in southern Serbia, and I'm sure you're aware of the situation there. Nearly all the Kosovar Albanians that we've had anything to do with here, people who have become acclimatised and learned Swedish and who have children in the Swedish school system – nearly all of them are now going to be deported. But it's not going to happen without resistance.'

'All the more reason not to go in and shoot him down. The hostage team of the National Criminal Police was on its way. Specialists, experts. Why in holy hell did you go in alone?'

Hjelm could no longer keep silent. 'To save his life, goddamn it!'

* * *

It was approaching eight P.M. Hjelm and Bruun were sitting in Bruun's office, the superintendent in his armchair and Hjelm in a semi-reclining position on the sofa. In front of them on the desk stood a large cassette recorder. The tape was playing. They heard: 'To save his life, goddamn it!'

Bruun practically swallowed his cigar. He hit the stop button with a swift chop.

'You, sir,' he said, pointing at Hjelm with the same abrupt movement, 'are a very foolhardy person.'

'It was stupid, I know . . .' said Hjelm from the sofa. 'Just as stupid as secretly taping an Internal Affairs interrogation.'

Bruun shrugged and started the tape again. First a brief pause, then Hjelm's voice resumed:

'That unit specialises in one thing, and you know that as well as I do: their directive is to render the perpetrator harmless without injuring the hostages. Render harmless, meaning eliminate, meaning kill.'

'Do you really want us to believe that you shot him in order to save his life?'

'Believe whatever the hell you like.'

Bruun glanced at Hjelm, shaking his head sternly; now it was Hjelm's turn to shrug.

'That's precisely what we're not allowed to do.' Grundström had spoken in his normal voice; the last couple of things he said had sounded different. 'We're here to determine right from wrong, to ensure that you haven't committed any dereliction of duty, and then clear your name without issuing any reprimands. That's how the justice system becomes undermined. If necessary, we may have to censure you. This has nothing to do with our personal beliefs.'

'For the record' – Hjelm – 'the shooting took place at eight forty-seven A.M., the special unit arrived at nine thirty-eight. Were we supposed to just sit there taking cover outside, and wait for almost an hour, with a desperate gunman, terrified hostages and a paralysed Hallunda shopping centre on our hands?'

'Okay, for the moment let's drop the question of why and take a look at what you *de facto* did.'

Pause. Grundström and Mårtensson had switched places then, while Hjelm pondered what sort of person says *de facto*.

The sharp voice was replaced by one that was significantly coarser. 'All right then. So far we've just skimmed the surface. Now let's get down to brass tacks.'

With a frown, Bruun switched off the tape recorder and turned to Hjelm with genuine surprise.

'Do you mean to tell me that they in all seriousness tried to pull that good-cop–bad-cop routine on you? When you're an experienced interrogator?'

Hjelm shrugged as fatigue overtook him. An already long day wasn't going to get any shorter. When Mårtensson spoke again, his voice merged with words and images from all the other layers of Hjelm's mind. For a brief moment as he hovered between wakefulness and sleep, these layers fought for dominance. Then he fell asleep.

'Okay, one step at a time. First, you shouted through

the door without any warning; that alone could have caused a disaster. Second, you claimed to be unarmed, even though your gun was sticking out of your waist-band. All he had to do was ask you to turn round, which would also have been a disaster. Third, you lied to the perpetrator. If he'd been aware of certain facts, again, disaster would have ensued. Fourth, when you fired, you aimed at a spot that was not according to regulations; that also could have led to disaster.'

'How is he?' Hjelm's voice.

'What?' Mårtensson's.

'How is he?'

'Who the hell do you mean?'

'Dritëro Frakulla.'

'What the fuck is that? The name of some kind of orange? A Transylvanian count? Just focus on the facts, for fuck's sake!'

'It *is* a fact. *That* is a fact.'

The pause went on so long that Bruun fidgeted, wondering if it was over. Hjelm was sound asleep. Then Grundström's voice piped up from the background.

'He's in the Huddinge clinic, under round-the-clock guard. His condition is stable. I can't say the same about your situation. We'll continue tomorrow morning at ten-thirty. Thanks for your time today, Hjelm.'

Sounds of chairs scraping, a tape recorder being switched off, papers shuffled, a briefcase snapped closed, a door shutting.

Superintendent Erik Bruun lit another pitch-black cigar

that had been unevenly rolled, and listened. Then came what he'd been waiting for. It was Grundström.

'He's incredibly cunning. Why the hell did you let him off so easy? "A Transylvanian count"? Damn it, Uffe! We can't let this guy slip through our fingers. A Dirty Harry who knows how to use the system and come out unscathed opens the door to hundreds of others all over Sweden, all of them more or less racist.'

Mårtensson mumbled something, Grundström sighed, chairs clattered, a door opened and closed.

Bruun stopped the tape and for a moment didn't move.

Outside the police station the bright spring day had dissolved into pitch-darkness. Slowly and laboriously he got up from his chair and went over to Hjelm, still in a deep sleep. Before taking in a big breath and blowing smoke right in his face, Bruun studied his subordinate and gently shook his head.

I won't be able to keep him here much longer, he thought. *One way or another, he's going to disappear.*

Hjelm coughed himself awake. His eyes were running, and the first thing he saw through the cloud of smoke was the combination of a reddish-grey beard and a double chin.

'Ten-thirty,' said Bruun, packing up his ratty old brief-case. 'You can sleep in. Try to be clear and concise tomorrow. Maybe a little better than today.'

Hjelm stumbled towards the door. He turned round. Bruun gave him a good-natured nod. It was his way of offering a hug.

* * *

What is it they usually say? Hjelm wondered as he opened the fridge and took out a beer. Middle-aged heterosexual men with full-time jobs and white complexions are the societal norm. It's on that set of features that all assessments of what is normal are based. And health standards. Another phrase appeared in his mind: *Being a woman is not a disease.* But it *is* a deviation. Not to mention homosexuality and youth and old age and dark skin and speaking with an accent.

That was how his world looked: inside the boundaries were all those heterosexual, middle-aged white policemen; outside was everybody else. He looked at the deviants sitting on the sofa: his – how old was she now? – thirty-six-year-old wife, Cecilia, and his twelve-year-old daughter, Tova. Public Enemy was playing from the opposite direction, clearly audible.

'It's on, Papa!' cried Tova. 'It's on now!'

He went into the living room, slurping the beer between his teeth. Cilla regarded this decades-old habit of his with a certain distaste, but turned her attention back to the TV. The theme music of the evening news programme was playing. The story was part of the headlines. *Way out of proportion*, he thought.

'A hostage drama was played out this morning at the Hallunda Immigration Office south of Stockholm. An armed man forced his way into the office just after it opened and threatened three staff members with a sawn-off shotgun. Fortunately, the drama had a happy ending.'

Happy, he thought. He said, 'The Botkyrka Immigration Office. Located in Hallunda.'

The women in his family looked at him, trying to evaluate his statement, each in her own way. Tova thought, *But that's not the point*. Cilla thought, *You always have to make a point of your own dissatisfaction by finding little factual errors; emotions become thoughts; perceptions become facts.*

The phone rang. Hjelm belched, then answered it.

'The Hallunda Immigration Office?' said Svante Ernstsson.

'Sawn-off shotgun?' said Paul Hjelm.

Laughter on both ends of the line, laughter only they shared. The Noble Art of Talking Shop Without Getting Noticed.

The requisite childishness.

The different types of laughter.

It's possible to hear from the sound that it's aimed only at somebody else.

It deepens if it's aimed inwards at the same time.

'How are things?' Ernstsson finally asked.

'So-so.'

'It's on now,' said Cilla, Tova and Svante in unison.

The weatherbeaten reporter was standing on Tomtbergavägen with Hallunda Square behind him. It was afternoon, in the dazzling spring sunshine. The square was swarming with people. Everything looked normal. A gang of football fans wearing AIK scarves stopped behind the enthusiastic figure of the reporter to make *V* signs.

'At eight-twenty this morning –' said the reporter.

'Eight twenty-eight,' said Hjelm.

'– a man of Albanian-Kosovar origin went into the immigration office in Hallunda, armed with a shotgun. Four staff members were present at the time, and the man took three of them hostage. The fourth managed to escape. The man forced the hostages up to the third floor and made them lie on the floor. After about twenty minutes, police officer Paul Hjelm from the Huddinge police department appeared . . .'

The ten-year-old photograph now filled the TV screen.

'Where did that come from?' said Hjelm.

'What a cutie,' said Ernstsson, over the phone.

'They came to the hospital,' said Cilla, glancing at him. 'Apparently your picture wasn't in any media archives. That's the photo that I have in my wallet.'

'Have?'

'Had.'

'. . . and entered the building. He made his way, unobserved, up the stairs and managed to get inside the barricaded room . . .'

'Barricaded,' said Ernstsson on the phone.

'. . . and he shot the perpetrator in the right shoulder. According to the three staff members, Hjelm acted in an exemplary fashion. Unfortunately, we haven't been able to reach Paul Hjelm for his reaction. Nor would his boss at the Huddinge criminal investigation division, Superintendent Sven Bruun, offer any comment.'

'Good old Svempa,' said Ernstsson on the phone.

The reporter continued, 'Bruun did tell us that the

investigation is ongoing and confidential. But you, Arvid Svensson, you were one of the hostages. Tell us what happened.'

A middle-aged man appeared next to the reporter. Hjelm recognised the staff member who had pressed the gun to the head of the unconscious Frakulla. He slurped the last of his beer through his teeth.

'I'll call you back,' he told Ernstsson, then went into the bathroom.

He studied himself in the mirror. A neutral face. No distinguishing marks. A straight nose, narrow lips, dark blond hair cut short, wearing a T-shirt, a wedding ring. No signs of balding. Early middle age. Two children approaching puberty. No distinguishing marks.

No marks at all.

When he laughed, his laughter sounded hollow. The one-sided laughter of a fired, lower-level police officer.

Ulf Mårtensson said, 'Two nasty bruises on the back of his head still haven't been accounted for.'

Paul Hjelm said, 'Haven't you talked to the hostages?'

'We'll take care of our job, and you take care of yours. Possibly. Although probably not. According to the medical examiner, the wounds on the skull were caused by the muzzle of the shotgun. Did you take the weapon away after you shot the man and use it to strike him on the head?'

'So you haven't talked to the hostages.'

Mårtensson and Grundström were sitting next to each other in an ordinary, cold, sterile interrogation room. Maybe they'd got wind of Bruun's manoeuvre yesterday with the tape recorder. Neither of them said a word as they waited for Hjelm to go on.

And he did. 'When Frakulla went down, the gun landed on the floor near the staff member named Arvid Svensson. Svensson picked it up and pressed it to the man's head.'

'And you let him do that?'

'I was fifteen feet away.'

'But you allowed this staff member to press a loaded shotgun with the safety off to the head of an unconscious man?'

'Nobody could know whether he was unconscious or not, so staff member Arvid Svensson did the right thing by taking the gun away from him. Although he shouldn't have pressed it to his head. That's why I yelled at him to stop it.'

'But you did nothing to stop him, took no physical action?'

'No. But after a moment he put down the gun.'

'After a moment . . . How long of a moment?'

'As long as it took me to throw up my whole fucking breakfast.'

A pause. Finally Mårtensson said slowly and maliciously, 'So in the middle of your unfinished freelance operation, when you should have been waiting for the experts, you're put out of commission by your own digestive system. What if Svensson had shot the perpetrator? What if the perp hadn't been rendered harmless at all? What might have happened? You left a lot of loose ends hanging, without securing the situation.'

'Sounds redundant to me,' said Hjelm.

'What?' said Mårtensson.

'It was because the perp *was* rendered harmless that I threw up. Because for the first time in my life I'd shot someone. Surely you must have encountered this type of reaction before.'

'Of course. But not in the middle of such an important and unilaterally determined solo operation.'

Mårtensson leafed through the papers for a moment, then went on: 'This is actually just a minor addition to an already long list of questionable actions. Taken together, it looks like this. One, you chose to go in alone, even though the special unit was on its way. Two, you shouted through the door without warning. Three, you claimed to be unarmed even though your gun was visibly sticking out of your waistband. Four, you lied to the perpetrator when you attempted to talk him down. Five, you fired a shot, aiming at a spot that was not according to regulations. Six, you failed to disarm the person you had shot. Seven, you allowed a desperate hostage to mistreat and almost shoot the perp. Are you starting to understand the dilemma that we're facing here?'

Grundström cleared his throat. 'In addition to this formal list, there are two more important elements that are worth taking a look at, pertaining to department policy and discipline. They have to do with discrediting the police department and with the immigrant question. Together they open the door to a freelance mentality, which has no place on the force. I'm not saying that you're a racist, Hjelm, but your actions and the flood of praise for you in the media risk legitimising attitudes that are latent in large sectors of the police force. Do you understand what I'm saying?'

'You want to set an example . . .'

'It's not a matter of *want*: it's something we *have to do*. The fact is that I think you're one of the least-corrupt members of the force. You speak your mind, and you're a thinker, maybe even too much of a thinker. But our job is crystal clear. The point is not to get rid of individual rotten apples on the force. We have to ensure that any unpleasant attitudes that may exist in the force are not given official sanction. Because otherwise we'd be damned near approaching a police state.

'It's the same with our whole society. The abyss is lurking inside us. We project our own failures, the voice of the people, the voice of simple solutions. But the skin of this societal body, so loosely held together, is law enforcement. We're way out on the periphery, closest to the crimes, the most exposed of all. If the skin is cut open at the right place, the entrails of the societal body will come pouring out. Do you realise what you may have started with your little freelance action? I really want you to understand.'

Hjelm looked Grundström right in the eye. He wasn't really sure what he saw there. Ambition and careerism at war with dedication and honesty, perhaps. Maybe even genuine concern about the attitudes that were doubtless simmering beneath the uniformed surface. Grundström could never be just another colleague; his role would always be special, outside. He wanted to be the superego of the police force. Only now did Hjelm understand what a top-level power they had sent after him. And maybe even why.

His eyes bored into the table as he said quietly, 'All I wanted to do was resolve a difficult situation as quickly and simply as possible, in the best possible way.'

'There's no such thing as a simple action.' Grundström sounded almost human. 'Every act is always linked to a multitude of other actions.'

'I knew that I could save him.' Hjelm looked up. 'That's all I wanted to do.'

Grundström gave him a penetrating stare. 'Is that really true? Look deep into your heart, Hjelm.'

They sat for a moment, studying each other. Time passed. Something happened, an exchange took place.

Finally Niklas Grundström got up with a sigh, and Ulf Mårtensson followed. As Grundström packed up his brief-case, Hjelm noticed how young he still looked, yet they were the same age.

'To start with, we'll need your ID badge and your service weapon,' Mårtensson said. 'Until further notice, you're on suspension. But the interrogation will continue tomorrow. It's not over yet, Hjelm.'

Hjelm placed his ID and service weapon on the table

and left the interrogation room. He closed the door, but left it slightly ajar, perfect for eavesdropping, and placed his ear to the narrow opening.

It was possible that he heard a voice say, 'Now we've got him.'

It was possible that no one said a word.

He stood in the pitch-dark taking a leak, for a very long time. Five late-night beers needed to be excreted in a single nightly piss. As he stood there and the stink of urine rose up from the toilet, the contours of the bathroom gradually emerged around him. There was just enough light for the dark to take shape. Thirty seconds earlier it had been so dark that the darkness didn't exist. Only when he shook out the last drops did it seem real.

As he flushed the toilet, he thought about the fact that the only urine that didn't stink was one's own.

He looked in the mirror again, a vague rim of light encircling darkness. In that darkness, in the dark that was always himself, he saw Grundström, who was saying, *'Look deep into your heart, Hjelm.'* Then Mårtensson appeared: *'It's not over yet, Hjelm.'* And Svante: *'Wait, Pålle. Don't do anything stupid.'* And then Danne, his son, within the encircling light, stared with the horrified eyes of puberty straight at him. Now Frakulla was there, saying quietly, *'I'm sacrificing myself for their sake.'* And Cilla was there too, in the faceless darkness, saying, *'Why the hell are you still disgusted by a woman's bodily functions?'*

'*Look deep into your heart, Hjelm.*'

So empty, so terribly empty.

Everything had fallen apart. Suspended, fired. No unemployment cheques. On the dole. Who'd want to employ a used-up police officer?

He remembered the coffee room at the station, the hatred towards welfare recipients there, the epithets about dark-skinned immigrants. Of course he had participated, levelling scorn at those who accepted welfare, the riff-raff living luxuriously on public support. Now he found himself in the same situation. There was no floor under his feet. He was floating in a dreadful emptiness.

Where were the police higher-ups? Everybody had abandoned him. He could kill them all.

Grundström: '*Then we'd be damned near approaching a police state.*'

The details of the bathroom had emerged from their dark haze, taken on depth, assumed their proper positions. The light was hauled forth from the night; his eyes had hauled it out. The features of his face should also have taken shape by now.

But they hadn't. They were still cloaked in darkness.

A silhouette.

'*Look deep into your heart, Hjelm.*'

5

He is sitting motionless in the darkness, which isn't truly dark. Through the balcony door light is seeping in from the street-lights below the luxury apartment. If he turned his head, he would see both of the big museum buildings resting quietly in the faint light issuing from inside. But he doesn't turn his head. The silence is absolute. His gaze is directed unwaveringly across the floor of the large living room towards the half-open double doors leading to the hallway. He has already surveyed the space. A tiled stove and a fireplace in the same room. Next to the fireplace a dull-black big-screen TV and the stacked units of a VCR and stereo. On the floor are three artistically hand-woven *rya* rugs, a dining table with two place settings and a five-piece ox-blood leather sofa group. On the walls hang genuine examples of modern Swedish art, three paintings by Peter Dahl, two by Bengt Lindström, two by Ola Billgren. Enthroned on the mantelpiece above the fireplace is one of Ernst Billgren's big mosaic ducks. A total of seven tiled stoves on both floors of the apartment. If the previous living room was ostentatious, this one is thoroughly stylish.

He sits in the same position for over an hour.

Then he hears the front door open. There is a fumbling with keys. He knows that the man is alone. The man swears softly out in the hallway, a noticeable but not extreme intoxication. More like the inebriation of a man who knows exactly where to find the point of greatest possible enjoyment and how to keep himself there all evening. He hears the man take off his shoes and methodically put on his slippers; he even thinks he can hear how the man unknots his tie so that it hangs loose, draped down the front of his silk shirt. The man unbuttons his jacket.

The man pulls open one side of the double doors, already ajar and almost ten feet tall. He enters the living room, stumbles out of one slipper, swears, bends down and manages to put it back on, then straightens up again and catches sight of him through the pleasurable haze. He tries to get a fix on him.

'What in holy purple perdition!' says the man pompously.

Famous last words.

He raises the gun from his lap and fires two rapid, silent shots.

The man stands still for a moment, stock-still.

Then he sinks to his knees and leans forward.

He stays there for ten seconds, then topples over sideways.

He places the gun on the glass table and takes a deep breath.

In his mind he sees a list. Mentally he ticks off a name.

Then he goes over to the stereo and turns it on. He lets the cassette door open and the tape slide down and the door close again, and the first piano notes glide through the room. The fingers wander up and down, the hands move up and down. Then the saxophone comes in and wanders alongside the piano. The same steps, the same little promenade. When the sax cuts loose and dances and leaps, and the piano starts to spread out the gentle chords in the background, the tweezers pull the first bullet out of the wall. He drops it into his pocket, then lifts the tweezers to the second hole – and waits. A couple of small drum rolls, and then that strange little Arabian-sounding twitter from the sax, a couple of seconds of Oriental digression. The piano vanishes. Sax and bass and drums now. He can see the pianist swaying as he waits. Yeah, u-hoo. He's waiting too. The tweezers are raised.

The saxophone keeps climbing towards the heights, faster and faster. Ai. Is the sax player himself producing those little cries that punctuate the crescendo?

And at that moment, with the applause, the audience murmuring, the transition from sax to piano – at that moment he yanks out the second bullet. At that very moment. Splinters fall out of the wall. The flattened lump drops into his pocket to join the first one.

The piano replaces the sax, starting off with a few

meandering intervals, apparently fumbling. Then it cuts loose from the established structures. The flights are freer and freer, more and more beautiful. Now he can hear the beauty. Inside himself. Not just as . . . a memory.

The bass disappears. The piano is meandering again, just like at the beginning. He should really be able to teach himself to understand this. The sax is now following.

The last repetition.

The applause, whistling.

He takes a small bow.

He will never grow tired of listening to it.

6

On the first day of April Paul Hjelm was sitting in the interrogation room, ceaselessly rubbing his hands together. The clock on the wall showed 10.34. Were they going to let him sweat for a while? Or was the whole thing an April Fool's joke?

He no longer knew what to say. He had shut down. Maybe Grundström was right. Maybe they really did need to set an example. He knew the attitudes that prevailed in the station; he was part of them, they were part of him.

The door opened quietly. He pictured the apologetic expression that Grundström would have on his face. He couldn't tell whether it would be sincere.

'I'm sorry, Hjelm,' Grundström would say. *'We made the decision earlier this morning. Your letter of resignation has to be on Superintendent Bruun's desk no later than three this afternoon. Since you're leaving the force voluntarily, there naturally won't be any question of severance pay or unemployment compensation.'*

Instead the face of a stranger appeared in the doorway.

The man studied him for a few seconds. He was in his late fifties, quite ordinary-looking, well dressed, clean-shaven and bald. His nose was enormous. He looked at Hjelm a while longer, his gaze searching, neutral.

Then he stretched out his hand. 'I'm Detective Superintendent Jan-Olov Hultin. I understand that you've been waiting for someone else.'

'Paul Hjelm,' said Paul numbly.

So that's how it was done. Their boss had to do it. The top brass, the appropriate chain of command. It was hard to imagine anyone higher up than Grundström. So this was what he looked like, the more or less secret boss of Internal Affairs.

'Where's Grundström?' Hjelm managed to say. He didn't recognise his own voice.

'Ah,' said Detective Superintendent Jan-Olov Hultin. 'Nothing but a memory.'

He pulled copies of Stockholm's two morning papers out of his briefcase and held them up, one in each hand. The ten-year-old photo adorned the front page of both. The headline in *Dagens Nyheter* said, HOSTAGE DRAMA IN HALLUNDA, with the subhead POLICE OFFICER RESCUES THREE. *Svenska Dagbladet* wrote, THE HERO OF NORS-BORG, and underneath, DETECTIVE INSPECTOR PAUL HJELM SAVES THE DAY.

It was a terrible mockery, staged by a seriously sadistic director.

'Have you seen these?' asked Hultin.

'No.' His response was meant to be brief and concise, but instead it came across as . . . curt.

Hultin folded up the newspapers: 'These headlines should never have occurred. Don't get me wrong, I'm *pleased* that they read the way they do. It means that we still don't have any leaks. The fact is that something much, much bigger is going on in the city.'

At the moment confusion felt like Paul Hjelm's middle name.

Hultin set a pair of half-moon reading glasses on his capacious schnozz and leafed through a dossier with Hjelm's name clearly visible on the brown cover.

'How were you able to spend so many years in this tough district without leaving any traces behind? No complaints filed against you, no commendations, nothing. I've seldom seen such a blank sheet in a file this old. What have you been doing here, anyway?'

Hjelm sat as if frozen. Hultin gave him an inquisitive look. He probably wasn't expecting an answer. But he got one.

'During these years I've raised and supported a family. Not all cops could say the same.'

The man with the big nose bellowed, directing the laugh both at Hjelm and at himself. Then he laid his cards on the table.

'Early this morning an entirely new unit was created within the National Criminal Police. For the moment it has been assigned a ridiculous name: the A-Unit. You might say it's structured to be the antithesis of the Palme

45

Assassination Investigation Squad. No big names, no constant changing of bosses, no fussing around with hierarchies. It's going to be a completely new type of unit – small, compact, composed of people from the outside; it will broaden the scope of the Criminal Police while at the same time compressing it a bit. Young officers, experienced and highly skilled, from all over Sweden will form its core.

'I'm in charge of the group, and I want you to join. When the media gets hold of the story, we're going to need the goodwill of the press that your actions attracted. I also happen to think that you did a damned good job. I've taken some of the material from Internal Affairs – liberated it, so to speak. This has been given top priority, and since the National Police Board is involved, even Internal Affairs has to kiss the ring.'

'I was about to get fired just a few seconds ago.'

Hultin gave him a searching glance. 'Forget about that. It's ancient history. The question now is whether you're up to joining this well-oiled machine. Overtime hours are going to be far more extensive than the normal work schedule. You're looking a little worn out.'

Hjelm cleared his throat. For a moment he thought he actually understood what it felt like to be happy. 'These past few days haven't exactly been a piece of cake. But give me the job, and damn it, I'll work my arse off. Literally.'

'Not too literally, I hope,' said Hultin, pausing a moment. 'We need some of that initiative that you demonstrated at the immigration office. But not too much of it. Above all, it's important to create a functioning group made up of individuals with imagination and conscience. Grundström's notes and tapes indicate that you have just such a personality hidden somewhere behind the blank pages that have filled your dossier all these years. I think this is an opportunity for you to allow it to blossom. There's also a chance that you'll get totally burned out.'

'What's this all about?'

'Serial murders. But not the usual kind, with little boys or girls or prostitutes or foreign campers. No, this is a whole new type and, by all indications, we've only seen the beginning.'

'Politicians?'

Hultin smiled faintly and shook his head. 'No. Good guess, though. No, this has to do with what we call the titans of business. On the night before you so heroically stormed into the immigration office, a man by the name of Kuno Daggfeldt was shot to death at his home in Danderyd. Even then, there were signs that this wasn't going to be the end of it. By all indications a cold-blooded killing that was either a professional hit or committed by someone beyond desperate, so to speak. We now have two situations that exhibit a remarkable number of similarities. Daggfeldt leaves behind two large corporations, a wife, two children and six homes, both in Sweden and abroad. Late last night it happened again. This time on Strandvägen, in one of the slightly smaller luxury

apartments, with a mere eight rooms, plus balcony. There
Director Bernhard Strand-Julén was killed in precisely the
same fashion. Two shots to the head. As with Daggfeldt's
killing, the bullets were dug out of the wall with pliers
or large tweezers. Not a single trace of evidence left
behind. An ordinary nine-millimetre handgun. It's impossible to be more specific, except that we're talking about
real firepower: all four bullets passed straight through the
skulls of the victims. So far we know nothing about how
the perpetrator managed to get in or out. Daggfeldt and
Strand-Julén have countless personal connections, and
every single one will need to be followed up. They moved
in the same social circles, were members of many of the
same associations, sailed with the same sailing club, played
golf at the same clubs, were members of the same
fraternal order, sat on many of the same boards, et cetera,
et cetera. On the surface nothing odd or abnormal.'

'Forming a special group is a rather extreme measure.
How does the Stockholm police department feel about
being pushed aside?'

'We don't know yet. We'll continue to cooperate with
them. And of course it's an extreme measure. But the
key players in the Swedish business world are being deci-
mated. And we have some nasty indications that organised crime might be involved. An utter professionalism
that I've never seen the likes of before in Sweden. If
we're smart, we'll jump on this right away. For a change.'
Hultin paused. 'Of course it's a bit unfortunate to start
up a new special unit on the first of April.'

'Better than on Friday the thirteenth, I assume.'

Hultin smiled faintly and then cast a quick glance at his watch. Hjelm could tell that the man was under a great deal of pressure, but he showed little sign of it. Hultin stood and shook hands with Hjelm.

'First meeting this afternoon at three o'clock, at police headquarters, the new building. Entrance at Polhemsgatan thirty. What do you say?'

'I'll see you there,' said Hjelm.

'All right then,' said Hultin. 'Now I've got to head over to Gamla Värmdövägen to pick up a certain Gunnar Nyberg from the Nacka district. Do you know him? Damned fine officer. Like you.'

Hjelm shook his head. He knew almost no one outside the Huddinge police force.

On his way out the door Hultin said, 'So you've got less than four hours to say goodbye to your colleagues for the foreseeable future and collect all your things. That ought to be enough time, shouldn't it?'

He disappeared, but came back just as Hjelm had sat down and taken a deep breath.

'I assume you realise that for the moment this is all top, top secret.'

'Of course,' said Paul Hjelm. 'I realise that.'

His first thought was to call Cilla to tell her what was happening, but he changed his mind. He thought about all the overtime hours and about the summer and his holiday, which would most likely be cancelled, and about the Dalarö cabin that they had rented at such a good price for the whole summer. But first he wanted to enjoy the moment.

Finally he went over to the break room, unable to hide his joy.

Four people were sitting there, stuffing themselves with the junk food that they'd brought for lunch. Anders Lindblad, Anna Vass and Johan Bringman. And Svante Ernstsson. They all looked at him with surprise. Maybe the expression on his face wasn't exactly what they'd been expecting to see.

'I've come to say goodbye,' Hjelm said solemnly.

Bringman and Ernstsson stood up.

'What the hell do you mean?' said Bringman.

'Tell us,' said Ernstsson. 'You mean to say those fuckers fired you?'

Hjelm sat down across from them and pointed at Ernstsson's lunch.

'Put the burger in the nuker. I told you – it's better if the sauce is warm.'

Ernstsson laughed with relief. 'Okay, so they haven't fired you! Tell us what happened.'

'I really have come to say goodbye. You might say I've been kicked upstairs.'

'What about Internal Affairs?'

'That ordeal is over. Now it's the NCP for me, hand in glove with the commissioner himself.'

'So they thought it'd be better to remove you from

the shitpile of the southern suburbs and the hordes of black-head immigrants?'

'Something like that, I guess. It's . . . top, top secret, as the man said. You'll probably be reading about it in the newspapers, soon enough. But right now it's all very hush-hush.'

'When do you start?'

'This afternoon, actually. Three o'clock.'

'Fucking great! I'll drive you over to Ishmet's bakery so you can buy the most expensive farewell honey-oozing cake that he's got.'

Bruun inhaled the brown smoke from a black cigar and smiled into his beard, which covered a considerable portion of his face. He stretched his arms upwards and growled faintly, and a few flakes of ash floated onto his reddish-grey mane.

'So, now I've produced yet another bigwig at the NCP,' he said with immeasurable conceit. 'And you know that once you're in over there, they'll never let you out. Except in a casket. Stamped NCP.'

Hjelm removed his ID badge and service weapon from Bruun's desk and fastened the shoulder holster around his chest.

'"Another bigwig"?' he asked.

'Hultin was here in the late Seventies. Didn't you know? A hell of a football player. Wooden-leg Hultin. The worst centre-back in the city. Absolutely no sense of the ball. Instead he specialised in head-butting and splitting open eyebrows.'

Hjelm felt a faint sensation of warmth creep through his veins. It was not altogether unpleasant. 'He said he'd read about me in the papers. Lots of goodwill in the media.'

'Oh yeah, Hultin the newspaper hound.'

'Are you still in contact with him?'

'Occasionally I give him a call to remind him of old favours, sure. I think he still plays. On the senior team of the Stockholm police sports league. When he has time, which isn't often. I can just picture him splitting open the eyebrows of his semi-retired colleagues. That'd be a sight for the gods.'

Hjelm decided to ask him straight out. 'It didn't happen to be you who . . . ?'

Bruun dropped the divine mental image of grey eyebrows gushing with blood and gave Hjelm a shrewd look. 'It was pure luck that they were setting up a new group right now. The top, top secret A-Unit.'

'There aren't many ways to get around Internal Affairs.'

'You have to take what you can get. Wooden-leg is always in the back of my mind.' Bruun took one last puff on his cigar, his mouth shaped like the hose of a vacuum cleaner. 'Just do a good job, all right? I don't want to have to go through this shit again.'

7

The A-Unit had its first meeting in one of the smallest conference rooms in the enormous complex of police headquarters, located within the rectangle formed by Kungsholmsgatan, Polhemsgatan, Bergsgatan and Agnegatan. The original headquarters building, constructed in 1903, still boasts dreams of power; its yellowish expanse faces Agnegatan. It is the central hub of the Stockholm police. The opposite side of the rectangle faces Polhemsgatan, mirroring the entirely different but equally absurd architectural ideal of the Seventies. That's where the offices of the National Police Board are located.

And it was there that Paul Hjelm was headed a few minutes before three P.M. He was expected. A guard showed him on a map near the entrance how to find his way to the small conference room. Hjelm wasn't paying attention, and so he arrived a bit late.

Five people were already in the room, sitting at a table and looking almost as bewildered as he felt. As

unobtrusively as possible, he slipped into a vacant chair.
As if on cue, a blond man in his fifties wearing a serious
expression and a custom-tailored suit appeared. He took
up position at the head of the table, placing his right
hand on the telescope-like arm of the overhead projector.
He glanced around, looking for a face that he didn't see.
He left the room again, clearing his throat. Just as he
closed the door behind him, the door on the other side
of the room opened, and in came Detective Superintendent
Jan-Olov Hultin. He too glanced around, looking for a
face that he didn't see.

'Where's Mörner?' he asked.

The constituents of what was evidently the proposed
A-Unit stared in confusion at one another.

'Who's Mörner?' asked Hjelm, not offering much help.

'A man was just here,' said the group's only female
member, a dark-haired woman from Göteborg who was
in the process of acquiring the first wrinkles on her face,
but clearly didn't give a damn. 'But he left.'

'That sounds like him,' said Hultin flatly. He sank
heavily onto a chair and set a pair of half-moon reading
glasses on his big nose. 'Waldemar Mörner, the commissioner of the National Police Board, and the official boss
of this group. He was planning to deliver a little welcome
speech. Oh well, maybe he'll come back.'

Hjelm had a hard time picturing this distinguished and
efficient man with the controlled, neutral voice as a
vicious soccer player.

'Okay, you all know what this is about,' Hultin continued.

'You are now members of what, for lack of a better term and for lack of much else, is going to be called the A-Unit. You answer directly to the National Criminal Police, or NCP, but you'll be working closely with the Stockholm police, primarily with their homicide department, which is housed in the Kungsholmsgatan wing, around the corner from here. Stockholm is the scene of the crime, at least for the moment. All right then.

'The point is that all of you, regardless of rank, are in a position of higher authority than those who will be assisting you, whether it's the Stockholm police or the NCP. This case has top priority, as they say on TV. Since you've been hand-picked from districts all over the country, I don't think you know each other, so let's start by introducing ourselves. As you know, my name is—'

The door was flung open, and the man they'd seen before entered again, out of breath and ill tempered.

'There you are, Hultin. I've been looking everywhere for you.'

'Is that so?' said Hultin. 'Well, here you have your A-Unit.'

'Good, very good,' Waldemar Mörner said impatiently. He took up the same position as before, standing at the head of the table and leaning one hand on the raised section of the overhead projector. 'So, gentlemen. And madam. You are a hand-picked unit consisting of six individuals – five men and one woman – and I assume that Detective Superintendent Hultin has already informed you of your assignment. So now you've got to get busy. It's of the utmost importance to the security of this nation that you stop this insane serial killer before Sweden loses all of its leading citizens. You, and you alone, can end this rampage through the country's streets. Yes, that's right. Yes, indeed. I can see that you are all young and ambitious, fully aware of what's at stake, and raring to take on this task. So let the game begin. May the guardian angel of police officers offer you protection.'

He left the room at the same whirlwind pace as he had arrived. Several jaws that had dropped open during his speech were now firmly back in place.

Jan-Olov Hultin closed his eyes and reached over his glasses to rub the corners of his eyes. 'All right, so now everybody knows what this is about,' he said calmly. It took a second before smiles began to appear around the table. It would take much longer before they fully understood Hultin's subtle sense of humour. 'Let's continue from where we left off. My name is Jan-Olov Hultin, and I've worked here for a number of years, often directly under the former, nationally known boss, whose name we no longer mention. They're just about to appoint a successor, with the new title of National Criminal Director, a title that carries the status of director-general. Gone are the police titles of the past. So why don't you introduce yourselves now? Moving clockwise.'

This abrupt transition caused more confusion. Finally a balding, rather stout man in his early fifties spoke up. He was sitting on the far right in the small, bare conference room. He tapped his pen lightly as he spoke.

'Yes, well, my name is Viggo Norlander, and I'm the only one here who has worked on this case from the very beginning. So I've been transferred directly from the Stockholm police criminal division around the corner. You might say that I'm the one who has travelled the shortest route to get here. I also see that I'm presumably the oldest one present, except for Mr Jan-Olov, of course.'

Hultin nodded slightly, without changing expression. They clearly knew each other well.

Next to Norlander sat the woman.

'I'm Kerstin Holm. As you can no doubt already hear, I've been imported directly from the North Sea coast. I've worked in the Göteborg criminal division all my adult life, and even before that.'

Then came the youngest and shortest member of the team, a dark-haired young man who couldn't be much over thirty. He spoke with great clarity.

'My name is Jorge Chavez, and until yesterday I was the only "black-head" cop in the entire Sundsvall police district. I'm leaving behind a real void, believe me. Apparently all the minorities have to be represented here. Including heroes, I see.'

He cast a meaningful glance at Hjelm, who sat next to him. Hjelm blinked a few times before attempting to speak. Off in the background he saw the shadow of a smile cross Hultin's lips.

'I'm here because of a foolhardy act and not because of some heroic deed, and we'll just have to see whether this assignment is meant to be a punishment or a reward.

My name is Paul Hjelm, and I'm from the Huddinge police. I'm sure you haven't missed the charming photograph from my youth that's been plastered all over the media the past few days.'

Quite a decent response, considering the circumstances, he thought, though he was sweating so much afterwards that he missed part of the next introduction.

The man on his left looked very Finnish. He appeared to be several years older than Hjelm, who immediately thought about Martti Vainio, the famed long-distance runner from Finland who had ended up testing positive for drugs and then became a conservative politician. The man's accent was minimal, but still noticeable, compared to Chavez's complete lack of accent.

'Arto Söderstedt, your typical Finnish buffoon,' he said laconically. 'Flown here from Västerås early this morning in the NCP boss's private jet.'

Then there was only one man remaining, a huge guy wearing slovenly clothes, muscular, but also with the rolls of fat often left by anabolic steroids when not combined with regular workouts. Hjelm tried not to draw any conclusions based on this initial observation.

'I'm Gunnar Nyberg from the Nacka police,' he said. They waited to hear something more, but nothing came.

Hultin took the floor again. 'We have five offices at your disposal: my office, this – what should we call it? – conference room, where we'll have our meetings. And three other offices. That means you'll have to share rooms, so you're going to be working in teams of two for a while.

That's nothing new. I suggest the following pairs: Norlander and Söderstedt in room 302; Holm and Nyberg in room 303; Hjelm and Chavez in room 304. In each office you'll find two desks, two phones, an intercom, two mobile phones and a fully equipped computer system. You'll find me hunkered down in room 301, and this is of course room 300. On each desk you'll find a file folder with a complete rundown of the case. With these administrative details now out of the way, I'll ask Norlander to present a summary of what's far more important, meaning the details relating to the police investigation. I'll hand out your work assignments afterwards. It's all yours, Viggo.'

Norlander got up and perched on the edge of the table next to Hultin. He took a coloured marker from the whiteboard behind him and fidgeted with it as he talked.

'There won't be a scrap of technical evidence to go on. The perp didn't leave a single clue, not even a strand of hair. The very lack of evidence has led us to believe that we're dealing with some sort of professional. So we can leave the technical reports until later. An ordinary nine-millimetre weapon. But big firepower. The bullets passed right through the skulls of the victims and were afterwards plucked out with some type of pliers. In both cases, the perp was sitting in the living room when the victim arrived home, and he fired the shots from that position. Even though in both instances the victim had a wife, it seems as if the perp *knew* that the victim would be coming home alone and also that he would arrive late in the evening. I'll make a sketch of both living rooms so you can get an idea of the similarity of the modus operandi.'

Norlander drew two blue rectangles on the whiteboard and then filled them in with a number of smaller squares and rectangles. Then he drew a short line that stretched diagonally from the same side of both rectangles.

'That's the living-room door,' he explained. 'As you can see, both rooms are basically square-shaped. The arrangement of the furniture and the layout are practically identical. It was here, on the sofa along this wall farthest from the door, that the perp was sitting. He waited until the victim moved slightly to one side so that the slugs would end up in the wall and not go flying off to some unknown fate outside the door. Then he fired two shots through the victim's head.'

Norlander drew a diagonal line through each square, indicating the path of the shots from the sofa positioned directly opposite the doorway.

'The similarity may have two functions. Either it indicates a ritual, meaning that we're dealing with a highly specific method of execution, and the intention could be for someone to recognise this method and feel threatened by it. Or else it's a trick, directed at us, to make us anticipate the same pattern the next time; if the symmetry is broken, we might then think that the crime isn't part of the series. But I think someone should do some checking on this MO with Interpol and the rest of the international contact network, to see if this is a recurring execution method used by any existing terror groups or mafia organisations.

'But right now our most important job is to predict who the next victim will be. It's not going to be easy. As I'm sure you can imagine, there are scores of connections between Kuno Daggfeldt in Danderyd and Bernhard Strand-Julén in Östermalm. We can divide them up into five parts: common enemies, common circles of friends, common leisure activities, common business interests and common board memberships. These areas will probably overlap somewhat, so they should just be taken as general guidelines.'

Norlander went back to his place at the table and sat down. Hultin nodded and took the floor.

'Okay, if we assume that this pattern also applies to time, then nothing is going to happen tonight. The first murder took place in the very early morning hours of March the thirtieth; the second sometime after midnight on April the first, today. I think Commissioner Mörner stated it quite clearly. If the pattern holds, though I grant you it's based on premises that are still much too vague, then murder number three will take place tomorrow night.

'It's unreasonable to think that before then we'll be able to close in on a suspect and put him under surveillance. But it would be good to at least narrow the field of possible targets so that we can then call on the willing assistance of the Stockholm police force and watch maybe five or six of the most likely candidates. Keep in mind the home-alone and arriving-home-late element.

'I suggest the following work assignments: Viggo will handle Interpol and the MO angle; Nyberg will try to track down any common enemies, with particular attention to the distant past, the Stockholm School of Economics and their paths to prominence. Holm will call people in their circles of friends and find out if there are any secret lovers or the like. Hjelm will focus on their leisure activities: sailing, golf, fraternal orders, and anything else that can be discovered. Söderstedt will tackle their business interests. And be sure to get all the help you need from the National Economic Crimes Bureau; that's probably going to be the toughest area to deal with. And Chavez will check up on the various board memberships that both victims have held, both now and in the past.

'I'll be in charge of the overall picture, the assignments, decision making, and so on. This damned whiteboard is going to fill up with flow charts. It's almost four o'clock now. I suggest we put in a few hours so we can set up an effective work plan for tomorrow.'

Hultin paused to think. Then he nodded slightly, as if to indicate that he'd said all he wanted to say. Just as he was about to stand up, Arto Söderstedt cleared his throat, and Hultin sank back into his chair.

'What's the work schedule going to be?' asked Söderstedt.

'Well, as I said, we're all going to be putting in a lot of hours until this thing is solved. You can forget about any union contracts and legal work hours for the time being. In principle, the entire group is on call twenty-four–seven.

You can choose to see it from the bright side – special loopholes have been created so that we can make use of the maximum allowable overtime. If this thing goes on for long, you may be earning a lot of extra pay. Or you can choose to see it from a negative point of view. Marriages and the like are going to suffer, especially if this goes on through the summer.'

Again Hultin made a motion to get up; again he sank back into his chair.

'Just one more question,' Söderstedt said. 'What about Säpo?'

Hultin nodded. It was impossible to interpret his brief pause. 'Right. Well, the Security Police will certainly be involved. As usual, they'll carry out their parallel investigation in secret, but the plan is for us to "exchange information".' Hultin's quote marks fluttered around the room like little death's-head hawkmoths. 'One day in the very near future, their group is going to show up here to introduce themselves and discuss the security aspects of the case. I've had certain indications, you might say, that the security division of the military will also step in at the slightest hint of any international military involvement. So we have several reasons to hope that this can stay on a national level.'

That was as far as Hultin's subjective opinion went.

He got up and went out to the corridor. They followed, in single file, well aware of what lay ahead of them, and disappeared, two by two, into their respective offices.

Jorge Chavez and Paul Hjelm went into room 304. It

was so small that it really had only enough space for the two desks, which had been shoved together. The computer stood on the crack between the two desks; the monitor could be turned to face in either direction. Squeezed into the corner of the room was a little table with a coffee-maker.

At least the minuscule room had a window facing the courtyard. Hjelm stepped over to the window and looked out. He could see sections of police headquarters surrounding a small, concrete yard. Under the window stood a little table with an old dot-matrix printer; the cables stretched like tripwires across the floor from the computer.

'If we quickly swallow our disappointment at not getting our own offices, this will probably do just fine,' said Chavez. 'Which desk do you want?'

'It doesn't look like it makes any difference,' said Hjelm.

Chavez sat down on the chair closest to the door, and Hjelm took the other. Both tested the chairs by rocking back and forth as they absent-mindedly leafed through the file folders on the desks in front of them.

'Better than Sundsvall,' said Chavez.

'What's better?'

'The chairs. At least they're better.'

Hjelm nodded, noticing the unanswered questions hovering in the air between them. He imagined that the other man noticed it too.

Chavez broke the rather oppressive silence by jumping up and asking Hjelm, 'Coffee?'

'That might be a good idea.'

Chavez lifted the lid of the coffee container sitting on the little table in the corner. Then he bent down and sniffed.

'Ah,' he said as he let the coffee grounds slide through his fingers. 'Ah. What is it they call this? The King's Coffee? Would you mind if I brought along a South American blend tomorrow instead?'

'Okay, but leave that one here.'

'Absolutely,' said Chavez as he returned to his desk with the empty coffee pot in his hand. He leaned towards Hjelm. 'But I think I'll be able to make you a convert to genuine Colombian coffee, hand-ground.'

Hjelm looked at the short, eager man. 'Can you brew that sort of thing in an ordinary Swedish coffee-maker?'

'Ah,' said Chavez. 'It has many unused capabilities.'

He disappeared out into the hallway, then returned carrying the pot filled with water. He went over to the corner table and gently tipped the pot towards the coffee-maker.

'That part about being a hero . . .' said Hjelm as he heard the first drops hitting the tabletop. One by one they landed on the floor. The rest of the water ended up, as intended, in the coffee-maker, which Chavez switched on as he stuffed a filter in the basket and dumped in several spoonfuls of the King's Coffee.

'It just slipped out,' Chavez said to Hjelm, with his back turned. 'That happens. It's an old defence mechanism.'

'Do you have reservations about working with me?'

'I don't even know you,' said Chavez to the wall.

'Give me a break,' said Hjelm.

Chavez turned around, went back to his chair and sat down, fixing his eyes on the desk. 'It's true that I know nothing about you. I have no idea what really happened during that . . . hostage drama. All I know is how people reacted.'

'In Sundsvall?'

'Let's just say this: I'm glad I'm here and not there.'

'With me?'

'In a closed room.'

'The media story isn't correct.'

'It doesn't matter.'

'It does to me. And it does in terms of our working relationship.'

Both fell silent. Neither man looked at the other. It started to get dark in the room. Hjelm got up to switch on the ceiling light. An unpleasant fluorescent glow gradually filled the office. Hjelm was still standing, garishly illuminated. 'Tomorrow I'll ask Hultin to find you a different officemate,' he said, and went out into the hall.

The men's toilet was right next door, and he stood there for a good long time after taking a piss. He shut his eyes and leaned forward against the wall. *'There are no simple acts.'* Damn Grundström. And Hultin, who'd obviously teamed him up with Chavez as a test. He picked a speck of dirt from the corner of his eye and flicked it into the toilet bowl. He flushed it away, and as he slowly and methodically washed his hands, he avoided looking in the mirror.

'Now I get it,' said Chavez when Hjelm returned. 'You're the one who wants to change officemates. Get away from the Sundsvall black-head with the big mouth.'

'Better a Sundsvall black-head with a big mouth than a world-famous black-head exterminator,' said Hjelm as he poured two cups of coffee.

'Just one question,' said Chavez, taking the cup Hjelm handed him. 'Would you have gone in if the guy was Swedish?'

'He *is* Swedish,' said Hjelm. For a moment neither of them spoke. 'So should we get to work?'

Chavez slapped the file folder against the desktop a few times. 'Let's roll,' he said, and then raised his index finger. 'And hey –'

'Let's be careful out there,' they both said foolishly, in unison.

'Our age is showing,' said Chavez, looking shamelessly young.

It was close to seven by the time Hjelm finished compiling his list. Kuno Daggfeldt and Bernhard Strand-Julén had both been members of the RSSS. Before finding out what the acronym stood for, Hjelm toyed with the idea that they had played in a punk band from the southern suburbs. But RSSS stood for the Royal Swedish Sailing Society, which had its headquarters in Saltsjöbaden.

Apparently lots of Swedish sailing enthusiasts were members, which meant this particular link wasn't of great interest. On the other hand, their sailing boats happened to be docked in the same place, provided they had already been launched for the season: in the Viggbyholm marina in Täby, north of Stockholm. The two men were also members of the Viggbyholm Boat Club. Hjelm wondered why Strand-Julén would dock his boat so far away when he had the Djurgården small-vessel marina practically at his doorstep. At any rate, a visit to Viggbyholm was on the agenda for the following day.

The two men were also both members of the Stockholm Golf Association, which was headquartered at the Kevinge Golf Course in Danderyd. And that was where they both played whenever they were in town. Hjelm would have to go out there as well.

Finally, the men were both members of the same fraternal lodge, the Order of Mimir. Since Hjelm didn't know one thing about fraternal orders, he was forced to do some serious checking up on the subject. This form of activity, which for all practical purposes was unknown to the general public, was apparently widespread among the upper classes throughout Sweden. The Freemasons alone had 25,000 members divided up among 125 lodges all over the country. After he'd read through the available material and become familiar with various orders of monks as well as military associations, with government groups and non-profit organisations, all of them orders, both big and small, and after he'd learned about a whole series of founders of orders from the Middle Ages onwards, and after he'd become familiar with the different training procedures and levels of promotion, each one more peculiar than the last, even then he didn't have a clue as to the true nature of the activities of these orders. Their real purpose was secret and kept hidden from public scrutiny with the help of strange laws, many centuries old, but the reference books hinted that the most obscure rituals took place within those high-class walls. In general, women were excluded.

The Order of Mimir was one of the smallest and least-known groups, which made this connection significantly more interesting than if the two men had been Freemasons or Good Templars (membership in the latter, it turned out, was impossible because of the gentlemen's drinking habits, which were apparently well known). There were no written materials to be found about the Order of Mimir, but Hjelm managed to track down an address via a tax-evasion lawsuit in which the order had been involved six years earlier. He blessed the search engine on the Internet.

No other common leisure activities showed up. As if three weren't enough for hard-working businessmen.

So Hjelm put together a short list of activities to be investigated further the next day: (1) The Viggbyholm Boat Club, Hamnvägen 1, Täby; (2) The Stockholm Golf Association, Kevingestrand 20A, Danderyd; and (3) The Order of Mimir, Stallgränd 2, Gamla Stan. Talk about stepping into another world.

69

Hjelm stretched. They had turned off the ceiling light. It was unusable for anyone who wasn't a masochist specialising in migraines. They were now working with the light from the two desk lamps, using ordinary forty-watt bulbs. The sky outside had not yet turned dark, although it no longer provided them with any appreciable light.

Chavez had lifted the computer keyboard to his side and was typing madly.

'Have you figured out any connections regarding their board memberships?' asked Hjelm as he stood up.

'Just a minute,' said Chavez, continuing to type. 'It's a hell of a mess.'

'I was thinking of taking off. Where do you live? Are you headed south?'

With an emphatic gesture, Chavez pressed ENTER, and the old dot-matrix printer started rattling underneath the window. He took a gulp of coffee and grimaced. 'I live here,' he said, then continued melodramatically, 'This is my home.'

Hjelm stared at him, his right eyebrow raised.

'It's true,' Chavez asserted. 'There's a room where I can spend the night two floors up. They're going to find me a proper place to stay tomorrow. At least I hope so.'

'Okay. See you in the morning.'

'Sure, see you,' said Jorge Chavez as he went over to the shuddering printer.

8

On the morning of 2 April, Paul Hjelm sat at the breakfast table looking at his family with new eyes. Yesterday
a destroyed man had consumed breakfast; today a resur-
rected man was telling them about his new situation.
They received his news about being transferred to the
city with moderate enthusiasm.

'That's not really surprising,' said Danne. It seemed
to Hjelm that his son was regarding him with the same
expression that he himself had displayed at the sight of
his wife's menstrual blood a few days earlier. 'You're the
Hallunda hero, after all.'

'Of course, it's a promotion to get out of this ghetto,'
said Tova, leaving the room before Hjelm could recover
enough to ask her where she'd heard that word.

From him? Had he been spreading a bunch of shit
around without even being aware that he was doing it?
Had he corrupted the minds of the next generation, which
had more experience than his own in dealing with what

was foreign, in becoming familiar with it, in learning not to fear it?

Look deep into your heart, Hjelm.

It had been exposed for a second, but only a second, and now he had to hide the sight behind tons of work. And no one in his family had a clue about how close to the abyss he had come. They saw the hero; he saw the corpse.

He had been saved, but he was also being transferred. Maybe an officer from an immigrant background would take his place in Fittja, and maybe the Huddinge police would benefit immeasurably from his replacement.

The children had left, and just as he was about to discuss it with Cilla, she too disappeared.

When he got up to leave for the city, he felt lonelier than he'd ever felt. But also ready – to become someone else.

Maybe he sensed that this case was going to be different from any he'd previously encountered.

Something foreign.

He picked up the newspaper and glanced at the headline: DOUBLE MURDER OF TOP BUSINESSMEN. ITALIAN MAFIA IN STOCKHOLM?

He sighed heavily and left.

Cool breezes that couldn't decide whether they belonged to the forces of winter or spring rippled the surface of the water. Slightly stronger swells lapped back and forth, shoving some of the boats a few extra feet. About a dozen small vessels were bobbing up and down on Neptune's shoulders, making dots of various sizes on the water of Stora Värtan, almost all the way out to the horizon.

'A horrible affair,' repeated the man wearing a captain's cap. 'For both of them. Two of our most outstanding members. What are we going to do when we can't even feel safe in our own homes? Will every decent citizen have to hire bodyguards?'

Hjelm and the man were standing on one of six long piers that stretched out from shore towards the breakwater. Together they formed the Viggbyholm small-boat marina. Only a few boats were actually in the water next to the piers, but on land a frenzy of activity was under way as boats were readied for the new season. Men garbed in work clothes were rushing around, and the heavy, stifling stink of epoxy and varnish rose up from the roaring electric sanders.

'So this is where Bernhard Strand-Julén's boat should be docked?' said Hjelm, pointing down at the water.

'Yes, and Daggfeldt's should be over there, at pier three. It's still a little too early to launch the boats. I must say that it was a real shock to open the paper this morning.'

'It was for me too,' said Hjelm.

'Such headlines! Is a Sicilian mafia hitman really planning to eradicate all the business leaders in Sweden? Or – as the other paper reported – has the Baader-Meinhof terrorist group resurfaced? It seems incredible. And what are the police doing about it?'

'This is what we're doing about it,' said Hjelm the police officer as he turned back to shore.

'I didn't mean that as a criticism,' said the man, following with a somewhat swaggering gait. 'I just meant, what *can* the police do against forces like that?'

'This is what we're doing about it,' repeated Hjelm.

They went inside the imposing building on Hamnvägen that housed the boat club. The man showed Hjelm into his office. He sat down at his desk, but his thoughts were elsewhere. He picked up a letter opener and sliced open an envelope. Hjelm cleared his throat.

'I'm sorry,' said the man, putting down the letter opener and envelope. 'I'm not feeling very well.'

'So did you know them personally?'

'Not really. No more than other members of the club. We talked a bit about boats, about good sailing areas, winds, weather forecasts. Things like that.'

'Did they know each other? Did they spend time together here at the club?'

'I don't really know. They were very different kinds of skippers, so I'm inclined to think that they didn't. Daggfeldt was a family sailor; he always took Ninni and his children along when he went sailing in the *Maxi*. I remember that his older daughter, she must be eighteen or nineteen, was getting a bit tired of it all, and the son, who's a couple of years younger, wasn't particularly amused either. And Ninni would get seasick before she even left the pier. But she was always cheerful and enthusiastic. "Hearty but seasick," Daggfeldt used to say with a laugh.

'But it was important to him to have his whole family along. That was probably the only time they were all together. Though things could get a bit testy out among the skerries. That was my impression, at least.'

Hjelm was surprised at how much this man had been able to learn from a few chats about sailing areas and weather forecasts. 'What about Strand-Julén?' he asked, to keep him talking.

'That was a whole different story. A serious-minded skipper. He had one of those Swan boats, not the large kind, so it could still squeeze into the small-boat marina. Always with a crew that seemed very professional, two or three young men with the best equipment, different each time. Fancy new clothes, the best brands.'

'Different each time?'

'The crew. But they always looked well trained. Highly skilled, the type of guys who take part in the Whitbread Round the World Race, just to mention the one that everybody would know. But younger, of course. They had a certain look about them. Like swimmers do – you know how they all have the same body type.'

'In this case very young and blond and tanned? And the equipment was newly purchased each time?'

The man blinked a few times and frowned. Probably at his own loose tongue. But his reaction was a little too strong for that. *There's more going on here*, thought Hjelm. *Better lay it on thick.*

'Okay,' he said, taking a chance. 'I don't give a shit about whether Bernhard Strand-Julén was a paedophile and liked to have thirty-five young boys in – what should we say, the sack? – at the same time. But do you have any idea where I could find any of those boys? The man is beyond the reach of the law now – he's untouchable.'

'His reputation isn't untouchable. Standing in judgement over a dead man, and so on. And he does have a wife, you know.'

'It's possible,' ventured Hjelm again, 'that you never actually played the role of pimp. But if you don't give me a little more information, I'm going to see that every detail of the situation is investigated. Homosexual procurement activities, possibly involving minors, at one of Sweden's most prestigious boat clubs. So let's try again. The rumour is enough. You know that, Mr Lindviken.'

The man chewed on his knuckles. The interview had taken a most unpleasant turn.

Exploit the guy's confusion, thought Hjelm. *Somewhere behind it all there's some form of guilt.*

'Ten seconds. Then I'm going to take you down to headquarters for a proper interrogation.'

'Good Lord, I haven't done anything wrong! All I've done is keep my mouth shut about what I've seen. A big part of my job down here is not to see or speak.'

'At the moment, it looks like you personally, Arthur Lindviken, are behind a big paedophile operation in Viggbyholm. The more names and addresses you can produce within the next ten seconds, the greater the chance that you won't have to see this appalling suspicion reflected in the eyes of every single member here. Not to mention the judge. Seven seconds left. Five.'

'Wait!' shouted Lindviken. 'I have to get . . .'

He stumbled over to a painting that hung on the wall and lifted it off. Then he wildly spun the dial on the combination lock of a wall safe, got it open, took out a thick accordion file and reached into the pocket labelled *S*. He pulled out a postcard adorned with a statue of Dionysus that was impressive in every sense of the word. A truly erect god. Written faintly in pencil was the name 'Strand-Julén', and then in ink from a ballpoint pen, 'We're going now. You can always call. 641 12 12. P.S. You're the biggest Billy-Goat Gruff.'

'He dropped this in my office by chance. I keep all lost items here. And label them, in case the owner wants them back.'

'Lost and found in a wall safe . . . Do you have any items filed under *D*?'

'Daggfeldt? No.'

'Take a look.'

Lindviken opened his eyes wide as he stared at Hjelm.

'Don't you think I know exactly what I have in here?'

He opened the pocket marked *D* and showed it to Hjelm. It was empty.

Hjelm stood up, waving the Dionysus postcard in his hand. 'I'm taking this with me. I'm sure you won't have any more use for it. But hang on to the rest of the contents in that file. I may need to see it again.'

When he passed by the window, he peered inside and saw Arthur Lindviken still seated at his desk. The accordion file was on his lap, and it was shaking.

For a moment Hjelm wondered if he'd been too hard on the man. He was used to people who'd undergone police interrogations dozens of times and knew the rule book inside out. People who were familiar with all the tricks and loopholes, who knew when to keep quiet and when to lie.

The wind had picked up considerably. The small sailing boats had vanished from Stora Värtan, as if blown away.

It was still before noon when Hjelm parked his unmarked police vehicle, a Mazda, at Kevinge Golf Course. A surprising number of people were there, putting away one bucket of golf balls after another in the early April morning. He took out his mobile phone and punched in a number.

'Directory enquiries,' replied a woman.

'08 641 12 12, please.'

'One moment,' said the woman. A moment passed and she was back. 'Jörgen Lindén, Timmermansgatan thirty-four.'

'Thanks,' said Hjelm, jotting down the information. He wrote down the number four in front of the address. It was now the fourth item on his list of things to do. He'd have time to get out there before the unit meeting at three o'clock.

He climbed out of his car and trudged up the stairs to the clubhouse.

A young girl sat behind the front desk. 'Hi,' she said.

'Hi.' He showed her his ID. 'Criminal investigation department. It's about two of your former members.'

'I think I know who you mean,' she said, nodding at the copy of *Svenska Dagbladet* on the counter.

Hjelm nodded too. 'They were members here, right?'

'Yes. They played here quite regularly. They would always say hello when they came in and stop to chat.'

'Do you know whether they played golf together? Did you ever see them together?'

'Hmm . . . I don't think they were regular golf partners. I can't remember ever seeing them together. But sometimes, afterwards they'd join a larger group. Those types of golfers often sit down after a game to discuss other matters.'

'What do you mean by "those types of golfers"?'

'Bad golfers.'

Hjelm paused. 'So you're a competitive golfer?'

'Uh-huh.'

'And you don't like the kind of people who come here to, well, hobnob and network and meet up with colleagues? Even though you're a true Danderyd girl, you have trouble with these "bad golfers", since they give the sport its persistent image of an indolent rich man's game.'

'Quite a psychoanalytical interpretation,' said the true Danderyd girl.

'So how do things work here? Do the members just

go out and start playing as soon as they arrive, or do they have to register somewhere?'

'We have a guest book, and everyone who wants to play has to sign in first.'

'May I have a look at it?'

'You're leaning on it. Excuse me, I have to see to the guests who just came in.'

'No, you don't,' said Hjelm. 'While I leaf through the pages for the past few weeks, you can take a quick look in that fancy computer of yours and find out when Daggfeldt and Strand-Julén became members.'

'I'm sorry, but I'll be with you in a minute,' she said over his shoulder to a couple of grey-haired men wearing classic checkered lambswool golf sweaters. Hjelm eavesdropped on their conversation as he glanced through the so-called guest book.

'Good Lord,' said the older man. 'What'll it be next? Have you seen today's *Svenska Dagbladet*?'

'Yes, by God. Does every decent person have to rely on a security firm nowadays? They were fine, upstanding men, I'll tell you that, brother, fine men. Both Daggfeldt and Strand-Julén. I knew them personally. Do you think the Communists are behind it?'

Hjelm left the two men to their not entirely unpredictable fate as the girl handed him a handwritten note and then turned with a smile to her guests.

Hjelm stopped her. 'I'm not quite done here. Mr D. joined in '82,' he said cryptically in order not to attract the attention of the two men. 'Mr S.J. didn't become a member until '85. Do you have the guest books from that period?'

The girl again apologised to the guests, who were easily seduced by her dazzling white teeth.

'What a great girl,' Hjelm heard them say behind him. 'Ranked number ten in Europe, I've heard.'

'Could we go into your office?' said Hjelm. They went into the office. 'Ranked number ten in Europe?' he exclaimed.

She smiled. 'Nope. Those dear old men have me mixed up with Lotta Neumann. She's older than me, but ten years give or take doesn't mean much at their age.'

'So do you still have the old guest books?'

'Yes, they're in the storeroom. I can get them for you.'

'Good. All of them. Starting with 1982, that is. I'll need to take them with me, but you'll get them back. And I'll need to take the current book that you've got out there on the counter, so you'll have to start a new one. As soon as we're done with all of them, you can have them back. It'll just be a matter of a few days, at most.'

'I can't let you have the one on the counter. We're using it.'

Hjelm sighed. He had hoped to avoid resorting to the language of intimidation.

'Just listen to me. This has to do with a double murder, and there are likely to be more. Pretty soon your whole clientele could be wiped out. I have powers of authority invested in me that would make even those old guys out there start talking about a police state. Okay?'

She slunk off.

He never ceased to be amazed at how close ordinary speech could come to the language of intimidation. A few minor shifts in the wording, and the deed was done. Quite acceptable when spoken by the right person. Quite horrific if uttered by the wrong one.

Hjelm emerged into suddenly radiant spring sunshine, lugging a big box filled with guest books. There wasn't a trace of wind. Perfect golf weather, or so he assumed.

The only indication that he'd arrived at the right place was a yellowing old label, handwritten and partially torn away, next to one of the buttons. 'Mimiro,' it said. There were nine other buttons in the low entryway, half a flight of stairs down, on Stallgränd in Gamla Stan. He pressed the button. Through a rusty little grating on the building intercom, a stentorian voice bellowed, 'Yes?'

'I'm not sure that I'm in the right place. I'm looking for the organisation called the Order of Mimir.'

'This is the Order of Mimir. What can I do for you?'

'I'm from the Criminal Police. It has to do with a couple of your members.'

'Come in.'

The lock buzzed, and Hjelm pushed open the worn door. It was so low that he had to stoop to enter. The hall was narrow and dingy, the air dusty and damp. It was a medieval building that looked as if it had never been remodelled. He paused for a moment to allow his eyes to adjust to the dark.

In a doorway appeared a tall, sinewy old man wrapped in a strange, lavender-coloured cloak. He held out his hand towards Hjelm. If he hadn't studied up on the nature of these organisations, he probably would have tried to twist the man's arm out of its socket and at the same time avoid baring his throat.

'How do you do?' said the man, whose voice was no more of this world than he himself seemed to be. 'I'm David Clöfwenhielm, Guardian of the Order of Mimir.'

'Paul Hjelm.' As Hjelm expected, the man had a firm handshake, though not exactly like the Freemasons, if a comparison were permitted.

'You haven't yet seen the inner sanctum.' The words resonated from David Clöfwenhielm's golden throat. 'And you may never see it. How close you come depends on the reason why you're here.'

'Guardian,' said Hjelm. 'Is that something like a Grand Master?'

'We don't use that sort of outmoded title. We don't want our order to risk being considered a lesser variant of the Freemasons. By the way, do you happen to know who the Grand Master of the Freemasons is here in Sweden?'

Hjelm shook his head.

'Prince Bertil,' said Clöfwenhielm.

'Is he still alive?' said Hjelm.

Clöfwenhielm emitted a thunderous sound, and only

after it had echoed ten times was it possible to identify it as a laugh. Apparently there was some animosity between the two organisations. 'Come in, inspector.'

'Thank you,' said Hjelm with no intention of correcting him as to his proper title. Any sort of promotion was undoubtedly useful in this situation.

They slowly descended a long, winding staircase. The massive stone walls were dripping with moisture, and the ceiling was so low that the lanky Clöfwenhielm bent nearly double as he led the way. Here and there a damp-resistant torch was affixed to the wall. Finally they entered a small room with several coats of arms scattered over the walls, thick velvety drapery on the far wall and an enormous oak desk. On the desk stood two plastic cheese bells; rivulets of moisture formed and dripped off the outside of the misty, opaque surfaces. Clöfwenhielm lifted up one of the cheese bells and took out a small, ultra-modern laptop, a miracle of an anachronism. He sat down at the desk.

'I assume that you want to consult our directory for some reason,' he rumbled. His voice, which had seemed so out of place upstairs in the relative light, was now in its proper element. 'Please have a seat, superintendent.'

At this rate I'll be the chief of police in another fifteen minutes, thought Hjelm as he took a small chair facing the Guardian.

'Your assumption is quite correct, Guardian,' he said in an ingratiating tone. 'It has to do with two of your members. Both have been murdered within the past few days.'

Clöfwenhielm didn't look especially shocked, although perhaps a bit wary. He straightened the collar of his lavender cloak.

'The brothers of the Order of Mimir usually hold positions in society where acts of violence are extremely rare. Are you insinuating that it had something to do with the Order of Mimir?'

'Not at all. We're looking into every possible connection between the two victims, and our primary concern at the moment is to prevent another murder. The fact that they were both members of this organisation is one of these connections.'

'I understand. So what is this about?'

'You don't read the newspapers, Guardian?'

'Very seldom any more,' said Clöfwenhielm. 'Having decided to devote myself to the organisation, I retired not only from my job, but also from those parts of the outside world that I find repulsive. That's permissible when you reach a certain age.'

'And a certain financial status.'

'Of course,' said Clöfwenhielm, his tone neutral.

'How many members does the Order of Mimir have?'

'Sixty-three,' and he said, 'all very carefully chosen. Well, sixty-one, now,' he corrected himself.

'Of course,' said Hjelm, his tone equally neutral. 'Do you know all of them personally?'

'What goes on within the order has very little to do with anything personal. We are preoccupied with what is above and beyond the personal. And besides, during

85

the rituals we usually wear cloaks, rather like the one I'm wearing now, and masks of various types representing the Nordic gods. I seldom see anyone's face. But now we're touching on proprietary information.'

'Top, top secret.'

'Precisely,' said Clöfwenhielm, without for a second questioning the odd choice of words.

'There's one thing I'm curious about,' said Hjelm. 'Can you explain to someone who's a complete outsider what makes these kinds of organisations so attractive to certain groups in society?'

'I could give you an idealistic answer and say that we're united by a desire to expand our consciousness, to open pathways into the unexplored parts of our souls. But that wouldn't be entirely in keeping with the truth. Many by-products of the world I've left behind follow the brothers here from the outside: prestige, the feeling of being one of the chosen, an attitude of superiority, the desire to make connections, freedom from women and an often artificial sense of tradition.

'The Order of Mimir can be traced back to Geijer's Gothicism of the early 1800s, which marked a resurgence of interest in Nordic mythology. But ninety per cent of the members have no clue about this. If I required of the brothers the same purity and enthusiasm that I expect of myself, I would be sitting here chanting all alone. And that might not be such a bad idea.' Clöfwenhielm sighed a bit before returning to his usual thunderous tone of voice. 'All right, so what are the names of the two departed brothers?'

'Kuno Daggfeldt and Bernhard Strand-Julén.'

The Guardian of the Order of Mimir let his fingers wander over the computer keyboard. 'I see,' he said hesitantly. 'Once again we have taken a small step across the magical border into secrecy.'

'Do you mean that we're touching on confidential matters?'

'We're bordering on that, in any case. Allow me to think for a moment.'

David Clöfwenhielm was allowed time to think.

'All right,' he said at last. 'Assisting the authorities in a murder investigation concerning two of our brothers must be given priority. Come over here, Hjelm.'

Hjelm looked at the screen over Clöfwenhielm's shoulder.

'As you can see, I'm scrolling through the names relatively quickly so that you won't be tempted to memorise too many of them. Sometimes you'll notice an asterisk flashing past in front of a name. There's one in front of both the ones you mentioned. Here we have Daggfeldt, and here's Strand-Julén. An asterisk next to each. There are ten of them altogether. You can sit down again, Hjelm.'

Hjelm did as he was told. He felt like a schoolboy. All the elevations in title had apparently collapsed.

'The asterisk indicates, to put it simply, that they're no longer members of the Order of Mimir.'

'Do you mean that they've forgotten to pay their annual dues?'

Once again the Guardian uttered an ear-splitting

bellow of laughter. 'This is a fraternal order, my boy, not
a country club. No, I put the asterisk there myself for
quite another reason. The men in question have chosen
to establish a subgroup within the Order of Mimir, the
so-called Order of Skidbladnir. In lay terms, their group
functions as a subsidiary, independent, but at the same
time always answerable to the parent company. They
wanted to develop certain ritualistic ideas that were not
found acceptable by the Order of Mimir, meaning by
me, but they didn't want to leave entirely. And let me
emphasise that there was no real conflict behind the
formation of the Order of Skidbladnir.'

'No grumbling in the corridors?'

'There are no corridors here, nor any grumbling. Any
antagonisms that have arisen have been on a more
personal level, and as I mentioned, that sort of thing
doesn't interest me.'

'Do you recall who or what was the driving force
behind the secession?'

'When the matter was presented to me, and this was
about six months ago, we were all wearing our masks
after an intense ceremony here. I have no idea who or
what prompted the whole thing. But I accepted their
proposal; I'm not running a reformatory here, you know.
The administrative arrangements seemed quite acceptable. But I was expecting to receive certain reports
regarding their progress, et cetera, and so far nothing
has been forthcoming.'

'What are the differences between the Order of Mimir

and the Order of Skidbladnir? What did the other men want to develop?'

'You won't be able to entice me any further into our secret domains, officer. It's a matter of specific details in the rituals. Nothing radical. A desire to develop certain ceremonial aspects a bit further.'

'I'm sure you'd be willing to give me a list of the names with an asterisk,' said Hjelm, aware that he'd now been drastically demoted to the rank of officer.

Two taps of the keys, a rustling sound under cheese bell number two, and then David Clöfwenhielm, Guardian of the Order of Mimir, lifted off the lid and let a microscopic inkjet printer pump out two pages of A4 paper.

'I assume that the same tact and finesse that you have demonstrated here today, Hjelm, will be shown regarding these pages. I would be very upset to hear that the media had got hold of them.'

'I would too,' said Hjelm.

They both stood and shook hands.

'I'd like to thank you for all your help, Guardian,' said Hjelm. 'Just one little question. What is it that this organisation actually does?'

'Does?' said Clöfwenhielm in surprise. Then he really let loose.

The periodic bursts of laughter moved like shock waves, seeming to propel Hjelm up the stairs and out onto Stallgränd.

* * *

April weather, thought Hjelm, peering through the rain trickling down the windows of the café. *As capricious as fate.* Occasionally someone crossed Västerlånggatan with the collar of his coat or jacket turned up, dashing along the wall of the building, vainly seeking shelter under balconies that didn't exist. The rain lashed against the big windows of Café Gråmunken, and light was noticeably absent. He squinted his eyes, staring at the Order of Mimir printouts. A flash of lightning abruptly lit up the café, leaving behind a lavender light that blocked his vision for a moment.

'Shit. Thanks a lot,' said Hjelm to the lightning.

'Shit yourself, and here you are,' said the girl with the white apron as she poured him another cup of coffee. He looked up at her in surprise. She was nothing but a lavender silhouette.

When his vision returned to normal, he went back to skimming the list. It included the home and business addresses of all the brothers in the strange separatist faction called the Order of Skidbladnir. He found two addresses in Gamla Stan: one residential address on Prästgatan, and one business address. Since it was only a few minutes past noon, he chose the work address, a computer company on Österlånggatan. Not waiting for the rain to let up, he gulped down the rest of his coffee and rushed out.

When he found the address, he pressed the intercom for ComData. A secretary answered, then reluctantly buzzed him in. He walked up two flights of stairs and entered a five-room apartment that had been converted for office use. The secretary was a woman with too much make-up, her hair pulled into a bun. When he showed her his ID, it dripped rain onto her neatly stacked papers, curling the edges.

'Put that away,' she said indignantly.

'Criminal Police. I want to talk to Axel Strandelius.'

'The director is unavailable at the moment. I assume that you don't have an appointment?'

'You have thirty seconds to tell him that I'm here. After that I'll just barge in on my own.'

It had worked earlier in the day, and it worked now. A door opened, and an impeccably dressed man in his fifties whose demeanour practically screamed 'CEO' showed Hjelm into his office without a word.

'Sara said you're from the police,' the man said as he sat down behind the desk. 'How can I be of service?'

'Are you Axel Strandelius?' asked Hjelm.

'Yes,' said the man, 'that's precisely who I am.'

'Are you a member of the group known as the Order of Skidbladnir?'

Strandelius was silent for a moment. 'Now we're touching on proprietary information.'

Hjelm recognised his choice of words. 'I know the rules. The only proprietary information has to do with the rituals. Membership is public information.'

'Except that the group in question is not yet public.'

'You know why I'm here. I see there a copy of *Dagens Nyheter*, over there *Svenska Dagbladet* and here *Dagens*

Industri. All three have the story on the front page. This isn't some kind of game or police harassment; it's a matter of life and death. Your life and your death. Daggfeldt and Strand-Julén were part of the little separatist group that about six months ago broke away from the Order of Mimir. That means that you too are at risk.'

Strandelius clearly hadn't thought that far and shrank a couple of inches in his chair. 'Good God. But the Order of Mimir is the most innocuous organisation you could imagine. There couldn't possibly be anyone who—'

'The strongest link we have between the two men who were murdered two days apart and in the exact same way is this little Order of Skidbladnir. Both of them belonged to the group, which has a total membership of twelve. Or had. That goes a long way in my book. There are two questions I want you to answer. One: What were the driving forces behind the secession? Two: Which members were most fiercely opposed to the secession?'

Strandelius paused to think. He was a data guy. He spent a couple of minutes organising and analysing. When he replied, he used the enumeration that Hjelm had used.

'One: Daggfeldt and Strand-Julén were the driving forces, but the idea actually came from Rickard Franzén. He was probably also the strongest advocate in getting the idea pushed through. At about the same level as Daggfeldt and Strand-Julén was Johannes Norrvik. First and foremost Franzén, then Daggfeldt, Strand-Julén and

Norrvik. The rest of us just thought it sounded exciting and joined in. Two: I'm afraid I can't help you much in that area. There was a general undercurrent of opposition, which the otherworldly Clöfwenhielm never even noticed. But I think it was Franzén who took the brunt of it. He would at least know who most opposed the whole idea. If, and I say *if*, this has something to do with the murders, then Franzén would most likely be the next victim.'

'Very nicely summarised,' said Hjelm and then said goodbye.

The rain was now gone. It didn't just *seem* to be gone; it was in fact gone. The violent spring weather had sculpted whitecaps on the surface of Saltsjön.

April weather, thought Hjelm.

He was stopped at the red light up near Södermalmstorg, looking across Slussen towards the shape of the Gondolen Restaurant hovering overhead, more like a subway car on the rack rather than an actual gondola.

The hanging gardens of Babylon, thought Paul Hjelm as the light changed to green.

He moved into the left lane, no doubt unable to avoid the red light at the next intersection, and turned onto Timmermansgatan.

The locked door had a number code. Annoyed, he punched in a bunch of random numbers. He stood there for two minutes, pressing hundreds of made-up codes.

Nothing happened. He took a step back and found himself standing next to a young girl with straggly black hair wearing a leather jacket. She gave him a suspicious look.

'Police,' he said.

'Is that how you solve your cases?' said the girl.

He glared after her as she walked away.

'Yes,' said Hjelm, and went back to wildly punching in numbers. Finally the little red LED lit up, and the lock emitted a faint clicking sound. *My day in a nutshell*, he thought as he stepped inside, found the name on the board posted just inside the door and went up four flights of stairs.

It said 'Lindén' on the mail slot. He rang the bell. Once. Twice. Three times. After the fourth time, a thudding sound was audible from inside, and a blond youth of about eighteen opened the door and peered out. A sloppy Champion jogging suit more or less covered his body, and his hair was standing on end.

'Did I get you out of bed?' said Hjelm, holding up his ID. 'You're Jörgen Lindén, right?'

The guy nodded, trying in vain to focus on the ID, which kept flapping back and forth before his eyes. 'What's this about?' Lindén's voice was groggy with sleep.

'Mass murder,' said Hjelm, pushing past him into the apartment.

'What the hell did you say?' Lindén followed him, stuffing his shirt into his trousers. On the sofa was a rumpled blanket. In the other room the bed was meticulously made up. *Two sides of the same coin*, thought Hjelm, resorting to cliché, and opened the window to let in some fresh air from the tidy back courtyard with small trees and wooden benches.

'It's one o'clock in the afternoon,' he said. 'Do you always sleep this long?'

'I don't know what you mean by "this long". I was out late last night.'

'What sort of work do you do?'

Lindén scrupulously folded up the blanket and sat down on the sofa. 'I'm unemployed.'

'You seem to be getting by quite nicely on your unemployment cheques.'

'What is it you want?'

'I assume that you haven't read today's paper?'

'No.'

'Bernhard Strand-Julén was murdered.'

In spite of his youth, Jörgen Lindén was the most experienced of all of the people Hjelm had interviewed that day in terms of dealing with the police. He managed to maintain an expression of vague, innocent confusion, although perhaps his eyes were a shade brighter. The wheels had started to spin in his brain.

'Who?'

'Director Bernhard Strand-Julén. You know.'

'No, I don't know.'

Hjelm took the postcard showing the highly virile Dionysus out of his jeans pocket and held it up. 'Quite a hard-on, don't you think?'

Lindén looked at the picture without saying a word.

Hjelm went on, 'Is this your advertising trademark, or what? Marketing? Do you hand these cards out in the subway?'

Lindén still didn't speak. He was looking out the window. The storm was making the low-lying cumulus clouds practically race past.

Hjelm stubbornly continued. 'So if we flip over the steak, what do we find? Here it says: "We're going now. You can always call." And then a phone number that happens to be the same as that one.' Hjelm pointed at the cordless phone next to the window. 'But what's this? There's more. A little P.S. "You're the biggest Billy-Goat Gruff." I think a comparison of this handwriting with that notepad on the phone table will prove very interesting.'

Hjelm sat down in the armchair facing Lindén.

'"And then the big Billy-Goat Gruff rushed at the troll, lifted him on his horns and flung him in a big arc through the air, hurling him so far that the troll was never seen again. Then the goat ran up to the mountain pasture. There was so much good grass, and the goats grew so fat, that they didn't have the energy to go back home. And if they haven't lost that fat, then no doubt they're still up there today."'

Jörgen Lindén still didn't utter a word.

Hjelm went on: 'The land of childhood. I read that story to my children almost ten years ago, every night. I remember every word of it. What sort of troll was it that flew in a big arc through the air and disappeared for good out there on the Swan boat? The troll of poverty? The troll of abstinence? Are you still up there in the mountain pasture?'

Lindén closed his eyes, but remained silent.

'My son is only a few years younger than you. At least I hope he is. Answer me right now, or I'm taking you in. What sort of troll was it that the big Billy-Goat Gruff Strand-Julén chased away?'

'Not the troll of poverty, at any rate,' said Lindén glumly. 'He didn't want a repeat. Never wanted to see us again. The cash lasted me a couple of months, no more than that. And drugs are out of the question. I'm clean.'

'No rave parties, no Ecstasy? Like last night?'

'That's a different story. It's not addictive.'

'Of course not.' Hjelm leaned back in his chair. 'But if you keep working as a prostitute, pretty soon you're going to need something that *is* addictive. Okay, I don't have time for this right now. Here's my most important question: have you ever performed any services for an executive by the name of Kuno Daggfeldt in Danderyd?'

'I don't always know their names.'

'Here's what he looks like,' said Hjelm, holding out a photograph of an imposing man who was struggling to carry his fifty years with dignity, a battle that a couple of days ago had horribly failed. *Nothing exposes vanity more clearly than death*, thought Hjelm, convinced that he was quoting somebody.

'No,' said Lindén. 'I don't recognise him.'

'And you're a hundred per cent sure about that? Take a good look through your internal files.'

'I remember them, believe me. I remember them all.'

'The whole herd of Billy-Goats Gruff? Okay, give me the name of your pimp.'

'Come on—'

'Under other circumstances I would probably have picked you up off the street, lifted you up by the scruff of your neck like a little kitten . . . and tossed you home to your parents –'

'That would be difficult.'

'– but right now the situation is different. All I'm after is as much information as you can give me about Daggfeldt and Strand-Julén. So I need the name of your little pimp. And I need it now.'

'Do you know what he'll do to me if he finds out that I've squealed?'

'He'll never find out from me, I can guarantee it.'

'Johan Stake. I don't know if that's his real name, and I don't have any address. Just a phone number.'

Lindén wrote the number on a piece of paper and handed it to Hjelm.

'One last thing: Strand-Julén's sexual preferences. And be as specific as possible.'

Lindén gave him a pleading look and then started to cry.

The language of intimidation, thought Hjelm, not sure what he himself was feeling.

A hailstorm pounded the windowpanes for ten long seconds. Then it was gone.

April weather, thought Hjelm and sneezed loudly.

* * *

It was two o'clock by the time he rang the bell of the Nockeby villa. He listened to the first five notes of 'Ode to Joy' play three times inside, hating Beethoven's deafness. Immediately behind the villa, the property dropped down towards Lake Mälaren, at the spot where it was most beautiful. This particular villa was not the most palatial in Nockeby, but it still deserved inclusion in this oasis of a western suburb, upon which the April sun had chosen to cast its fickle light.

The door was finally opened by an old woman, whom Hjelm assumed was the housekeeper.

'Criminal Police,' he said, starting to feel sick and tired of the words. 'I'm looking for Rickard Franzén.'

'He's taking a nap,' said the woman. 'What's this about?'

'It's extremely important. If it's not too much trouble, I really must ask you to wake him.'

'It's up to you,' said the woman cryptically.

'What?'

'It's up to you to decide whether it's too much trouble to ask me to wake him. But maybe you've already indirectly answered the indirect question and just as indirectly asked me to wake him up.'

Hjelm stared at her, his mouth agape.

She invited him in with a wave of her hand, smiling up her sleeve, as it were. 'Don't mind me. I'll always be a language teacher, to the end of my days. Sit down and I'll go get my husband.' She disappeared up the stairs, moving with surprising agility.

Hjelm remained standing in the enormous vestibule,

trying to make sense of what had just ensued. '*If it's not too much trouble, I really must ask you to wake him.*' Surely that was an acceptable way to say it?

There went his language of intimidation.

After only a couple of minutes the woman came back down the stairs, followed by an obese elderly man wearing a bathrobe and slippers. The man held out his hand.

'Rickard Franzén,' he said. 'Ninety per cent of my afternoon nap involves trying to fall asleep and ten per cent trying to accept that I won't be able to. So I wasn't asleep. It's hard to get used to being retired after a whole lifetime of working. And I assume that you've already noticed that the same is true of my wife.'

'Paul Hjelm,' said Hjelm. 'From the Criminal Police.'

'The Stockholm police?'

'No, NCP.' Hjelm had forgotten that the man used to be a judge.

'Some sort of new special unit?'

'Yes.'

'I thought so. And I also think I know why you're here. Fast work.'

'Thanks. So what's your view on the matter?'

'I think it's entirely possible that I'm potentially the third victim. We talked about that this morning, my wife and I. Birgitta thought I should call the police. I was more reluctant. And I won the argument. That's not always the case, let me tell you.'

'Do you think that someone in the Order of Mimir is behind these murders?'

'I wouldn't venture to speculate about that, but I can understand that, in your eyes, there must be a connection.'

Franzén's amenable attitude allowed Hjelm to get right to the point. He opted for blunt language instead of the language of intimidation.

'We have an important investigative meeting at three. Might I request that you accompany me to police head-quarters so that we can ask you a number of questions about the Order of Skidbladnir and also decide on the surveillance measures for tonight?'

Franzén paused to consider it. Then he said, 'Of course. The pattern. You think that the spatial symmetry indicates a temporal similarity as well, and that the third murder is going to take place tonight. Forty-eight hours between each of them. You could be right. Just give me a few minutes.'

He disappeared into the bathroom. Without a doubt, the Swedish judicial branch had suffered a major loss. In Hjelm's eyes, Rickard Franzén had clearly been a very good judge.

Birgitta Franzén came over to Hjelm. 'Do you think his life is actually in danger?'

'I don't really know, but it's quite possible. Will you be home tonight?'

'I rarely go out.'

'What about your husband?'

'He's going to visit an old colleague. They usually get together once a month.'

Hjelm nodded. 'Does it usually go late?'

She gave a little laugh. 'Very' was all she said.

'And your bedroom is on the next floor up?'

'Two floors up.'

'What about the living room? Is it on the ground floor?'

'You're practically standing in it. The vestibule narrows to form a corridor over there on the right and then opens onto the living room.'

Hjelm headed to the right. A short distance away the vestibule formed a sort of funnel shape, then widened to become the living room. It was a very unusual floor plan that a murderer would have to know about in advance in order to act. Against the window on the opposite wall in the living room stood a long, sectional leather sofa.

Hjelm returned to the vestibule and found Rickard Franzén fully dressed. He looked resolute, practically enthusiastic.

'Have you taken a look at the proposed murder scene?' he asked with a smile.

He gave his wife a hug and then led the way out to Hjelm's car, ready for a temporary but much-longed-for comeback in the machinery of justice.

The sun was still shining.

9

Jan-Olov Hultin again made his entrance through the mysterious door on the far side of the room, which Jorge Chavez somewhat ironically called 'Supreme Central Command'. The half-moon reading glasses were already perched on the wide bridge of his nose. Hultin turned to face the assembled members of the A-Unit. Everyone was leafing through their papers and notebooks.

'So this morning the whole thing was made public,' said Hultin grimly. 'In all the newspapers simultaneously, by the way. Somebody was busy making calls. Or else there's some sort of cooperation among all sectors of the media. We haven't yet located the leak. Maybe it was simply impossible to keep such a major case secret. At least we had a day's head start.'

He went over to the whiteboard, twisted the top off one of the felt markers and got ready to fire. The pen was now his service weapon.

'At any rate, it looks as if some feverish activity has

been going on inside your A-Unit brains today. Let's see the results. Norlander?'

Viggo Norlander bent over his dark-blue notebook. 'Modus operandi,' he said. 'I've been in contact with everybody from the FBI to Liechtenstein's security force and done a whole bunch of cross-checking through the worldwide phone network. Three of the groups that are currently active consistently use shots to the head when it comes to blatant executions: a branch within the American mafia, under the mob boss Carponi, in Chicago, of all classic gangster cities; a semi-extinct separatist group from the Red Army Faction, under the command of Hans Kopff; and a minor Russian-Estonian crime group led by Mr Viktor X, which you might call a segment of the Russian mafia, whatever that label is now worth. Most cases have been executions of traitors or snitches; no instance has involved two, and only two, shots. So far I haven't been able to track down any examples of two shots to the head. I'll keep looking.'

'Thanks, Viggo,' said Hultin. He'd already filled a corner of the board with notes. 'Nyberg and the enemies they had in common?'

The imposing Gunnar Nyberg seemed uncomfortable as he gripped a pen in his big right hand.

'It looks like a dead end,' he said dubiously. 'I haven't found any common enemies. Both men attended the Stockholm School of Economics, but Strand-Julén was seven years older, so they weren't there at the same time. That's the place where people tend to make friends and

enemies for life. A couple of decades ago Daggfeldt
kicked a colleague out of a business that they'd started
together under the name of ContoLine. The man's name
is Unkas Storm. I located him, in a highly intoxicated
state, at a small scrap-metal company in Bandhagen. He
still harbours a deep hatred towards Daggfeldt. He said
that he, quote, "danced on his coffin", unquote, when
he heard about the murder. But he doesn't know Strand-
Julén.

'The latter has an ex-wife by the name of Johanna,
whom he left without financial means after their divorce
in '72. Nobody could be as filled with hatred as she is,
but it's a strictly personal hatred. She hopes, quote, "to
eat his liver before they cremate the swine, and that really
should have been done while he could still feel the
flames", unquote. I spoke with the family members, who
showed varying degrees of grief, and came to the conclusion that of the two, Daggfeldt, in spite of everything,
will be missed more. Both his son, Marcus, aged seventeen, and his daughter, Maxi—'

'Maxi?' Hjelm interrupted him.

'Apparently that's her given name,' said Nyberg,
throwing out his hands.

'Sorry. It's just that Daggfeldt's sailing boat is called
the *Maxi*, so that's why I . . . Go on.'

'Marcus and Maxi, who's nineteen, seem to be genuinely mourning their father, even though he made himself
practically invisible at home. His wife, Ninni, is taking
his death with what we might call great composure.

Speaking of the sailing boat, she asked whether she would be allowed to sell it immediately. I told her yes. The same is true of Strand-Julén's widow, Lilian. Great composure, I mean. Evidently she'd already more or less moved out of their apartment on Strandvägen, even though divorce was, quote, "out of the question", unquote. She'd seen what had happened to his first wife, the one named Johanna. She made certain insinuations about Strand-Julén's sexual preferences. And I quote: "Compared with my husband Saint Bernhard, the paedophiles in Thailand are God's own angels." Unquote. That may be something we should follow up.'

'I'm beginning to see a red thread,' said Hjelm, 'regarding their leisure activities. If you're finished, that is?'

'I'd like to finish by saying that I haven't been able to get in touch with Strand-Julén's children. A daughter, Sylvia, thirty years old, from his first marriage, and Bob, age twenty, from the second. Both are apparently employed abroad.'

Then it was Hjelm's turn. 'Strand-Julén's Swan boat was evidently a pleasure craft, in the most literal sense of the word. I've talked to one of the members of his ever-changing crew, consisting of blond young boys. I don't know how nauseated you'd like to feel, but I have a detailed description of what took place on that boat.'

'A rough summary will do,' said Hultin laconically.

'And rough it is. He liked to watch and give orders, creating little, quote, "tableaux", in which the crew members were supposed to freeze in the middle of the act while he walked around to study the scene. One boy, for example, might have another guy's dick or some similar object stuck up his arse for fifteen minutes without being allowed to move an inch until Strand-Julén gave permission for the activities to resume. He himself never participated, other than as stage director. But there doesn't seem to be any connection with Daggfeldt. I'll keep looking. I have a lead on the procurer.'

'Holm and the circle of friends,' Hultin moved on to the next topic he had assigned. His notes already filled a significant area of the whiteboard. His handwriting was gradually getting smaller.

Kerstin Holm's melodic Göteborg accent rippled through the room. 'Nyberg and I have been crossing into each other's territory; it can be difficult to distinguish between friends and enemies. At the risk of falling into cliché, I can say that people in the upper echelons seldom make friends with someone just because they happen to like each other. Of course, it's an advantage if they do, but that's mostly of secondary interest, an extra bonus.

'In short, they acquire friends in order to exploit them. For the sake of prestige, to demonstrate what a large and impressive circle of friends they have, and for the sake of business, in order to expand their contact network – which is the alpha and omega in their lives – as well as for the sake of sex, to establish contacts with the former, sex-starved housewives of other men. The impression I get reinforces what I know from the other side of Sweden, meaning Göteborg: that the trading of marital partners is so sanctioned and so common that you can talk about generations of inbreeding and bastard progeny. Do you think I'm exaggerating?'

'Go on,' said Hultin with inscrutable terseness.

'Ninni Daggfeldt hinted at a number of strange but heterosexual escapades that her husband engaged in while he was travelling around the country and especially while he was abroad, in Germany, Austria and Switzerland. But at home he seems to have been quite monogamous. And he always spent his holidays on the famous sailing boat with his family – no one but his family.

'As mentioned, the daughter was named after the boat, which they've had since the early Seventies. The type of boat, that is, not the actual vessel – they've traded up to a larger version approximately every three years. Ninni hated, quote, "that disgusting dry dock", but she decided to make the best of the situation. Daggfeldt had a standing joke about her and the boat that he never failed to cite.' Holm leafed through her notebook.

'"Hearty but seasick,"' said Hjelm.

She gave him an appraising look and then went on. 'Precisely. So Ninni put up a good front, but she was disgusted, and I quote again, "by the cloying family intimacy that was supposed to appear like a letter in the mail for two weeks a year, but never existed at any other time". Lilian Strand-Julén was even more blunt. Gunnar has already quoted the Saint Bernhard passage and – Paul, is it? – has with the utmost clarity reported the facts of the Swan boat expeditions. It's possible to imagine that the two widows, who are now free and financially independent for the rest of their lives no matter what they decide to do, might simply have joined forces to hire a professional hitman. If that's the case, the whole idea of a serial killer is moot.

'But the problem is that they don't know each other. They have plenty of friends and acquaintances in common – they frequent the same social circles – but neither has any recollection of meeting the other. So they claim. Of course we'll continue to check this out.

'A woman named Anna-Clara Hummelstrand, wife of George Hummelstrand, vice president of Nimco Finance, seems to be close friends with both of them. She left for Nice this morning, which may be of interest. Mrs Hummelstrand could have acted as a sort of intermediary between Ninni and Lilian. In general, there are numerous potential motives on both sides, but no real link.'

'Thank you,' said Hultin as he finished writing a flurry of words on the board. 'Hjelm.'

'I'd like to give the rest of my report last, if that's okay. We need to finish with a discussion of how to carry out the surveillance tonight.'

'Do you have such a strong candidate that we'll need to do a stake-out tonight?'

'That's what we have to decide. But I think it'd be good if we heard all the other reports first. Provided that Söderstedt and Chavez don't have an equally strong candidate, of course.'

Both men shook their heads.

Hultin gave a slight nod. 'Okay,' he said. 'Söderstedt?'

'I've been thinking about this idea of a serial killer,' he said, speaking with a Finnish intonation. 'From an international perspective, we're a bit premature. Two similar murders really means nothing more than two similar murders—'

'Granted,' Hultin interrupted him. 'But in the guidelines presented by Commissioner Mörner and the NCP director, as well as the inner circle of the National Police Board, the aspects of protection were emphasised. That's why we're treating this as a serial murder case even before it officially takes on that definition. Besides, I'm convinced that that's what it is. And when it comes right down to it, my judgement is what steers the direction of this investigation.'

Whoops, thought Hjelm. *That's Detective Superintendent Jan-Olov Hultin's first display of power.*

But Söderstedt wasn't about to budge. 'I was just thinking about the fact that serial murders are very "in" at the moment. It's easy to be led astray by American perversities. That madman Jeffrey Dahmer was sentenced to life in prison for having killed, dismembered and eaten seventeen black youths. His father wrote a best-seller about what it was like to have such a monster for a son. Both the father and Dahmer himself have become rich on the crimes. Sympathisers, some of them from South Africa, have sent him money in prison, and plenty of magazines in the United States make heroes out of serial killers and mass murderers. It's related to the fact that their society is on the verge of collapse. A widespread feeling of general frustration makes it possible for an entire nation to empathise with extremists and sick outsiders. Their disregard for all social rules exerts a strong fascination, so strong that people will even send money to a mass murderer. Sort of a retroactive reward. But the victims are always small and weak, and their only shared characteristic, as reported in the media, is the fact that they became victims. We need to ask ourselves what sort of effect this kind of mess could have on the national soul of the Swedish people. There's no such thing as a simple act.'

Hjelm flinched.

'Söderstedt, I've heard from Västerås that you have a tendency to go off on tangents,' said Hultin, his tone neutral. 'Let's stay on topic. What about the financial aspect?'

'I just think we shouldn't lose perspective,' muttered Söderstedt as he looked through his thick stack of print-outs. 'As you mentioned, Hultin, it's a real hotchpotch. I've only been able to scratch the surface. Daggfeldt had two large companies that were under his sole ownership: the finance firm of DandFinans AB with four subsidiaries; and the import company MalackaImport AB. He was also part owner of eight other smaller enterprises, three of them holding companies. And he had a huge stock portfolio, primarily with shares in all five of the country's biggest export corporations. Strand-Julén's main company is called simply Strand-Julén Finans AB, with a bunch of interlocking holding companies attached to it. His business ventures are even more difficult to delineate than Daggfeldt's, if that's possible.'

'One question,' said Hjelm. 'What's a holding company?'

All eyes of the A-Unit seemed to turn on him at once.

'All muscles and no brains,' he said apologetically.

'A holding company is a management company that owns shares in other businesses,' said Söderstedt.

'Is that all it does?'

'Yes. The only company that I've found with any connection to trade and industry – to the production of goods – is Daggfeldt's import firm, which imports canned goods from the Far East. You can find them in any well-stocked grocery shop. And that's only *indirect* production. We still use industrial yardsticks when we look at the post-industrial world of business. So in that sense Strand-Julén owned shares en masse, but he also had a personal portfolio comparable to Daggfeldt's. I haven't been able to find any link between their business activities. But both owned stock in Electrolux, Volvo and ABB – as do so many people. Perhaps the most interesting connection is the fact that they both owned shares in the little glass factory Hyltefors in Småland. Maybe that has some significance.'

'Have you checked with the financial police?' asked Hultin.

'That's the first thing I did. Both men were involved in ongoing tax cases – the kind that drag on for years and then simply go up in smoke, as the bite is gradually taken out of the tax laws. Daggfeldt ruined his first partner, Unkas Storm, as Nyberg mentioned, and was accused of fraud. He was acquitted. Otherwise nothing.'

'Chavez,' said Hultin. 'The board memberships.'

'Also a mess,' said Chavez, getting tangled up in a long sheaf of printouts, 'although on a smaller scale. They were on a total of seventeen boards, either separately or together. They were both members on eight of them: Sandvik, 1978–83; Ericsson, 1984–87; SellFinans, 1985; Skanska, 1986–88; Bosveden, 1986–89; Sydbanken, 1987–91; and MEMAB, 1990. During the period before they were killed, they sat on only one board together, which is not without a certain irony: the Fonus Funeral Company, from 1990 on.'

'So at least we now know which undertaker will be hired,' Söderstedt remarked.

'But doesn't this imply that they knew each other?' said Viggo Norlander.

'They must have known each other,' said Hjelm.

'On the other hand,' said Chavez, 'plenty of people sit on any given board of directors, and they hold regular meetings only a few times a year. It's possible to be on the same board with somebody without exchanging a single word, and maybe without even knowing that the other person exists.'

'Don't the membership periods seem rather short?' said Holm. 'A few years with each board?'

'What I've reported are the years when they were *both*

on the same board,' said Chavez. 'Each of them was generally a member for a longer period of time. For example, Daggfeldt was still a member of the Skanska board up until his death, while Strand-Julén had left in 1988. On the other hand, he'd been a member since 1979. It's much the same situation with the other boards.'

'And the Fonus connection doesn't lead anywhere?' said Norlander.

'Just into the coffin, maybe . . . Of course it's of interest that they were both on that board when they died. Daggfeldt was a member for eight years, while Strand-Julén had been on the board for fourteen.'

'Okay,' said Hultin, writing and drawing arrows. 'Hjelm's turn.'

'I didn't find any connections at the boat club, but a man by the name of Arthur Lindviken had an entire file of blackmail-worthy items in his wall safe. Apparently he's seen all sorts of things going on at the Viggbyholm small-boat marina. Under *S* I found a rather stiff post-card.' He held up the picture of Dionysus. 'A guy by the name of Jörgen Lindén wrote his phone number on it along with a cosy little greeting. He was the one who told me about Strand-Julén's escapades on his boat. There was nothing in the file folder under *D*.'

'Have you picked up Lindviken and Lindén?' asked Hultin calmly. 'Both appear to be felons.'

'No,' said Hjelm.

'Good,' said Hultin.

'At the golf course I found no direct connection either,

just the fact that both men seemed to be frequent guests. But I did confiscate the club's so-called guest books, in which the golfers write down their names before they play. I haven't gone through them yet. The third leisure activity shared by both men was membership of a small organisation that goes by the name of the Order of Mimir. It apparently carries out some sort of Nordic pagan rituals, but the rites are top, top secret.'

Hultin frowned.

'I visited their cellar stronghold in Gamla Stan, without being allowed to enter the inner sanctum. The Guardian, David Clöfwenhielm, kindly informed me, in accordance with the motto of most fraternal orders, which is "obedience to higher powers", that a small breakaway group had been formed within the Order of Mimir. It's called the Order of Skidbladnir, named for the ship that belonged to the god Frey. It was supposed to be large enough to accommodate all of the gods and yet so small that it could be folded up and stuffed into a sack.'

'So what the hell does *Mimir* mean?' asked Chavez.

'Don't you know your Nordic mythology?' said Hjelm.

'As you might have guessed, I'm better at old Inca mythology.'

'Mimir was the guardian of the spring of wisdom beneath Yggdrasil, the world tree. It was from that spring that Odin drank in order to become the wisest of all the gods.'

'Get to the point,' said Hultin.

'Twelve out of the approximately sixty brothers in the

Order of Mimir formed the as-yet-unconsolidated Order of Skidbladnir. As I understand it, not everybody in the Order of Mimir appreciated the secession; it was viewed as a betrayal of sacred lifelong oaths. Four individuals were mainly responsible for the secession; one at the top, so to speak, and three others. They were Johannes Norrvik, Kuno Daggfeldt and Bernhard Strand-Julén.'

Hjelm paused to study the effect of this revelation. No reaction. He went on.

'Johannes Norrvik, a professor of commercial law, is currently on an academic sabbatical in Japan. But the leading force behind the secession is now sitting in room 304, sniffing suspiciously at Jorge's Colombian coffee beans. I think you know him, Hultin. The retired judge of the Svea Court of Appeals. Rickard Franzén.'

'Aha,' said Hultin forcefully, without changing expression.

'So what do you think? Should we regard this connection as sufficient reason to spend the night at the Franzén villa in Nockeby? The former judge is supposed to go out this evening, alone. And he won't be home until late.'

Hultin sat in silence for a moment, running his index finger along his nose. 'What do the rest of you think?' he asked without looking at anyone specific.

A democratic tactic, thought Hjelm, then said, 'I can't see any other clue that bears the same weight.'

'Me neither,' said Norlander.

'Ultimately, it depends on whether we think a minor

controversy within this type of organisation is sufficient grounds for murder,' said Holm. 'It seems a bit vague.'

Chavez nodded. Gunnar Nyberg said nothing as he stared down at the table.

'Gunnar?' said Hultin.

'Sure,' said Nyberg. 'It's just that I had other plans for tonight.'

'I'll think about whether we can do without you. The rest of us, at any rate, will be going out there. Separately and incognito. Not a word to anyone. We don't want the press lurking in the Franzén raspberry bushes. So shall we bring in the highly esteemed judge?'

'Use the intercom,' said Hjelm.

Hultin pressed 304 and said, 'Come on in, Franzén. Room 300.' He went over to the whiteboard, now covered with scribbling, and pulled down the covering. 'The last thing to fade away on old dispensers of justice is their eyesight,' he said.

The door opened, and the corpulent former judge of the Svea Court of Appeals made a stately entrance. He walked right over to Hultin and shook hands.

'Superintendent Hultin,' said Rickard Franzén at once, 'I hope the years have healed the wounds between us.'

'I'll need a rough sketch of the layout of your house and the surroundings,' Hultin merely replied, 'and a description of how you're planning to spend the evening. Don't change your plans. Our man undoubtedly knows what they are. Is it possible to gain entrance to your house from the rear?'

Franzén studied him for a moment. Then he took a fountain pen out of his waistcoat pocket, leaned forward and began drawing on a blank piece of paper on the table.

'The house,' he said, pointing. 'The pathway, road and both neighbouring houses. The trees, shrubbery, fence, gate. In here the stairs, vestibule, hallway, living room. My wife sleeps two floors up. A kitchen door opens onto the terrace at the back. Here. There are never any cars parked on the road, so you should avoid parking there. I'm supposed to be at the home of my old colleague Eric Blomgren in Djursholm at seven o'clock. He's someone else you know, Hultin. I always take a taxi out there and back. We play chess until around midnight, put away half a bottle of Rémy Martin and reminisce about the old days. I have a feeling that we're going to be talking about you tonight, superintendent. Was that all?'

'For the time being. Now I'd like to ask you to return to the other room and wait. Hjelm will be there in a minute to take another statement from you. Thank you for your cooperation.'

Rickard Franzén laughed loudly as he left Supreme Central Command. Everyone except Hultin stared after him in astonishment.

'All right,' said Hultin, his voice devoid of expression. 'We'll go in the back way, in case the killer is already out there somewhere, keeping watch. I assume it's possible to gain access from some distance, through neighbouring properties. And we need two men tailing Franzén in the taxi and out to Djursholm, just in case the pattern is broken. Chavez and Norlander in two cars. You'll rendez-vous out on Drottningsholmsvägen.'

They both looked disappointed.

Hultin went on, pointing at Franzén's sketch. 'Two of you will watch the front of the house from outside, one from each direction on this road. What's it called?'

'Grönviksvägen,' said Hjelm.

'Grönviksvägen,' said Hultin. 'It's going to be a cold job. Söderstedt and Holm, with walkie-talkies in the most appropriate shrubbery.'

They too looked disappointed.

'Hjelm and I will be inside the house. We also need to keep watch on the old lady and the kitchen door and the windows on the ground floor. Do you think we can manage that on our own, or do we need Nyberg to help out? I'm afraid we're going to need Nyberg. Do you think you can cancel your plans for tonight?'

'Sure, sure,' said Nyberg, frowning. 'It's a dress rehearsal.'

'Do you sing in a choir?' asked Holm.

'How'd you know that?'

'I do too. In Göteborg. Which choir is it?'

'The Nacka Church choir,' said the huge, lumbering Gunnar Nyberg, suddenly enveloped in a whole new light.

'Sorry,' said Hultin. 'Dress rehearsal cancelled. I'm sure you know your part. Okay, we'll stop now. I suggest you go downstairs to the cafeteria and get something to eat. The operation starts at seventeen-thirty, in a little less than an hour. Hjelm, I'd like to see you for a minute.'

Hultin and Hjelm remained in the room. Hultin was packing up his papers and said without looking up, 'Good work, man.'

'Everything came together perfectly, if that's what you mean.'

'That's what I mean,' said Hultin, and exited the room through his mysterious door on the left.

10

He was lying in a sticky brown mire. He tried to get up but couldn't, tried to crawl but couldn't, tried to squirm forward, but couldn't even do that. The more he moved and fought and struggled, the tighter the mud squeezed around his body, pulling him downwards. He opened his mouth and was just about to scream when the brown murk started pouring into his throat. As his nose sank into the mud and his nostrils filled up, and only when the horrible last minute of death by drowning remained, did he notice the stench for the first time.

'What shitty—' Nyberg began, and then sneezed.

Hjelm gave a start, an unreasonably strong reaction.

'Try and stay awake, will you?' said Hultin.

'I wasn't asleep,' Hjelm said groggily.

Nyberg blew his nose and tried again. 'What shitty weather,' he said from the hall window. The April storm rattled the pane alarmingly as it swept in from Lake Mälaren. 'I'm grateful to have an indoor assignment.'

'It might be possible to accuse us of nepotism,' said

Hjelm. 'Shivering outside in the car are the Stockholm detective and the Sundsvall black-head, and out in the bushes the Västerås Finn and the officer from Göteborg are shivering even more. While here we sit, inside this warm house with our southern suburban past, drinking coffee. There must be a connection.'

'Paranoia is the worst side effect of our profession,' said Hultin, downing a cup of Birgitta Franzén's superb espresso in one gulp. 'Damn, that's strong!'

'It's espresso,' said Nyberg. 'You're supposed to take little sips.'

'That's why the cup is so small,' murmured Hjelm, trying to be helpful.

'I've got other things on my mind,' said Hultin, raising his walkie-talkie to his ear. They all had them, hanging from a strap across their chests. 'Hello – is the first team in place?'

They heard static, then Chavez's voice.

'We're parked on Gubbkärrsvägen, right behind the church. Waiting. Is it nice and comfy inside?'

'The taxi was ordered for eighteen-forty,' said Hultin curtly. 'How's it going with the bush people? I'm going to take the liberty of pointing out just once the import-ance of keeping the earpiece in your ear and keeping all sounds and movements to an absolute minimum.'

'Oi,' Söderstedt's voice crackled. 'And here I was hanging by my knees from the pear tree, making jungle noises.'

'That might be a lot smarter than what we're doing,'

said Holm, shivering. 'I don't think I can squat here in these spiny bushes for hours on end. The wind is really fierce right now.'

'If you don't want to have a third of your force laid up with pneumonia, you might want to think of another plan,' said Söderstedt.

'You're right – this is no good. The weather gods aren't on our side. You'll just have to slip inside once in a while and get warmed up. One at a time, and put on as many warm clothes as you can find here in the house.'

Rickard and Birgitta Franzén came down the stairs. He was wearing an ancient but still elegant pin-striped suit, complete with waistcoat and pocket watch. As he straightened his tie, he leaned to one side to see past Nyberg's substantial bulk and out the window.

'It's dismal weather for an outdoors stake-out,' he said as the taxi pulled up. 'You'll have to relieve your colleagues now and then, the three of you. Three big strong fellows in here and a woman outside. Very nice. Now take good care of my wife. She's the most precious thing I have.'

The old couple gave each other a quick kiss. Then Franzén put on his overcoat and went out into the wind. She stared after him for a long time.

'The cab arrived a little early,' Hultin was saying into his walkie-talkie. 'It's turning around now and heading off. A black Mercedes, licence number CDP four-four-three.'

'Black Mercedes, CDP four-four-three,' Chavez repeated.

Hultin let go of the walkie-talkie so that it hung from

the leather strap in the middle of his chest. He turned to Mrs Franzén.

'All right, from now on it's going to be risky for you to be seen downstairs. I hope you'll be comfortable on the upper floors and won't come down again unless absolutely necessary.'

Birgitta Franzén stared at Hultin for a moment, as if she were trying to place him in a different context, but failed. Then she gave a slight nod and swiftly made her way upstairs.

When she was out of sight, Hultin said, 'I'm afraid, gentlemen, that Franzén was right. You're going to have to relieve the others when they come inside.'

Nyberg sneezed, sighed heavily and tapped lightly on the storm-lashed windowpane. Then he headed out to the kitchen to keep an eye on the kitchen door and the windows facing the back garden. In spite of the bad weather, he would have a fine view of Lake Mälaren at dusk.

Hjelm went off to Franzén's study, where he checked the windows, and moved on to the two smaller rooms in that wing of the ground floor. Everything was normal.

Hultin went into the living room and sat down on the leather sofa. He gave Söderstedt and Holm the good news about their anticipated replacements.

It's the waiting, thought Hjelm as he leafed through one of the law books in Franzén's study. Everything in the room looked to be still in use. Obviously the man had refused to stop working. Maybe there was nothing besides work for him – nothing but the yawning abyss. Maybe that was why Franzén had wanted at all costs to rejuvenate the Order of Mimir. Hjelm listlessly read an ordinance regarding tools that were permitted and not permitted for picking berries, until it got too dark to read.

He went out to the kitchen to find Nyberg and caught him with a glass of white wine in his hand. 'There's an open bottle in the fridge,' said Nyberg, holding out the glass. 'The lady of the house said to help ourselves.'

'Compensation for missing the dress rehearsal?' said Hjelm, opening the fridge. He peered at the label. A Moselle. 1974. That didn't mean anything to him.

'And now I've got to go out into the cold and feel my vocal cords clench up,' muttered Nyberg.

'Life is tough.'

'You can say that again.'

The whole conversation was part of the waiting. Completely meaningless phrases that they never would have said otherwise. They were talking while their thoughts were elsewhere. Everything could happen very fast. At any moment something life-threatening could go down. They had to stay loose, but at the same time be alert. A strange, double-edged and stressful state.

'You married?' asked Hjelm, eating a banana as he looked to see what else was in the refrigerator.

'Very divorced,' said Nyberg. 'You?'

'The last time I saw my wife I was still married, at any rate.'

The sun appeared just as it was about to sink beyond

the choppy waters of Lake Mälaren. The layers of clouds were moving at varying speeds, one above the other. The April storm was still at work.

Nyberg lit a cigarette and offered one to Hjelm. He took it, and they sat in the dark, smoking.

'I don't actually smoke,' said Nyberg.

'Neither do I,' said Hjelm.

He put on some coffee, working in the beam of a little pocket torch. An ordinary drip coffee-maker stood next to the astoundingly huge espresso machine.

'Such a big machine to produce such a tiny cup,' he muttered to himself in the dark. Nyberg didn't seem to react.

A crackling sound came from their walkie-talkies. Kerstin Holm whispered, 'Solitary man passing. Thirty feet to the gate.'

Hjelm set down the pot filled with water and went out to the hall. He took a drag on his cigarette and felt a slight nicotine kick. Through the window he watched the individual pass the gate and continue up Grönviksvägen. After a moment Hjelm heard Söderstedt's crackling walkie-talkie voice issuing from his chest: 'He's gone past me now.'

Hjelm poured water into the coffee-maker, put in a filter, measured out some ground coffee, plopped one spoonful after another into the filter and then pressed the red button. He did everything slowly and methodically, making no unnecessary movements. He smoked calmly and took a swing down the funnel-shaped corridor to the living room. Hultin was sitting in the murderer's position on the leather sofa against the far wall. A muffled darkness had settled over the room.

'I've put on some coffee.'

'Regular brew?'

'Yes.'

'Good.'

Time rolled by in long, viscous waves. Their eyes slowly adjusted to the dark. Soon they were like nocturnal creatures, their eyes open wide to take in the night.

Hjelm made a round in the other direction. He was getting used to manoeuvring by touch instead of sight. He got to know all the nooks and crannies in order to move quickly and easily. In the faint glow of the torch, with the beam on low so as not to disturb his night vision, he emptied a couple of wardrobes of heavy sweaters and coats and jackets, gloves and caps and blankets, piling everything onto the kitchen table.

After an hour and a half of wandering around and drinking coffee, with six or seven false alarms, Holm reported from outside: 'Requesting a replacement. I'm coming in.'

'I'll do it,' Hjelm told Nyberg, who nodded.

Hjelm had almost finished dressing when Holm knocked on the back door. She was shivering violently. Nyberg handed her a cup of coffee, and she accepted it greedily, using both hands to raise it to her lips. Once the warmth had spread through her body, she said, 'I was seriously about to turn to ice.'

Hjelm draped a blanket around her shoulders, then pressed the earpiece into his ear and the plug into his walkie-talkie. He put on a wool cap and a pair of grotesque mauve gloves and stepped out into the stormy evening.

It was pitch-black outside. Keeping low, he ran for Holm's spiny thicket. He could see exactly where she'd been sitting, huddled next to a rosehip bush with a perfect view, through a peephole, of the road. The outermost edges of the light cast by a street-lamp several yards away just grazed the section of road visible through the peep-hole.

There he sat for two hours. While all his senses went numb, ten cars and an equal number of bicyclists and pedestrians went by. He reported three solitary pedes-trians, but all of them passed by the gate.

Kerstin Holm came out to meet him, looking signifi-cantly more alert. At the same moment he saw Söderstedt's figure slink across the other side of the garden.

Hjelm and Nyberg arrived back in the kitchen at about the same time. Both were more or less out of commis-sion for several minutes, and Hjelm cursed the idea, whoever had thought of it, that they change shifts simul-taneously. The coffee-maker was on. They each managed to fill a cup and guzzle down the hot brew. Warmth returned to their fingers and toes, then spread through the rest of their bodies. *Isn't it usually just the opposite?* thought Hjelm, fumbling to remove the hotchpotch of outerwear. He didn't want to face the murderer looking as if he were part of Amundsen's expedition to the South Pole.

He went into the living room. Hultin was sitting in exactly the same place as before. They looked at each other in the dark without saying a word. *If it's going to happen, it will happen soon*, said their expressions. Hjelm went out to the hall and stood next to the window. He stared out at the dark. The wind was no longer blowing so hard, something he hadn't noticed outside.

He's walking along the deserted street. The houses are set far apart. His hands are in his pockets. He touches the cassette tape, and the two loose keys in his left pocket clink against each other. In his right pocket is the gun with the silencer attached. He is utterly calm.

'I've got something here,' whispers Kerstin Holm into her walkie-talkie. 'A lone pedestrian. Male. Passing me in a minute.'

He knows exactly where he is. His steps are firm. Here is where the fence begins. He crosses the road. The wind howls in his face. He adjusts the bag hanging from his shoulder and places his hand on the gate.

Holm again: 'It's him. He's opening the gate. Now.'

'He's coming now,' Söderstedt whispers almost at the same time.

He opens the gate slowly, without making a sound. Closes it. Moves away from the garden path and walks carefully in the grass along the edge, heading towards the house. He takes out the keys and goes up the steps.

'He's got the keys out,' whispers Söderstedt. 'He's putting in the first one. Now.'

He puts the first key in the lock and turns it soundlessly. Then the second, also soundlessly. He presses down the door handle with one hand, holding the gun in the other.

The door slides open.

They take him.

Hjelm seizes the man's hands and twists them behind his back. Nyberg tosses him onto the floor and presses his face into the carpet. Hjelm holds his arms behind his back. Hultin switches on the light, a lightning bolt frozen in place, and aims his service weapon at him. Hjelm has already snapped on the handcuffs. It's over.

'What the hell?' says the man in surprise. Then he screams.

Holm and Söderstedt rush in with their guns drawn. Birgitta Franzén appears on the stairs. She stares at them with a wild expression.

'Rickard,' she whispers.

'Rickard?' all five officers say in unison.

'Mama,' the man manages to say before he faints.

He goes in through the door and closes it behind him. It's completely dark, completely quiet inside the villa. He takes off his shoes, places them in his bag, and heads straight for the living room. He sits down on the leather sofa against the far wall, facing the door, places his gun on the table and waits.

He sits there motionless.

He's waiting for the music.

11

The scent, just the scent of ordinary female skin. Tiny, tiny hairs tickling his nose. Nothing else.

He needs absolutely nothing else.

She grumbles when he touches her. He's still cold.

'There's a stranger in my bed,' she manages to say, seventy-five per cent asleep.

'No, no,' he says, pressing closer. 'There's a stranger in *my* bed.'

It's like a formula. They've said the same thing hundreds of times.

It *is* a formula.

'Open, sesame.'

Sesame hesitates. Does she feel like it? Only a couple more hours of sleep left. To do it while half-asleep. As if dreams themselves were forcing their way in, she once said. That was a long time ago.

He instantly gets an erection. Click. And he thought he was too tired. *It just said click*, he thinks drowsily. The rest of him is asleep. The blood has collected in one place. That part isn't asleep.

He warms up his hand as best he can by sticking it under his armpit and then tentatively touches her bare hip. She doesn't push it away. She doesn't react at all. She's asleep. He makes one last attempt, slipping his hand under her T-shirt. He cups his hand around one breast. Slowly he starts to circle the nipple. She'll think either that the tickling is annoying and push him away, or that it feels lovely and let him continue. Or else she'll just keep on sleeping. Anything is still possible.

The nipple stiffens. She stirs. She lets him continue.

He loosens his underwear and runs his penis lightly along her backbone and down over her buttocks. At the same time he circles his finger over her nipple, squeezing it gently. His penis softly moves down her hip, past the waistband of her pants and down to her thigh. There it turns and moves upwards, then farther down, rubbing softly along her pants, slowly across her anus and up to her backbone again. Circles.

She turns onto her back and arches up onto the soles of her feet. He tugs off her pants and can smell the scents. He tugs off his underwear, and she grabs hold of him with both hands, guiding him inside.

His tongue on her lips. She sticks out her tongue. They touch each other. He sinks slowly inside her, opened wide, and is enveloped in moistness. They lie there for a minute without moving. Fulfilled. Their skin touching everywhere.

Then he pulls out, almost out, and plunges back in, all the way.

It's not over yet, Hjelm.

He had put down his helmet and was Paul. Simply Paul.

Breakfast. Paul and Cilla and Tova were sitting at the table. He blearily scanned the morning paper. Tova gulped down the last of her orange juice and jumped up to look in the mirror.

'Ohhhh,' she groaned.

She pulled the rubber bands off her pigtails and ruffled her hair, frantically dragging a comb through her tresses.

'That looks great,' Hjelm said. 'Come here.'

She dashed over to the table, gave him a quick hug and ran back to the mirror. She grabbed her shoulder bag just as the doorbell rang. She opened the door, and Milla came in.

'Hi,' she said.

'Hi,' said Hjelm.

'Come on, let's go!' yelled Tova. 'We're already late!' The door banged shut.

Danne came downstairs and gave them a sullen look.

'You're home?' he said to his father, then left. The door rattled for a while after he slammed it behind him.

Cilla sighed deeply and said, with half a piece of liverwurst sandwich in her mouth, 'So the whole thing went to hell?'

'Yes.'

'Want to talk about it?'

'Oath of confidentiality,' he said, giving her a droll look.

'Oh, right,' she said, her expression exactly the same as his. That happened frequently. He recognised his own facial expressions in hers and could never figure out which of them had influenced the other.

'We were at the wrong place. It was as simple as that.'

'Do you think something happened somewhere else?'

'I'm absolutely convinced it did. You'll probably be able to read about it in the noon edition of the evening paper. At any second, that phone is going to ring,' he said, pointing at his mobile on the table. He finished his coffee, went out to the coat rack in the hall and took down his denim jacket with the sheepskin collar. He was holding it as he went back to the table and gave her a little kiss. 'Are you working tonight or are you off?' he asked.

She shook her head, playfully admonishing him. 'I'm working tonight.'

He pulled on his jacket, blew her another kiss, opened the door and stepped outside, heading for his unmarked Mazda. Before he closed the door, she cleared her throat. She was holding his mobile between her thumb and index finger, her expression slightly disgusted. It was ringing. She dropped it onto the table.

With a chuckle he picked it up and answered. He didn't say a single word during the entire conversation.

'Exactly as I said,' he told her, slipping the mobile into his jacket pocket. She blew him a kiss as he stepped out into what looked, strangely enough, like a midsummer day.

No wind. Bright sunshine. Only in the shade was it possible to feel that it was still a hesitant spring.

Love, he found himself thinking, to his surprise. *Love and daily life. Daily life and love.*

He turned the key in the ignition and drove out towards Norsborg.

It was time, once again, to exchange the southern suburbs for the north.

12

It was 9.03 A.M. on 3 April. The same date on which
Gustav IV Adolf was crowned king of Sweden in the
year 1800 in Norrköping, somebody thought, thus devi-
ating from the group's otherwise synchronised thoughts.

Although at that particular moment everyone's
thoughts were quite disparate, not to mention listless.

Jan-Olov Hultin, on the other hand, looked very
composed. No evidence of the previous night's misfor-
tune. With great care he set his reading glasses on his nose
and leafed through a stack of documents that were far
from kind.

Hjelm looked around in the grandiose kitchen. The
other members of the A-Unit were displaying various
effects from the day before. Gunnar Nyberg sneezed
loudly; he was thinking about singing in the choir with
inflamed vocal cords. Viggo Norlander merely looked
annoyed. Kerstin Holm was having what used to be called
a catnap, but had become commonly known as a micro-
nap after various politicians had been discovered asleep

in the parliament chambers. She was dozing with her elbow propped on the table supporting her head. Arto Söderstedt was without a doubt on some other planet. He was standing at the kitchen window, looking out and pondering mysterious coincidences.

The day on which the first murder occurred was the anniversary of Emanuel Swedenborg's death in London in 1772.

Söderstedt let his thoughts evaporate and flutter upwards into the ether of the clear April sky.

The only people at work inside the villa were a medical examiner, a couple of crime techs and Jorge Chavez, who was studying every last inch of the house. Every once in a while the techs would chase him out of the living room, but he kept returning, again and again, to the scene of the crime, like some stupid criminal.

The officers who had arrived first had now gone back to the police station on Golfvägen. A couple of NCP plain-clothes assistants were keeping watch at the police cordon outside. Strangely enough, the media hadn't yet got wind of what had happened. Aside from the technical team at work in the living room, the A-Unit was able to sit in the villa undisturbed.

That is, until two well-built gentlemen in their forties wearing identical leather jackets came stomping into the kitchen.

'Don't say a word,' said the blonder of the men to Hultin. 'We just want to see the crime scene for ourselves.'

'You'll have my report as soon as it's done, as usual,'

Hultin told him. Much against their will, he introduced them to the rest of the group.

'Gillis Döös and Max Grahn from Säpo.'

'The Security Police,' said the man who apparently did all the talking. Evidently he was Döös. 'We won't disturb you.'

They went into the living room and carried on a low-voice conversation with the pathologist and the tech in charge. Then they walked through the house, peering in all the nooks and crannies. All of a sudden they were gone – their car gave an audible screech as it pulled away.

'We may have more to do with them from now on,' said Hultin, keeping his tone neutral. Nobody cared to think about what that might entail.

Chavez came into the kitchen and sat down next to Hultin. 'It's exactly the same,' he said.

'Not really,' said Hultin. 'We need to hear more from the techs. Apparently one bullet was left behind.'

They were sitting in the kitchen of a huge mansion in the suburb of Djursholm, just a couple of blocks from the house owned by Eric Blomgren, the retired judge, with whom the other retired judge, Rickard Franzén, had spent an uneventful evening over a chessboard while drinking cognac. It was at the latter address that Chavez and Norlander had sat in their police vehicle, keeping watch all evening. Presumably that fact bothered both of them.

The villa belonged to a man by the name of Nils-Emil Carlberger. His body was discovered in the living room just after eight-thirty in the morning, when his house cleaner arrived. She called the police and then vanished. Nobody knew who she was or where she was now. In all likelihood she was a refugee who was supposed to be deported and thus had gone underground, making a living by cleaning houses for minuscule wages. The Carlberger family consisted of a wife and two grown sons. They would be notified shortly. The wife, Nancy, was staying at the family summer house outside Halmstad, getting it ready for the season. The sons lived in Landvetter and Lund, respectively. Neither of them was active in the business empire owned by Nils-Emil Carlberger. One was an air-traffic controller and the other a doctoral candidate in sociology. Nancy had been a secretary in one of the firms belonging to the Carlberger conglomerate before she gave it up to become a housewife. She was not the mother of his two sons.

That was about all they knew so far.

The elderly pathologist came into the kitchen, vigorously scratching the back of his neck.

'As far as I'm concerned, everything seems identical,' he said. 'Two shots through the brain. Death seems to have been instantaneous. I'll get back to you, of course, with more details after the autopsy, but I don't think you should hope for any big revelations from my side.'

'We're not expecting anything like that, Sigvard,' said Hultin quietly. 'Is Svenhagen almost done?'

The pathologist, Sigvard Qvarfordt, shrugged.

They went back to waiting. The venetian blinds were

losing their battle against the sun, which seemed filled with the promise of spring, and the kitchen table was streaked with thin bars of sunlight.

Hjelm opened the kitchen door onto the terrace. Chavez followed as he stepped outside.

'See that chimney over there? The tallest one?' said Chavez, squinting and pointing across the two neighbouring gardens. 'That's Blomgren's house. That's where we sat yesterday, freezing in Norlander's Volvo. He was here, creeping around almost next door. Maybe he saw us and laughed to himself.'

Hjelm shrugged.

'Maybe we should have felt his presence,' muttered Chavez, drinking in the sunshine. '*Como en casa*,' he said with pleasure.

'Like home?' said Hjelm. 'Where's that?'

'Rågsved,' said Chavez, and went back inside. '*Nací aquí*,' he said over his shoulder. 'I was born here.'

In the kitchen Brynolf Svenhagen, who was in charge of the crime-scene techs, was looking through his notebook, but spoke in standard phrases guaranteed not to be included in his notes.

'Naturally we'll be going over the whole house with a fine-toothed comb today. But it looks like no evidence has been left behind, as usual. Except for the bullet. He removed one bullet, but not the second. That gives us something to go on. We'll analyse it as soon as possible. What I can tell you right now is that I don't recognise it. It's not one of the six or seven most common types.'

He went back to the living room, where both his subordinates were still crawling around on the floor and over the sofa. Hjelm saw the black-covered stretcher slip past, out in the hall, under the supervision of pathologist Qvarfordt.

A sleepy mood rather than an air of resignation had descended over the kitchen. It had been a long shot, and things hadn't worked out. That happens. Although it was too bad that Rickard Franzén Jr had suffered a cut to the face when Nyberg shoved him down onto the *rya* rug. Commissioner Waldemar Mörner had already set up an account in the budget for the anticipated legal claim for bodily harm.

'So we're just going to have to start over again,' said Hultin matter-of-factly. 'CEO Carlberger actually fits the pattern better than the incorruptible judge. It should be crystal clear by now that this whole thing somehow has to do with business. Hjelm, you'll check up on whether this castrates the Mimir lead and, if so, follow up on the significantly less castrated Dionysus angle instead. And don't forget about the golf-course guest books. The workload is going to increase dramatically for those of you working on the business aspect. We'll probably have to bring in a few more people, Nyberg. Holm, you'll keep working on the personal angle. Norlander will continue with the international. According to what the good Svenhagen said, the bullet could be foreign. That remains to be seen.

'And then there's the inexplicable fact that the bullet

was left in the wall. Was he interrupted? Did he intentionally leave a clue behind? If so, did he do it to play
with us, to lead us astray, or because for some reason he
actually wants to get caught? Or did he make his first
mistake? There's undoubtedly a reason. The bullet will
soon be on its way to the lab. I want all of you to think
about that. To summarise quickly: Norlander, the international aspect; Holm, the personal; Chavez, Söderstedt,
Nyberg, the business angle; Hjelm, the sexual. As soon
as I hear the slightest peep from Mr Crime Tech Boss,
Brynolf Svenhagen, I'll call you in for a proper rundown.
Questions?'

No questions.

At any rate, none that Hultin could answer.

They left the magnificent villa in the care of the crime
techs.

Hultin heard the first peep from Mr Crime Tech Boss
Brynolf Svenhagen at 11.22 A.M. on 3 April. By 11.51 the
team had gathered in Supreme Central Command –
Chavez's name for it had been officially adopted, as
Waldemar Mörner had given it his 'full approval'. They
had all been in their offices when Hultin called on the
intercom at 11.23. All except one.

At that moment Hjelm was sitting in a basement on
Stallgränd in Gamla Stan, where no mobile-phone signals
could reach. Guardian Clöfwenhielm typed in the name
'Carlberger, Nils-Emil' on his little cheese-bell computer,

but got no hit. Nils-Emil Carlberger was not, and never had been, a member of the Order of Skidbladnir or the Order of Mimir or any order whatsoever.

At 11.35 Clöfwenhielm drew aside the heavy drapery covering the entrance to the order's inner sanctum. At 11.41 Paul Hjelm came out and made a sacred vow never to reveal what he had seen inside. He would keep his word. At 11.42 he emerged into the narrow alleyway and took a call from Hultin on his mobile, notifying him of the meeting. At 11.51 he entered the room now known as the Supreme Central Command, with its capital letters. At 13.09 he laughed loudly at this label, when Chavez, also laughing, told him about it.

But before then, the following took place.

Jan-Olov Hultin informed them that news of the murder of Nils-Emil Carlberger, the head of the Carlberger conglomerate, had not yet reached the media. Apparently, and to Hultin's great relief, as he said without changing expression, the media leak was not due to anyone within the A-Unit.

'As I suspected,' said Hultin modestly, 'there's something very special about the bullet that was left in the wall. Svenhagen has conducted some sort of incomprehensible but irrefutable chemical analysis of the shattered bits of lead and found a most particular chemical component. It's a damned inferior bullet, and those types of inferior bullets stem from a small, second-rate weapons factory in a town called Pavlodar in present-day Kazakhstan. Vladimir Smirnov's country, you know.

'Svenhagen has personally been in contact with Interpol's forensic-data centre this morning, and here's what he found out. The weapons factory ran into trouble when the Soviet Union collapsed and then the market economy came in and imposed its "infallible natural selection", to quote Svenhagen. There was simply no market for the factory's shoddy ammunition. But apparently there was a huge bankruptcy inventory. No one knows what happened to it. But Interpol's response is unequivocal: the mafia.'

Hultin paused. Possibly he was waiting to see the effect of his words. But no one reacted. Possibly he was just catching his breath. After a moment he went on.

'The Russian mafia is, as we know, a very heterogeneous organisation. In reality we know far too little about it. It's almost frightening how little, considering that it has made its way across the Baltic and dominates large parts of the underworld in Helsinki. There are indications that Stockholm is its next big market. In the largest faction are a bunch of crackpots who have seized upon the more extreme aspects of the market economy. Survival of the fittest.

'But the more sophisticated factions are branching out to the top national echelons in Russia and the Baltic countries. They also have close contact with top mafia bosses in Italy and the United States. The presence of this ammunition in the home of the third victim of a serial killer who has attacked Sweden's top capitalists within a few days of one another presents us with a frightening prospect. But presumably we're not the first to reach this conclusion. We've already seen the odd demonstration put on by Säpo at the Djursholm villa – as if they suddenly wanted to step out of the shadows and show their presence. Apparently they're working at top speed in the military security division, in even deeper cellar vaults on Lidingövägen and elsewhere.'

Hultin sighed, gulped down some water and went on in the same droning tone of voice: 'If we now combine this ammunition with the execution method, we have real reason for concern. As you heard yesterday, Norlander has ferreted out three international organisations that consistently execute their victims with a shot to the head. One of them, as you heard, is a small Russian-Estonian criminal band, led by an anonymous commander, known only as Viktor X. It's not clear what their connections are to the mafia. We need to look into it further. That's going to shake up our work assignments a bit. Right before the meeting I ran into Mörner in the hall. He told me that due to the, quote, "appalling link to the Soviet state mafia", he has appointed two more officers to the unit. Both are from the Finance Police. They'll be helping out with the financial aspects, because that's where we need to be looking.

'We also need to expand that part of the investigation – and this is important – to include any business connections to the Russian mafia. Eventually I'm hoping to release those of you working on the business angle to work on something else, to do a little moonlighting, as

Hjelm is doing. We should by no means fixate on this Russian lead. And Nyberg, before you get too involved in the financial side of things, I'm going to send you over to Norlander to chart the Viktor X gang. So we're going to be working on two flanks: one from the ex-Soviet viewpoint, and the other from the Swedish. At some point these two flanks will meet up to assume positions for the final battle.'

'You've been spending too much time with Mörner,' said Hjelm.

'No doubt,' said Hultin.

There was a knock on the door, and two faces peeked in: a tall man so fair that his skin was almost transparent and who couldn't be over thirty; and an equally young, dark-haired woman who was a good deal shorter than average. They were definitely an odd couple.

'Good. Come in,' said Hultin. 'Have a seat. We're just about to discuss Carlberger's life and lifestyle. So these are the new members of the A-Unit: Billy Pettersson and Tanja Florén. We've managed to clear out room 305 for them. All right, does anyone have any information on Carlberger outside his business dealings? Anything that we don't already know? Kerstin?'

Holm shook her head. 'His wife and sons will be arriving soon,' she said. 'I'm going to interview them.'

'What about leisure activities? Hjelm?'

'Just like Daggfeldt and Strand-Julén, Carlberger played golf and owned a boat, although his was a motorboat, apparently a real luxury cabin cruiser docked at the marina in Lidingö. Don't ask me why. But the golf connection is rock-solid: just like the other two, he was a member of the Stockholm Golf Association and played mainly at Kevinge. He wasn't a member of the Order of Mimir, or any other order, as far as I know.'

'So we can probably set that lead aside for a while,' said Hultin, making a chequered pattern on the whiteboard. The previous day's little fiasco was noticeably absent from everything he said, and there was an implicit command in his silence. He turned to the new members. 'Arto Söderstedt is handling the corporate aspect. Söderstedt?'

Arto Söderstedt cleared his throat and straightened up a bit, as if preparing to give a lecture or a sermon. For a moment Hjelm thought the thin, pale figure was someone quite different from a low-level police officer. The wrong man in the wrong place. A wolf in sheep's clothing. The clichés raced through his mind as Söderstedt took the floor.

'So what we're dealing with are three individuals each in charge of a group of enterprises that border on, but don't quite constitute, a genuine financial empire,' he said. 'Our victims are – were – rich and powerful, but weren't part of the general flood of celebrities. The structure of their conglomerates is similar. At the centre are a couple of wholly owned financial companies, and on the periphery a cluster of various co-owned firms that are also financial companies.

'Keep in mind that all three of our corpses are capital-ists of the new breed that were first given a great deal of leeway in the Eighties, meaning that they were men of non-productive business ventures. Money-movers whose wealth benefits no one but themselves, either in the form of job creation or tax receipts. What only a few years earlier was the domain of bandits – laundering money, moving it around and lending it at exorbitant rates – has now become a legitimate business endeavour. With the deregulation during the Eighties, it actually became possible to shovel money out of the country.

'All that prosperity was nothing but an empty balloon that imploded during a seriously confused decade. Government authorities misinterpreted the plus columns, reading the figures through the old, discarded lenses of industrialism, and cheered. The financial sharks cheered too, but for completely different reasons. They sucked the juice out of the national economy, as it uttered masochistic moans of joy.'

Söderstedt fell silent. The members of the A-Unit looked at him in bewilderment. What an odd explanation of Carlberger's business ventures.

'Let's try to keep the political opinions to a minimum,' said Hultin, his tone neutral.

Söderstedt looked around the room, as if suddenly remembering where he was. Hjelm could almost see smoke rising out of his shirt collar. He pulled himself together and went on in his resonant Finnish accent.

'There are two things I'm trying to get at here. First, the general coupling of this social climate with what I said earlier about the serial-murder boom in the United

States, the hero-worship of outsiders who have cast aside the system of norms that is increasingly showing its cracks and revealing the chasm behind it for one simple reason: money. We're sitting on a powder keg.

'Second, the specific link to our case. What if we're dealing with an individual who has quite simply seen through, or thinks he has seen through, the whole damn game. Or to put it another way: an individual who assumes he has seen the real face of the invisible power and doesn't give a damn about ripping it away and putting it on display. An individual who is both intelligent and insane, the worst possible combination. He has seen the connections, the more or less mysterious correspondences, and begins his exposé of these connections, most likely by accident, on the anniversary of Swedenborg's death.'

'For the sake of clarity,' Hultin said, 'do you think these murders are politically motivated? Leftist terrorism?'

'Not terrorism. No, I wouldn't think so. But in a sense they *are* political. Someone who has been affected in some way, someone who has thought deeply and drawn certain conclusions, who is quite correct in terms of analysis, but completely wrong in terms of action. Let's think about this. We've just come through the worst possible financial crisis. Many people were affected by it, but perhaps everything is becoming clear only now.'

No one said anything for a long time. Without a doubt Söderstedt's torrent of words contained certain valid points. Both newcomers, Billy Pettersson and Tanja

Florén, were trying not to yawn, wondering where on earth they'd landed. In a lecture hall at the university? In a discussion group for conspiracy theorists? Or in the presence of a police officer whose obstinate intelligence had always prevented him from advancing within the force?

'Three representatives of the new capitalism,' Hjelm summed up. 'Various possibilities. Indications pointing to Eastern Europe. Problems with the mafia establishing itself in the Baltics? Use of business contacts from the Baltics? Although one of the three doesn't have much to do with Eastern Europe. A purely political motive? Some sort of revenge? Personal or professional? What else?'

Silence. Clearly there was nothing else. Was there anything they had overlooked? The fraternal order, a fine old classic straight out of an Agatha Christie novel, had gone up in smoke – that type of puzzle intrigue belonged irrevocably to the past – and instead they had landed squarely in the present day: post-industrial capitalism, Eastern European mafia and the collapse of Sweden's financial regulatory system in the 1990s.

Paul Hjelm preferred the fraternal order.

'All right, shall we discuss Carlberger's conglomerate?' said Hultin, pouring oil on the waters of the A-Unit.

Söderstedt instantly switched from the verbose and voluble to the terse and concise. Hjelm had the feeling that the abrupt change was something deeply anchored in Söderstedt's character. In the latter approach there was an answer, a solution, and he wanted to present it as clearly and distinctly as possible. In the former approach there was no answer, no solution; there the 'truth' trickled through the cracks between the words, in the ghastly connections. That was how society was, this post-industrial society at least, in the eyes of the eloquent Finnish buffoon.

'The Carlberger conglomerate,' he said. 'At the centre is the Spiran financial firm. Surrounding Spiran are ever weaker, concentric circles formed by increasingly inaccessible subsidiaries, and subsidiaries of subsidiaries. In less than an hour I discovered one connection, and with professional help' – Söderstedt gestured towards Pettersson and Florén – 'I'm sure more will come to light. My connection has to do with Strand-Julén, who was part owner in one of the affiliates of a Carlberger subsidiary, Alruna Holding AB.'

He fell silent.

Nobody could tell whether he had finished. But he was looking slightly burned out, so Hultin said, 'Okay, we thank Söderstedt for an unusually inspired report. Chavez?'

Chavez chuckled. 'I'll be brief. Carlberger was a member of three boards of directors concurrently with Daggfeldt and Strand-Julén. Our three victims were members of the same board at Ericsson in 1986–87; Sydbanken in 1989–91; and MEMAB in 1990. That's the connection between our three stiffs as regards boards.'

'What's MEMAB?' asked Holm.

'No idea,' said Chavez.

'I can tell you,' said Tanja Florén, speaking in a deep alto voice. 'What's your guess?'

'A financial company,' said a very weary Finn.

'That's right,' said Florén.

13

As far as Paul Hjelm was concerned, his work now entered an entirely new phase. After standing on the front lines, he had now been pushed to the very back of the pack. The investigation was progressing along two flanks: the Russian mafia lead, via Norlander and Nyberg; and the business angle, via Söderstedt, Chavez, Pettersson and Florén. Holm was carrying on intensive interviews with the relatives and friends of the departed magnates, leaving the secondary interviews to the foot soldiers in NCP and the Stockholm police force.

And Hjelm was spending his days leafing through the pages of the golf association's guest books. *The criminal landscape of the past*, he thought bitterly. No one was murdered any more because of intrigues within fraternal orders or at golf clubs. Nowadays it was kinky sex, drugs and money-laundering that brought people down.

The phone number for the purported pimp with the fitting name of Johan Stake had been disconnected without any forwarding number. And a return visit to

Timmermansgatan, together with innumerable phone calls, revealed that the young male prostitute, Jörgen Lindén, had fled the scene.

The autopsy performed by pathologist Qvarfordt on Nils-Emil Carlberger produced nothing other than signs of an incipient brain tumour. Nor had Svenhagen's crime techs turned up any solid leads. Once again the perp had left no evidence behind – except the damned bullet in the wall.

Hjelm was making his way backwards through the golf association's guest books. The hours dragged along. Among the signatures written in varying degrees of legibility, he soon learned to recognise Daggfeldt's meticulous handwriting, Strand-Julén's expansive scrawl and Carlberger's backward slant. They appeared frequently in the books, but never anywhere near each other. Hjelm had made his way back to 1990 and was getting ready to accept that none of the three corpses had ever played golf with any of the others, when he suddenly saw the meticulous squiggles right next to the scrawl. After a moment he discovered nearby the backward slant.

Daggfeldt, Strand-Julén and Carlberger had actually once played golf together, just the three of them. That opened up interesting prospects. Hjelm checked with Chavez; apparently the joint golf game had taken place immediately following a MEMAB board meeting on 7 September 1990. It was, oddly, the only golf game that the lodge brothers Daggfeldt and Strand-Julén had ever played together. They had both belonged to the inner circle of the Order of Skidbladnir; they had been members of the same eight boards of directors since the late Seventies; and they had belonged to the same golf association. Yet they had played golf together only once. And on that one occasion the third golf partner had been the third murder victim.

It was extremely puzzling.

'Three men play a round of golf in the autumn of 1990,' said Hjelm aloud. 'It's the only time they ever play together. Several years later, all three of them end up on ice, put there by the same perp, within a week's time. What does it mean?'

Chavez continued to type on the computer. 'What?' was his inspired reply.

'I'm not going to repeat myself. Your subconscious heard me.'

Chavez stopped typing and turned to look at him.

He ought to have a moustache, Hjelm surprised himself by thinking, sensing the old, deeply buried prejudices stir inside him.

'It doesn't mean shit. Maybe just the fact that there are close ties between all sectors of the business world.'

'Or that somebody doesn't like golf.'

'That's it,' said Chavez calmly and went back to typing. 'The whole mystery is solved. Some golf-hater stood there brooding outside Kevinge Golf Course on an autumn day in 1990, caught sight of the three arrogant upper-class gentlemen who were boasting about themselves on the fairway and decided, "I'm going to kill those fuckers, those three right there, in one fell swoop." He waited several long years before he decided to act. But then he moved quickly.'

'A caddy, perhaps?'

'I was joking,' said Chavez.

'I realise that,' said Hjelm. 'But if we make a few changes in your story, it sounds more serious. The three men show up right after a tedious board meeting. They've had time to relax and chat a bit on the cab ride over, maybe had a few whiskies in the bar, and all the usual business bullshit comes pouring out of them. They're fucking awful. Even the flowers wilt as they pass by. Their tongues are so loose, they flap. Okay? So maybe the caddy is a little late to arrive and starts off by making some mistake, who knows, but they start in on him, badgering him, or her for that matter, and laughing good-naturedly. Then for the rest of the game they treat him like shit, inescapable, but revolting. It's possible that sexual harassment takes place. They casually force him or her so far down that it takes several years for the caddy to recover and start fresh.

'Maybe their behavior was some sort of – what's it called? – catalyst that ignited a bigger reaction already in process. Maybe this caddy had previously spent a few years in a mental hospital or something like that. And then he was let out with the rest of the lunatics during the general wave of cutbacks and release legislation. Finally he's got hold of his life and figured out what triggered his persecution mania. Okay? He's beyond desperate, everything seems clear, and then he takes them out, one by one, simply, quickly, elegantly. Sweet revenge.'

'Very imaginative,' said Chavez. He had stopped typing. 'And not without a certain interest.'

'I'm going to make a call,' said Hjelm, and quickly punched in the number.

'But if you're right, then the killing is over now. And it doesn't explain the Russian bullet. Plus it eliminates the whole financial angle.'

'Hello, this is Paul Hjelm from the NCP. Who am I speaking to?'

'Axel Widstrand,' said the voice on the phone. 'Secretary of the Stockholm Golf Association. Are you the one who took all of our guest books? Lena doesn't have the authority to release them. Are you going to be done with them soon?'

'*I* gave her the authority. Do the golfers normally use a caddy when they play a round at the club?'

'I'd like to have those books back.'

'Three of your members have been murdered in less than a week, and you want to have the books back? What kind of world are you living in?'

'Oops,' said Chavez. 'Breach of confidentiality.'

Hjelm took the noon edition of *Aftonbladet* out of his top desk drawer and placed it in front of Chavez. The headline screamed: EXTRA. EXTRA. THE POWER MURDERER STRIKES AGAIN. THREE CEOS KILLED. DIRECTOR NILS-EMIL CARLBERGER'S BODY FOUND BY MYSTERIOUS WOMAN.

'"The Power Murderer"?' Chavez held up the tabloid by one corner, as if it had been steeped in day-old vomit. 'Newborn, yet already baptised.'

'Might as well start using the name. Everybody else is going to,' said Hjelm grimly, and went back to his phone call.

'Just answer the question.'

'Caddies?' the secretary of the Stockholm Golf Association echoed on the other end of the line. 'Sometimes.'

'Sometimes?'

'It's rare that anyone would use a caddy for an ordinary round of golf. But it does happen.'

'How do the players get hold of one?'

'We usually provide them. But you have to make the request in advance.'

'So if three men are going to play a round of golf, then you find a caddy for them. Is that right?'

'As I said: if they make the request in advance. It takes a few hours to set it up. And in the case you mentioned, there would be *three* caddies. One for each of them. One caddy can't carry clubs for three people, of course.'

Hjelm suddenly had an idea. It was a long shot, but he had to try.

'Is Lena a caddy?'

'Lena Hansson? She used to be. But now she works inside.'

'Was she active as a caddy in September 1990?'

Axel Widstrand, secretary of the Stockholm Golf Association, was silent for a moment. Hjelm could hear a murmuring, as if the man had covered the receiver and was talking to somebody nearby.

'Yes, she was. She didn't stop until last season.'

'If you've got her there on your lap, could you ask her if she remembers caddying for Kuno Daggfeldt, Bernhard Strand-Julén and Nils-Emil Carlberger when they played a round on the afternoon of 7 September 1990?'

'I must say that I don't appreciate your attempt at a joke. If that's what it was.'

'Ask her.'

Again a muted murmuring on the line.

'No,' said Widstrand.

'Her memory is that good?'

'Is there anything else?'

'Is there any marking in the guest books that would indicate whether the players used a caddy?'

'No. The players sign their names, and that's all. Is there anything else?'

'Not at the moment,' said Hjelm, hanging up the phone and writing the name Lena Hansson in his notebook.

For future use.

The theory about a lone, persecuted caddy vanished as quickly as it had appeared. It was rare to use a caddy at all, and if the men, contrary to custom, had decided to do so, then there would have been three caddies, not just one. He drew a line through Lena Hansson's name. If the murders stopped, he would return to the idea.

'Listen to this,' said Chavez, deeply immersed in the

evening paper, which was no longer published in the evening. '"There should be no doubt whatsoever that we're dealing with the first real terrorist action to occur in Sweden in a very long time. Not even during the heyday of the Red Army Faction did we see anything like this. Now top Swedish businessmen are being executed one after the other by this 'Power Murderer.' We may be facing the worst crime ever to take place in Sweden. The only thing we know for sure is that the police are clueless." Which is their way of saying,' Chavez added, as he put down the paper, 'that since they're not being told anything, there's nothing to know.'

'They forgot to mention the West German ambassador,' said Hjelm. 'But you're too young to remember all that.'

Jorge Chavez stared at Hjelm. 'Paul. If you persist in concocting old-fashioned intrigues and fiddling around with equally old-fashioned detective work – meaning if you refuse to accept that this has to do with moving money via global computer networks and professional hitmen, probably hired via the same computer networks – then you need to find out more about the people involved. Instead of relying on clichés about business bullshit and flowers that wilt as the potentates pass by. This is about real individuals, after all, not cartoon characters.'

'A very touching speech. What sort of suggestions are you hiding behind your concern for the lost honour of these gentlemen?'

'You don't know enough about them. Go see Kerstin. Borrow her tapes. Learn about them.'

Chavez returned to the computer screen. For a moment Hjelm watched him working diligently. He saw the new breed of policeman, and for the first time he realised what a gulf existed between him and his officemate; it really had nothing to do with their backgrounds. Chavez, computer-literate, international, rational, without prejudices, able to maintain a certain distance, enthusiastic. If it was true that Hjelm was looking at the future of the police force, then it was not exactly a bad thing. When he thought it was possible that there might be a certain lack of heart and soul, he realised at the same instant that he was once again working from a cliché. For a moment he thought that his whole world consisted of nothing else. What the hell could he say about his own heart and soul? He felt old. What he saw in front of him was quite simply a man who was a better police officer than he was. With black hair and a Spanish surname.

Look deep into your heart, Hjelm.

One of his tasks was to purge Grundström from his thoughts.

He went down the hall to the bathroom. He had a spot on his cheek. He tried squeezing it, but nothing came out. Instead, the skin around it split and began to flake off. He put a little water on his finger and dabbed the flakes of skin away. Then he went back out to the corridor, walked past his office and stopped outside room 303. He knocked and went in.

Gunnar Nyberg was tapping away on the computer keyboard, a woolly mammoth jabbing at a spaceship. The giant of a man looked as if he'd landed on the wrong planet.

Kerstin Holm was wearing a headset and typing on a small laptop. She turned off the Walkman lying next to her computer and turned to face Hjelm. Nyberg kept on typing, slowly, doggedly, reluctantly – but with great tenacity. Hjelm thought he was witnessing a basic personality trait.

'A visitor,' said Holm. 'How unusual.'

'What's that?' asked Hjelm, pointing at her laptop.

'Haven't you ever seen one of these?' she asked in surprise, seeing his expression darken. Then she gave him a slightly ironic smile. He'd never thought of her as beautiful before.

'I brought in my own,' she said. 'It's faster.'

For three more seconds he thought how beautiful she was: the loose-fitting black clothes, the tousled brown hair, her alert eyes an even darker brown, the charming wrinkles that she didn't try to hide, the perpetually ironic smile, the textbook-pure Göteborg accent. Then he blinked all these thoughts away. 'I'd like to listen to your tapes,' he said.

'Is there anything in particular you want to hear?'

'Not really. I want to see if I can get to know them better. Avoid clichés, if that's possible.'

'Maybe. Maybe not,' said Holm, pointing to a skyscraper of cassette tapes in front of her. 'Maybe a lot of clichés actually apply.'

'What's your own opinion?'

'We can talk about that afterwards,' she said, pushing the unsteady tower of tapes across the desk.

The tapes weren't labelled, so Hjelm chose one at random and stuck it into his newly purchased Walkman.

Kerstin Holm's voice said, 'All right. Interview on 3 April with Willy Eriksson, born William Carlberger, 8–14–63. So you're the son of Nils-Emil and Carlotta Carlberger?'

'Yes. Although her last name is now Eriksson. Carla Eriksson. That was her maiden name.'

'And you've taken the same name? And officially changed your first name too?'

'Yes.'

'But your brother is still named Carlberger, Andreas Carlberger. What's the reason behind the name change?'

'Hmm. I don't know. I guess I just feel closer to my mother.'

'You're a doctoral candidate in sociology in Lund. Are you a Marxist?'

Willy Eriksson chuckled. 'If I was, you wouldn't have to ask the question.'

'Was there some sort of ideological conflict between you and your father?'

'I suppose you could call it ideological, even though I'd be a bit cautious about using that term. What you're trying to get at, and I might as well make it easier for you, is the question of whether I hated that sweetheart of a man, Nils-Emil Carlberger. The answer is no. No hatred involved.'

'No hatred and no sorrow?'

'Exactly.'

'Tell me about him. What was he like? Was he the classic capitalist? From a purely sociological perspective?'

'An elegant way to steer the conversation into my own field of interest. *Touché*. Get the guy to talk.'

'That's enough. If you really want to make things easier for me, then help me out here. Otherwise we're just going to waste a lot of time that neither of us can spare.'

'If such a thing as a "classic capitalist" exists, from a "purely sociological perspective", then I think that's what he was. A materialistic and disciplined childhood with sporadic visits by the authoritarian father figure. Nothing new under the sun. No hugs, but no visible violence, either. Everything had to do with money and its shiny display. Andreas and Mama and I were all part of the shiny display. Andreas a bit more than I, and I a bit more than Mama. She was always a little too grey and plain to shine, no matter how much he tried to polish her up. And no matter how much I try to find redeeming features, or even any individual traits, I can't find any. I'm sorry.'

'I'm the one who's sorry. Did he have any special interests or something that might present an alternative picture?'

'I've really searched for something. When I was ten or

eleven, when the inferno was raging at home the year before their divorce, I once asked him what exactly they made in his factory. He laughed and said, "Money". I was hoping for something slightly ridiculous, and redemptive, behind all that accumulation of wealth: condoms or teddy bears or back-scratchers or nose-hair clippers or whatever the hell it might be. But of course it was a purely financial enterprise, from beginning to end. There's not much comedy in money.'

Hjelm was getting bored, so he fast-forwarded. A crackling female voice said:

'But Kuno, he was a real family man. He was.'

Hjelm rewound to the start of the interview: 'Madame Hummelstrand, *s'il vous plaît*,' said Kerstin Holm.

There was a rustling sound, and off in the background an angry female voice could be faintly heard: *'Touche pas le téléphone! Jamais plus! Touche seulement moi-même!'* Finally an emphatic voice spoke into the receiver:

'Allô!'

'Is this Anna-Clara Hummelstrand, wife of George Hummelstrand, vice president of Nimco Finance?'

'Who wants to know?'

'Kerstin Holm, National Criminal Police in Stockholm. It has to do with the murders of Kuno Daggfeldt and Bernhard Strand-Julén.'

'Oh, I see. *Une agentinne, n'est-ce pas?*'

'C'est peut-être le mot juste, madame,' said Holm, her voice ice-cold. 'I want to point out that this conversation is being recorded. Let me begin: phone conversation with

Anna-Clara Hummelstrand in Nice on 2 April at 17.02.'

'Tally-ho!' said Anna-Clara Hummelstrand. Only now was it clear how drunk she was. '*On dit peut-être agentesse . . .*'

'Maybe I should get back to you after the fog has cleared,' said Holm.

'After what?'

'After the haze has lifted.'

'*Croyez-moi, une agentesse humoriste!*' shouted Anna-Clara Hummelstrand. '*Tirée! Tirée, ma amie! Immédiatement!*'

'Okay. Let's give it a try. Is it correct to say that you are close friends with both Ninni Daggfeldt and Lilian Strand-Julén?'

'As close as anyone can get. We exchange information about our gynaecological exams. That's the definition of a deep female friendship. *Tout à fait.*'

'Do they know each other?'

'*Ninni and Lilian?* Not directly. I try to keep my girl-friends separate, *à ma honté.* Then they can't gang up on me. But of course they know about each other through gossip.'

'And their husbands?'

'Well, neither of the poor dears had it easy, I can tell you that. They didn't know how to handle their little boys the way I do. Lilian's situation was well known, of course. Saint Bernhard's little puppies. If she was the one who got rid of him, she has my full support. She had moved out, with *his* full support, but divorce was out of the question, as she always said. We all know how things went for little Johanna. Besides, it was an arrangement that suited Bernhard. But Kuno, he was a real family man. He was. No escapades that I know of, and what I don't know about isn't worth knowing, let me assure you, *ma petite*. On the other hand, he worked way too much. More than Bernhard, I'm positive about that. Never home.'

'Yet he had time to play golf and attend meetings of a fraternal order.'

'Right. The Order of Hugin or Munin, or whatever it's called. So cute. George is a member too. He's told me about the little rituals, how they put on Nordic god masks and strange robes, or whatever they're called, and engage in sheer bacchanalia. It's been a long time since he engaged in sheer bacchanalia with me, that's the truth. I have to arrange my own. *Pas vrai*, Philippe? He's nodding. But in general I think they regarded both golf and the order as work. I think the good Sir George, my own little dragon-slayer, also considers them part of his work time.'

'Have you ever heard George talk about something called the Order of Skidbladnir?'

'Dear God, no. That sounds ghastly.'

'How did you hear about Daggfeldt's and Strand-Julén's deaths?'

'My husband called me last night. He sounded a bit shaken, *mon grand chevalier*.'

'Was he involved in business deals with them?'

'I've never been interested in George's business affairs. As long as there's plenty of money in the bank account,

I'm happy. Terrible, right? I must be the classic object of hatred for feminist advocates like yourself, Miss Holm. Oh, whoops, I see that little Philippe is preparing for other activities. Have you, Miss Holm, ever seen a magnificent, olive-brown Gallic pole rise up from an absolutely slack condition to an absolutely stiff one? A marvellously prolonged moment of slow, slow, economical expansion? I guarantee that it affects a person's ability to carry on a sensible conversation with a female Swedish police officer. *Mais Philippe! Calmons!*'

The conversation was cut off. Hjelm heard Kerstin Holm sigh. Then the same crackling telephone sounds behind Holm's voice.

'Part two, Nice, 3 April, 10.52 A.M.'

'*Encore,*' said a tremendously lacklustre Anna-Clara Hummelstrand.

'Do you know a Nancy Carlberger?'

'Nancy? A wonderful little town in Lorraine—'

'Are you awake, Mrs Hummelstrand?'

'*Peu à peu.* Nancy Carlberger? Nils-Emil's little trophy wife? I've met her a couple of times. Didn't much care for her. What is it now? Has Nils-Emil kicked the bucket too?'

'He was murdered last night. I'd like to point out that until further notice this information is to be considered confidential.'

'*Mon dieu!* This is starting to feel like that Agatha Christie story *And Then There Were None.* Have you talked to the servants? The butler?'

'As a matter of fact, we're trying to locate his house cleaner.'

'That must be little Sonya, the poor thing. She takes care of most of the houses in Djursholm. Was she the one who found him? She didn't murder him, that much I can guarantee. I've never met anyone so timid since I saved the life of a wagtail in my sadly so-distant childhood. Åke was his name, Åke Wagtail.'

'Does Sonya clean your home?'

'No, we have a different little woman, a Turk who's been with us for years now. Iraz. Iraz Effendi. No, Sonya is black. From Somalia, I think. I'm not entirely sure that she has all her documents in order. Although officially you didn't hear me say that.'

'Did she clean the Daggfeldt home, or the Strand-Juléns'?'

'No, she works only in Djursholm. You know how quickly word spreads through an area if there's a nice, cheap, reliable cleaning woman. Don't try to tell me that you don't know that.'

'And you have no idea what Sonya's last name is? Or where she lives?'

'No, but Nancy would know, of course. Why do you keep calling me, by the way? I do hope George isn't in the danger zone . . . Speaking of which, I think I must have said a lot of nonsense yesterday. I hope you can erase whatever doesn't have a direct bearing on the case. You know, George . . .'

'Do you mean this passage? And I quote: "Have you,

Miss Holm, ever seen a magnificent, olive-brown Gallic pole rise up from an absolutely slack condition to an absolutely stiff one? A marvellously prolonged moment of slow, slow, economical expansion"?'

'You delightful creature!' Mrs Hummelstrand blurted out with glee. Hjelm had finally heard enough when she went on: 'Did you sit there and masturbate at the thought of Philippe's remarkable organ? Shame on you!'

While Hjelm changed tapes, he couldn't quite rid himself of the thought of Kerstin Holm masturbating because of Philippe's remarkable organ. He pictured her sitting alone in her office. Night had descended over police headquarters. She had propped up her legs, one on either side of the laptop, and eased down her loose-fitting trousers. Her hand moved calmly and methodically up and down inside her pants. Her dark eyes were completely glazed over as she opened them wide and then threw back her head with a half-stifled moan.

What a child I am, Hjelm thought as he let his slight erection deflate. He heard the sound of a teenage girl's shrill, defiant voice in his ears.

'How do *you* think it felt? Mini, midi, maxi. Maxi-deep. Maxi-horny. Of course there were other people who had fucking stupid names. One of the girls in my class was named Angel, Angel Jakobsson-Flodh, old hippies who fixed up a luxury collective in Danderyd to keep the dream alive – alongside their computer company, of course. But nobody else was ever named after a damn boat! People name their boats after women, but they don't fucking name women after boats!'

'Did you hate your father because he gave you a name like that?'

'When I was an adolescent, sure. Now I actually think it's rather cool.'

'Did you hate the boat?'

'I've actually never hated the boat. It was the only time when Papa relaxed. He was always fussing about, trying to make sure that we all had a good time. Okay, my mother was always throwing up, and that could get really disgusting, you know, but Marre and I kept out of her way and just played our silly guess-the-word game.'

'Did your father ever hit your mother?'

'I don't know.'

'You don't know?'

'No. He would get so incredibly disappointed when he saw that all his efforts had no effect on my mother. They shouted and screamed, so we stayed out of their way, hid in a corner, out on the island where we docked, pulled a quilt over ourselves and played guess-the-word.'

'How do you feel about your father's death?'

'I've been crying a lot . . .'

Hjelm fast-forwarded, thinking how impossible it was to get any sort of insight into another person's life. What is it that drives somebody's life, what is it that forms all these connections with other people?

Everything spreads out like rings in the water.

He changed the tape again, making another arbitrary selection.

He went on and on and on, amazed at Kerstin Holm's diligence. Secretaries, family members, employees, friends all swept past in a never-ending stream.

Now a man was speaking with some sort of semi-west-coast accent.

'You're from Göteborg? Then you must know Landvetter Airport quite well.'

'More or less,' said Holm, not sounding particularly interested. 'Why is it that Willy changed his last name, but you didn't?'

'Hmm. I have nothing against Carlberger. It has a certain . . . ring to it. William took the divorce much harder than I did. He was twelve, while I was fifteen. We went to live with Mama, and our life changed radically after that. From the luxury of Djursholm to the poverty of Danvikstull, so to speak. It was lucky that I was already practically grown-up. William was more susceptible. Besides, he quickly managed to turn his personal problems into an ideological conflict. I think it's called "projection". A way to survive.'

'How did you react when you heard that your father was dead?'

'I don't know. I guess I was dumbfounded. It's not everybody whose father is liquidated by the Russian mafia.'

'Why do you think it was the Russian mafia?'

'That's what it said in *Göteborgs Tidende*. I read the newspapers on the plane. In *Aftonbladet* it said something about the Red Army Faction. *Expressen* claimed it was the Sicilian mafia. What are we supposed to believe?'

Hjelm switched off the tape and studied the hard-working Chavez for a moment. It was beginning to get dark outside.

Then he decided that the next tape would be the last. He put it in and Kerstin Holm said:

'Conversation with Rickard Franzén at 12.16 P.M. on 3 April.'

'I want this on tape too,' said the retired judge sternly, 'so I can make my view perfectly clear. How dare you come here, my dear, after what you did to my son last night?'

'I'm truly sorry about what happened, but you might have informed us that you had a son, and that he had keys to the house, and that in the middle of the night he might come tromping in with his nostrils rimmed white with cocaine.'

'I never thought that . . .'

'Here's my first question. One member of the Order of Mimir who was not part of the Order of Skidbladnir is named George Hummelstrand. Do you know him?'

'George? Of course.'

'How did he feel about you forming a separate group?'

'He wasn't at all in favour of it. Do you mean to say that you're still following the order lead? In spite of what happened to Carlberger?'

'How do you know about that? It hasn't been officially announced yet.'

'I have my contacts, damn it! That lead is a dead end!'

'Tell me about Hummelstrand.'

'Without a doubt he was furious about it. For him the by-laws of the Order of Mimir were inviolable. We were traitors. He belonged to the little hate group. It was because of them that I accepted your suspicion that I would be the next victim.'

'Give me more names.'

'Oscar Bjellerfeldt, Nils-Åke Svärdh, Bengt Klinth, possibly Jakob Ringman.'

'What was the whole thing about? Really?'

'Ritual details. Ultra-secret. Especially from women.'

'Is it true that in 1978 Jan-Olov Hultin, who back then was a detective inspector with the Stockholm police, on the narcotics squad, arrested Rickard Franzén Jr for drug possession and dealing; that Hultin was as stubborn as hell and managed to get him arrested and arraigned in spite of tremendous opposition; and that your son was convicted by both the district court and the county court, but was acquitted by the Svea Court of Appeals, where you were then serving as judge?'

'I was not the judge for my son's case!'

'No one said you were. Is it also true that Hultin was transferred to the Huddinge police after this incident?'

There was silence for a moment. Hjelm imagined serious eyebrow-raising. Franzén's voice reappeared, faintly from the background.

'I didn't think Hultin was the kind to tell tales . . . Well. It was an open-and-shut case. My son was acquitted. There wasn't enough evidence.'

'Hultin hasn't been telling tales. I reviewed the details of the case myself. There's nothing out of the ordinary. Since then Rickard Jr has been picked up a dozen times and released.'

A rattling sound started up, and it got worse. The judge said in a shrill, quavering and utterly grotesque voice:

'I think you'd better start looking around for a new job, young lady. I know one that would be very suitable.'

'Let go of the tape recorder, judge,' said Kerstin Holm calmly.

Hjelm knocked cautiously on the door and went in. Nyberg was gone. Holm was still sitting at her desk, listening to a tape and typing on her laptop. It was quite dark in the room. She looked up and took off the headset.

'Yes?' she said, her tone of voice much the same as when she had said 'Let go of the tape recorder, judge,' a few hours earlier. It was late.

Hjelm put the pile of tapes on her desk and shook his head. 'Hopeless,' he said. 'But Franzén was an unexpected bonus.'

'That might have been stupid.'

'You went there to give him a scare.'

'He's been supplying that son of his with money for drugs all these years, and he's bailed him out so many times that it's become a standing joke down at the jail.

He's never going to let him go through the Passageway of Sighs again.'

Hjelm perched on the edge of the desk. The Passageway of Sighs was the underground tunnel between police headquarters and the courthouse, through which prisoners with bowed heads had passed for almost a century.

'What a hell of a lot of work you've done,' he said.

'So did you ever manage to get beyond the clichés?' she asked.

'I've never felt so far removed from other people.'

'I know what you mean. New threads keep appearing that you can track down further; new shoots keep growing out of the stalks. But the stalks themselves remain inaccessible. Maybe a human being merely consists of a bunch of threads and external connections. Who knows?'

'In any case, that's all that's left.'

Kerstin Holm closed her laptop, stretched and said into the dark, 'You have a spot on your cheek.'

'It's not a spot,' said Hjelm.

14

They came from the cellar.

They poured out of a plain grey delivery van and rushed soundlessly towards the stairs. They carried submachine guns.

They opened the door and wound their way up the stone steps in the insulated stairwell. They moved in complete silence.

At every landing the first man barricaded the door leading to the apartments. The lift started up somewhere outside.

At the seventh landing they stopped for a moment to assemble. The man at the door threw it open, and they spread out among the apartment doors on the eighth floor.

They rang the bell on a door labelled 'Nilsson'.

No one opened it. Not a sound was heard.

A rough cement cylinder was brought forward. Affixed to one end was a thick metal plate, and there were two handles on either side. Two men grabbed the handles, and on a signal they rammed the cylinder against the door.

It shattered into pieces around the lock.

They forced their way into the apartment, once again without making a sound. It was dark inside; all the blinds were drawn.

In the closest bed of the small two-room flat lay three little black children who had been awakened by the crash. Lying on mattresses on the floor were four more children. Five of the children had already started to cry.

They continued into the second room. On beds and mattresses lay four black adults, gaping at them. Half of the men stopped there with their guns raised. The rest made their way into the kitchen.

At the kitchen table sat a black man and a white pastor with cups of coffee in front of them. Paralysed, they stared at the sub-machine guns, which were all pointed at them.

'What the hell!' said the pastor. Otherwise no one spoke.

Two well-built gentlemen in their forties wearing identical leather jackets came stomping into the kitchen, cast a quick glance at the pastor and the other man, then continued into the bedroom.

'Sonya Shermarke?' said the blonder of the men.

One of the women lying on the mattress on the floor sat up and looked at him in terror.

'Search her for weapons,' said Gillis Döös to his men.

'And drugs,' said Max Grahn.

15

Hjelm studied his face in the left rear-view mirror and saw that the scaly red patch on his cheek had got bigger. He thought about skin cancer.

The sun was spreading a thick, illusory layer of summer as the police car struggled up the steep incline of Liljeholm Bridge. Hornstull Beach and the cottages of the Tanto allotment gardens basked in the spring sunlight, and he wondered for an instant whether the mini-golf course was open. In the other direction the little pier of the Liljeholm swimming area stuck out into the bay.

One beach is as good as another, thought Hjelm nonsensically, flooring the accelerator in order to make it over the crown of the bridge and head down towards Södermalm. He ended up in a rather chaotic line of cars that was forming down near the intersection. A shimmering metallic Saab 9000 had tried at the last minute to make it through before the light turned red, and ended up in the middle of the intersection while the traffic blared its horns for him to get out of the way.

'I told you we should have stayed on the Essinge road,' Gunnar Nyberg admonished as Hjelm leaned on the car horn.

He'd picked up Nyberg at his small, three-room bachelor apartment near Nacka Church. *Car-pooling*, he thought as he squeezed the Mazda past the stranded Saab. It'd been a long time since anyone had used that term.

'This is a nicer route,' said Hjelm, swearing loudly at a bicyclist wobbling past.

'A nicer traffic jam, you mean,' said Nyberg. 'They're not exactly the same thing.'

The line was at a standstill nearly all the way to Långholmsgatan, and only close to Västerbron did the traffic ease a bit. Then they rolled past the square where the new Swedish jet had crashed one summer not so long ago, during the infamous air show for which no one was willing to take responsibility. Hjelm had actually been in attendance, along with his entire family; even Danne had enjoyed it. They were standing in the fourth row, almost directly across from City Hall, and saw the plane bank sharply to the left, watched as the pilot ejected, saw the plane slowly tilt towards the ground, saw the cloud of smoke rising up and listened as the absolute, dead silence morphed into a shocked and aggressive but liberating chatter. Yet another blow to the national self-confidence, he thought afterwards, but during the entire episode he had remained utterly passive, devoid of all thought. After a moment Danne pulled away from his father's arm, which Hjelm, out of a primeval but futile protective instinct, had placed around his son's shoulders.

'Cool,' Danne had said.

'Cool,' said Gunnar Nyberg. He was looking first at the waters of Riddarfjärden to the right and then at the channel of Mariebergsfjärden to the left.

One bay is as good as another, thought Hjelm nonsensically, and agreed with his colleague. It was a sight for the gods, as Erik Bruun would have said. Stockholm's waters glittered faintly in the morning sun. Not a cloud in the sky, the building facades were brilliantly coloured in the almost horizontal rays of light, and a few dazzling white excursion boats chugged between the flashes of sun on Lake Mälaren. Two sailing boats were out early, with rainbow spinnakers. City Hall self-consciously swaggered with its three gleaming crowns. The vegetation was already starting to sprout at the bridge abutment on the Kungsholmen side, in Rålambshov Park, at Smedsuddsbadet, in Marieberg Park. The promenade down by Norr Mälarstrand was filling up with people out for a stroll.

Neither of them was upset when the traffic came to a complete halt on the very crest of the bridge.

Life was returning to the city, coming out of hibernation. With death in tow, thought Hjelm melodramatically.

'I have to go out and pick up some small-time thugs today,' said Nyberg. 'Want to come along?'

Hjelm shifted into neutral and put on the hand brake. He glanced over at the gigantic figure sitting next to him, who was making the Mazda tilt precariously to the right.

'Informants?' he asked.

'Partly. The police districts have gone through their files on snitches and other loose-lipped individuals and come up with several likely candidates.'

'With knowledge of the mafia?'

'About mafia murders in general and the Russians in particular. They're possible candidates, but real long shots. And most likely it will be deeply and sincerely pointless.'

The traffic jam abruptly cleared. Västerbron swerved sharply, and the Mazda did as well. Together they passed over Rålambshov Park. Small clusters of people, for some reason not at work, were spread out over the grass, which was not yet particularly green.

'My leads have kind of dried up lately,' said Hjelm. 'Maybe I can tag along with you. I need to track down something that thrives in the undergrowth. A Stake, actually.'

'Oi,' said Nyberg. 'When'd you lose it?'

'Johan is his name. Johan Stake. And he's not mine.'

They fought their way across the numerous intersecting streets and took the right-hand route around Kronoberg Park, and turned onto Polhemsgatan. Ahead of them loomed police headquarters. Hjelm parked the car a block away and walked alongside his giant of a colleague towards Stockholm's version of the Taj Mahal, glittering harshly in the sunlight.

* * *

Hultin sat and stared at them, peering like an owl through his half-moon glasses.

'News from the higher-ups,' he said. 'The cleaning woman who reported Carlberger's death has been found. Sonya Shermarke, a Somali who was due to be deported. She and her family were hiding with some relatives in Tensta, under the protection of the church. She was making a living by cleaning houses in Djursholm and getting paid under the table. Early this morning a unit from another law-enforcement department located her and arrested everybody they found in the apartment, including seven children, six adults and a pastor from Spånga Church. All of them have been held in custody for the past three hours, being strenuously interrogated by our colleagues.'

'Should I guess which other department we're talking about here?' asked Söderstedt.

'No, you should not,' said Hultin calmly. 'All right. I just had a talk with Sonya Shermarke. She speaks decent Swedish, so we managed without an interpreter. She arrived at the villa, as usual, around nine o'clock, took a quick look at the living room to see what needed to be done, and discovered Carlberger lying in a pool of blood. She called the police without identifying herself other than to say that she was the 'cleaning woman'. Then she panicked and immediately returned to her hiding place. Our colleagues are still trying to pump her relatives for information about where the Russian gun was hidden.'

He paused for a fraction of a second, then continued.

'Right now we'll take time only for a very, very brief summing up. In all likelihood a fourth victim is going to end up in a pool of blood in his living room, so we have a lot to do. Don't forget that we have access to plenty of assistants, as a matter of fact the entire Stockholm police force. I shouldn't have to remind you that you now have much greater powers than your rank would normally permit, but don't try to do all the shit-work yourself. Make use of the foot soldiers as much as possible. And by the way, Mörner and his superiors will keep the press away from the unit, at least for the time being. First, does anyone have a likely victim for tonight?'

No one in Supreme Central Command stirred.

'Okay. If you exceed fifty words, I'm going to give you the "time's up" signal. Holm?'

'Tons of interviews, nothing serious. Minor leads to follow up on.'

'Exceptionally concise. Hjelm?'

Hjelm glanced down at his notebook. There he read a number of names: Lena Hansson, George Hummel-strand, Oscar Bjellerfeldt, Nils-Åke Svärdh, Bengt Klinth, Jakob Ringman, Johan Stake, Sonya X. He crossed out the last name. 'Not a damned thing.'

'A little more detail, please.'

'Our three victims played golf together once, just the three of them, in the autumn of 1990. If the killing spree does *not* continue, then that's a lead. If Kerstin isn't going to take on George Hummelstrand, the husband of

Anna-Clara, who is friends with the widows, then I'd like to have a go at him.'

Holm shrugged ambivalently. Hjelm tried to understand what she meant by that.

'He's one of the remaining links to the Mimir lead,' he went on, 'along with a few others. Then there's Strand-Julén's pimp, Johan Stake. I was thinking of tagging along with Nyberg on his foray into the underworld in order to locate him. How many words?'

'Close to a hundred. But okay, go along with Nyberg. And now, Nyberg?'

'Spent all day yesterday working with the Stockholm police. We cross-checked various grey-zone files and came up with some potential Russian contacts, aside from those already convicted. I talked to several of those serving time in various prisons yesterday, but they weren't very communicative. Hjelm and I will tackle the others today. Pubs, gyms, video stores, and so on.'

'That's good. Norlander?'

The finicky Viggo Norlander gently rubbed his balding pate. 'I've been in regular contact with customs about hits on post-Soviet smuggled goods, but have essentially drawn a blank. It seems that it's never possible to track down the sender, but I do have several addresses that I'm going to check out. I've also talked to the police in Moscow, St Petersburg and Tallinn regarding the mafia in general and the Russian-Estonian Viktor X gang in particular. It hasn't been easy to find out anything, but all indications are that we're dealing with a branch of the larger mafia, and that it's already here in some form, in Stockholm. The most cooperative was an Inspector Kalju Laikmaa in Tallinn. I'll be getting in touch with him again today, and I hope that—'

Hultin had put the palm of one hand perpendicular to the other to form a *T*.

Norlander fell silent.

'The economists?' said Hultin.

'Chief economist Söderstedt reporting,' said Söderstedt. 'I'll speak for Pettersson, Florén and myself. Chavez can make his own report. We've located a number of interesting things in the terrible corporate mess that the three gentlemen have left behind. The lawyers should be rubbing their hands together: there's enough to keep them busy for years to come. But the occasional irregularities that we've come across are of a different nature from crimes of violence. We'll get back to you when we know more. All we can say now is that there are more connections among the empires of the three men than we originally thought.'

Hultin was just about to make his 'time's up' sign when Söderstedt stopped talking of his own accord.

Chavez then took the floor. 'There are three boards of directors that included all three victims during the late Eighties and early Nineties. I'm checking up on everyone who was a board member at Ericsson, Sydbanken and MEMAB during the same period. It's quite a list. Right now I'm leaning towards MEMAB, partly because it had – and still has – the smallest board of directors, a purely mathematical-statistical distinction; partly because Paul's golf lead is connected to MEMAB, which is a more gut-level distinction; and partly because membership on that particular board seems to have aroused a bit of competition, not to mention hostility. So to put it simply, I'm looking for enemies among the board members. So far nothing concrete, but a few nibbles at MEMAB.'

Chavez delivered the last two statements at breakneck speed since he was looking at Hultin's hands in a *T* as he spoke.

'Let's get busy, then.' Hultin removed his glasses and left the room through his special door.

On his way out, Hjelm stopped Kerstin Holm. 'If you want to take Sir George, go ahead. I was out of line bringing that up. I guess I'm just obsessed with the Order of Mimir.'

'Fine,' she said curtly, then disappeared into room 303 just as Nyberg came out with his jacket in hand and gave Hjelm a wave. Like Laurel and Hardy, they trudged down the hallway and out into the sunshine.

It turned out to be a long and tiresome day. Hjelm drove Nyberg around, following a list of names in Nyberg's notebook, which soon filled up with ticks. The names ticked off consisted partly of a bunch of well-informed snitches, partly of shady characters with possible Russian contacts for access to cheap booze and drugs: pub owners who slept in the daytime, notorious pushers, steroid-popping gym owners, less-than-honest art dealers, owners of illegal gambling clubs. All of them well known to the police, but impossible to catch.

Nyberg's personality changed before Hjelm's eyes. From one second to the next the bass singer in the Nacka Church choir switched from a good-natured teddy bear to a furious grizzly, then back again when it was time to tick off another name.

'How the hell do you do that?' asked Hjelm after tick number eight, just as fruitless as the previous seven.

Gunnar Nyberg chuckled. 'It's all a matter of harnessing the steroids,' he said. He stopped laughing and stared out the car window with a far-away look in his eyes. After a moment he went on quietly.

'I was Mr Sweden in 1973. I was twenty-three and tossed down all the pills that anyone handed to me, as long as they would increase my muscle mass. While I was on the Norrmalm police force from 1975 to '77 I was charged three times for police brutality, but managed, with the proper help, to wriggle my way out of it each time. The reports just disappeared, so to speak, in the bureaucratic process. I stopped doing serious bodybuilding, meaning with drugs, in 1977 after the last charge of assault and battery, which was a really close call. Even I could see that. I'm never going to get over it. For a time I struggled with sudden outbursts of anger. I left my wife and lost custody rights to my kids. But I conquered that angry shit. At least I think I did. But I still don't know whether

I pretend to be enraged, or whether it actually takes over for a moment. I don't know. But it seems very controlled, don't you think?'

Hjelm would never again hear Gunnar Nyberg say so much all at one time.

'Very,' he said. Nyberg never crossed the line. His violence was indirect. With almost 300 pounds of potential assault and battery looming over them, most small-time thugs quickly turned submissive.

They continued all day long and even into the evening, traversing Stockholm and its environs. Hjelm's main role was to drive, but he usually slipped his brief questions regarding pimps into Nyberg's interrogations. Just before three in the afternoon Hjelm had a brief phone conversation with Hultin, who had decided to skip the three o'clock meeting; there wasn't anything new to discuss. Hjelm reported on the duo's meagre results:

The owner of a gym in Bandhagen had bought a large supply of anabolic steroids from a couple of 'ferocious Russians' who called themselves Peter Ustinov and John Malkovich.

One of the more prominent drug-pushers at Sergelplattan had once received a load of first-rate stuff, sent in plastic bags that had Russian letters printed on them. That was all they could get out of him before he started spitting up blood.

The owner of a small basement pub in Söder had made several purchases of Estonian vodka via a strange Russian pair calling themselves Igor and Igor.

A self-proclaimed art dealer in Järfälla had been offered big money from a 'Russian-speaking gangster type' for a Picasso, then in the possession of the financier Anders Wall. He had declined the offer.

An amphetamine-babbling proprietor of a video store with private viewing booths in Norrmalm had cheerfully offered them some child porn films with Russian subtitles, even though they had shown him their police ID. He was arrested. He spoke Swedish with a Russian accent, but he wasn't Russian. With thirty confiscated child-porn films, it wasn't going to be difficult to get him arraigned quickly. They would be talking to him again later.

That was all they had come up with just before three P.M. on 4 April.

Their search continued until seven. By then every name and address on Nyberg's list had been ticked off.

The latter half of their search was depressing in terms of the Russian mafia lead, since it brought in no results whatsoever. But after an utterly absurd marathon chase all the way from Tessin Park to Värtahamn, they had caught up with a terrified dealer. They learned from him that the man who went by the name of Johan Stake had actually been baptised Johan Stake, and one of his many enterprises was a phone-sex company with an 071 pay-by-the-minute number. The company was called JSHB, for Johan Stake Handelsbolag, and it was located in Bromma. They had big ads on the phone-sex pages in all the tabloids.

When Hjelm and Nyberg drove back across the Liljeholm Bridge, the lights of the city were already turned on. Everything had settled into an eerie silence; they both noticed it, although it might have existed only in their own minds. They both knew that they would sleep badly.

They knew when and how, but not who or where.

That night another person was going to be murdered.

16

All during breakfast Paul Hjelm's attention was focused on the mobile phone that lay like a defective slab of cheese among the others on the kitchen table. Even though he didn't take his eyes off it even once, he could feel the annoyed glances that Cilla directed at him, only to be dismissed over and over again. Finally her gaze grew so sharp that he was forced to look up.

'Maybe he hasn't been found yet,' he said, his thoughts still on the mobile phone.

But the look on her face wasn't her usual give-me-some-attention-too expression. It had been transformed into something else, something he'd never seen before. A strangely lonely expression, a look of final surrender. So desolate. He was totally bewildered. A feeling rushed through him, the same one that had stunned him as he listened to Kerstin Holm's cassette tapes: the dreadful, unbearable feeling that we can never really reach anyone else. Never ever, not even those closest to us.

The horrifying sensation of absolute existential lone-liness.

And now he saw this same emotion in Cilla's eyes.

For a brief second they were paradoxically united by this overwhelming emotion.

When they finally managed to speak, they were both fully aware that what they said had nothing to do with what they really wanted to say. For *that* there were no words.

There at the kitchen table, on that ordinary morning, they shared, while being unable to communicate it in any way, an almost mystical experience that their very language was assigning them roles that they would never be able to escape.

Did those few minutes in the kitchen draw them closer together? Or had a final chasm opened up between them? It was impossible to say, but something decisive had taken place; they had looked right into each other's naked loneliness.

And perhaps that was the most shocking development during that whole eventful week.

Nothing else happened. His mobile phone didn't ring once during the drive over to police headquarters, but Hjelm didn't care. For the other members of the A-Unit, the day passed in an intensity of waiting, but the murder victim remained conspicuously absent, and Hjelm still didn't care. The investigation seemed paralysed by the broken pattern, and Hjelm was paralysed too, in his utterly personal, utterly lonely way. Towards the end of the day Hultin tried to normalise the group's mood as they all gathered around the table in Supreme Central Command.

'All right then,' he said calmly. 'If there's no undiscovered victim lying in some monumental living room somewhere in the city, then we have to accept that we're faced with two possibilities. One: for some reason the perp has changed his MO; or two: it's over.'

Paul Hjelm didn't hear what he said. He stayed sitting there until the others had gone home. All alone in Supreme Central Command, he wondered what *he* was going to find when he arrived home.

But what he came home to was a reasonably normal family life. The looks that he and Cilla exchanged would never be the same, and he never stopped wondering whether the return to normal was artificial, whether it might contain a ticking time bomb. Nevertheless, he regained a foothold on life after that strange day spent teetering on the edge of the void, even though he continued to wonder what sort of ground he was actually standing on, and his interest in the case rose back to normal levels.

But nothing new came to light. The case returned to normal, just as his life did. But in neither instance did the ground feel entirely trustworthy.

* * *

Almost a week after the first murder, Paul Hjelm, for once, was having lunch in the cafeteria at police head-quarters. He was notorious for skipping lunch. But for once the whole core group was present at the same time: Söderstedt, Chavez, Norlander, Holm, Nyberg. The six of them formed a closed unit at one long table, and if they'd had the slightest tendency towards paranoia, they would have thought they were surrounded by hostile faces.

They did think they were surrounded by hostile faces.

'So here's the thing,' said Söderstedt resolutely, rubbing his white cheek that showed almost no sign of stubble. In one hand he held a forkful of gristly and fatty beef stew, dripping with gravy. 'The Stockholm detectives hate us because we took the case away from them. The national cops hate us because Hultin chose a bunch of low-ranking outsiders for one of the most important investigations in the history of Swedish crime. And they all hate us because we're deviants: a pale Finn, a black-head, a west coaster, a fifth columnist, a Goliath meat mountain and a media hero.'

'Fifth columnist?' said Viggo Norlander sullenly.

'So you recognised your place in the terrarium?'

'I've never betrayed the Stockholm detectives, and I never will.'

'You know what they say,' said Hjelm, hating the bite of stew that he had just put in his mouth. 'Once you become part of the NCP, you never get out. Except in an appropriate casket.'

'Who the hell said that?' said Chavez.

'I don't remember,' said Hjelm, surreptitiously spitting a lump of fat into his napkin.

Chavez turned to Söderstedt. 'How's it going with the apartment, Ärtan?'

Ärtan? A nickname? Hjelm suddenly realised that he had missed out on a lot. When the hell did they have time for personal conversations?

He looked around. The time they'd spent together had been strictly of a professional nature. Who were these people really, with whom he was spending such obscenely long workdays? Again a chill rushed through him, from the cassette tapes and from his own kitchen in Norsborg: no one could ever understand anyone else. Way off in the distance he caught a glimpse, for the briefest moment, of Grundström.

He gave himself a shake.

So how was the camaraderie now? The work pace had slacked off a bit, and he could see the members of the A-Unit as something other than cogs in the machine.

Jorge Chavez was a pleasant colleague; they worked well together. An ultra-professional, modern police officer, well dressed in a sporty sort of way, solid and above all young. If time allowed, Hjelm should be able to establish strong teamwork with him. Although from a personal point of view, they might be too different. Hjelm knew only that Jorge was single and that he'd recently moved out of one of the apartments available for temporary lodgings at police headquarters. He'd said nothing about his tenure with the Sundsvall police force. All Hjelm's attempts to find anything out had fallen flat. He got the feeling that it had been a nightmarish period that Chavez preferred to forget. Sometimes Chavez seemed to think he'd landed in paradise.

Who else? Gunnar Nyberg, the former Mr Sweden and bass singer in the Nacka Church choir, had almost become a friend. At any rate, they *car-pooled* together. Hjelm liked that phrase; it made him happy. But when it came right down to it, he really didn't know Nyberg either. Divorced after abusing his wife while taking steroids – wasn't that how all the hints could be interpreted? And he hadn't seen his children since they were very young. In reality, Nyberg lived for his singing. But in his own way he was also an exceptionally effective police officer, a model of potential assault and battery.

Viggo Norlander was someone Hjelm couldn't get a handle on. A real stickler for detail, very old-school. An arch-Stockholmer. Seemed to like rules and regulations. Believed in the law books the way religious people believed in the Bible. Wore suits that had been elegant twenty years earlier, but now merely smelled of dust and sweat. Tall, but with a slightly sluggish body. Unattached. Getting a bit paunchy. Hard to get to know. Maybe there wasn't anything inside to know.

And then there was Kerstin Holm. He couldn't ignore the attraction. In many ways she was Cilla's opposite. Everything dark: dark eyes, dark hair, dark clothes. An incredible . . . well, integrity. Enormously professional

– he couldn't stop thinking about the finesse with which she had carried out the interviews on the tapes; her conversation with Anna-Clara Hummelstrand in France ought to be in a textbook. Holm was staying with a relative in Stockholm and refused as staunchly as Chavez to talk about her past. From what Hjelm could understand, something had happened over there in Göteborg, something unpleasant that was not to be mentioned. Sooner or later it would be mentioned. He gave her a furtive glance. A fabulous woman.

And then Söderstedt. Arto Söderstedt. A unique specimen. Hjelm had never seen a police officer like him. The pale Finn, as he candidly called himself, was a special creation. Hjelm couldn't quite get it into his head that Söderstedt was a police officer. Not that he was unprofessional in any way; on the contrary. But he acted and talked more like a . . . well, an intellectual, a fearless academic, daring to voice his political opinions boldly in the middle of their meetings.

Just as Hjelm was thinking about it, Söderstedt replied to Chavez's question, although it was hard to remember what the question had been.

'I wouldn't exactly call it an apartment, but it's close by. On Agnegatan, in fact. A one-room place with a kitchen in an alcove, while my whole family is back in Västerås. I have five children,' he added, looking at Hjelm.

Hjelm's feeling of being out of the loop soared to astronomical heights. He pushed it aside.

'Five?' he exclaimed, thinking that his voice sounded convincing. 'Is Västerås really that boring?'

'Oh, yes. But two of them were conceived in Vasa.'

'You were working in Finland? How was that?'

'No, well, I wasn't . . . a police officer back then. I became a cop rather late in life. Some people think I never should have joined the force.'

Hjelm felt a bit smug about his intuition. He tried to interpret the mood around the table. Maybe Söderstedt meant some colleague in Västerås had criticised him, or maybe he meant someone sitting at the table. It was impossible to tell. Hjelm had a vague impression that he was the only one who didn't know what Söderstedt was referring to. But it turned out that he needn't have taxed his brain over the subject.

'All I said was that you don't need to give a campaign speech for the Communists,' Viggo Norlander muttered testily. The fork he was holding started to shake.

'No, that wasn't all you said.' Söderstedt fixed his eyes on Norlander.

'Okay, boys,' Kerstin Holm said suddenly.

Norlander slammed his fork down on the tray and rose, carrying it away without another word. Even in that state of monumental anger, he felt compelled to put the tray in its proper place on the rack, crumple up his napkin and toss it into the proper wastebasket.

Hjelm glanced around the staff cafeteria. A few openly sarcastic smiles came from the neighbouring tables. He smiled grimly.

To be an outsider even among the outsiders.

Right in the eye of the storm.

Holm said to Söderstedt, 'Cut that out. We have other things to do than pick fights in the sandbox.'

'He socked me right in the jaw,' muttered Söderstedt sullenly. For a second, a bucket and shovel might have been visible in his hands. When they disappeared, he went on: 'And then he dragged in the whole foreigner thing. Except for the black-head, of course.' Söderstedt ran his hand over his thin, chalk-white hair.

Hjelm laughed. He didn't know why, but Nyberg joined in. Söderstedt also chuckled a bit. Holm smiled that ironic smile of hers, as did Chavez. The peace pipe went around the whole group.

'To exclude the political aspects of this case would be like working on only half a case,' said Söderstedt at last. 'Come on, give me some support, somebody!'

'I agree,' said Chavez. 'But there are different ways to handle it. To back up a bit, what exactly happened in Vasa?'

'Oh no. No, no,' said Söderstedt, laughing. 'We're not on those kinds of personal terms yet. How's it going with *your* hole in the wall, by the way?'

'Mine is definitely not an apartment. Just a room rented from an old woman at the intersection of Bergsgatan and Scheelegatan. Like when I was in training.'

'So what about you, Kerstin?' asked Söderstedt. 'Where are you staying, my dear?'

'With my ex-husband's second ex-wife in Brandbergen,'

said Holm. 'We get on well together. We share an identical and highly productive hatred.'

More laughter, about everything and nothing. About the fact that they had taken a small step closer to each other. About the fact that nobody had been murdered in several days. About themselves and their absurd situation at police headquarters.

Nyberg left, followed by Chavez and Söderstedt. Holm finished her light beer and was about to get up when Hjelm said, 'Kerstin. Did you get hold of George Hummelstrand?'

She sank back down onto her chair, giving him a surly look. 'I really didn't like the fact that you took credit for the Hummelstrand lead,' she said.

'I've already apologised. Besides, it's not really a matter of taking credit, is it? I was still on the track of the Mimir lead. I'll apologise again, if that's what **you want**. And again. And again.'

A reluctant smile appeared on her disturbingly beautiful face.

'And again,' he said, feeling rather pleased. 'So. How did it go with George?'

The smile abruptly vanished. Her dark eyes seemed to X-ray right through him. 'Are you happily married?' she asked.

'What?' he said. For a moment Cilla's desolate expression obscured his field of vision.

'Happily married?' said Kerstin Holm with the utmost seriousness. 'Really happily?'

'Why do you ask?'

'I don't know who you are,' she said inscrutably, and got up and left.

The image of Cilla slowly faded.

Finally the whole world went pale.

17

Viggo Norlander was sitting in a warehouse in Frihamnen, waiting.

Waiting, he thought. *Waiting to wait. Waiting to wait to wait. Waiting to wait to wait to wait.*

In other words, he was feeling tired.

He felt even less inclined to put on the kid gloves. He'd already taken out the other kind of gloves.

The boxing gloves. Metaphorically speaking.

Something has to happen now, he thought. He was damned sick and tired of all the desk work and all the phone calls to condescending Interpol officers and recalcitrant former Soviet policemen and burned-out customs agents. He'd been waiting long enough.

He'd forced entry into the small office of the warehouse and was crouched down behind a cabinet. There he'd been sitting for three hours, and it would soon be evening. He was extremely angry.

Soon everything was going to have to proceed at an entirely new pace.

He kept his anger alive by thinking about Arto Söderstedt, that Finnish bastard, who came from somewhere out in the sticks and despised everything that he'd ever believed in. Of course money had to be coming in so that it could be divided up. If Swedish companies made the money, then it would benefit the Swedish people. It was as simple as that.

He fanned his anger by thinking about his own name. Viggo, for God's sake, the hearty little Viggo, Viggo the fucking Viking. It was his only inheritance from the travel-happy Danish seaman who for some inexplicable reason had become his father. A quick ejaculation into the womb of a starving woman, and then he was on his way again. No responsibility. No responsibility at all. Like Söderstedt, he thought. Exactly the same.

His thoughts weren't following any particular order.

Once in his youth he'd tried to find out something about this loathsome name of his. Its origin went back to the thirteenth century when the Danes' great history writer, Saxo Grammaticus, latinised the Danish word *vig*, meaning 'battle', and gave the name to one of King Rolf Krake's men.

Viggo, Jan-Olov Krake's henchman, Norlander thought incoherently as the door opened. A man with a ponytail and wearing a jogging suit came in and sat down at the desk a couple of yards away. Norlander took a few seconds to ascertain that the man was alone.

Then he rushed out and slammed the man's head against the desk.

Once, twice, three times, then four.

Taking a firm grip on the man's ponytail, he stuck his service revolver deep into his ear and snarled, 'Little Strömstedt, you've got three seconds to give me the name of your mafia contact. Otherwise you're dead, big-time. One. Two.'

'Wait, wait, wait!' cried the man. 'Who the hell are you?'

'Three,' said Norlander and pulled the trigger.

The gun clicked.

'There's a bullet in the next chamber,' said Norlander. 'Be damn quick about it now!'

The man was like jelly in his hands, thought Norlander with a rush of adrenaline. He was shaking all the way down to the bottom of his dark soul.

He laid it on thick: 'A shipment of 120-proof Estonian vodka from Liviko intended for little Strömstedt was confiscated by customs a couple of months ago. Who sent it to you?'

'I'm just a middleman,' said little Strömstedt, shaking. 'Damn it, I've told them everything. I don't know anything!'

'Right now there are other factors in play. Every complaint for police brutality that you submit is going to end up in the wastebasket. You hear me? Top priority. National security. Spit out everything you know. Now. The bullet's in the chamber.'

'Who the fuck are you? Dirty Harry?'

Norlander took a chance and shot little Strömstedt's computer to smithereens.

'You fucker!' he bellowed, trying to twist his body

around. Norlander, in turn, took an even tighter grip on the man's ponytail until he felt the roots pull halfway out. Little Strömstedt let out a scream.

'Igor and Igor!' he screamed. 'That's all I know! They do their own pickups!'

'Igor and Igor are your Russian mafia contacts? Is that right?'

'Yes, yes, yes! Damn it, that's all I know!'

'I know all about you,' said Norlander. 'You speak Russian. You know what these guys Igor and Igor said to each other. I need more!'

Norlander lowered his gun and aimed the barrel at the man's hand lying on the desk.

'A little more, please,' he said, and fired.

The bullet passed between the man's middle finger and ring finger, singeing the skin. Strömstedt screamed even louder.

'Gotlanders!' he wailed.

'Go on,' said Norlander, moving the gun until it was pointing at the man's wrist.

'The Gotland black-head smugglers! They belong to the same gang! That's all I know, I swear! They talked about Gotland and how clumsy the guys had been down there!'

Viggo Norlander lifted Strömstedt up by his ponytail, yanked on the door handle behind his back and hurled the man into the nearest cupboard. Then he barricaded the door and left him there. He could hear a flood of curses coming from inside.

He thought they were Finland-Swedish.

A barrier, thought Norlander as he sped away from Frihamnen. He received the go-ahead from Hultin on his mobile to drive straight out to Arlanda Airport.

A barrier had been lifted.

Now he was really going to be fucking dangerous.

Viggo Norlander was forty-eight years old, divorced, with no children. End of story. The bare spot on the top of his head had long ago acquired its final shape; not so his stomach, which slowly continued to grow. He wasn't fat, just pre-fat.

There wasn't a single blot on his record. Nor much of anything else. He'd always been an exemplary if not always terribly active officer, whose only guides through the journey of life had been the police handbook and the book of law. He'd always believed in legal methods, in defending established society and in the slowly grinding wheels of the justice system.

His life had stagnated and, like his bald spot, had long ago achieved its final form. It was a deliberate stagnation. The humdrum was his very essence, the correct, the legal, what could be described in black and white. He'd always believed that people were generally like himself: hard-working, never making up excuses to take sick days, paying their taxes without complaint, and following the universal rules, with no extremes, either highs or lows.

Everything else was shit and had to be removed.

And in his world all law-abiding citizens intuitively wanted the shit removed, and naturally they appreciated his efforts to get it off the streets.

No matter what he happened to encounter in the course of his daily work in the Stockholm criminal division, he still managed to retain these crystal-clear guidelines in his job and in his life. He'd always been quite satisfied both with himself and with the police force in general. In spite of occasional slumps and increases, everything was moving in the right direction and at the right speed, which meant at a steady pace: growth, progress, development. A stable societal advancement.

He was a tranquil man.

He would never be able to put his finger on where the rupture first appeared, or where the wall had finally burst.

Not even if subjected to torture would he admit to the presence of a rupture, simply because it didn't exist in his worldview.

But it did exist in his present world of action.

Now as he walked through Visby, on the island of Gotland, moving along the medieval ring wall in the morning mist, his beliefs were still intact. Conditioned by trust. The lingering vestiges of the previous days. What he had done and was about to do were necessary. No more unsolved Palme murders. *Legal security*, he thought. Trust. Societal responsibility. Daggfeldt, Strand-Julén, Carlberger. That was enough. He would see to that.

He was defending the most important thing of all.

Even though he didn't really know what it was.

After a long walk through an almost-deserted Visby, encircled by a sort of Mediterranean morning mist as much as by the ring wall, he reached the police station. It was seven-thirty A.M.

He went inside and was directed to the jail. There he found an officer on duty who was about his own age. They immediately recognised the policeman in each other. That was how he looked – Policeman with a capital P. And Swedish.

'Norlander,' said Norlander.

'Jönsson,' said Jönsson, speaking with a distinct accent stemming from both Skåne and Gotland. 'Vilhelm Jönsson. We've been expecting you. Peshkov is ready whenever you are.'

'I assume that you're aware of the gravity of this investigation. There is nothing more important in Sweden today.'

'I'm aware of that.'

'So how do we do this? Does he speak English?'

'Fortunately, he does. An old, international seaman. I assume that it would have been inconvenient to have an interpreter present. If I understood you correctly.'

'We certainly do understand each other. Where is he?'

'In a soundproof room, as agreed. Shall we?'

Norlander nodded, and Vilhelm Jönsson led the way along several corridors, recruiting a couple of guards from the break room as they walked past. Then they all went down to the basement. The four men stopped outside a grey-painted steel door with a peephole.

Jönsson cleared his throat. 'As you've explained,' he said, 'because this investigation is classified, and for other reasons as well, we won't be allowed to participate in the interrogation, but we'll stand guard outside. Here's the panic button. Press it and we'll be inside in a second.'

Norlander accepted the little box with the red button. He put it in his pocket. 'Don't look unless you have to,' he said calmly. 'The less you know, the better. That way any eventual complaints will be directed to NCP management. It's for the best.'

They unlocked the door and let him in. A table, two chairs, padded walls. Nothing more. Except for a small man wearing prison garb sitting on one of the chairs. A sharp face, skinny biceps. *The sinewy, ropy muscles of a sailor*, thought Norlander, assessing the man's potential strength to resist – it wouldn't be in his body, at any rate. The man stood up and greeted Norlander politely, 'How do you do, sir?'

'Very brilliant, please,' said Norlander, placing a notebook and pen on the table before sitting down. 'Sit down, thank you.'

The conversation proceeded, although not without certain linguistic infelicities. In the same knotty English, Norlander continued, 'Let's get right to the point, Mr Alexey Peshkov. During a bad winter storm you and your crew ditched a hundred and twelve Iranian, Kurdish and Indian refugees in two rubber rafts hundreds of yards off the east coast of Gotland, then headed back to Tallinn in your fishing boat. But the Swedish coastguard managed to stop your vessel before it left Swedish waters.'

'Very straight to the point,' said Peshkov.

Since irony wasn't Norlander's strong suit, his attempt to imitate Hultin's icy tone came out a bit abruptly. 'I need information,' he went on, 'about the serial killings of Swedish businessmen that have occurred in Stockholm over the past few days.'

Alexey Peshkov's jaw dropped. After he managed to close it again, he blurted out, 'You must be joking!'

'I am not joking,' said Norlander and continued in the same calm manner. 'If you don't give me the information I want, I have the authority to kill you right here and now. I'm specially trained for that. Do you understand?'

'I'm not buying this,' said Peshkov, eyeing Norlander's slightly flabby build. At the same time, Norlander's utterly composed steadiness of purpose brought a dubious expression to the man's face. Norlander hammered home the point:

'We know that you're part of a Russian-Estonian crime group headed by Viktor X, and that a couple of booze smugglers calling themselves Igor and Igor are in the same group. Correct?'

Peshkov didn't say a word, but now he was on the alert.

'Correct?' Norlander repeated.

Still not a word.

'This is a soundproof room. Nothing that takes place in here will be heard by anyone else. The powers that I've been granted have no limit; they come from the highest authority. I want you to understand that and think carefully before you answer. Your personal welfare depends on the next answer you give.'

Peshkov closed his eyes; he seemed to think that he must be dreaming. This was something quite different from the good-natured Swedish police officers he'd met so far. Maybe he saw the glint of something monstrous in Norlander's eyes. Maybe he'd seen that glint before.

'This is a democracy,' he said cautiously.

'Of course,' said Norlander. 'And it's going to remain so. But occasionally every democracy has to defend itself by using undemocratic means. Any sort of defence is actually by definition undemocratic. This is one instance when that will be made abundantly clear.'

'I've been in here for two months. I know absolutely nothing about any serial murders in Stockholm. I swear it.'

'Viktor X? Igor and Igor?' said Norlander, in exactly the same tone. Somehow he realised that it was import-ant not to change it.

Alexey Peshkov calculated the risks.

Norlander clearly saw that the man was contemplating the best way to postpone his own death for as long as possible. He gave him time to think, but also slipped his hand into his jacket pocket. The sound of him clicking off the safety on his gun seemed to echo off the walls.

Peshkov sighed deeply. 'I was a seaman on inter-national routes during the entire Communist era. I kept out of the clutches of the KGB and GRU by constantly changing my identity. I scraped enough money together to buy my own fishing boat when the regime fell. For about a year I was an ordinary Russian-speaking fisherman from Tallinn, a bit oppressed, but free.

'You might say that was our only free year, because then other forces came into play. I was contacted by anonymous protectors. First it was just money they wanted, payment for not setting fire to my boat or blowing it up. The usual protection racket. But soon it began to escalate. I was ordered to take on . . . transports of this type. This was my third. Tens of thousands of desperate refugees are stuck in the old Soviet Union, just waiting to be fleeced.

'I've never been anywhere near the boss; Viktor X is just a name, a myth. My contact was an Estonian by the name of Jüri Maarja. He's supposedly close to Viktor X. I've never heard of any Igor and Igor, but the group has lots of booze smugglers, as well as all sorts of other smugglers in Northern Europe.'

Norlander was surprised by the man's sudden volubility, but didn't let it show. 'Addresses? Contact places?' he said quietly.

Peshkov shook his head. 'They keep moving them around.'

Norlander studied Peshkov for a good long time. He couldn't decide whether the man was a victim or a criminal or both. He slapped his notebook against the table and stuck his pen in his breast pocket. 'I'll be leaving for Tallinn now. If it turns out that a single detail of what you've told me is wrong, or if it turns out that you haven't told me everything, I'll be back. Do you understand what that means?'

Peshkov stared down at the table without saying a word.

'Last chance to change or add anything,' said Norlander, standing up.

'That's all I know,' Peshkov said, sounding resigned.

Viggo Norlander suddenly held out his hand towards Alexey Peshkov. The Russian-Estonian fisherman reluctantly got up and shook hands.

'How do you do, sir?' said Norlander.

Peshkov gave him a look that he would never forget.

Tallinn was a crazy city.

That's what Viggo Norlander thought after being there only fifteen minutes. Later on he would by no means change his opinion.

He had trouble getting a rental car at the airport. Finally he headed out into the chaotic afternoon traffic, struggling to find his way with the help of an English-language tourist map. He ended up in Old Town, on the slopes of Toompea Hill, circling around as if inside a medieval labyrinth. Since he kept coming upon ancient walls with magnificent tall defensive turrets, he almost thought he was still in Visby.

But in reality the city was nameless, a mere backdrop for his single-minded purpose. Street signs, traffic signs, billboards in a foreign language – it was like in a film. He was a stranger and wanted to stay that way. Everything should remain nameless, no more than a backdrop. Nothing would be allowed to distract his attention. He felt as if new blood were pumping through his body. This was what he was meant for. Enduring all those idle hours in life just so that he could arrive at this specific moment.

Finally he located the big, modern police headquarters. He parked illegally and went inside. He entered the reception area, a small room where the old Soviet bureaucratic drabness fought in vain against the modern Western interior design. In the same way, the duty officer was both accommodating and dismissive in a strange mixture that Norlander had never encountered before. Under other circumstances he might have been surprised. Now he was merely stubborn.

'Superintendent Kalju Laikmaa,' he said for the third time in his broken English. 'He's expecting me.'

'I don't see any Swedish police officer in my authorisation documents,' said the young man, managing to sound both stern and apologetic. 'I'm sorry,' he added for the third time.

'At least give him a call,' said Norlander with composure, using the icy tone that had proved so successful at the Visby jail. Finally the duty officer did as he asked. He sat for a while with the phone receiver expertly held between his shoulder and chin as he stirred his cup of coffee. When he finally spoke, his words sounded like

Finnish with a bunch of misplaced *o*s. Eventually he hung up and said with politely disguised annoyance: 'The superintendent will come down and get you, Mr Norrland.'

'Please,' said Mr Norrland courteously.

It took only a minute before he heard the lift in the lobby of police headquarters, and out stepped a fair-haired man wearing a wrinkled corduroy suit and glasses of the type that were handed out free of charge when Norlander was doing his military service in the distant past.

'Norlander, I presume,' said the man, holding out his hand. Norlander shook it. The man had a firm handshake. 'I'm Laikmaa.'

They got in the lift and rode up to the fifth floor.

'You could have told me that you were on your way,' said Laikmaa, speaking with an elegant East Coast American accent. 'Then we could have avoided all the trouble.'

'I wanted my arrival to go unnoticed, as much as possible,' said Norlander, resorting to the icy tone that was by now well practised. 'There's too much at stake.'

'I see,' said Laikmaa drily. 'Over here businessmen as well as others are dying in hordes. We're living in a new climate of violence. Everybody interprets the laws of the market economy any way they like. What was suppressed under the Soviets is now bubbling up with all the force we had expected. Our job was undoubtedly easier when we were the tools of the oppressor, but hardly more pleasant. We now live in a state within a state that has exactly the same ability to infiltrate as the union of states did in the past. It wouldn't surprise me in the least if your arrival is already known within certain circles. We need to be very careful at all times about what we say and reveal. Just like before. There are ears everywhere. Come in.'

They went into a pleasant little office. Dead plants lined the sills of the windows facing Old Town and the castle with its imposing tower, called Pikk Hermann. But for Norlander the view didn't exist. He sat down in the visitor's chair in front of Laikmaa's desk.

'The day starts with an electronic sweep of my office,' said Laikmaa, lighting a cigarette. 'To make sure that no listening devices have been planted during the night. But of course that doesn't prevent long-distance bugging. In my position as head of the nominal fight against the mafia in this country, I'm a popular target. As far as the mafia is—'

'You of all people should know,' said Norlander coolly.

'The more I know, the more I realise how much I don't know,' Laikmaa said sagely. 'Cases dealing with all forms of organised crime land on my desk, from simple protection and collection rackets to matters that reach all the way up to the highest imaginable levels. The only common denominator is the desire to exploit the new opportunities. Some think we're looking at the naked face of the market economy; others say it's the natural continuation of state terrorism. In either case, what's most apparent is the complete lack of, shall we call it empathy, or perhaps an intrinsic sense for the essence of democracy. As always, people are grabbing as much as possible for themselves, at others' expense. It makes no difference whether the state is an absolute power or non-existent.'

Laikmaa rummaged through the multitudes of documents and somehow managed to find the right one.

'All right,' he said. 'Regarding your earlier questions on the phone, I don't exactly have anything new to offer. The Viktor X gang is a constellation of Russians and Estonians operating primarily in Tallinn. They've started making forays into Sweden since the Finnish market will soon reach saturation point. We don't really know how far they've got – whether a contact network has already been established, or whether a regular smuggling operation is under way – but we do know that there's no lack of ambition.

'As we've said, they execute traitors with a shot to the head; that's a consistent trademark, and I've never seen any deviations. They use ammunition from the weapons factory in Pavlodar, Kazakhstan, as we've already discussed. There's no doubt about any of this. But you need to know that most of the groups use the same ammunition and that here in Tallinn the evasive Viktor X's group is quite a small, marginal enterprise. Seven or eight gangster rings have divided up Tallinn and eastern Estonia into districts, and they avoid crossing each other's boundaries.

'We know very little about their contacts higher up

with the larger intra-Russian mafia. If we disregard Yugoslavia, right now Estonia tops the charts for European murder statistics. We have more than three hundred homicides a year in this country, and Tallinn has one of the highest murder rates in the world. That's the background that you need to be aware of when you step out onto our streets.'

'Is it your department that's known as Commando K?' asked Norlander.

'No, we're the criminal police. Commando K is our anti-terror group. They're our extended arm – and the only actual physical weapon that we have against our gangsters. They do have a tendency to go a little too far, but they remain our only real force. We're the ordinary criminal police, handling the investigations. Commando K is purely an assault team.'

Laikmaa fell silent, rifling through the papers to pull out another document.

'What we know is that Viktor X is mixed up in the protection operation for a Swedish media firm that's trying to establish itself in Russia and the Baltics by producing a daily business newspaper, among other things. Internationally, the firm calls itself GrimeBear Publishing, Inc. I don't know what it's called in Sweden, but I think they have almost a monopoly on the media in your country. Seems rather strange for a democracy. Or am I mistaken?'

Norlander hadn't a clue about any of this. He jotted it down in his notebook and then abruptly changed the subject. 'I've got a new lead. A Jüri Maarja. He's behind the smuggling of refugees to Gotland.'

'He's not alone.' Kalju Laikmaa looked pensive.

Norlander saw that he'd mentioned a sensitive topic. Laikmaa was apparently considering how much he could reveal. Norlander decided to help him out. 'We're not interested in the refugee traffic itself. It is what it is. We're only interested in the connection to the serial killings.'

'And what sort of connection is that?' Laikmaa asked sceptically.

Norlander didn't reply. He tried to appear inscrutable rather than uncertain.

Only now did it occur to him how vague that connection actually was.

'So,' said Laikmaa when he realised that he wasn't going to get an answer, 'you get to keep your secrets and I have to reveal mine. Is that what our contract looks like?'

'*Ich bin* sorry,' Norlander managed to say. 'This investigation has to do with national security. And as you said yourself, this office may be bugged, long-distance.'

'I was being sarcastic,' said Laikmaa, beginning to understand the nature of the man with whom he was talking. 'Never mind. Jüri Maarja speaks Swedish, which may be of some interest to you. He lived in Sweden for many years without ending up in any police records. He's close to Viktor X; that much we know. We also know that he's one of many who deal in smuggling refugees. We have orders from the highest authority not to be too rigid when it comes to that particular type of smuggling. The Baltic countries are overflowing with refugees who think that Sweden is heaven. Apparently they're using an old map.'

Norlander gave him a stony look. Laikmaa evidently had more on his mind.

'There's something more,' said Norlander coldly.

Laikmaa sighed heavily and looked as if he were trying to think about good Baltic-Scandinavian relations, and about their dependence on Swedish aid. He was really thinking about the deportation of Baltic refugees back to the Soviet Union and about Swedish business interests in the Baltics.

The multifaceted meaning contained in that sigh went right over Norlander's head. He heard only Laikmaa's response.

'I've spent days interrogating one of Maarja's more prominent drug dealers, one Arvo Hellat. But in vain. We're going to have to let him go in a couple of hours, for lack of evidence. He speaks Swedish. From Nuckö, if that means anything to you. Would you like to have a try?'

Norlander stood up without a word. He was getting closer.

Laikmaa led the way down corridors, both above- and below-ground, to the prison. Accompanied by a couple of guards, they arrived at a steel door, where they stopped.

'I think it's best if I'm present,' said Laikmaa. 'Don't worry, I don't speak a word of Swedish. But it violates the rules to allow a foreign police officer to be alone in an Estonian cell. I'm sure you understand.'

Norlander nodded, hoping that his disappointment wasn't too obvious.

They went in. The man in the cell had long hair and looked Finnish. Viggo Norlander pictured Arto Söderstedt in his mind and let the image stay there.

Arvo Hellat studied both mafia fighters and said something sarcastic in Estonian. Laikmaa replied tersely and pointed at Norlander, who cleared his throat and began talking. It was liberating to speak Swedish. No more '*Ich bin* sorry.'

'You're close to Jüri Maarja, and that means you're close to Viktor X. What do you know about the murders of three Swedish businessmen during the past week?'

Arvo Hellat looked surprised. He glanced at Laikmaa, who shrugged and said something in Estonian that meant either 'answer' or 'the man's insane'. Hellat replied in a strange Estonian-Swedish accent with peculiar diphthongs and *t*s and *g*s and *k*s that came in odd places. Norlander could barely understand him.

'I have no idea what you're talking about,' said Hellat. 'What do those murders have to do with me?'

Norlander was really only there to look. *Window-shopping*, he told himself. He wasn't going to let this man out of his grasp.

'The good superintendent doesn't understand a word we're saying,' Norlander said in the icy tone that by now almost came naturally to him. 'Is Viktor X involved in the murders of the Swedish businessmen? Let me point out that I'm here on a special assignment and have the power to make things very unpleasant for you.'

Arvo Hellat was even more astonished. He stared at Norlander for a good long time, then burst into loud laughter. 'You don't know what you're playing with!' he blurted out. 'By comparison, fire is ice-cold!'

Norlander left the cell with the image of Hellat engraved on his mind.

Laikmaa followed, astonished, as they walked down the corridors. 'Did you find out anything?' he asked in his American-tinged English.

'Enoff,' said Norlander.

They returned to Laikmaa's office. The superintendent sat down to continue their discussion.

Norlander remained standing. 'I'm going home now,' he said.

Laikmaa frowned. 'You've only just arrived. We still have a lot to discuss.'

'I'm satisfied. Thanks for all your help.' He headed for the door, then turned around and asked, 'Oh, that's right. Do you know anybody calling themselves Igor and Igor?'

Kalju Laikmaa just stared at him and shook his head.

Norlander closed the door and then he heard Laikmaa pick up the phone.

He went out to his rental car, tossed the parking ticket onto the ground without a second thought and drove off.

He drove three-quarters of the way around police headquarters and then parked near one of the walls that couldn't be seen from Laikmaa's window. It was near the prison entrance; he had carefully taken note of its location.

He sat there for three hours, fully alert. Dusk arrived. He was hungry. He sat there for another hour, feeling drowsier.

Then Arvo Hellat came out the door, tossing back his long hair with a feminine gesture. Norlander hunched down behind the wheel. Hellat went over to an old green Volvo Amazon, a vintage model that Norlander hadn't seen in God knew how many years. He drove off.

First he stopped at a Greek restaurant in Old Town. He made a phone call, ate a good-size portion of moussaka and drank a beer. That took almost an hour. Norlander sat outside in his car, freezing and starving. Twilight swept away the last remnants of Tallinn light. The lights came on in Old Town, perched on its hill.

Hellat came out and drove off in his absurd Amazon – hardly a suitable car for someone holding a top position within the mafia. He drove out of Tallinn, heading southwest in the direction of Keila. In that small town he went inside the restaurant at the train station, made another phone call and had another beer. Norlander watched him the whole time through the window. Then Hellat returned to his car, got back on the highway and drove towards Tallinn. It was eleven o'clock by the time he re-entered the Estonian capital with Norlander's rented

Skoda in tow. He drove into Old Town again, choosing the sections that were more dimly lit, and stopped outside a decrepit building that looked abandoned and ready for demolition. Not another car was anywhere in sight, not a person on the sleazy streets.

Mafia territory, Norlander thought as Hellat slipped inside the ramshackle building. The big Swede slid his gun back into the shoulder holster, took the little pistol out of his waistband at the small of his back, flicked off the safety, put it back and checked to make sure that the big hunting knife was still easily accessible, attached to his shin.

Blood was pumping wildly through his veins.

This was Viggo Norlander's Moment, with a capital *M*. Viggo the Viking.

He entered the building with his service revolver raised, the safety off. He heard Arvo Hellat climbing the rotting stairs a couple of floors above. Then Hellat took five steps and went through a door. After that, silence.

Norlander crept soundlessly up the stairs in the murky light. The steps didn't creak even once.

Two flights up he found three doors: one right next to the staircase, one at the far end of the corridor and one five steps away. He crept over to the last. It was closed, but he could see that it opened inwards.

He took a deep breath, hyperventilated a couple of times, then kicked open the door with all his strength and rushed in, gun raised.

Eight men were standing in the light along the walls, aiming machine guns at him.

'Please drop your weapon,' said an Estonian-Swedish voice from the dark section of the room.

A desk was standing there. Two men were seated behind it. It was impossible to see their faces. But perched on the edge of the desk was Arvo Hellat, smirking. Norlander had him in his sights.

'Drop your weapon or die,' said the voice again. It wasn't Hellat speaking. Hellat merely smiled. 'One second,' said the voice.

Norlander dropped his gun.

He had never felt so disarmed.

Shaking his head, Hellat came over and removed the rest of his arsenal. Then he went back to the desk and sat down, dangling his legs like a child.

'It took some time to assemble a decent force,' the voice went on. Now Norlander could tell that it was coming from one of the men seated behind the desk. 'And to find suitable premises. We sent Arvo on a little trip to Keila while we made the necessary arrangements. So what do you think you're doing? Is this some sort of private vendetta?'

Norlander didn't move. He was ice-cold inside.

'I really must ask you to tell us what you're up to,' the voice insisted courteously, stepping into the light and becoming a body. A large body, a large face adorned with a moustache and a good-natured smile.

'Jüri Maarja?' Norlander managed to say.

Jüri Maarja came over to him, pressed lightly on Norlander's stomach, ran his hand over his bald spot and then gave him a searching look.

'Interesting,' he said. 'An interesting person for a vendetta.'

Maarja said something in Russian and received a muttered reply from another man sitting in the dark behind the desk.

'Tell us everything you know and everything you think you know,' said Maarja, still very polite. Norlander recognised the chill in the voice. He couldn't even bring himself to hate the similarity. 'I insist,' Maarja went on.

Viggo Norlander closed his eyes. His last chance to be the hero would be to remain silent in the face of this courteous monster.

But the hero option was no longer on Norlander's list. It had been crossed off, never to return.

'Right now Swedish businessmen are being murdered one after the other in Stockholm,' he said hoarsely. 'They're being executed with your ammunition and with the method that you use to kill traitors. Viktor X!' he shouted at the shadow behind the desk. Nothing moved.

Jüri Maarja looked genuinely surprised and blurted out a few Russian syllables. He received a few more in return from the desk.

'It's possible that you've just saved your life, Detective Inspector Viggo Norlander.' He read the name aloud from Norlander's police ID, which he'd plucked from his pocket. 'We need to inform Stockholm of our innocence in some way. But of course we can't simply let you go without some form of punishment. That would go against our policy. Now listen closely, and memorise these words. We're going to write a note and pin it on you. We'd never do anything so incredibly stupid as to kill Swedish businessmen in Sweden. Is that understood? We have nothing to do with this matter. To the extent that we might have a presence in Stockholm, it's extremely important for us to stay as low-profile as possible.'

Maarja went over to the desk to accept a piece of paper and a pen from the man in the shadows. He shoved Hellat off the desk and proceeded to write for an uncomfortably long time. Then he said, 'Now it's time for us to make our departure. In case the good Laikmaa has seen fit to send a man after you. Although of course he knows better than to get involved. And it takes time to assemble Commando K.'

Then he said something in Estonian, and the men holding the guns flung Norlander to the floor. He stared up at the ceiling as they bound his arms and legs. He couldn't move.

Then came the first pain. It was almost liberating. He screamed. For all sorts of reasons.

The second pain was annulled by the next two.

He became an illuminated bundle of nerve impulses. He saw himself light up with a final light.

Damn it, he thought in surprise. *What a sleazy way to die.* Then he felt himself disappear.

18

The sunny spring morning did not reach its fingers into Supreme Central Command. Only the hands of the A-Unit reached that far, and for the moment they seemed to be tied.

Somebody farted.

No one claimed responsibility.

Everyone glanced around suspiciously as the smell dissipated.

Hultin made his usual entrance through his mysterious boss-only door and slapped his mobile phone down on the table. 'In case Norlander decides to report in from Tallinn,' he said to head off any questions.

Somebody burped.

There was a rather lax mood in the room. Hultin noticed it. 'Okay. The investigation has stalled. But we're used to that happening, right? You're experienced and hand-picked officers. Keep your spirits up.'

The previous day had felt like a hangover. All activity had seemed muted, and everyone had moved as if in slow motion – except for Norlander, apparently, who had gone to the opposite extreme.

'Señor Chavez?' Hultin began his systematic run-through.

Chavez sat up straight. 'I'm still working on the MEMAB lead. If you can call it a lead. But I'm convinced that it is.'

The mobile phone rang. Hultin held up his hand and answered it. 'Viggo? Is that you?'

A faint murmur spread through the room.

'How does it feel to sing in the Maria Magdalena Church?' Holm asked Nyberg.

'Magnificent acoustics,' said Nyberg. '*Missa papae Marcelli.*'

'How divine,' Holm said dreamily.

'What the hell is that on your cheek?' Chavez demanded of Hjelm.

'A blemish.' Hjelm had been practising saying that word.

'Yes,' Hultin said in English into the mobile phone, waving his free hand at the team members. Silence descended over Supreme Central Command. Hultin turned round and stared at the wall as he again said, 'Yes.' Then he didn't say a word for several minutes. Everyone could tell by looking at his back, perhaps from the way it was hunched up and leaning forward, that something had happened. No one spoke. Finally Hultin said, 'Yes,' for a third time and put down the mobile phone. At that moment the small fax machine whirred and churned out a piece of paper. Hultin held on to it as the machine released it. He read the message, then closed his eyes for a moment. Something dramatic had happened.

'Viggo Norlander has been crucified,' he said, his voice failing for a second. 'The Russian-Estonian mafia nailed him to the floor in an abandoned building in one of Tallinn's roughest neighbourhoods.'

Everybody exchanged wide-eyed glances. They were still missing the most important piece of information. Then it came.

'He's alive,' said Hultin. 'That was Superintendent Kalju Laikmaa from the Tallinn police. Norlander apparently set off on a fucking one-man vendetta against the mafia. And he ended up nailed to the floor. Laikmaa had put a tail on him, since he suspected something like this would happen. When his men, the so-called Commando K unit, entered the building, Viggo had been lying there like that for about an hour, with nails through both hands and both feet. Fortunately he was unconscious.

'The nail driven through one of his hands held this message, written in Swedish. I'll read it to you: "To Detective Inspector Viggo Norlander's boss, Stockholm. We are the group that you know as Viktor X's group. We have nothing to do with any murders of businessmen in Stockholm. We prefer to keep more serious crimes of violence within our own borders, as you can see. We're returning your Lone Avenger to you without even a broken bone. We'll only put the nails through his flesh."

It's signed Viktor X, and then there's a P.S.: "If this is the way you choose to proceed, then we can understand why the case hasn't been solved. But good luck. It's in our interest that you solve it quickly."'

'What in hell was he thinking?' exclaimed Chavez.

Hultin shook his head. 'Clearly he'd picked up a couple of leads. He's still in a serious condition, but he sent word via Laikmaa that a big Swedish media company, known internationally as GrimeBear Publishing, Inc., has been under heavy pressure from the protection racket of Viktor X and others, and that a couple of the racket's booze smugglers, by the name of Igor and Igor, are operating in Sweden. Let's try to get hold of these gentlemen, and check up on what this GrimeBear is all about.'

Hjelm looked at Nyberg. Nyberg looked at Hjelm. Igor and Igor. They'd already come across those two some-where.

Hultin finished his summing-up. 'Norlander also said that he's done playing Rambo.'

Again the team members exchanged glances.

'I didn't know he'd started,' said Holm.

Hjelm drove with Nyberg over to Södermalm, to a small basement pub on Södermannsgatan, and went to the apartment directly above. They'd been there before. They rang the bell twelve times before a man, bleary-eyed with sleep, stuck out his head. Within a tenth of a second he was wide awake at the sight of Gunnar Nyberg.

'Don't kill me,' the man said submissively.

Hjelm thought about Nyberg's menacing an-assault-is-imminent technique and the deepest bass voice in *Missa papae Marcelli* in the Maria Magdalena Church.

'Don't try to suck up to me, Bert,' said Nyberg. 'We need a little more information about Igor and Igor. What exactly did you buy from them?'

'I told you last time,' the voice said faintly from the door opening.

'Tell us again.'

'Estonian vodka, 120-proof, from Liviko. Four shipments at various times last winter.'

'When and how much?'

'The first time was in . . . November, I think. The last time in early February. I haven't heard from them since then.'

'Should you have?'

'They came in November, December, January, February. Not in March. Each time I bought a few cases. I knew I could sell it. Besides, you can water it down quite a lot without anyone noticing. It's become something of a favourite with the regular customers – a bit unusual for a vodka, being Estonian and all. But I've run out now, and I haven't heard from them again. Unfortunately. It was really cheap.'

'You're going to have to come down to the station with us and help put together some pictures of the Igor brothers,' said Nyberg.

The not-very-heroic trio then made their way from Söder to Kungsholmen.

Hultin tapped on the table a few times and held up two classic police sketches. The one on the right showed a thin man with unmistakably Slavic features and an equally unmistakable Russian moustache. The man on the left was clean-shaven, stout and powerful-looking, not unlike Nyberg.

'These are two of Viktor X's booze smugglers in Sweden,' Hultin began his three o'clock meeting. 'They call themselves Igor and Igor. The photographic composites didn't turn out too well, so we had to drag out the old sketch artist from the museum corridors. The drawings were made based on information provided by a Mr Bert Gunnarsson, a pub owner in Söder, who has purchased smuggled vodka from them on several occasions both this year and last. I've also been in contact again with Kalju Laikmaa in Tallinn. He identified them at once. Neither of them is named Igor. The thin guy is Alexander Bryusov and the fat one is Valery Treplyov. Both are small-time Russian gangsters active in Estonia until six months ago, when they apparently came to Sweden in the employ of Viktor X. The fact that they broke off contact with Gunnarsson in March may have significance.'

'Are we going to accept the damn official explanation for Norlander's stigmata?' said Söderstedt.

'Stigmata?' said Billy Pettersson.

'Wounds that appear in the same places as on the body of the Lord Jesus Christ,' said Kerstin Holm pedantically.

'That explanation can't steer the investigation,' said Hultin. 'We're going to have to ignore it, even if we believe it. So let's try and get hold of these two Igor gentlemen. They're our only solid link to Viktor X.'

Time now took on a new form, calmer and more protracted, more methodical. They published the drawings of Igor and Igor in all the newspapers, but with no results. Messieurs Alexander Bryusov and Valery Treplyov remained nothing more than sketches.

There were several current hypotheses: (1) only Daggfeldt was the intended victim, and the other two were red herrings; (2) only Strand-Julén was the intended victim, and the other two were red herrings; (3) only Carlberger was the intended victim, and the other two were red herrings; (4) Daggfeldt and Strand-Julén were the real targets, and Carlberger was the red herring; (5) Strand-Julén and Carlberger were the real targets, and Daggfeldt was the red herring; (6) Daggfeldt and Carlberger were the real targets, and Strand-Julén was the red herring; and (7) all three were the intended victims.

Number 6 applied to the newly acquired GrimeBear lead. The media company known abroad as GrimeBear Publishing, Inc., turned out to be none other than the huge, powerful and venerable Lovisedal AB, which evidently was now experiencing mafia problems in the former Soviet Union. Daggfeldt and Carlberger had both been members of the Lovisedal board of directors during the same period, from 1991 until 1993. Strand-Julén was not, and hence he could be the red herring. It was conceivable, for instance, that Daggfeldt and Carlberger were killed because Viktor X wanted to make an example of the Lovisedal corporation, due to their antipathy to the protection racket in Russia and the Baltics.

The enormous Lovisedal media factory had expanded beyond Sweden, had started a daily Russian-language business newspaper and was exploring the Baltics, as so many other Swedish companies were doing. The free market intersected with an even freer market, was subjected to daily threats and disruptions, and then to fight the mafia turned to private Russian security services consisting of people who had been trained during the Soviet era. The Swedish companies were financing a minor civil war between ex-Soviet entrepreneurs. Foreign aid, it might be called.

Chavez followed up on the Lovisedal lead along with the MEMAB lead. This meant that he talked to all the board members from the relevant time periods, then tried to narrow his focus to potential suspects. His efforts didn't produce much. Hjelm often accompanied him when he had to drive somewhere.

Hjelm had ended up in a real vacuum. His days seemed to centre mostly on the red blemish on his left cheek. It was growing, slowly but surely. Cilla, who was a nurse, dismissed it with an ambivalent laugh. It was now about three-eighths of an inch across, and he was seriously beginning to consider the fateful word: *cancer.* Malignant melanoma. But he rejected any suggestion that he have the blemish checked out.

Kerstin Holm had hardly spoken to Hjelm since their strange conversation in the staff cafeteria. She spent most of her time with her tapes, coordinating them with the interviews of neighbours and employees that she'd assigned to the less-than-pleased Stockholm Criminal Police.

George Hummelstrand, the foremost opponent of the secession from the Order of Mimir, seemed – contrary to Judge Franzén's observations – to have quite a sceptical attitude towards the Order of Skidbladnir. In fact, he thought the whole thing was ridiculous. His manner of speaking was much like that of his wife Anna-Clara, sprinkling semi-lewd Gallicisms into the conversation and constantly hinting at remarkable erotic relationships with other women. He kept on emphasising what a 'Free and French' relationship he and Anna-Clara enjoyed. At first Holm thought he was trying to seduce her, but she was soon convinced that he must be impotent. It was with relief, but also with some fascination, that she crossed Mr and Mrs Hummelstrand off her agenda.

Söderstedt, Pettersson and Florén had become more and more immersed in their own world of audit reports and stockbrokers, shell companies, pseudo-businesses, covert dividends and new stock issues. Even when

Söderstedt sat down in the cafeteria and talked about convertible promissory notes so that it sounded like a public lecture, he revealed a weariness that was easy to see. Sometimes the finance group would appear at the meetings with diagrams and charts that got progressively less comprehensible and made Hultin's increasingly messy scribbles on the whiteboard look like a miracle of precision. Söderstedt felt more and more alienated from the obvious enthusiasm exhibited by the two finance officers as they mapped the business affairs of the three wise men, Daggfeldt, Strand-Julén and Carlberger. He wanted to be a cop again. Or at least be able to think.

Nyberg was burrowing his way like a mole through the underworld. In spite of his carefully devised methodology, he was unable to come up with any results at all. He was the first to have real doubts about the investigation. Either they were doing something fundamentally wrong, or else they were dealing with another Palme murder. Nobody in the murky world of small-time criminals, which was always filled with rumours and gossip, knew the slightest thing, either about the perpetrator or the crimes that had been committed. Both seemed to be far removed from the underworld, in the classic sense of the word. On the other hand, the underworld, in the classic sense of the word, was becoming passé. The truly violent crimes were being committed by other groups, primarily within the institution of the family, which was at the true core of crime in society; the family was the eternal recipient of all the frustrations of adult life.

Burglaries were committed almost exclusively by drug addicts, while robberies were carried out by strange paramilitary organisations, often with a racist bent, in order to finance their own operations. Fraud was now an entire division within the service sector, just like any other division. The old small-time crooks stood on the sidelines, looking on and feeling positively honourable. Desperation and frustration were flourishing like never before in a society in which hordes of young people had been shut out of the job market without ever getting even a whiff of it. Nyberg wanted a holiday.

What Hultin was doing or thinking was just as mysterious as the door through which he entered and exited Supreme Central Command, the door that was always locked if anyone tried to follow him out. When they asked him about it, he merely laughed.

One evening Chavez and Hjelm slipped out to Stadshagen Field with its artificial turf to catch a glimpse of a match between senior players of the Stockholm police soccer team and the Rågsved Alliance team.

When Hultin head-butted Chavez's father and split open his eyebrow, they left.

Hjelm, who had thrown himself into the 24/7 job to avert the personal crisis he had felt approaching, suddenly had a great deal of free time on his hands. He gazed at his lonely image in the mirror, hating the evergrowing blemish on his cheek.

Who is this man? he stopped himself from thinking, yet the thought stayed with him.

By the end of April he was showering a surprising amount of attention on his family. Danne thought it was disgusting, Tova was mostly startled, and as for Cilla – he had no idea what she thought. The strange experience in the kitchen still hovered between them like an untouchable wound. Was it starting to ooze? Was it becoming inflamed?

In early May the family moved out, at least part-time, to the little cabin that they'd been lucky enough to rent on Dalarö, the island that wasn't really an island at all, but rather a whole string of islands. Cilla spent almost every night out there, commuting to Huddinge Hospital. Her much-anticipated holiday would begin in June – she would have the whole summer free. The children were also out there at weekends. Danne had evidently decided to hide away from reality during this last summer of his childhood. Paul managed to get a free weekend at the very beginning of May and spent a couple of unusually pleasant days in the spring sunshine, basking in the bosom of his family, and in Cilla's embrace. The latter took place on a blanket on a deserted pier in the midst of a fiery red sunset, with an empty wine bottle rolling around next to them. She was silent and sad afterwards. Unapproachable. The preposterous beauty of the sunset seemed to have bored its way into her. A deep red layer had spilled across the motionless surface of the sea. The red contours, clearly delineated against the surrounding black, had slowly contracted; an evaporating pool of blood above an abyss. Before long only the abyss remained. Cilla began trembling, a deep, unfathomable shivering. He watched her for a long time through the gathering dusk. He tried to share her experience, tried to see what she saw, feel what she felt. But he couldn't. The red was gone. Only black remained. He tried to get her to go up to the cabin, but he got no response. He was forced to leave her there on the pier, all alone with an experience of utter solitude. He went inside and climbed into bed, but didn't sleep all night.

Early in the morning he went back down to the pier. She was still sitting there, wrapped in the blanket. He returned to the cabin without making his presence known.

Before the move out to Dalarö nothing much happened, from a professional standpoint. It was the period of working on details and consolidating findings. Besides collaborating with Chavez and Nyberg in both the upper- and the underworld, respectively, he completed two tasks still on his list, the second more important than the first.

First he called an 071 number and encountered the first phone-sex in his life. In a simpering voice a woman exhibiting some symptoms of dyslexia read from a script what she would do with his penis. Since the aforementioned organ remained completely limp the whole time, it would have been difficult to implement any of these acrobatic manoeuvres. He then called the business registry at the Patent and Registration Office, but the only address for the simpering company JSHB was the post-office box listed in the newspaper ad, a box number in Bromma. So he ended up having to drive over to the post office on Brommaplan and simply wait. He positioned himself so that he could see the post-office boxes through the window and smoked a couple of cigarettes in a sweltering heat more typical of the height of summer than the month of April. Temperatures that had undoubtedly been stolen from July and August. And he waited. He kept box number 1414 in his sights for almost three hours before a short, fox-like man in his forties stuck his key in the slot and opened the box. By that time Hjelm was feeling worn out and had no energy left to tail Johan Stake to see whether his 071 premises actually housed a bordello. Instead, he went up to the man and said, 'Stake?'

The man didn't hesitate for even a second. He slipped past Hjelm and took off fast. Hjelm stuck out his leg and elegantly tripped him, making his face slam into the glass door. Stake fell next to a well-groomed little poodle that was tied up outside. The dog began yapping wildly. Hjelm hauled the man to his feet. Stake had a split lip, and blood was gushing out over the shrieking poodle's mane.

'So unnecessary,' said Hjelm as he snapped handcuffs on the man and dragged him over to the car. He hoped Stake wasn't thinking of bleeding all over his vehicle, just when he'd got it broken in.

* * *

Jorge Chavez was present when Hjelm interviewed Johan Stake. They kept things informal by conducting the interview in their office.

'I have a lot of questions about those 071 ads, which in happier times used to cover entire pages of the tabloids,' said Hjelm, seeming to fumble around a bit. 'Why do they put the address in the ad? Is that how pimping and bordello operations work nowadays?'

'There are laws about this,' said Johan Stake belligerently as he touched his taped lip. 'Don't you know the laws? What the hell am I doing here, anyway? You have no legal right—'

'Officially you've been arrested for resisting an officer.'

'In that case, I have the right to a lawyer. "Provision of legal aid precedes interrogation."'

'You seem to be extremely knowledgeable about the justice system. The problem is that a much more serious charge is hovering in the background. Promoting prostitution. Acting as a pimp for underage boys.'

Stake looked shaken. 'In that case, I really do want a lawyer.'

'Then the prosecutor will have to indict you and take you to court. But there's another option.'

'Wait a minute. You don't have any proof. You'll have to release me.'

'How do you know we don't have any proof?'

Stake didn't reply.

Hjelm calmly went on, 'Early this morning we picked up a young guy by the name of Jörgen Lindén as he boarded the first train to Göteborg. He was carrying a big suitcase, as if he was about to flee from somebody, and I don't think it was the police. He's now sitting in jail. Not ten minutes ago he was ready to testify. Detective Inspector Chavez here conducted the interview brilliantly, but not entirely without . . . shall we say, some persuasion.'

Chavez went over to the coffee-maker and poured himself a cup to hide his astonishment. He took a few seconds to compose himself, then returned with an expression of persuasion etched on his face.

Good job, thought Hjelm. Good lies should always be as detailed as possible. Then they will convince anybody.

Johan Stake seemed convinced. He didn't say a word as he sat thinking. Apparently the scenario wasn't the least bit improbable.

'But there's another option,' Hjelm repeated.

Stake remained silent. He was no longer calling for a lawyer.

Hjelm completed his attack. 'Step one on the road to immediate release: tell us about Bernhard Strand-Julén.'

Johan Stake cleared his throat and squirmed a bit on his chair. 'Can you guarantee that you'll let me go?'

'We're the only ones who know that you're here. No formal charges have been filed. You're free as soon as you spit out what we want to know. We have much bigger fish to fry than you and your bordellos. We'll let both you and Jörgen go if you cooperate. That's step one.'

'Strand-Julén . . . I got boys for him. A crew for his boat, as he insisted on calling them. Healthy, blond boys about sixteen or so, athletic types. Two or three at a time. Always new ones. During the summer season almost every weekend. Never during the winter. That's when he went into hibernation.'

'Step two. Were your services ever used by Kuno Daggfeldt or Nils-Emil Carlberger?'

'Carlberger,' said Stake, looking as though he'd been expecting the question. 'He got my number from Strand-Julén. That was six months ago. He sounded damned nervous when he requested a boy. I had the impression it was his first time. An attempt to widen his horizons maybe, a little Socratic boy-love. What do I know?'

'Do you know how it went?'

'I talked to the kid afterwards. He got a little . . . central stimulation.' He laughed loudly. 'Carlberger was like a little boy, totally inexperienced, either a hundred per cent hetero or else a hundred per cent impotent. But he paid well.'

'And that was all? What about Daggfeldt?'

'No.'

'Can you tell us anything else about Strand-Julén or Carlberger? Think carefully.'

Stake thought for a moment. 'No, I'm sorry. That's all.'

They let him go.

'You could have warned me,' said Chavez, sipping his coffee.

'If I had, would you have agreed to go along with it?'

'No.'

They allowed themselves a good laugh at their peculiarities, both their own and each other's. Then Hjelm crossed off Johan Stake from the investigation.

Two hours later Stake called to compliment him. It was very strange, but he'd just spoken to Jörgen Lindén, who hadn't understood a word of what he was talking about. Stake praised Hjelm for the impressive lie and then hung up. Hjelm stood for a long time, staring at his phone.

By now Paul Hjelm was almost certain that the murders had stopped with victim number three. One morning it was raining for the first time in what seemed like a premature summer. So it was time to drive out to the Kevinge Golf Course. It was deserted. The whole clubhouse was deserted too.

Except, that is, for Lena Hansson, who was in her place at the reception desk. At first she didn't recognise him, but when she did, her expression changed, which was precisely what he was hoping for. He instantly mobilised his heavy artillery. 'Why did you lie about the fact that you were a caddy for the three corpses on 7 September 1990?'

She stared at him with a frankly naked expression; it was obvious that she'd been expecting him. For a month. 'They weren't corpses back then,' she said hesitantly. 'On the contrary. You might call it an . . . over-the-top life they were living.'

'But not without an oversexed component, right?'

'That's right.'

'Shall we sit down for a moment? The customers are conspicuous by their absence.'

'And what a glorious absence it is.' She sounded older than her years. She went into the closed club restaurant and sat down at a table. Hjelm followed.

Lena Hansson fiddled with the wax of a burned-out candle in a small holder. Hjelm said:

'There were three of you working as caddies, am I right?'

'Yes. That's what they requested. A guy named Carl-Gustaf something-or-other. Some kind of aristocratic last name. I don't really remember, but I can look it up. And my friend Lotta. Lotta Bergström. She was really upset. It was because of her that I didn't say anything.'

'What do you mean?'

Hjelm permitted himself a cigarette. He blamed the elegant setting, but more likely the 'no smoking' sign had enticed him.

'Lotta was . . . going through a hard time. A horrible childhood. An even more horrible adolescence. I got the job for her. We were both seventeen, in the same class in school. I felt guilty. She . . . well, she killed herself in '92. I don't really know if it had anything to do with this. Probably not. But I still feel like it was my fault.'

'What they did?'

'Yes. That Carl-Gustaf – he didn't believe it could happen. He was from some really old upper-crust family.

You know the kind, people who still care about good breeding and etiquette, and not just as a role that you play when you go to fancy dinners and things like that. For them, it's all part of their daily lives, both private and professional. Good breeding and etiquette and an ancient moral code seem to be injected into their genes. They're often quite pleasant to be around. Carl-Gustaf was too. He laughed politely and shyly during the first four holes, then he shut up, letting that Strand-Julén badger him for four more holes. At the ninth green he set the golf bag down so that Strand-Julén's putt struck the bag. Then he simply left. I've never seen him again. If he'd been a real gentleman, he would have taken us with him.'

Carl-Gustaf, wrote Hjelm in his mental notebook. 'But Lotta and you stayed?' he said.

'Seventeen, properly brought up, insecure. Of course we stayed. After Carl-Gustaf left, they began tossing around nouveau-riche jokes about the arch-conservative nobility. It was a form of jealousy.'

'Could you be a little more precise? What exactly did they do?'

'They'd had a lot to drink here in the restaurant before the game. They seemed – I don't know, speedy, almost, as if they'd snorted some coke in the men's room or something like that.'

'Or in the cab on the way over,' said Hjelm, unprofessionally.

'At any rate, they started telling dirty jokes and making insinuating remarks, on a polite level that allowed at least

Carl-Gustaf to join in the laughter. Lotta and I were mostly just embarrassed. There was hardly anybody else on the golf course, so they could carry on as much as they liked. After a while Strand-Julén focused his remarks on Carl-Gustaf, which let us off the hook for a time. The remarks were mostly about the size of Carl-Gustaf's noble organ. Then he made his heroic departure, and the two of us ended up in the line of fire. Really. I've never in my life been so badly treated, and I'll never let it happen again. I promised myself that.'

'So what did you do?'

'What do you mean?'

'Did you shoot them?'

She laughed loudly, her voice shrill and unnatural. 'Oh, sure,' she said at last, as she wiped away the tears. 'I can't say that I was sorry when I heard that they'd been shot. All three of them, one after the other. It was wonderful, to be quite honest. Magical, like in a fairy tale. The unknown avenger. But good God, I've never fired a gun in my life.'

'But somebody you know might have.'

She was silent for a moment, mulling it over. 'I don't think so,' she said quite calmly. 'Maybe somebody Lotta knew. That would be more likely. I was just furious, fucking furious, and that sort of anger doesn't go away. But I wasn't seriously affected. She was. She was already in a fragile state, and things just got worse.'

'Okay, so what happened?'

'They started pawing and groping us on the tenth and

eleventh fairways. It got much worse when we were over by the woods. They were really worked up – they must have still been high on drugs – and that's when they started going at us. They tore off Lotta's sweater, and one of them pushed her down on the ground and lay on top of her. Daggfeldt, I think. Carlberger sat nearby and watched. Strand-Julén grabbed hold of me.

'I managed to pull loose and got hold of a golf club, which I slammed against the back of Daggfeldt's neck. He rolled off Lotta, and I went over and tried to comfort her. Daggfeldt lay there, writhing. I think he was bleeding from the back of his head. The other two just stood there, thinking. Doing some problem-solving. They'd sobered up awfully quick. Started apologising and saying how sorry they were and offering us money to keep our mouths shut. And we let them buy our silence. It was as expensive as hell. Several thousand kronor. Besides, we wanted to keep our jobs. Well, Lotta got fired shortly afterwards. She made another suicide attempt a couple of weeks after that. She'd already tried twice before. The seventh time she finally succeeded, a couple of years later. I don't know whether she really meant to die. And I have no idea how big a role all this played in what she did. But I've given it a lot of thought. Those fucking pigs! I'm glad they're dead.'

'And they continued to play golf here? Afterwards? All three of them?'

'Yes. Apparently they would have missed out on important contacts they made here otherwise. But they never played together again.'

'The last time we talked, you said about Daggfeldt and Strand-Julén, who by then were dead, and I quote: "They would always say hello when they came in and stop to chat." But that didn't really happen, did it?'

'No, I lied. I don't think any of them ever even glanced at me again. They looked a bit worried when I moved inside to work in the reception area. But I think they were convinced that they'd bought my silence.'

'And had they? Have you ever told this story to anyone else? To your lover, for example? What's his name? The golf association secretary. Axel Wifstrand?'

'Widstrand. No, especially not him. He would take it . . . in the wrong way.'

'React violently?'

'Just the opposite, I think. He would think I was lying. No, I haven't told anyone. They bought my silence. But I don't know whether they bought Lotta's.'

'Did she have a boyfriend? A brother? A father?'

'If I understood correctly, her father, Bengt-Egil, was at the root of all her problems. She would never have told him about it, and he would never have tried to avenge her honour. And she never had a boyfriend – that was another source of anxiety. But she was close to her brother, Gusten. In fact, Gusten and Lotta were inseparable.'

'Do you think he knew?'

'We lost contact when she got really sick, so I don't know. But if Gusten is behind this, then I'm grateful to him. I'll visit him in prison.'

Hjelm paused to think. Gusten Bergström.

'Shall we find out what Carl-Gustaf's last name was? After that I won't bother you any more. At least I don't think I will.'

Lena Hansson got up and stretched. He saw a pride that he hadn't noticed before. Once a possible witness, now a whole and complete human being.

'Keep the anger alive,' he found himself saying to her.

She gave him a sarcastic look.

Count Carl-Gustaf af Silfverbladh had moved in 1992 to his family's estate in Dorset, England. Having sown his wild oats, he sought to obtain a proper education at Oxford, as his father and grandfather had done. He hadn't returned to Sweden, and in all likelihood never would.

Hjelm wondered how the English would pronounce the man's last name.

Gusten Bergström was twenty-eight, a few years older than his sister Lotta would have been had she lived. His apartment was on Gamla Brogatan in central Stockholm. He worked as a computer operator for Swedish Rail in the long-distance office at Central Station.

He doesn't have far to go every morning, thought Hjelm as he rang the doorbell of Bergström's apartment, which was a couple of floors above the old Sko-Unos shop.

A shadow appeared in the door's peephole. *Not a great idea to have a peephole near the window*, he thought.

'Police!' he bellowed, pounding on the door.

The man who opened it was as thin as a stick, with a

haircut that looked like a toupee but probably wasn't. He wore glasses with thick lenses. He looked like a combination of a teenage hacker and a middle-aged accountant.

Hjelm looked at Gusten Bergström with dismay. This was no murderer. He'd bet his life on that.

'I'm from the Criminal Police,' said Hjelm, showing his ID.

Gusten Bergström let him in without saying a word. The apartment was spartan, to say the least. The walls were bare, and at one end of the room a computer was on. Before Bergström could go over and turn down the light, Hjelm caught a glimpse of a naked woman on the coloured screen, incredibly true to life. It made him feel old.

'Have a seat,' said Bergström politely.

Hjelm sat down on a quasi-antique sofa and Bergström on a matching armchair, if it could be called that.

'I'd like to talk to you about your sister,' said Hjelm cautiously.

Bergström got up at once and went over to the bookcase near the computer. From one of the shelves he took down a photo in a gold frame and showed it to Hjelm. A girl in her mid-teens was smiling at him. It was astonishing how much she looked like her brother.

'This is Lotta before things went bad for her,' said Bergström sadly. 'On her seventeenth birthday.'

'Very pretty,' said Hjelm, feeling ghastly. The photograph was taken about the time of the golf-course incident.

'What's this about?' said Bergström, pushing up his glasses.

'When she was seventeen she worked as a caddy at the Kevinge Golf Course. Do you remember that?'

Bergström gave a slight nod.

'Did she ever tell you anything about her job?' asked Hjelm.

'No,' he said with a sigh. There seemed to be something shattered about him.

'Nothing at all?'

For the first time Bergström looked Hjelm in the eye. Each of them was looking for something in the other.

'What's this about?' Bergström repeated. 'My sister has been dead for a couple of years now. Why are you coming here and talking about her as if she were alive? I've just got used to the idea that she's gone.'

'She was fired from her job at the golf course in the autumn of 1990. Do you recall that?'

'Yes, I remember. The season was over, and the golf course was about to close for the winter. She was still at school, so it was no big deal to lose a seasonal job.'

'But you don't recall anything she told you about her time at the golf course?'

'She got the job through a friend; I don't remember her name. I didn't feel very comfortable in Danderyd, to be honest. I didn't know anyone there. She didn't really, either. It wasn't a happy time, not at all.'

'Shortly afterwards she tried to take her own life for the third time. Is that right?'

'How sensitive of you,' Bergström said glumly. 'Yes, she did. A razor blade, for the first and last time. When she actually succeeded, it was by taking Alvedon. Did you know that all it takes to kill the liver and kidneys is one blister pack of Alvedon and some liquor? Lotta knew that. Nobody knew what she had planned. There were no warning shots or cries for help or any bullshit like that. She really did try to kill herself seven times. It was like a . . . miscarriage. As if she weren't meant to be born. As if there were something seriously wrong with her view of life.'

'Do you know why?'

'I don't know anything, and I don't understand anything,' Bergström said tonelessly. 'I'll never understand anything.'

'Do you know about the murders of the three businessmen here in Stockholm?'

Bergström was off somewhere else. It took a moment for him to return. 'How could anybody not know about that?'

'Did you murder them?'

Gusten Bergström looked at him in surprise. Then a strange spark appeared in his eyes, as if a gust of life had suddenly been blown into his withered lungs. *The spirit is willing, but the flesh is weak*, Hjelm thought blasphemously.

'Yes,' said Bergström proudly. 'I murdered them.'

Hjelm studied the luminous figure. Something seemed about to happen in Gusten Bergström's dreary life. His face would appear on newspaper placards. He would be in the spotlight for the first and last time in his life.

'Come off it,' said Paul Hjelm, and the spark was extinguished.

Gusten Bergström seemed to crumple, sitting on the armchair's hard upholstery, as if he were its long-absent stuffing.

Hjelm poured a little oil on the waters of disappointment. 'Why did you kill Kuno Daggfeldt, Bernhard Strand-Julén and Nils-Emil Carlberger?'

'Why?' said Bergström, shrugging his hunched shoulders. 'Well, because – because they were rich.'

'You don't have the faintest idea what those three men did to your sister at the Kevinge Golf Course on 7 September 1990, a month before she made her third suicide attempt and was locked up in Beckomberga Hospital. Do you?'

'What the hell are you talking about?'

Gusten Bergström got up abruptly and tried to find something to hold on to. There was nothing. His fingers clutched wildly at the air.

'On that particular day, that trio of murdered men tried to rape your sister when she was acting as a caddy for them.'

Bergström's hands stopped grabbing. 'If I'd known,' he enunciated very clearly, 'I would have killed them. But they wouldn't have been allowed to live this long, I can promise you that.'

'But you didn't know?'

'No,' he said and sat down. Then he got up again, standing in the midst of the evening light flooding in from Gamla Brogatan. 'Now I understand,' he said, lighting up for one last time. 'Now I understand.'

'What do you understand?'

'It's Lotta! Lotta herself has taken her revenge! For a couple of days she stretched out her hand from the realm of the dead. Then she went back to that better world.'

Extremely agitated, Bergström went over to the bookcase and pulled out a worn, old book, holding it up and shaking it.

'Do you know about the Erinyes?' he asked without waiting for an answer. 'They're the most gruesome creatures in Greek mythology, but also the most awe-inspiring. The ultimate hand of justice. They hunt their prey day and night until the grave opens up. Let me read you a short passage: "The Erinyes are nothing more than the murdered victim's spirit, which, if no other avenger exists, take vengeance into their own hands, mercilessly and relentlessly, as the spirits of the dead are contained in their wrath."'

He gave Hjelm an urgent stare. Hjelm didn't say a word.

'Don't you understand?' shouted Bergström. 'There are no avengers, so she had to do it herself. She waited for an avenger, but none came. Everything fits! Those three men who hurt her were the ones she killed in quick succession all these years later. It's amazing! Your killer is a murder victim's spirit! An avenging goddess!'

Hjelm sat there for a moment, fascinated by Bergström's onslaught. Without a doubt, the parallels were striking. The avenger who left no traces. The divine, posthumous avenger from the realm of the dead.

But the thought of a highly tangible bullet from Kazakhstan in a wall in Djursholm brought him back to the world of crass reality: 'The Erinyes may have had a physical intermediary who pulled the trigger. Do you know if she might have talked about the incident at the golf course to anyone else?'

'There wasn't anyone else! Don't you understand? It was just the two of us, just Lotta and Gusten. Gusten and Lotta.'

'Papa? Mama? Anyone at the hospital?'

'My father? Oh, sure, that's really likely!' laughed Gusten. He had now crossed a line. 'Mother? That woman who could see no evil, hear no evil, speak no evil? All three monkeys in one. Absolutely! Someone at Beckis? Where everybody sits in a separate corner, rubbing their private parts all day long? Highly likely! There you have your cold-blooded murderer! The Beckomberga man! The expert killer from the loony bin!'

Hjelm could tell it was time to leave.

Under other circumstances Hjelm would have gone over to the computer, turned up the light and laughed crudely at the computerised figures, who by now were undoubtedly in the midst of fucking. But he didn't.

In some ambiguous way, that was a victory.

Hjelm spent the next few days pursuing the golf lead. He drove out to Beckomberga Hospital and talked to the staff, to find out who Lotta's friends were. She'd never had any. The only staff member who was still there from the early Nineties, a stony-faced male nurse, remembered Lotta as an extreme loner. Morbidly withdrawn, a total introvert. The only person that Lotta Bergström could have conceivably told about the incident was her brother, and apparently she hadn't done that. Or else Gusten Bergström was the best actor that Hjelm had ever seen.

He also directed his enquiries at Lena Hansson's family and circle of friends. With equally disappointing results. She had truly allowed Daggfeldt and his pals to buy her silence. The only possibility that seemed to be left after a number of days of fruitless searching was that Lena Hansson had hired a professional killer. He let that lead drop.

At the same time he received a summons to appear in court for the trial of Dritëro Frakulla. It was not something he was looking forward to. A couple of weeks after Frakulla seized the hostages at the immigration office in Hallunda, the refugee policies had suddenly changed, and several hundred Kosovar Albanians who had been threatened with deportation were allowed to stay in Sweden, including Frakulla's family. But after his desperate attempt to save them, he would be forced to leave the country as soon as he had served his prison sentence. The irony of fate seemed to Hjelm an understatement.

He sat in the chair in the courtroom of City Hall, giving his testimony. He tried to be as clear and objective as he could, almost managing to ignore the press, who harassed him before, during and after the trial. But he couldn't escape Dritëro Frakulla's surly gaze directed at him from the defendant's bench. Frakulla still had his arm in a sling, and he never took his eyes off Hjelm. It was not an accusatory look, but rather an open, candidly shattered gaze. Even so, Hjelm couldn't rid himself of the impression that he was being accused; perhaps that emotion was to be found only within himself. He thought that Frakulla was not accusing him of having shot him, but of not having killed him. If he had been killed, his family would have been able to stay; now they would loyally follow him back to the Serbs in a few years' time. Frakulla's lawyer was a jaded old man who asked all the right questions. Why hadn't Hjelm waited for the special unit? Why hadn't the Department of Internal Affairs investigated the case? Apparently Bruun and Hultin and Mörner had managed to erase all trace of the interrogation conducted by Grundström and Mårtensson. And yet the lawyer's attacks were nothing compared to Frakulla's unyielding eyes.

When Hjelm stepped down from the witness stand and walked through the courtroom between the rows of spectators, he met the gaze of a little boy. His expression was identical to his father's.

It took a while before Paul Hjelm could think again about the investigation.

A couple of days later Viggo Norlander suddenly appeared at Supreme Central Command during a morning meeting. He was actually still on sick leave, but he came in, hobbling on crutches and looking quite subdued. Something had been extinguished in his already extinguished expression. Gauze bandages were wrapped around his hands. They all greeted him warmly, and Kerstin Holm jumped up to get the bouquet of flowers that they had bought. They'd taken up a collection and were planning to deliver it to him that evening. Norlander looked genuinely touched and sat down in his usual seat at the table.

It had been left vacant. No one had replaced him.

While he was convalescing in the hospital in Tallinn and then in Huddinge, he had been convinced that Hultin had kicked him off the investigation and that Internal Affairs might even be after him. When he sank down onto the chair, he understood that he was . . . forgiven. He couldn't come up with any other word. He wept openly.

Norlander looked like a broken man. They wondered if he should have come back to work, but when he looked up at them with his red-rimmed eyes, they saw happiness beneath the tears, sheer happiness.

The more they got to know each other, the harder it became to understand each other. As always.

As they were leaving Supreme Central Command, Hjelm saw out of the corner of his eye Söderstedt go over to Norlander, put his arm around his shoulders and say something. Norlander laughed out loud.

Not much had been said during the meeting, no new progress had been made. They were now working from the theory that the killing spree was over, and that the deficit for the Swedish business world was going to stop at three and only three entries: Kuno Daggfeldt, Bernhard Strand-Julén and Nils-Emil Carlberger.

They were wrong.

19

The acrid smoke has settled; the pungent smell has disappeared. The man has finally been put to rest. It took a bit longer this time.

It has been a long day.

Now it's night.

It's night in the living room.

As the first notes from the piano slide out into the room, he is leaning back against the sofa, looking at the man. The piano notes walk up and down, back and forth; the saxophone comes in and walks at the piano's side. The same steps, the same little promenade.

When the sax takes off and the piano starts scattering the seemingly indolent chords in the background, it's as if the man rises up off the floor. A couple of little drum fills. And when the sax continues to chirp with a few dissonant notes, it's as if he's bending over a void. The saxophone jabs, chops, works its way up in higher and higher spirals. The blood is running out of the man's head.

It's as if he's slamming his fist right into the abdomen of the void in front of him. When the piano falls silent, the other, harder blow slams against the void's stomach.

It's a pantomime, a peculiar dance of death.

Yeah. Whoo-ee. The first kick. At the knee.

The saxophone climbs even farther, faster and faster. Ai. The second kick. To the groin.

It's so choreographed. Each blow, each kick at the void's invisible body, has been predetermined, occurs in exactly the right place.

He has envisioned it so many times before.

And right there, when the applause comes in, that's when the big punch is delivered. The audience is murmuring; the piano takes over. The blow falls at that very instant. The void's teeth are rolling under the tongue, and that's when it happens. At that precise moment.

The piano begins by taking a tentative step. Then it cuts loose. Ever freer wanderings, ever more beautiful. He is certain of the beauty now. It's as if the man aims a kick at the prostrate void. It's as if he kicks once, twice, three times, then four. The piano sings, lingering.

The void no longer exists.

The bass disappears. The piano is strolling again. Just like in the beginning.

It's as if the man is aiming a fifth kick – when the front door opens out in the hallway.

'Papa?' shouts a girl's voice.

The man collapses flat. Returns to a prostrate position.

He's already out of the room, out of the house, out of the garden.

He's so far away that he doesn't hear the heart-rending scream.

That's why he ran.

20

Gunnar Nyberg was jolted out of the double bed, which was still there, a symbol of hope in his three-room Nacka apartment. Viggo Norlander was wrenched from the more basic cot in his three-room place on Banérgatan. Kerstin Holm was pulled from the mattress on the floor in the little apartment belonging to her ex-husband's ex-wife in Brandbergen. Jorge Chavez was yanked up from the little drop-leaf table in the kitchen alcove of his rented room at the intersection of Bergsgatan and Scheelegatan, where he had fallen asleep, holding a full wine glass in his hand and resting his face on the remains of his meal. Arto Söderstedt got up from his chair in his apartment on Agnegatan and took off his reading glasses. And Paul Hjelm was hauled out of the unpleasantly empty double bed in his terraced house in Norsborg.

Jan-Olov Hultin had already been roused out of bed. He was waiting for them in a kitchen in Rösunda, Saltsjöbaden.

Chavez was the last to arrive, looking unashamedly fresh, a night flower in the pitch-black May darkness.

'What the hell? Did you take a shower?' asked Hjelm, holding a big coffee mug.

'Don't ask,' said Chavez curtly. 'Okay, who is he?'

'Have you had a look inside?'

'It looks the same as usual. Have the techs started working?'

'I called all of you here before I contacted the techs,' said Hultin. 'Among other things because I want you to see everything untouched. There were two shots to the head, right?'

A couple of the team members nodded. 'The bullets are still in the wall,' said Söderstedt.

Hultin nodded. 'All right. We finally have something to go on. A different sort of society big shot. His name is Enar Brandberg. He became a member of parliament in the last election. Before that he was general director of a small government agency.'

'The General Direction Fund,' said Söderstedt. 'It's not really a government agency, but almost. Then he became a member of parliament, representing the Folkeparti.'

Hultin gave him a sidelong glance. 'His daughter, Helena Brandberg, eighteen years old, arrived home a few minutes past one A.M., so about forty-five minutes ago. She heard jazz playing in the living room and thought it strange, since her father never listened to any kind of music. She went into the living room and saw the curtains fluttering in front of an open window. Outside a dark, unidentifiable shadow was running full tilt across the lawn and out to the street. In sheer bewilderment, she went over to the stereo and turned it off. Only then did she catch sight of her father lying on the floor. She screamed so loudly that the neighbours were over here in a matter of minutes. A family named Hörnlund. They have a daughter the same age as Helena Brandberg, and the two girls are best friends. Helena was clearly in a state of shock, and it was difficult to get any sort of eyewitness account from her. I mostly had to rely on the second-hand report from the Hörnlund family. Helena's mother died of cancer this past year. The Hörnlund family accompanied the girl to the hospital. I've been out in the garden to take a look around; there seem to be a number of footprints in the grass.'

'So that's the end of leaving no evidence behind,' said Chavez.

'The Erinyes assume bodily form,' said Hjelm.

Everyone stared at him for a moment. Söderstedt raised his left eyebrow and was just about to say something, but changed his mind.

'Okay,' said Hultin, summing up. 'This time we have both bullets still in the wall and a good number of footprints. But above all we have the cassette tape.'

'Cassette tape?' said Holm.

'The music. Jazz. In the tape player in the living room there's a tape that in all likelihood belongs to the murderer. It's not Brandberg's at any rate. Neither he

269

nor his daughter listened to jazz, and the tape was playing when Helena came home while the killer was still in the room. Apparently the music is part of our man's set routine. After the murder he sits down on the sofa to listen to some jazz. Since Helena stopped the tape, we know which tune was playing. Since a couple of unit members here are interested in music, I thought we could try to figure out right now what he was listening to. That was one of the reasons that I waited to contact the crime techs. We probably have about twenty minutes before we're locked out of the living room.'

'I don't know much about jazz,' said Gunnar Nyberg.

They went into the room, stepping over the body on the floor. Wearing a latex glove, Hultin rewound the tape to the beginning of the tune.

After the first three or four piano notes, before the melody had even begun to stroll over the keys, two people said in unison, '"Misterioso."' Kerstin Holm and Jorge Chavez looked at each other in surprise.

Hultin stopped the tape. 'One at a time.' How unlikely was it that two of the attendant members of the A-Unit were jazz fanatics?

'It's a standard,' Chavez said, after Holm nodded to him. 'The Thelonious Monk Quartet. Monk on piano, Johnny Griffin on tenor sax, Ahmed Abdul-Malik on bass. And what's the name of the guy on drums again?'

'Roy Haynes,' said Kerstin.

'Exactly,' said Jorge. 'It's the title track on the album *Misterioso*. If I remember right, it's the sixth and last track on the original. Ten or eleven minutes long. Amazing sax-playing by Griffin, and Monk is in top form. Of course Monk wrote the piece, as usual. What else can I tell you?'

Kerstin Holm picked up where he left off. 'All the tracks on the album were recorded on a magical summer evening in 1958 at the classic jazz club, the Five Spot Café, in New York. On the CD, a couple of other tracks were added from an earlier recording made during the same summer. One of them is also a standard, "Round Midnight". We can tell whether it's the CD or the original album that our man put on tape. If it's from the CD, "Round Midnight" will come right after "Misterioso". Otherwise, there won't be any other tunes.'

She fast-forwarded to the final piano and sax promenade in 'Misterioso'. After the applause and the whistling, a new tune started up, significantly more chaotic, free and ecstatic, as if born of that very moment of inspiration. *Not like a tune at all,* thought Hjelm, feeling ignorant. The sax and the piano inciting each other to something that was either a great achievement or sheer chaos. He couldn't decide which.

'No, no, no,' said Chavez. 'That wasn't "Round Midnight".'

'I've never heard that piece before,' said Holm. 'How odd.'

'What does it mean?' said Hultin.

'He could have taped something entirely different right afterwards,' said Chavez dubiously.

'Although that's certainly Monk playing,' said Holm.

'Those blue notes with even bluer notes on top. That's him. His hands are lying practically flat on the keys.'

'It sounds like a direct continuation,' said Hjelm, expecting to hear sighs and groans from the experts. 'I didn't hear a real space in between.'

'Actually, there wasn't,' Chavez surprisingly agreed. 'Either our man is a damned good mixer—'

'Or else,' Holm finished, 'this is a one-of-a-kind recording.'

'How the hell do the two of you know so much about all this?' asked Hjelm.

'Haven't you ever heard what jazz musicians say?' asked Kerstin Holm. '"Those who talk don't know, those who know don't talk."'

'I know somebody, a fellow Chilean.' Chavez mentioned his country of origin for the first time. 'He's a real *experto* on unusual jazz recordings. He has a little record shop in Rinkeby. We can go over there in the morning.'

Hultin had already worked out a plan, as usual. 'Okay, since this is our best lead so far, I want all three of you on it. Holm, Chavez and Hjelm. But after you've heard what your Chilean friend has to say, Jorge, I want you back on the board-of-directors angle. That still could provide the best leads. But this murder may put an end to the business angle,' he said to Söderstedt, who didn't look the least disappointed. 'We may send Pettersson and Florén back to the finance division. We'll see. Arto, I want you to find out, of course, whether there are any business connections between these four men, but I think that this time we're dealing with a different type of victim. We're going to keep working in the same way. Nyberg will drag his notorious nets through the sea of snitches again and generally keep bottom-fishing. Norlander, if you're ready to get back to work, I want you to stay on the mafia lead, as if nothing had happened.'

Norlander nodded emphatically.

'The more important question is obvious,' Hultin added. 'Why has he started up again? After waiting more than a month?'

'What about the tape?' Hjelm asked, instead of answering the question. 'We can't let the techs sit on it for weeks. And leak it to the press.'

Hultin ejected the tape from the player. He held it in his hand for a moment, weighing the possibilities and risks. Then he tossed it to Kerstin Holm.

'If we know our man correctly, then there won't be any fingerprints. It looks like an ordinary Maxell tape, of a slightly older type. Probably untraceable. Am I right?'

Hjelm, Chavez and Holm all looked at the tape.

'Yeah, you're right,' said Chavez.

'Okay,' said Hultin, with a little sigh. 'Take good care of it.'

21

'Misterioso' was playing on the door speakers, over and over again, like a self-fulfilling prophecy.

'Did you guys get any sleep last night?' asked Jorge Chavez.

They were sitting in Hjelm's unmarked Mazda. Hjelm was driving, and Holm was sitting next to him, playing the Thelonious Monk piece non-stop on the car stereo. Chavez was just as constantly popping up from the back seat.

Hjelm and Holm replied only with slight movements of their heavy eyelids, which were trying to stay open, but also keep out the relentless glare of the summer-like sunshine. An impossible task.

It was 18 May.

'Monk would turn over in his grave if he knew that his marvellous music had inspired someone to commit a series of murders,' Chavez went on, not sounding particularly sad. They were on the trail. At last.

Again he received no answer from the front seat. That neither stopped him nor annoyed him.

'I went over to headquarters last night, to look at the members of the boards of directors again. Intensive computer work. There are four ways to proceed from here. The most interesting is Sydbanken. All four men were actually on the board at the same time for a brief period in 1990. On the whole, that's really the most promising lead. But maybe it's even more interesting that Enar Brandberg was on the Lovisedal board at the same time as both Daggfeldt and Carlberger in 1991, the same media conglomerate that's having problems with Viktor X's protection racket today – GrimeBear, you sleepyheads. Assuming, of course, that Strand-Julén was a red herring. On the other hand, if our murderer has presented us with a red herring at this late date by killing Brandberg, then Ericsson and MEMAB will still have to be under consideration.'

Still no answer.

And once again it had no effect on Chavez's enthusiasm. 'I'm sure that Hultin is right, that one of these corporations is the key to the whole mystery.'

The car stopped for a red light.

'Turn at the OK petrol station,' said Chavez. 'On Rinkeby Allé. We can park where it dead-ends and walk across the square. I need to buy some fresh garlic.'

Hjelm drove down the avenue and parked the car. 'You seem a little hyper,' he said.

'The only way to stay awake,' Chavez said.

They crossed the lively square in the summery sunshine. The vendors' stalls were bursting with vegetables and fruits of all sizes and types, seldom seen in ordinary grocery shops. Hjelm thought about the ban on pesticides in vegetables from abroad, compared to the Swedish ones. He felt grey and dreary in the midst of the bustling, colourful crowds.

Chavez bought a bulb of fresh garlic and waved it in front of Hjelm's face. 'Begone, you blasphemer, Nosferatu.'

Hjelm, who felt as if he were about to fall asleep on his feet, climbed out of his coffin with a foolish grin.

They walked a few blocks to the heart of the Rinkeby district. Half a flight down, in one of the buildings that all looked the same, was a small shop with no visible signage, but extremely dusty windows. The shop turned out to be much larger than expected, and it was packed. People of all races were looking through the endless rows of CDs, containing music from every corner of the globe. A group of teenage boys of various colours, united by their baggy clothes and their baseball caps turned backwards, occupied the big hip-hop corner. And at the very back, behind the counter, sat a dark South American in his fifties, filing his nails.

'Alberto!' exclaimed Chavez, going over to hug the man, who stood up and proved to be gigantic.

'Jorge, Jorge,' said the man after they'd embraced for at least thirty seconds, then spoke rapidly in Spanish. Hjelm was able to catch the name 'Skövde', to which Jorge answered, 'No, no, Sundsvall.' Chavez pointed at his colleagues. Kerstin Holm had just dipped into a stack of Gregorian chants; she said a few words in her slightly faltering Spanish. Alberto laughed loudly. Hjelm smiled at him, noticing that the shop smelled of incense. A stick of it was smouldering in a pot of dried flowers on the counter.

'Come with me,' Alberto said to Hjelm and Holm, then continued in broken but essentially correct Swedish, 'Let's go into my inner sanctum.'

They entered a small, dimly lit room. An exquisite stereo system occupied the absolute centre of the space.

'Do you know that Jorge is one of this country's finest Swedish-Chilean jazz bassists?' said Alberto from the dark.

'¡Esto con chorradas!' cried Chavez merrily, stepping inside.

'Yes, that's true, that's true,' laughed Alberto loudly. 'May I borrow the tape?'

Holm was the last to enter the room, holding three CDs in her hand. She pulled the tape out of her bag.

'Do you dare leave the shop unattended like this?' she asked as she handed it over.

'Nobody steals from me,' said Alberto ominously, sticking the tape in the player. It started playing towards the end of 'Misterioso'. 'Really poor quality,' he continued. 'Copied two or even three times, I'd guess. Not from any CD. And there aren't any typical LP clicks, either. The original is probably a classic Fifties reel-to-reel tape.'

'Here it comes,' said Chavez as the applause and cheering began. Then came the wild improvisations.

Alberto's face lit up in the dark. 'Aaaahhhh,' he said, then uttered an excited flood of Spanish.

'Speak Swedish,' said Chavez.

'Sorry. Of course. This is very, very rare. Even I don't have a copy. Wait a sec. Let me listen to the whole thing.'

For three minutes, hardly more than that, the chaos continued. Towards the end the playing seemed less chaotic. It was as if the musicians had jointly found a form or shaped a form. It was highly remarkable; even Hjelm could hear the themes looping and passages meeting and combining and melding. Three very strange minutes had passed.

Alberto cleared his throat and stopped the tape.

'"Misterioso", taped by the producer and Monk-fanatic Orrin Keepnews and the technician Ray Fowler on that magic night, 7 August 1958, at the Five Spot Café in New York. On the CD, after Monk died, Keepnews added a couple of numbers that they'd rejected from the earlier Riverside taping on 9 July. They're not included on this tape.

'This must be the thing I've heard people talk about, but never actually heard before. It seems that this snippet ended up on the tape because Ray Fowler was drunk and fell asleep when he should have turned off the tape recorder. But that might be a myth. This improvisation was given a name afterwards: "Risky". That's what it's called. *Arriesgado*, Jorge! Neither Keepnews nor Monk wanted to include it on the album, and it's not on the collectors' edition, either, *The Complete Riverside Recordings*.

It was magical when it was born, but it died soon afterwards, or so they thought. As you can hear, that wasn't
the case. Somebody dragged this out of a deep cellar
vault and copied it.'

'You've heard people talk about it?' said Hjelm. 'When,
where, how?'

'I had an offer to purchase a copy sometime in the
mid-Eighties. By an American jazz musician living in
Sweden. But he wanted a thousand dollars. I didn't go
for it.'

'Who was he?' asked Chavez.

'You know him, Jorge. You almost played with him a
couple of years ago. Jim Barth Richards.'

'The tenor man?'

'Exactly. White Jim. The whitest skin I've ever seen
on a jazz musician. A little like Johnny Winter. He stayed
here in Sweden. Better treatment here, as he said when
we met a year or two ago. He has to go into detox practically every other month. Then he can play again. I don't
know whether he's playing anywhere right now or if he's
in rehab.'

They thanked Alberto, got the tape back and were
heading towards the door.

Alberto said from the dark, 'A copy in exchange for
those CDs.'

Kerstin Holm glanced down at the Gregorian CDs in
her hand. She had forgotten all about them.

'How long will it take?' asked Chavez, just as Hjelm
was about to object.

Alberto laughed and punched a button to open the second cassette door. He took out a tape.

'Already done,' he said with a big smile.

Jim Barth Richards did, in fact, have the whitest skin that Hjelm had ever seen. They were lucky enough to find him relatively sober, in a crappy one-room apartment in Gamla Stan that suited his persona. He was in his fifties, and his hair was as white as his complexion. He was sprawled out flat on a mattress on the floor, wearing shorts and a T-shirt.

'I'm sure you've heard of the new jazz schools in the States,' said Chavez. 'The anti-self-destructive movement. The Marsalis brothers and some even more radical young guys. Don't you think it's about time to put this outsider myth on the shelf?'

'Traditionalists!' spat White Jim, in his American-accented Swedish. 'They think they can create music by cramming down the whole fucking history of jazz. As if it were a school subject. Where does your fucking pain come from! Books? Fucking mama's boys! Those who talk don't know, those who know don't talk.'

Hjelm and Holm exchanged quick glances.

'They create something new by knowing about everything,' Chavez insisted. 'That's not so damned strange. They're familiar with every riff, every little passage, every damn run in the history of jazz. That's where they get all the power and all the pain they need. They can build on your conquests without having to repeat your mistakes. It's a whole new way of relating to art.'

'It's an *ancient* way of relating to art!' said Richards, barely keeping his fury in check. 'One that we've finally managed to escape. And now they want to go back to the whole damned era of repetitions. I'm glad you never got to play with me, Jorge.'

'You're the ones who are repeating yourselves, precisely because you don't know your own history. You think you're creating something new just because you're too drugged out to notice that you've done it all before. The personally unique expression is one long, damned repetition, the worst kind of self-delusion. The only way to really create something new is to become familiar with everything that has already been done. Then you can talk about a new beginning. The dawn of history again, but a dawn that contains within it all previous dawns.'

'Theoretical bullshit,' said White Jim, boiling over. 'All the pain comes from in here!' He slapped his bony chest, where every rib was visible through the dirty T-shirt. The slap produced a disquieting echo. 'You can never replace direct feeling!'

'That's exactly the point!' shouted Jorge, beginning to pace in the filthy apartment. 'There's no direct outlet from in here. That's not where you get it from. The pain always has to take a path through various forms. It's just that you don't see it. You mistake the fog of drugs for emotion and try to invent the wheel over and over again, and each time you think you've done it. Authentic bullshit!'

Hjelm was starting to get worried that they might lose White Jim before they even reached him. There seemed to be a high risk that they'd get thrown out at any moment. But instead, Richards sat up, uttered a loud bellow of laughter and patted the palm of his hand on the mattress.

'Sit down, for God's sake!'

Jorge sat down, accepted the bottle of Jack Daniel's that White Jim had conjured up from somewhere and took a big gulp.

'You should have gone in for music,' said White Jim. 'Instead of all that.' He pointed at Holm and Hjelm. 'You take it seriously.'

'Those two know more about music than you do,' said Chavez. They both laughed for a long time. Hjelm understood very little. Kerstin Holm said calmly, 'For example, we know about a tape of a little improvisation called "Risky", played by Monk, Griffin, Malik and Haynes, which you tried to peddle ten years ago.'

White Jim looked at her in astonishment. Then he roared with laughter. 'Quite a long investigation, I must say. But all the priorities in the right places. Three cops come after an old sax has-been for a triviality. I'm deeply honoured, people!'

'We're not here to arrest you. We just want to know who your customers were.'

'Not many people actually bought a copy, you know. When Red Mitchell brought me here in the mid-Seventies, I'd heard that you were a small country up by the Arctic Ocean and that you loved jazz. So I made as many copies as I could of that session, plus a number of other original tapes that Griffin had turned me on to in the early Sixties. I was playing a lot with Johnny back then, you know, young and green and enthusiastic. He told me there was a lot of unreleased material from the Five Spot period, like "'Round Midnight" and "Evidence" and "Risky" and plenty of other motherfucking tunes. Most of them have been released by now, when . . . what's his name? The producer? Keepnews. When he needed cash.

'But "Risky" and a few others are my babies. They haven't been released. So yes, goddamn it, I brought ten different tapes like that from the States, and every once in a while I tried to sell them. This "Risky" tape was one of the last, sometime in '85 or '86. By then I knew who my customers were. There were only three; nobody else was willing to hand over big money for semi-lousy pirated recordings. It was fucking illegal, you know. I had no rights to them at all. I still have a couple of tapes left, by the way. For my retirement.'

'Do you still have the addresses of the people who bought copies of the "Risky" tape?' Holm asked doggedly.

'Sure. Since the beginning of the Eighties, the buyers have always been the same people. Jazz lovers, maybe. Lovers of rare items, absolutely. If you're not planning to arrest them, I'll give you the addresses. Two in Stockholm and one in Växjö. Somewhere I've got a little fucking yellow notebook . . .'

They searched through Richards's disgusting mess of an apartment, casting aside the most astonishing objects: the dried head of a boa constrictor that turned to dust in Hjelm's hands, filthy clothing, a shoebox containing Polish zloty bills, more dirty clothes, antiquated Finnish porn magazines with black patches hiding the genitals, still more dirty clothes, a number of throwing knives from Botswana, another huge pile of dirty clothes, thirteen unwashed Guinness beer tankards that had been scattered around, an LP with no album cover but with Bill Evans's autograph etched across the tracks, and thick stacks of pub receipts.

'Why are you saving all these pub receipts?' Chavez asked as he pulled the yellow notebook out of a pair of appallingly disintegrating underpants.

'For tax reasons,' said White Jim as he let the Jack Daniel's burn its way down his throat.

Just like in a B-movie, thought Hjelm.

Chavez wrote down the names and addresses on the back of a pub receipt and handed the notebook back to White Jim, who tossed it into the room, belched and then fell asleep sitting up.

Chavez and Holm laid him down on the floor, then pulled a blanket over the chalk-white body.

'That guy,' Chavez said as they came out into the sunshine, 'is a truly great musician.'

Holm nodded.

Hjelm wasn't sure what to believe.

* * *

Chavez returned reluctantly to police headquarters. Hjelm dropped Holm off at the nearest Stockholm address on White Jim's list, then continued on to the address that was farther away.

Holm went to see the retired major Erik Rådholm on Linnégatan. He was a distinguished-looking gentleman in late middle age, with a passion for unusual jazz recordings that was as monumental as it was unexpected. As Holm later described him, he looked more like a Sousa admirer, a man for whom rhythm meant marching in step. But that was not the case. He had an enormous collection of illegal pirated recordings from the most obscure little clubs, from Karelia in Finland to the interior of Ghana.

At first he didn't want to admit to anything that might be considered illegal. But by using methods that Holm refused to reveal, she got him to relent and, even with a certain pride, show her his impressive collection, hidden behind a bookcase that could be opened out into the room. He swore on 'his country and his flag' that he would never dream of copying a single one of his unique recordings. Holm both saw and listened to Major Rådholm's copy of Jim Barth Richards's 'Risky' tape. She stayed for two hours and also heard Lester Young in Salzburg and Kenny Clarke at the Hudiksvall Hotel.

Paul Hjelm drove to Märsta and visited the severely handicapped Roger Palmberg, who had been run over by the Stockholm-to-Luleå train; not entirely unintentionally, as Palmberg himself admitted, talking through

ARNE DAHL

his electronic speech apparatus. The only thing still intact was his hearing, but that was even better than before. They listened to White Jim's 'Risky' recording, and Roger Palmberg explained every little nuance, telling him exactly what was happening and precisely where it occurred and why.

Hjelm felt bewitched. He had serious doubts about the expression 'Those who talk don't know, those who know don't talk.' Inside that devastated body was the most subtle listener he'd ever met, and not just a music listener, but a listener in general. Simply by giving Hjelm his undivided attention, Palmberg managed to get him to reveal almost everything about the case. Palmberg thought that the cassette-tape lead sounded incredibly interesting. He swore that he was innocent, and in return he received a promise that Hjelm would get back in touch once the case was solved. No one else had ever heard Palmberg's copy of the recording, until now; he admitted point-blank that it was because no one ever came to visit him. He lived a solitary life, a situation that he had accepted. It was to music that he applied his innate capacity for listening.

So they listened to a couple of recordings of Jim Barth Richards from the late Sixties, and Hjelm began to realise who it was he had visited in that repulsive one-room apartment in Gamla Stan. By the time he finally left Roger Palmberg in his relatively handicap-friendly Märsta apartment, he'd acquired a new friend in northern Stockholm.

22

Paul Hjelm picked up the pace as soon as he was on the scent. He had no time now to stand in front of the mirror to see how much the blemish on his cheek had grown over the past week, no time to see himself as a void, a hole in a robust and constantly changing environment; no time to notice the peculiar cracks in his marriage. The spoor from the cassette tape was sufficiently strong to make all other smells evaporate.

He got ready to travel to Växjö to meet the remaining owner of the Thelonious Monk tape with the 'Risky' improvisation at the end like a thousand-dollar tail. Hultin had calmly accepted his and Kerstin's conclusions with regard to Rådholm and Palmberg. Neither of them was the murderer, and neither of them had copied their tapes for anyone else. They all agreed that the one remaining tape owner could be the killer. Ex-major Rådholm's proud refusal to make copies of his tape was apparently an attitude shared by this type of jazz fanatic. It was highly likely that there weren't many copies of the copies.

In the office next door, Kerstin Holm was getting ready to accompany Hjelm to southern Sweden. Presumably her field of vision had also narrowed; he thought he knew her well enough to say that. Tunnel vision had begun to set in. Everything else was shoved aside.

Then came the call from Dalarö.

Hjelm answered the phone, his voice sounding stressed. Chavez looked at him from the other side of the desk and saw the red patch on Hjelm's face become even brighter; except for that little spot, his whole face went pale.

Hjelm didn't say a word during the call. He just turned white as chalk. Chavez thought the blemish on his cheek looked like a pulsing heart. Hjelm dropped the phone twice before he managed to put the receiver down properly.

Jorge waited.

'Cilla has left me,' said Paul quietly.

Jorge didn't say a word. He put his pen down on the desk.

'She was calling from the cabin. She doesn't want me to come out there again this summer. She needs time to think.'

When Kerstin Holm opened the door, she found the two men hugging each other.

She closed the door, without making a sound.

In the taxi to Arlanda Airport she asked only one question: 'Are you sure you're up for this?'

Hjelm nodded numbly.

She thought the red blemish on his cheek looked like a hobo symbol, that little slanting parallelogram.

She couldn't remember what it stood for.

On the plane to Växjö some of the colour returned to Hjelm's face. The blemish became a little less noticeable, and just as the outline was starting to fade, Holm recalled what the hobo symbol meant. Hoboes used the parallelogram to warn each other, drawing it on houses occupied by cruel and inconsiderate people.

But now it was almost gone.

Tunnel vision had returned to Hjelm, more focused than ever before. He had felt his field of vision physically contract from one extreme to the other. After the call from Cilla, it had expanded *in absurdum* so that he thought he could see 360 degrees all around him, a totally undirected gaze that took in everything without being able to focus. A terrible state to be in. Complete collapse. And then the total opposite, the fiercely censoring tunnel vision of self-defence.

From the airport in Växjö, Hjelm called home and had a long talk with Tova about what had actually happened. Danne had picked up the phone, but merely snapped at him; in Danne's eyes everything was clearly his father's fault. On the other hand, Hjelm was also personally to blame for everything else that was wrong in his son's pubescent inferno of a world. Cilla had told Tova that she and her father needed to live apart for a while, that was all. Tova had hardly recognised her mother's voice. Hjelm tried to explain as best he could, but after a while he realised that he was simply uttering clichés. *Our language divides up the roles*, he thought grimly. He asked his daughter if they'd be able to get by on their own for a few days. Tova laughed and said that they'd been doing exactly that ever since Mama had moved out to Dalarö while Papa was working 24/7.

As Hjelm held the silent phone in his hand, it struck him that until now he hadn't given a thought to his children's situation.

Växjö was a classic small town in the heart of Astrid Lindgren's Småland. The idea was to find the third man on the list in White Jim's 'little fucking yellow notebook', a task that shouldn't be too difficult considering that the man bore the rather unusual name of Hackzell, Roger Hackzell, and he even co-owned a restaurant in the small city centre. But no one was home in his house on the outskirts of town, and the restaurant was closed.

Hjelm knocked on the door so hard that he appeared to be a bit demented. Then Holm said, 'I actually need to be back in Stockholm tomorrow morning.'

'It can't take that long to find the fucker.' Hjelm kept on knocking.

They talked to neighbours and everyone they could find with even a remote connection to Roger Hackzell, but still he couldn't be found. As the day turned to night, Hjelm finally managed to control his frustration. The two police officers sat down in a restaurant across from the one called Hackat & Malet, which as the day wore on had started to look even darker and more silent. But not any more. They started talking. Really talking. After a while they ceased to care about the missing fucker Roger Hackzell or his fucking restaurant.

At first they mainly talked about their work. About Daggfeldt, Strand-Julén and Carlberger. About Anna-Clara Hummelstrand's personality. About the relatives who had displayed so little grief. They proposed alternative names for the strange creation known as the A-Unit: The Alienations-Unit. The Attack Force. The A-Kids. The A-Team. The A-Bonds. The Antipathetics. They spent a long time talking about Norlander's one-man assault in Tallinn, with a certain gallows humour regarding the hero who had been nailed to the floor and then returned, like a Second Coming of Christ. They speculated about what might have happened to Arto Söderstedt back in Finland.

They ventured into slightly more personal territory. Kerstin talked about her passion for music. Paul talked about his children; he studiously avoided mentioning Cilla. He talked about Dritëro Frakulla, about the hostage drama and the trial, and about Grundström from Internal Affairs.

Then he said, 'What did you mean when you asked me whether I was happily married? "Really happily" was what you said.'

She looked at him over her wine glass with her coal-black eyes. They each puffed on the cigarettes that they were smoking to celebrate the occasion.

'I just had the feeling that you weren't.'

'I always thought that I was. Very.'

'You were projecting something through your job, through the police work itself; I couldn't really put my finger on it. I still can't. It was a little clearer than with the others; I guess that's why it was interesting. The whole time you seemed to be searching for something different through your work, as if you weren't really conducting a police investigation. Maybe I recognised the same thing in myself.'

'So you've been studying me that closely?'

She smiled faintly. 'I study everyone I meet. Maybe that's typical for female cops. Don't take it personally.'

'Maybe I'd like to take it personally.'

She leaned forward. 'Don't forget that you're feeling a bit confused right now. It's the turbulence. Everything has been pulled out from under you. I don't want to be some sort of . . . surrogate.'

He leaned back and took a drag on his cigarette. He downed the last of his wine, staring up at the ceiling and beyond. Far beyond.

As they walked through the warm May night they put their arms around each other, without consciously planning to. They joked a bit and laughed.

'Did you really do it?' he found himself asking her.

'Do what?'

'What Anna-Clara Hummelstrand suggested with regard to the olive-brown Gallic organ?'

He met her eyes. Was it disappointment he saw?

A shadow passed through him, just for a second.

But she merely said calmly, without taking her arm away, 'When I start masturbating at the thought of the erect male organ of a French gigolo belonging to the wife of a wealthy Swedish businessman, then I'll know that things have really gone south for me.'

They laughed as they walked down the street to their hotel, which was just around the corner. Inside the hotel window on the corner sat a dinner party of seven people. A very well-dressed gentleman was standing up, giving a speech. They were glad that they'd decided not to eat at the hotel. They walked down to the canal and peered at the filthy water. It wasn't particularly exciting. After a while they went in, took out their respective room keys and climbed the two flights of stairs. Their rooms were right next to each other. They stood in the hallway for a moment, vacillating. Then she stuck her key in the lock and said, 'This is probably best.'

She blew him a kiss and left him alone with his ghosts.

The Erinyes, he thought hazily as he entered the dark room that was trying to imitate the cosiness of home.

Could a woman whose soul has been murdered haunt a person even though she's still alive?

Although he didn't really know what Cilla was blaming him for.

He took off his denim jacket and trousers, but fell onto

the bed with his shirt still on. In a fog he saw himself making love to Cilla on the Dalarö pier in the twilight with an empty wine bottle rolling next to his thigh. The whole time her gaze was far away, hollow-looking in the crimson dusk.

Right next to them sat Kerstin Holm with her feet propped up on her desk, her legs wide apart. He was still on the pier. His underpants were pulled off. Or did he do that himself? He saw her lying next to him on the bed. She was masturbating.

Was that her interpretation of what he wanted? Was this a wish fulfilment? His or hers?

Then she disappeared.

The next day he didn't know whether it had really happened or not.

23

When Paul Hjelm woke up the following morning, it wasn't morning at all. It was noon or even later, and nobody had looked for him. He wasn't sure whether he should be more surprised than irritated. But the indecision ended abruptly as he found a note that had been slid under his hotel door. It said:

> *Paul. Thanks for yesterday. You were sleeping so sweetly when I left, so I'll make do with this note. See you back at the notorious Supreme Central Command. Hugs, Kerstin.*

Thanks for yesterday? You were sleeping so sweetly when I left? That didn't actually answer the question about whether she'd been in his room during the night. Everything could have just as well been played out inside his own imagination. He really couldn't tell.

'Thanks for yesterday' could be referring to the dinner they'd had in the restaurant, and 'You were sleeping so sweetly when I left' could mean that he hadn't responded when she knocked on the door. And besides, how would she have got in? She didn't have a key to his room. But maybe he hadn't closed the door properly . . .

He hated not knowing; that was a solidly imprinted reflex. Yet at the same time there was something appealing about the uncertainty. Something inside him resisted having a definitive answer. And he had to settle for that.

For the time being.

He looked at the map and found himself across the street from Hackat & Malet. And it was open. Presumably the place also served lunch, so perhaps he'd be able to get hold of Hackzell right away. The restaurant was quite small, and for all practical purposes the lunch rush was over – it was almost two o'clock. The premises contained a jukebox, several rifles hanging on the walls with their barrels crossed, a dartboard, advertising signs for various types of beer and a couple of Andy Warhol posters. Rather conventional decor. The broad-shouldered man sporting a moustache behind the bar emanated such authority that Hjelm was convinced he had to be one of the owners, either Roger Hackzell or Jari Malinen.

It turned out to be Roger Hackzell himself.

Hjelm asked him about the cassette tape, trying to be as detailed as he could. He missed Kerstin's and Jorge's expertise. While Hackzell pondered his answer, Hjelm on impulse asked for a triple vodka, straight up. Hackzell peered in surprise at this police officer who was apparently a serious alcoholic, then poured him a big glass of venerable Swedish Absolut. Then he said, 'I'll go see if I can find that tape. I've still got some of those strange recordings that White Jim forced upon me. Just wait a sec.'

Hjelm picked up the glass and sniffed the contents suspiciously. The moment the last customers left the restaurant, he went over to their table, grabbed an empty Ramlösa bottle and returned to the bar. He poured the vodka into the bottle, took a cork from a little basket on the counter and stuck it in the mineral-water bottle, which he then slipped into his pocket.

After a moment Hackzell came back. 'I'm sorry,' he said. 'I couldn't find it.'

Hjelm nodded, paid for the vodka and went out into the sunshine.

He went over to the state off-licence and asked the sales assistant, 'Is it possible to tell the difference between various types of vodka, or do they all taste the same?'

'I haven't got a clue,' said the assistant, in a broad Småland accent. She looked puzzled.

'Could I speak to the manager?' He showed her his police ID. That was always the easiest way to avoid fuss.

A serious-looking middle-aged man wearing a suit came out to the counter. Hjelm repeated his question.

'I don't really know,' said the man. 'Vodka is the purest liquor available, with the least flavour. I would think the only thing that would make any difference would be the alcohol content.'

Hjelm thanked the manager and went back out to the

street. He was very tired. He sat down on a park bench outside the shop and closed his eyes.

Roger Hackzell had looked scared shitless when Hjelm showed his ID and mentioned the NCP; that much he was sure of. When he started talking about the tape, his fear had decidedly diminished.

When Hjelm opened his eyes again he found sitting next to him on the bench a very young wino, a man that he might almost have mistaken for a muscular body-builder. He was greedily eyeing Hjelm's bulging jacket pocket.

'Have you got something there?' said the muscular alcoholic in the purest Småland dialect.

'Yes,' said Hjelm. 'One question first. You're an expert, right? Is it possible to tell the difference between various types of vodka, or do they all taste the same?'

'After I've had half a bottle, I can start concentrating on the taste,' said the young alcoholic slyly. 'I'm actually a connoisseur of hard liquor.'

'If I buy you half a bottle . . .'

'Then I'd be happy to undertake a more sophisticated taste test.'

This man didn't seem the usual blabbering alcoholic, so Hjelm went back inside the off-licence and bought a half-bottle of Explorer. The bodybuilder-wino downed the entire contents in six minutes and afterwards looked extremely alert.

'We're the A-Unit,' said Hjelm sleepily while the man drank.

'Yes, we certainly are.' The man set down the empty Explorer bottle. 'Now let's see about your taste test.'

Hjelm took the Ramlösa bottle out of his pocket and pulled out the cork. The steroid-pumped wino sniffed at it, shook the bottle, took a gulp and let it swirl around in his mouth like a professional wine-taster.

'Diluted,' he said. 'Otherwise the usual strength.'

'Do you mean that a stronger vodka has been watered down?'

'That's right,' said the man, taking another swallow. 'Finer than Explorer, that much is obvious.'

'It came out of an Absolut bottle.'

'No, no. It's definitely not Absolut. This one has a more direct kick. Not Swedish at all. Or Finnish. And absolutely not that American junk, Smirnoff. No, this is genuine East European vodka with a touch of a chemical factory. Probably 120-proof. Diluted, of course.'

'Do you really know what you're talking about or are you just blathering until you've drunk the whole bottle?'

The dedicated alcoholic looked immensely offended. 'We can just drop the whole thing, if you want,' he said morosely.

'Can you tell me anything more?'

'No. Russian or Lithuanian or Estonian, 120-proof. Plus a lot of water.'

Surprised, Hjelm thanked him and went straight over to the police station. It took a while before he was able to speak with an officer in charge. The man who came to meet him introduced himself as Detective Inspector Jonas Wrede, and he didn't look older than twenty. He was blond, well built and provincial.

And very computer-literate, as it turned out.

'NCP,' said Wrede dreamily after they'd sat down in his office. 'This doesn't have anything to do with the Power Murders, does it?'

'With what?'

'The Power Murders. That's the label that the NCP has assigned to those big-shot murders in Stockholm.'

'You've got to be shitting me,' said Hjelm in surprise.

'It's in the paper. Today's press conference with the commissioner, Waldemar Mörner, and Inspector Algot Nylin.'

'Who the hell is Inspector Algot Nylin?' exclaimed Hjelm, realising that he didn't know a single thing about the media and the power game surrounding the A-Unit's investigation. The only thing he paid any attention to was his work. In the power brokers' plus column, at any rate, was the fact that they'd managed to pull off the feat of largely keeping the A-Unit's existence out of the media for a month and a half.

'Does this have something to do with that?' Jonas Wrede persisted. 'We haven't had anyone from the NCP here since that incident up at the bank in Algotsmåla. So are you here because of the Power Murders?'

'I'm not authorised to divulge that,' said Hjelm, hoping that the authoritative tone of his voice would help, by indirectly confirming the fact.

And it did. Wrede straightened up.

'What do you know about the gentlemen who own Hackat & Malet here in town?' asked Hjelm. 'Roger Hackzell and Jari Malinen.'

'Offhand, I'd say that they're clean,' replied Wrede pensively. 'At least I can't recall any incidents.'

A favourite word of his, thought Hjelm and let his mind float into a better world while Wrede consulted his computer, his fingers flying over the keyboard. In the better world there were women, both fair and dark, who changed places with each other.

'Yup, both clean,' said Wrede, with a certain smugness. 'No incidents. Not since they've been in Växjö, that is.'

'What about the big national database?' asked Hjelm without letting go of the women's faces he was seeing in his mind.

'Well, that'll take a little longer . . .'

'Do I need to keep reminding you of the priorities here?' said Hjelm, even though so far he hadn't said a thing about priorities. Wrede looked impressed and began typing. Then they waited for a while. Wrede looked as if he wanted to say something; Hjelm looked as if he would never say another word. He was quite simply gone, beyond all hope.

Finally they received a response.

'No,' said Wrede. 'Nothing. Both are clean. Although there's an asterisk next to Malinen's name. A cross-reference to Finland. A possible incident, perhaps?'

'Is there some way to find out?'

Wrede's face lit up. A higher-up from the NCP was taking note of his computer expertise.

The higher-up from the NCP yawned loudly.

'It's possible that we can get in via the Nordic co-operative database,' said Wrede enthusiastically. 'Not many people know how to do that,' he added.

Hjelm thought he should offer some words of encouragement, but he didn't. He hadn't really returned to the real world yet.

Wrede began typing again. If his eminent colleague was daydreaming, Wrede was definitely in his element.

'Malinen, Jari, 13–6–52. Oh yes, there's an incident, all right: smuggling. Let's see now: yes, 1979 in Vasa, Finland. Convicted of smuggling goods. I'll see if I can find any more details.'

'Fucking great,' said Hjelm.

'All right, here's something that looks like records of a trial. Malinen was found guilty of smuggling on 12 February 1979, along with Vladimir Ragin: they had smuggled booze from Leningrad, as it was then called. Both got eighteen months in a minimum-security prison; Malinen was released after twelve months, while Ragin served the full sentence. Then there's a list of names: the judge, K. Lahtinen; lay assessors, L. Hälminen, R. Lindfors, B. Palo; defence lawyer, A. Söderstedt; prosecutors, N. Niskanpää, H. Viiljanen; witness for the defence—'

'What?' Hjelm dived into the ice-cold water of this world. 'What was the name of the defence lawyer?'

'A. Söderstedt,' repeated Wrede.

'Can you look up more about him?'

'I'll see if I can find anything in the legal society's registry, or somewhere like that.' Wrede looked like a fourteen-year-old hacker who'd just got into the Pentagon.

Another period of waiting. Then a liberating little ping.

'Arto Söderstedt, 12–1–53, law student at Åbo University 1972 to '75; finished a five-year degree in three; hired by Vasa's most respected law firm of Koivonen & Krantz right after graduating in 1975, at the age of twenty-two. For several months in 1980 the firm was actually called Koivonen, Krantz & Söderstedt. He became a partner at the age of twenty-seven. By the end of 1980 the firm was again known as Koivonen & Krantz. After 1980 there is no Söderstedt in any list of lawyers.'

Hjelm laughed long and loud. Scandinavia was such a small world.

Wrede looked at him sceptically. Was this man really what he purported to be? The Hallunda hero? The Power Murders investigator?

'Okay.' Hjelm wiped away tears of laughter. He was back. 'Damn it if I'm not thinking of recommending you to my bosses. You really know your way around a computer. I'm very grateful.'

Detective Inspector Jonas Wrede stood at the window and watched as Hjelm headed off towards Hackat & Malet. His face was shining with unrealised ambitions.

There was a mirror in a display window on the main walking street that cut through Växjö's central area. Hjelm caught sight of himself and stopped. The scaly, red blemish had grown even bigger. It now almost covered his cheek. It looked like a question mark.

Hackat & Malet had closed for the night, but Roger Hackzell was still there, drying glasses like a traditional bartender. Hjelm tapped lightly on the windowpane. The space around Hackzell seemed to freeze, but he managed to skate over to the door and open it.

'A triple vodka,' said Hjelm when he came inside.

Hackzell stared at him, returned to the bar and poured another glass from the Absolut bottle.

Hjelm sniffed at the clear liquid. 'No,' he said simply. 'This isn't Absolut Vodka from Vin & Sprit. I'd guess that it's diluted 120-proof Estonian from the Liviko distillery.'

Hackzell's face fell. It seemed to be lying on the counter, gasping for breath, as Hjelm completed his attack.

'You're a first-time offender and presumably basically clean. That's why you're reacting so strongly. Malinen would probably have been significantly more cool-headed, with that record of his. But I'm not here to get you or Malinen. Answer my questions correctly and you won't lose the restaurant and end up in jail. Think carefully before you answer, because I know a lot more than you thought, and if I discover even the smallest lie in what you tell me, I'll arrest you and take you back to Stockholm for a proper interrogation. Is that understood?'

The man with no face nodded mutely.

'Where did the vodka come from?'

'There are a couple of vendors who show up now and then. Russians. They call themselves Igor and Igor.'

A peculiar calm came over Hjelm. He'd guessed right. He could even allow himself to daydream a bit during the rest of the interrogation.

'Do you know anything more about them?'

'No, they just show up. For safety's sake, they don't have any schedule or specific delivery dates.'

'Haven't you seen the sketches of Alexander Bryusov and Valery Treplyov in the newspapers? They've been on all the news-stand placards too.'

Roger Hackzell blinked in surprise. 'They were? In that case, the sketches must not look much like them.'

'The caption clearly states their names, Igor and Igor.'

'I didn't read anything about them, just saw the placards. It was all about the Power Murders in Stockholm, you know. That didn't have anything to do with them. I didn't know there was any sort of connection. I swear it.'

'All right. But now at least you realise how important this is. You're already mixed up in it. There are police officers who would lock you up for good just because of the link between you and Igor and Igor. You get me?'

'Oh, dear God,' said Roger Hackzell, sounding like a real native of Göteborg.

'So now let's talk about the important thing. The cassette tape.'

'Oh, Jesus Christ,' Hackzell blurted out with a wild look in his eyes. 'Damn it to hell! That's right! The last time they were here, they took some of my old tapes. Partial payment, they said. Real tough customers. I gave Jari hell for dragging us into their fucking mafia deals. Are they the ones who did it? It wouldn't surprise me at all.'

'And you don't know anything else about their Swedish or Russian or Baltic connections?'

'For me they're just a couple of ruthless fucks who show up once a month or so and more or less force us to buy their booze. I'm telling you, I don't know anything else.'

'When were they last here?'

'It was quite a while ago, thank God. In February. I thought that I was finally rid of them. And now this—'

'And it was back then, in February, that they took the tapes?'

'Yes.' Hackzell leafed feverishly through a book that he took out of a drawer. 'It was on February the fifteenth. Early in the morning.'

'Where's Jari Malinen now?'

'In Finland. His mother just died.'

Hjelm took the cassette tape out of his pocket and handed it to Hackzell. 'Is this it?'

Hackzell studied it closely. 'It looks like it. White Jim copied a whole bunch at the same time back in '87 and '88. It was a Maxell tape.'

'Okay, do you have a cassette player? I want you to listen carefully to a tune and try to recall if you can associate it with anything in particular. Anything at all.

Maybe something that happened here in the bar. Calm yourself, listen and try to think.'

The introductory ascending piano figure of 'Misterioso' glided out into the restaurant. Hackzell tried to concentrate, but seemed mostly to be in shock, as if his world were crumbling. Hjelm watched him intently, trying to picture him as the ice-cold murderer in the living rooms of the financiers. He couldn't.

The ten minutes of 'Misterioso' passed. Hackzell was incapable of standing still for even a second longer. When the tune was finally over and the subsequent improvisation started, Hjelm switched off the cassette player.

'No. I don't know,' Hackzell said. 'I know nothing about jazz. Sometimes the customers want to hear something and I put it on. I can't tell the tunes apart. They all sound the same to me.'

'And you can't remember anybody in particular who requested jazz?'

Hjelm didn't know where he was going with this. Igor and Igor were already the focus of the investigation: the tape, the Kazakh ammunition, Viktor X, the threat against the Lovisedal conglomerate.

'Not at the moment, no.' Hackzell looked as though he'd lost his brain as well as his face. 'I'll have to give it some thought.'

'Okay, here's what we're going to do. If you have a blank tape, I'll give you a copy of "Misterioso", this Monk tune, and then I want you to do some real thinking. Make a list of everyone who asked to hear that particular tune, or jazz in general. Under no circumstances are you to leave Växjö. If you do, we'll put out a nationwide alert to track you down, and then you can say goodbye to the restaurant, and you'll end up in the slammer. Do you understand?'

Roger Hackzell nodded numbly. Hjelm made a copy of the tape for him. Then he took the train back to Stockholm, feeling quite satisfied with himself during the entire ride home.

24

With a real lack of sensitivity, Jari Malinen was picked up in the middle of his mother's funeral. The Finnish police simply entered the church during the service and whisked him away. They put him in a little cell in Helsinki overnight. He told them everything.

He'd come into contact with the Soviet mafia back in the late Seventies, made a so-called fiscal blunder, for which he served time. Then he went to Sweden, partly to escape from the mafia. It so happened that he'd dragged one of the Russians into the trap, a certain Vladimir Ragin, and he wasn't sure whether the mob blamed him for that or not. He didn't dare take any chances.

He went to Göteborg, borrowed some money and acquired a small restaurant; that was how he came into contact with another restaurant owner, Roger Hackzell. After some time they decided to join forces and go into business together. They found a nice spot in Växjö and opened Hackat & Malet in the late Eighties.

Suddenly the mafia contacted him again, this time the Russian-Estonian mob, and since he'd involved one of the Russians, he was terrified and agreed to everything. During the trial in Vasa, both he and the Russian had certainly had a brilliant young lawyer on his way up, whose name he couldn't remember. And they'd got off with much lighter sentences than he thought possible in a society based on the rule of law, but that hadn't diminished his fear. Then Igor and Igor turned up in Växjö and began delivering Estonian vodka. That was all.

Hjelm kept his eyes fixed on Söderstedt as Norlander told the story. The pale Finn sat staring at the table the whole time.

'Hjelm did an excellent job in Växjö' was the surprising remark with which Norlander finished his report to the unit.

This was a new Viggo Norlander sitting before them. A healed man. The crutches had been tossed aside, and the gauze bandages were gone from his hands. His wounds had closed up, and the scars shone a naked pink, like tiny flowers in the middle of his hairy hands. He moved them with a new lightness. *Healed and reborn*, thought Hjelm. *Stigmatised, healed and reborn.*

Hjelm and Holm had exchanged a few glances, each without being able to interpret what the other meant.

Hultin cleared his throat loudly and added another arrow to the whiteboard whose pattern had grown even more grotesquely labyrinthine. The arrow pointed to Växjö.

'Does everyone agree that we should prioritise Lovisedal now?' It sounded like a genuine question, not just a rhetorical statement. Hultin even waited for a reply. Maybe he thought he was on his way up to midfield.

He received no verbal response, just a general murmuring. He went on:

'Okay, that's where the perpetrator and his victims met, except for Strand-Julén. The other three, Daggfeldt, Carlberger and Brandberg, all sat on the Lovisedal board of directors for a period of time. So we're suggesting the following scenario. The Lovisedal conglomerate tries to establish itself with a tabloid publication in Tallinn, just as it has already done in St Petersburg. The company receives some prodding from Viktor X, refuses to accept the so-called protection that's offered and is threatened. It continues to resist, and then as a warning the henchmen Igor and Igor – alias Alexander Bryusov and Valery Treplyov – start executing members of the board. They take a break after three murders, two of them intended (Daggfeldt and Carlberger) and one of them an error (Strand-Julén) to see if Lovisedal will react. The company doesn't – it stubbornly continues to resist. Then Igor and Igor set to work again, on direct orders from Viktor X. Brandberg is presumably the fourth victim in a new series. Does this sound reasonable?'

'It's hard to see anything more reasonable,' said Gunnar Nyberg.

'There's just one catch, aside from Strand-Julén,' said Jorge Chavez. 'Daggfeldt, Carlberger and Brandberg sat on the Lovisedal board together for only a brief period in 1991. Daggfeldt was a member from 1989 until 1993; Carlberger from 1991 until his death; and Brandberg from 1985 until 1991, when he was elected to parliament. The only year they had in common was 1991. At their deaths, only Carlberger was still a board member. One out of four.'

'The point is presumably that it was in 1991 that the company started probing the Estonian market,' said Hultin. 'It's the board from that time period that they're after. Maybe they simply have an old list, or maybe it's deliberate: maybe they're saying it was that year, in 1991, that the company made the mistake of a lifetime when it tried to force its way into territory that had already been claimed. In any case, it's the most reasonable explanation we have.'

'There's one other catch,' said Viggo Norlander. 'Jüri Maarja and Viktor X allowed me to live as a means of proving their innocence. You've all read the letter that was pinned to me, so to speak.'

'That doesn't prove or disprove anything,' said Hultin.

'I saw the surprise on Maarja's face when I accused them. It was absolutely genuine.'

'Your Jüri Maarja is a smuggler of refugees. It's possible that he doesn't have Viktor X's ear in all matters. *He* was surprised, okay, but was Viktor X surprised? You never saw his face, if it really was him at all. Igor and Igor may be acting on direct orders from Viktor X, with no intermediaries involved. That's entirely possible, don't you think?'

Viggo Norlander nodded, but remained unconvinced.

'Chavez has a list of the Lovisedal board members *anno* 1991,' Hultin continued. 'How many are still alive?'

'Seven on the list, six are still alive. One died of natural causes.'

'Six individuals. We have to keep an eye on those six at all costs. No one is a more likely victim.'

Hultin looked at his notes.

'Of the six, I'll take Jacob Lidner, who was then chairman of the board; he still is. There are five more for you to divide up. Put some pressure on them, find out whether they know anything, whether they're scared and whether they have any security protection. They're going to have to get some, like it or not. As of tonight, we're putting the entire Lovisedal board under round-the-clock surveillance. And of course we've put out a juicy all-points bulletin for Igor and Igor. In all likelihood, they're our Power Murderers. All right then, let's get going.'

Hultin exited through his mysterious door, and the A-Unit gathered around the table to divide up the board members among themselves. The previous timetable, in which a murder occurred every other night, apparently no longer applied. If it did, then the previous night, sometime on the nineteenth or twentieth of May, which Hjelm had spent in a strange, fitful slumber in a little overnight room in police headquarters, would have produced a new corpse. The old theory about a specific pattern had fallen like a house of cards; the only constant now remaining was the fact that the murders were committed at night, so they probably had plenty of time during the day to talk to the board members. The important thing was to find the next potential victim before it was too late.

'I'm wondering whether there's any system behind the selection,' said Söderstedt. 'If we disregard Strand-Julén, we have Daggfeldt, Carlberger and Brandberg, in that order. D-C-B. Are there any names that start with A?'

There weren't. They divided up the board members. One person would be off the hook. Nobody wanted to be off the hook. Finally they agreed that Söderstedt and Hjelm would share one of the board members.

Hjelm went to Söderstedt and Norlander's office; he already had on his denim jacket and was ready to go. Norlander left, eager to start on his first real assignment since Tallinn. He was alive, but not exactly kicking – he was still limping slightly on his stigmatised feet.

Söderstedt reached for his lumber jacket, on a hook just inside the door.

Hjelm stopped him and pulled the door closed. 'There's just one thing I've been wondering about,' he said as he studied A. Söderstedt, formerly a top lawyer in Finland, and Jari Malinen's defence lawyer, hired by the mafia in February 1979. 'Why the police?'

Arto Söderstedt returned his gaze as he took down his jacket. 'What do you mean?' he asked without really asking. He slowly put on his jacket.

'And why Sweden?'

Söderstedt gave up. He sat down heavily on his chair

and said dully, 'Why I chose Sweden is simple: I was already a marked man in Finland; my name was known. I was the ambitious young lawyer who rescued citizens with fat wallets from the worst possible jams. I had no way out in Finland.'

He paused for a moment and stared at Hjelm. For the first time the gaunt Finn looked completely serious. He grimaced slightly, then went on.

'Why I chose the police is harder to explain. In 1980 I was twenty-seven years old and had just become a partner in the firm. Koivonen, Krantz & Söderstedt. Fucking cute name. Everything that I'd been striving for in my short and extremely goal-oriented life had now been achieved. Then I got a case representing a real fucking bad guy. That wasn't anything new – I'd been defending that type of person all my adult life. But this time something went over the line. Behind the man's respectable facade, the most repulsive sort of business you could imagine was going on: a type of sex-slave trade, it was beyond description. Finland was a closed country, the land that almost always refused to accept any immigrants, yet a steady stream of drugged Asians was coming in, sold at what might be called . . . auctions.

'Naturally I got him off so that he could continue to conduct his business, but something happened inside me. In that proper-looking man with his elegant facade and his loathsome attitude, I saw my entire future. The upholder of facades. That's when the whole shitload came down on me. I moved to Sweden with my family, became a Swedish citizen and tried to go underground. After a few dog-years I decided to join the police force, maybe to try to change the system from inside – the system I thought I'd seen in its entirety, from above and below.

'But things don't allow themselves to be changed from inside. During my time in Stockholm I became known as a controversial cop; then I was exiled to Västerås, and that's where I stayed. You might say I went underground again. The police work became routine. I acquired a large family, and I read books instead of putting any real energy into my work; the job just took care of itself. Somehow Hultin found me by looking through the records – don't ask me how. The end.'

Söderstedt stood up.

He had undergone a transformation in Hjelm's eyes. Gone was the buffoon. Here instead was a man who had suffered the consequences of taking a moral stand. He had given up millions of kronor in salary, he had accepted the fact that he'd thrown his life away, and for the sake of this insight he had changed his country and language and life. *Integrity*, thought Hjelm.

'The last one to the car is a frog with no legs!' shouted the man with integrity as he dashed off.

On that sunny morning of 20 May Jacob Lidner, chairman of the board at Lovisedal, was home in Lidingö. Jan-Olov Hultin arrived at the magnificent villa in his Volvo Turbo and rang the bell, which blared long and loud and with a slight delay through all the rooms of the mansion and out into the garden at the back. It was from there that Lidner came marching around the corner of the building. He was an impressive old man with an imperious gaze, wearing a white, monogrammed bathrobe. His white hair was a dishevelled mane, as if he'd just climbed out of the bath. Up close he smelled of chlorine.

'Stop pestering me,' he said to Hultin and then continued without giving the superintendent a chance to get a word in edgeways. 'I've had enough of publicists. I'm just an ordinary retiree who wants to wait for death in peace and quiet. Stop harassing me about the troubles on the board. I know you want press people on the board at all costs, but this happens to be a business we're running.'

Finally he paused to catch his breath.

'Do I look like a reporter?' said Hultin, putting on his half-moon reading glasses.

'You certainly do,' said Lidner. Then a light went on in his head. 'But you're not, are you?'

'I'm Detective Superintendent Jan-Olov Hultin. I'm in charge of the investigation of what the mass media have labelled the Power Murders.'

'Aha,' said Lidner. 'The A-Unit. An appropriate name. To distinguish you from the A-media of the Social Democrats.'

Hultin was thrown off balance, but managed to hide it. 'That's not information that the media has had access to . . .'

Lidner laughed briefly. 'Good Lord, superintendent, surely you know that a matter like that can't be kept secret. It's our social circles that are being threatened, after all.'

'Not just your social circle in general,' said Hultin, in an attempt to regain the initiative. 'The Lovisedal board of directors, *anno* 1991, in particular.'

Lidner again uttered a brief laugh. 'What has made you come to such a specific conclusion? Director Strand-Julén was certainly a good friend, but he never had anything to do with the company. You should be looking at the board of Sydbanken instead. All four of them were members for a while in 1990.'

Lidner's insight into the inner workings of the investigation was astounding. Hultin controlled himself as usual and struck: 'As far as I know, Sydbanken hasn't been in close contact with the Russian-Estonian mafia the way Lovisedal has. Because you're still refusing to cooperate with the mafia, aren't you?'

Lidner gave him a somewhat peeved look, the way a person looks at a fly that's disturbing him when he's busy with important matters. 'Of course,' he said curtly. 'They continue to be an annoying element. But if you think that the mafia is behind the murders, then you're really out of bounds.'

'Why would you say that?' Hultin retorted.

'In particular because of what happened to your private detective in Tallinn.'

Hultin was on the verge of boiling over. He cast a

determined glance at Lidner's bushy eyebrows. 'I need to ask how you happen to have such insight into our investigative work, Mr Lidnér,' he said, keeping his tone as neutral as possible.

Pronouncing someone's name in the wrong way can be just as effective as using the wrong title, but Lidner didn't seem to let it bother him. Whether the fly shits or not makes no difference; in either case, it's just as annoying. Until you take out the fly-swatter.

Lidner took out his. 'You're free to ask, and I'm just as free not to answer.'

Hultin gave up. 'We're going to bring in our own men as well as detectives from the Stockholm police to give you round-the-clock protection. I hope you can put up with their presence for a few days.'

'As usual, the taxpayers' money could be put to much more effective use,' said Jacob Lidner, and he turned on his heel and left.

It took almost two full minutes before Jan-Olov Hultin did the same.

25

A week passed in which almost nothing happened. After that came an event that should have been decisive.

The criminal division of the Stockholm police made a routine raid on an illegal gambling club in the city centre. An alert officer by the name of Åkesson recognised one of the gamblers, even though he had affected a trendy goatee, was wearing horn-rimmed glasses and had shaved off all his hair.

The gambler was Alexander Bryusov, the slimmer half of Igor and Igor.

He was now sitting mute in the city jail. The members of the A-Unit were peering through the peephole, one after the other, like curious schoolchildren.

Hultin turned to the officer who had arrested Bryusov. Åkesson was looking worn out; he was desperate to go home.

'Not a word?'

Åkesson shook his head. 'I've sat here almost all night

trying to get something out of him. He's pretending to be deaf and dumb.'

'Okay,' said Hultin. 'Damned good job, in any case, Åkesson. Go home now and get some sleep.'

Åkesson left. They hoped he wasn't planning to drive himself home.

The visiting schoolchildren of the A-Unit stood there, shifting from one foot to the other in the corridor of the jail. The guard was staring at them with a slightly indulgent expression.

'I'll go in with Söderstedt,' said Hultin, and asked the guard to unlock the steel door. 'The rest of you can leave,' he added, and slipped inside.

Söderstedt gave them an apologetic wave and followed.

No one left. They took turns looking through the peephole. The guard's expression grew progressively less indulgent.

Hultin and Söderstedt sat down across from Alexander Bryusov. He didn't look much like the police sketch.

It was Söderstedt who did the talking. He repeated each question he asked; first he posed the question in Swedish, then in Russian. But it was a very one-sided conversation.

Bryusov began by demanding a lawyer. The demand was denied with vague references to national security; an infallible excuse. The rest of the questions, including one about the Monk tape, Bryusov answered with an ironic smile. Once he said to Söderstedt, 'I recognise you.' Otherwise he remained mute, up until the question: 'Where is Valery Treplyov?'

Then Bryusov laughed loudly and said in crystal-clear Swedish, 'That, my good sirs, is a profoundly religious question.' After that he said nothing more.

The chief prosecutor didn't have an easy time of it at the indictment hearing.

Not only was there already an overwhelming lack of evidence. But when the case was presented in famed lawyer Reynold Rangsmyhr's rhetorically elaborated and sarcastic statements, it became downright ludicrous.

The members of the A-Unit were flabbergasted as they sat scattered among the spectators. They were far less concerned with whether one half of the Igor duet was going to be released than with the question of why the most prominent lawyer in Sweden, and definitely the most expensive, was defending a Russian booze smuggler.

What they witnessed was a battle royal, Tyson versus Anders 'Lillen' Eklund, which logically ended with the judge sternly admonishing both the office of the prosecutor as well as the police authorities for wasting the time and resources of the judicial system with a matter that could end in only one way. And the freed Alexander Bryusov actually managed to go underground while still inside the courthouse. No one even saw him leave the building.

'What just happened over there?' Gunnar Nyberg

dared to ask at the afternoon meeting in Supreme Central Command. A thick haze of disappointment hovered over the A-Unit. Through the fog they could just make out their badly lacerated, but not yet beaten commander, Hultin, sitting at the end of the table. He was deliberately rolling the shattered lance of his lead pencil between his fingers. Without looking up from this Sisyphean labour, he said grimly, 'The question is quite simple. Does the Viktor X group have sufficient resources and contacts within the Swedish judicial system to get Bryusov off so easily? Or what is it we're actually encountering here?'

The group tried as much as possible to relieve the Stockholm police and take over most of the night-time surveillance of the Lovisedal board of directors, *anno* 1991.

Hjelm had spent a night keeping an eye on a man by the name of Bertilsson, and another night guarding a man named Schrödenius. He'd also spent a couple of nights at home in Norsborg.

He'd had no contact whatsoever with Cilla, who was staying at the Dalarö cabin and remained an enigma. Apparently the worst thing he could do would be to try and reason with her. He had seen her loneliness. And Danne and Tova were living their own lives, with Danne spending most of his time in his room. Tova was often with her friend Milla, whose parents had cheerfully promised to look after her, but at the same time, it seemed to

Hjelm, had given him a number of reproachful looks. He stocked the freezer with food, wondering who was really to blame and for what.

Tova said that she thought the blemish on his cheek looked like an astrological sign, but she couldn't decide which one. Not until the following morning, just as he was about to leave for work, did she say that it was Pluto she meant – a *P* with a little line through the loop. He asked her what the significance was. She replied merrily and innocently that she had no idea.

'Are you coming to the closing ceremonies at school?' she asked him. 'Mama is coming.'

'I'll try,' he said, feeling a pang.

In the car on his way into town he thought about what Pluto might mean for Tova: a cute Disney dog, the most distant planet in the solar system or an archaic god of death.

When he entered the office, Chavez hadn't yet turned on the computer. That was very unusual. He was sitting at his desk, grinding coffee beans. 'It's going to be June soon,' he said tersely.

'Do you have plans for the summer that are going to end up frozen?' said Hjelm as he sat down.

'I suppose *frozen* is the right word.' Chavez looked out the window of the small office. The clear blue sky was peeking through the upper-right corner. Then he seemed to remember something. 'Oh, that's right,' he said, invoking his rather distracted memory banks. 'A guy called. Said he'd call back.'

'Who was it?'

'No idea. I forgot to ask.'

It was a fundamental dereliction of duty, but Hjelm stopped himself from criticising his colleague. 'What did he sound like?'

'What did he sound like? Someone from Göteborg, I think.'

'Ah,' said Hjelm with renewed hope. He punched in a long string of numbers and waited. 'Hackzell?' he shouted into the phone. 'Hjelm here.'

'I think I've come up with something,' said Roger Hackzell, his voice crackling on the line from Hackat & Malet in Växjö. 'Something actually did happen a couple of years ago when I played a jazz tape here in the restaurant.'

'Don't go anywhere!' Hjelm slammed down the phone. Already out in the hall, he said to Chavez, 'Tell Hultin that Kerstin and I have gone to Växjö. We'll be in touch.'

'Wait!' yelled Chavez.

Hjelm rushed into room 303. Gunnar Nyberg and Kerstin Holm were sitting there singing a complex Gregorian chant. He stopped and stared at them in astonishment. Without seeming to notice him, they sang to the end. Chavez threw open the door behind him and also halted abruptly. When they were done, Hjelm and Chavez applauded for a long time. Then Hjelm said, 'I think we've got a nibble regarding the cassette tape in Växjö. Want to come along?'

Kerstin Holm wordlessly put on her little black leather jacket.

'Is there room for me?' asked Chavez.

The three of them flew to Växjö. Jorge's presence made any intimate conversation between Paul and Kerstin impossible. Neither of them seemed to mind. Their tunnel vision had been activated.

Just after eleven o'clock they found Roger Hackzell inside Hackat & Malet. The restaurant had just opened for early lunch customers.

Hackzell showed them into his office, leaving the restaurant in the hands of a waitress. 'Misterioso' was playing loudly inside the office. Hackzell turned off the cassette player, which was set up to play the same tune over and over again.

'Yes, well,' he said, motioning for them to sit down on the sofa. 'A couple of days ago I got a feeling that there was something special about that tune, so I've been listening to it like a maniac. And then I remembered. It was late one night a few years back. We'd been running the restaurant here in town for several years and were the only place open until three A.M. It could get a little rowdy, with all the late-night partygoers gathered here. Later the rules were changed, and now we're open only until midnight. On that particular night, though, the restaurant was deserted, and I was just about to close.

'There were two men still here. One of them, Anton,

big as a house, requested that I play this tape again. I had just played it and then put in a new one with some rock music. But Anton had a kind of crazy look in his eyes, and he wanted the jazz back on. So I put in the tape again, and I'm positive that it was this tune. Then he started shouting wildly and lit into the other guy, punching and pummelling him.

'I remember it all very clearly now; it was as nasty as hell. Anton kept screaming the same thing over and over. I can't recall what it was, something really incoherent. He was as drunk as a skunk, and I was fucking scared. First he delivered a couple of blows to the stomach, then a kick to the knee and one to the groin, and finally a hell of a knockout punch right on the jaw, making the guy's teeth fly. He fell to the floor, and Anton kicked him as he lay there, again and again.

'But he was conscious the whole time, the guy who was lying there getting beaten; he just stared up at Anton with a strange expression. Then Anton stepped back to take aim for a fucking big kick that definitely would have killed the guy. I screamed at him. Anton stopped himself and instead picked up a bottle and hurled it against the wall. Then he left.

'I helped him up, the guy who was lying on the floor. He was beaten real bad, his teeth were rolling around under his tongue and he spat them out, one after the other. One arm was hanging limply, bent at an odd angle, and he had terrible pain in his stomach and abdomen. "I'm going to call the police," I said, "and an ambulance."

"No," he said, "he was totally justified." That's what he actually said about the lunatic who had just beaten him to a pulp: "He was totally justified." Okay, I thought, it was great not to have to bring in the police, because then we'd lose our nighttime licence. I helped him sop up the worst of the blood, and he left. And that was it.'

'I think that's good enough,' said Hjelm. 'This Anton, who is he?'

'Anton Rudström is his name. He'd opened a gym here in town – that must have been back in 1990. But when this happened it was about a year later, in the spring, and the gym had gone bankrupt. He'd got a bank loan without having to provide any collateral – you know how easy that was in those days – and then he couldn't pay it back. That happened a lot in the late Eighties. At the time of the episode in the restaurant, Anton had just started on his drinking career. Now he's a full-blooded alcoholic, one of the drunks who usually hang around outside the state off-licence.'

'Although he still looks like a bodybuilder,' said Hjelm pensively, amazed at the coincidence.

Roger Hackzell, Kerstin Holm and Jorge Chavez all looked at him in surprise.

'What about the other man?' said Chavez. 'The victim. Who was he?'

'I don't know. I'd never seen him before or since. I don't think he was from here in town. But he was a fucking expert at darts, I do remember that. Stood there for several hours, throwing them.'

'Throwing them?' said Kerstin Holm.

'Darts,' Roger Hackzell clarified.

He was sitting with a group passing around a bottle of cheap Rosita sherry. He was the youngest and the biggest on the park bench.

'I thought vodka was your poison,' said Hjelm.

Anton Rudström recognised him at once.

'Will you look at that!' he said jovially. 'The Stockholmer with the taste test. Gentlemen, you see before you the man who gave me a half-bottle of vodka so that I'd drink more vodka.'

'Hell, I was sure you were making him up,' said an old, toothless man, stretching out his hand towards Hjelm. 'I'd be willing to help with a taste test.'

'No taste test this time,' said Hjelm, showing them his police ID. 'Now clear out.'

Rudström tried to clear out too, but without success. 'Right now I want to hear a little about the fight in the restaurant Hackat & Malet in the spring of '91,' said Hjelm, sitting down next to the man. Chavez and Holm remained standing. Neither of them seemed particularly impressive compared to the enormous Rudström.

'I don't know anything about that,' he said sullenly.

'We're not here to arrest you. There's not even a police report about it. Just try to answer my questions as precisely as you can, and there'll be another half-bottle in it for you, I promise. First we'd like to know why you wanted to hear that particular piece of jazz called "Misterioso", by Thelonious Monk, while you beat that man to a pulp.'

Anton Rudström paused to think. He had to dive down through cubic yards of ethanol to return to the opposite shore. He fumbled his way along its shifting sands.

'I remember vaguely that I was about to kill somebody. That was after the plug was pulled for good.'

'You owned a gym, right?' Hjelm ventured.

'The Apollo,' said Rudström cockily. 'The Apollo Gym. Fuck.'

'Tell us about it.'

'Yeah, well, okay. Let me see. I'd been working out at Carlo's place all those years, and I finally got a job there. Then I happened to walk past a great vacant space in the centre of town, a little expensive, of course – an old boutique of some kind. Well, then I decided to go to the nearest bank and ask for a loan to open a gym there; it was just an impulse, I didn't have any collateral or anything. And suddenly I was coming out of the bank with a huge loan in my pocket. Everything was going so well back then; it was easy to get a loan.

'I bought the best equipment available and created a real fancy gym. Of course it wasn't going to make it in little Växjö. It took only six months or so for the whole shitload to go bankrupt, and I stood there with a fucking debt in the millions of kronor, with no idea how it all happened. I'd lost everything, just like that.'

Rudström snapped his fingers, then floated off to happier hunting grounds.

Hjelm cautiously prodded him back. 'It was about that time that you were in Hackat & Malet one night. The only people in the place were you, the owner and one other person. It was almost closing time. In the middle of the night. Do you remember?'

'Vaguely,' said Rudström. 'Shit, I need a drink.'

'You'll get plenty of drinks afterwards. Try to think back.'

Anton Rudström dived once again into the deep sea. 'He was standing in the corner, throwing darts. At least I think it was that night . . . I can't really recall.'

'Yes, it was. That's right. Go on.'

'Well . . . He was already there, throwing his fucking darts when I came in. The place was packed, but he stood over there in the corner, throwing one dart after another, for hours. It was starting to annoy me.'

'Why?'

'Somebody said something earlier that night . . . something that made me pay attention to him. Otherwise he'd have been easy to overlook. But somebody said that he was . . . that he . . .'

Rudström was about to fade away and slip through their fingers. All three noticed it.

'Was it something he said or did?' asked Chavez quickly. 'Some annoying behaviour? Or maybe something about him personally? Some trait? A particular type of person? Or profession? Was he an immigrant?'

'Something about him personally, that's what it was.' Rudström looked at Chavez in surprise. 'He *was* something that made me fucking mad, and the more beers I drank, the madder I got. I blamed him for all the shit that had been dumped on me.'

'Why him?' said Hjelm.

'He was a bank guy,' said Rudström clearly. 'That's what it was. Somebody said that he worked in a bank. Finally it drove me crazy.'

'He worked in town?'

'No, in some hole-in-the-wall town, I think. I'm not sure. He wasn't from Växjö, I know that. I have no clue who he was. But he was a real ace at darts. I hope he wasn't seriously injured.'

They exchanged glances, all four of them.

'It's possible that he was injured worse than you might imagine,' said Hjelm. 'But not in the way you mean.'

He pressed two hundred-krona bills into Rudström's hand. The man now seemed to be totally immersed in the memory that he'd initially thought the booze had drowned out for ever.

'My God, how I hit him,' he said. A couple of tears quietly ran down his steroid-scarred cheek. 'My God.'

They were just about to leave when Kerstin Holm crouched down in front of him. 'I have to ask you one thing, Anton,' she said. 'Why did you want to hear "Misterioso" while you beat him up?'

He looked her right in the eye. 'It was such a fucking great tune. But now I've forgotten how it goes.'

She patted his arm lightly. 'But he probably hasn't.'

★ ★ ★

They were so distracted that they ended up at what they thought was an outdoor café until they got their hamburgers with a big M on the wrapper. They found themselves sitting on the McDonald's terrace on the big pedestrian street in Växjö. It was afternoon.

'*Misterioso*,' said Kerstin. 'It's a play on words, typical Monk. There's an inaudible *mist* in the title. Behind the *mystery*, the *mysterium*, there's a *mist*. When you say the word, you don't hear the *mist*. It's hidden by the more-pronounced *mystery*. And yet it's there and has an effect. It's in the tune too. The mystery is immediately apparent, intangible, of course, and yet physically manifest. The mist inside is harder to distinguish. But it's there in the mist that we go astray.'

Hjelm had gone astray. There was something somewhere that he had overlooked, something that had passed him by and yet had been there the whole time; okay, he thought, something altogether physically manifest. Someone had said something. It was driving him crazy.

'Have you thought of anything?' asked Chavez, biting into his Quarter Pounder.

'It's there, just below the surface,' said Hjelm.

'I know how you feel,' said Chavez, chewing. 'It's like *Fawlty Towers*, right? A difficult guest is served the wrong dish three times. Basil's wife, what's her name? Sybil. She finally serves the wrong dish on purpose. Basil says between clenched teeth, "I know how she feels."'

'What does that have to do with any of this?' said Holm in surprise.

'Not a damned thing. Just making conversation, as I'm told it's called.'

A bank, thought Hjelm, digging through his own memory bank. He came up with nothing, not even a statement of account.

'What do we do if you can't come up with anything?' said Chavez. 'Line up every banker in Småland in a row and let Mr Serious Alcoholic take a look at them, one after the other?'

'He must have been treated for the teeth that were knocked out, and the broken arm, if that's what it was,' said Holm.

'This whole thing is still such a long shot.' Chavez smacked his lips. 'Not something we can present to Hultin, at any rate. He beat up a guy listening to Hackzell's "Misterioso" – but it's a big leap from there to actually *having* the tape.'

'There's a connection,' Hjelm said doggedly.

'Okay,' said Chavez. 'Does your connection have anything to do with Igor and Igor? It almost has to. The cassette is the only link between the beating in the spring of '91 in a restaurant in Växjö and the ex-Soviet bullets in the upper-class walls in Stockholm. And the path of the tape from the restaurant to the villa in Saltsjöbaden follows the same route as Igor and Igor. They took the tape from Hackzell, after all, as partial payment for the Estonian vodka on February the fifteenth.'

Hjelm shook his head. The whole thing was unclear. Misterioso.

'Let's start from the point of view of the banker who was beaten up,' said Kerstin Holm. 'According to Hackzell, right after the beating, as he's spitting out teeth, he said, "He was totally justified." About the guy who pounded him! Strange, don't you think? The years pass, the wounds heal, but at the same time the accumulation of distrust, insight, confusion, powerlessness grows—'

'Wrede!' shouted Hjelm, jumping to his feet.

Holm looked at him in surprise.

'Wrede. Jonas Wrede, from the Växjö police. He said something about an incident in a bank. I lost it in all the other damn incidents he kept talking about. Albertsboda, or somewhere like that. Shit, what time is it?'

'Three-thirty,' said Chavez. 'What's going on?'

'We have to go to the Växjö police station,' said Hjelm and dashed out.

Detective Inspector Jonas Wrede stood at attention three times, once for each member of the NCP Power Murders team that came into his little office. Finally he was standing so erect that the top button of his shirt popped off.

'Relax,' said Hjelm. 'Sit down.'

Wrede obeyed the command. Ordered to relax, he sat there looking like a sack of hay.

'The last time I was here, you said something about a previous contact with the NCP. It had to do with a bank incident somewhere.'

'That's right,' said Wrede hopefully. 'The bank incident in Algotsmåla. But of course you must know about that. The NCP sent a man down there. He never introduced himself, said his identity was confidential. He put a lid on the whole thing. Nothing got out to the press. I'm quite proud of that: no leaks from here whatsoever. Even the bank personnel kept their mouths shut. A matter of self-preservation, I assume.'

'What happened?'

'All the documents were confiscated by your man, so obviously you already know.'

'Just tell us everything you can remember.'

Wrede looked a bit disoriented, since he wasn't able to make use of his computer.

'Yes, well, let's see. It happened this year, on February the fifteenth. When the staff arrived at the bank that morning and opened the vault, they found a dead body inside. And a lot of money was missing. We immediately brought in Stockholm; it was a real mystery. Your man came down here and took over the whole investigation. That's all.'

'Our man . . .' said Chavez.

'February the fifteenth,' said Holm.

'Tell us about the dead man,' said Hjelm.

'I was the first officer on the scene, and I was the one who contacted Stockholm. I saw it as my duty to keep the whole staff there until your man arrived. He gave me high praise and imposed a gag order on the police officers on site as well as the bank personnel. Consequently

I was the first to examine the body properly. He was a big, stocky man, powerfully built. A long, sharp object of some kind, possibly a slender stiletto, had pierced his eye and gone right into his brain. A very unpleasant sight.' Wrede looked more excited than upset. 'But I'm sure that you already know all this,' he insisted.

'Okay,' said Hjelm. 'If you could arrange to have all the personnel who were present at the time come to the bank in Algotsboda, then we'll go out there right away.'

'Algotsmåla,' said Wrede, and put in a call to the bank office.

Jonas Wrede personally drove the police car that carried all of them about thirty miles from Växjö. The sun was sinking towards the horizon.

Wrede was all fired up and in full subtlety mode, meaning that he urgently prodded them to reveal what this was all about. None of the NCP officers said a word. All they saw was the narrowest of tunnels in front of them, the tunnel that would lead to a serial killer.

Wrede pounded fiercely on the locked door of the bank. A short, timid, middle-aged woman opened it. The only other person inside the minuscule bank office was an elderly gentleman wearing a pin-striped suit.

'This is the bank president, Albert Josephson, and the bank teller, Lisbet Heed.'

The officers looked at both with a certain scepticism. 'Is this the whole staff?' asked Chavez.

Lisbet Heed brought them cups of freshly brewed coffee. They accepted, without really paying attention.

Josephson cleared his throat and spoke in a shrill, pedantic voice. 'We lost a number of staff members in February this year, a cost-saving measure that also involved cutting back our business hours. It was part of the bank's austerity policy, as a result of the deplorable conditions at the end of the last decade and the beginning of this one.'

'So the basic staff,' said Hjelm, 'had to pay the price for the failed speculations and absurd borrowing practices instigated by the higher-ups, who later retired with their multimillion-kronor golden parachutes. Is that it?' He sounded like Söderstedt.

'Not an unreasonable way of viewing the matter,' said Josephson impassively. 'The fact is that this' – he glanced at Wrede – 'incident . . . occurred on the very day when the new business hours went into effect. And on the same day the staff had been cut in half. I opened the vault myself and found . . . the blinded man.'

The blinded man, thought Hjelm.

'Here's the vault,' said Josephson, pointing to the open vault. They went inside. There was nothing to see.

'So you found him lying inside the locked vault?' said Chavez.

'You can imagine what a shock it was,' said Josephson, without looking especially shocked.

'Do you remember what the . . . blinded man looked like?' asked Hjelm.

'Big,' said Josephson. 'Huge, in fact.'

'A real bull of a man,' said Lisbet Heed surprisingly.

'Worn out by the matador,' said Chavez, even more surprisingly.

Kerstin Holm dug around in her bag and took out the sketches of Igor and Igor.

Time for a decisive moment.

'Was it one of these men?' she asked.

Hjelm hardly recognised her voice. *A tunnel voice*, he thought.

'So that's why I thought I recognised the drawing!' cried Lisbet Heed. 'It was in the newspaper for days!'

Jonas Wrede froze. What an oversight on his part! Bye-bye to any chance of being transferred to the NCP.

'I knew I'd seen that face somewhere!' Lisbet went on. 'But I didn't even think about the man in the vault. I did everything I could to repress the whole thing. It was so horrible.'

'That's him, all right.' Josephson pointed at the sketch of Valery Treplyov's face. 'Even though his face looked slightly different, of course.'

'Wrede?' said Holm, wickedly, holding up the drawing to the pale man, who nodded mutely. Bye-bye, inspector training course.

Hjelm, Holm and Chavez gave each other meaningful looks. One important thing was still missing. Hjelm went to the back of the office, behind the wall that divided it from the public section of the bank.

He stopped in his tracks, then gestured for Holm and Chavez to join him.

ARNE DAHL

For a long time they all looked at the dartboard hanging on the wall.

Wrede, Josephson and Heed came over to stand next to them.

'Yes, it's still there,' said Lisbet Heed. 'I haven't had the heart to take it down.'

Chavez asked the question: 'What are the names of the two people who were let go on February the fifteenth?'

'Mia Lindström,' said Heed.

'And Göran Andersson,' said Josephson.

Göran Andersson, thought the three officers.

'Was it Andersson who played darts?' asked Chavez.

'Yes,' said Lisbet Heed. 'He was really good at it. He was the first to arrive every morning, and he always started the day with a . . . What was it called?'

'A five-o-one,' said Josephson. 'You start at five-o-one and work your way down to zero.'

'What happened to Göran Andersson after he was fired?' asked Hjelm. 'Did he stay here in town?'

'No,' said Lisbet, looking sad. 'No, he left his girlfriend high and dry and vanished. I don't think even Lena knows where he went.'

'Lena?'

'Lena Lundberg. They lived in a little house on the other side of Algotsmåla. Now she lives there alone. And she's pregnant, the poor thing. Göran probably doesn't even know that he's going to be a father.'

'Do you remember whether Göran was injured sometime during the spring of '91?'

'Yes.' Josephson had the personnel list filed in his mind.
'He was off sick for a couple of months back then. It
had something to do with his teeth—'

'I think he had to get a bridge, or something like that,'
said Heed. 'He mostly stayed indoors during that time.
He didn't want to talk about what had happened. But I
saw him with a plaster cast on his arm too. I think it was
a car accident.'

'One more thing,' said Hjelm. 'Had Göran Andersson
turned in his bank keys?'

'I don't think he'd done that yet,' said bank president
Albert Josephson, for the first time sounding a bit uncertain.

The three members of the A-Unit exchanged glances
again. Things were falling into place. Loose threads were
getting tied up.

Göran Andersson.

There wasn't much more to add.

Hjelm turned to Wrede. 'Do you have a sketch artist
in Växjö?'

'A police sketch artist?' said Wrede, still looking pale.
'There's an artist here that we sometimes use, yes.'

'The three of you are going to help each other produce
a drawing of the man from NCP who was down here
and took over the case. Be as specific as you can. But
first I want you to drive us over to see Lena Lundberg.'

It wasn't far to the other side of Algotsmåla. But while
sitting crowded together in a police patrol car, each of

them put all the information together in their minds to form one big picture.

In the spring of 1991 the bank employee Göran Andersson from Algotsmåla had been beaten up in a restaurant in Växjö. It was a result of the Swedish banking world's grotesque borrowing practices during the late Eighties: those borrowing practices contributed not only to the bank crisis and to Sweden's general economic crisis in the early Nineties, but also to scores of unnecessary personal bankruptcies. One of these bankruptcies was suffered by Anton Rudström, who at the sight of a banker went berserk and beat up the man. That man turned out to be Göran Andersson. Andersson apparently had already suspected that something was wrong with the bank's policies, because after the beating he said that Rudström's actions were justified. Yet he continued to work at the bank, maybe out of loyalty, or maybe because there simply wasn't any other job available.

Later, as a direct result of these shady business dealings, he lost his job, and that's when he snapped. Even though he'd been fired, he went to the bank just as he usually did, arriving before the normal opening time. He let himself in through the staff entrance, using the keys that he hadn't yet relinquished, *in order to rob the bank*. That would be his revenge.

But for some unknown reason, he opened the bank doors as usual. That was strange, because the opening hours at the bank had been cut back, and because he'd been fired and was in the process of robbing the bank.

Maybe it was the power of habit, or maybe he was distracted by a dart game that he'd started playing. Five-o-one.

To top it all off, he was robbed just as he was planning his own robbery. A brutal Russian mafia man by the name of Valery Treplyov came into the bank in the middle of Andersson's robbery and game of darts. The situation was grotesque. The world fell in on Andersson. The mafioso on the other side of the counter had the same gigantic build as the man who had beaten Göran up a couple of years earlier. Maybe he was holding the dart in his hand. Regardless, he threw it with infallible precision right into Valery Treplyov's eye.

Now Andersson had killed a man; in self-defence, of course, but no matter what, he was standing there with a dead body in his old bank office, which he was in the process of robbing. He dragged the body inside the vault and locked it. He had appropriated Treplyov's gun, perhaps in a state of confusion, and he'd emptied the man's pockets. In addition to a lot of ammunition from the notorious factory in Kazakhstan, he also found a cassette tape.

He took the money, locked the bank doors and left through the same entrance he'd come in, the back door, which was for employees only. In front of the bank was the truck containing Estonian vodka, ready to be delivered to other parts of the country. In the vehicle, the other Igor, Alexander Bryusov, waited for his partner to appear. After a while he might have gone over to the bank, only to find the doors locked and the place deserted. A mystery.

By then Göran Andersson had already driven off in his car, which he'd parked at the back, in the employees' lot. Maybe it was then that he popped the cassette into the car cassette player and listened to the very jazz tune he'd heard a few years earlier while he was being beaten up: the inexplicable hand of coincidence. It was as if some higher power were behind it all. An unexpected element that was simply impossible to explain. That absurd Russian – who had come into the bank while Göran was making a radical break with everything he'd ever believed in – had supplied him with not only a weapon, but also a motivation in the form of this music.

It was too much. He was transformed into the instrument of a larger power, seeking revenge against the banks, on behalf of the greater public, and at the same time against Anton Rudström, for himself personally. He decided to go after the bank's board of directors from the year when Rudström had so hastily been granted a loan, the year 1990. That loan had resulted in the beating in Hackat & Malet in the spring of 1991. Both banks were branches of Sydbanken, but it could just as well have been any of Sweden's larger banks. Göran Andersson presumably went to Stockholm on 15 February, right after the incident at the bank in Algotsmåla. There he planned the first of three murders to be committed in less than a month. He started on his path as the avenging angel between 29 and 30 March. After the first three murders, he retreated to his lair to plan the next series of killings. Which they were in the middle of right now. Göran Andersson was very determined, very accurate, very damaged and very dangerous. He was beyond desperate.

The mystery was gone. But the mist still remained.

Misterioso.

They got out of the police car in front of a small house on the edge of town. It looked tranquil and peaceful, basking in the evening sun. The police car drove away.

None of them wanted to be the first to go in and talk to the woman who was expecting the Power Murderer's child.

26

The underside of the crackle-glazed altocumulus cloud cover gleamed dark orange in the early summer evening. An infinite number of small, just barely separated wisps plunged Lilla Värtan and all of Lidingö into a strange, fractured, bewitching twilight. It was as if the sky were pressing down with superhuman force.

Gunnar Nyberg, sitting in a police car up on Lidingö Bridge, thought he'd never seen such a glow before. It had a fateful music about it.

Maybe it's my time to die, he thought, then shook off the idea.

He was on his way to the villa of Lovisedal board chairman Jacob Lidner in Mölna, located on the southern spit of Lidingö. Arto Söderstedt had the night watch; he would be gazing out across the water as he sat in that living room that radiated resistance to the police presence. Nyberg sympathised with the living room.

He had nothing to do and had decided on his own initiative to spend the night keeping Söderstedt company.

There were worse things he could be doing. Besides, he was feeling an acute need for human companionship. Loneliness had suddenly overwhelmed him and sucked the breath from his throat, propelling him inexorably out into this appallingly lovely early summer evening. The beauty on the Lidingö Bridge took his breath away again.

After the bridge Gunnar Nyberg turned right and took Södra Kungsvägen all the way out to Mölna. When he caught sight of Lidner's palatial villa, he stopped the car, parking it a safe distance away on the little entrance drive. Dusk had fallen. The peculiar cloud formations now glowed only faintly; then during the minute it took him to walk to the house, they disappeared entirely.

He reached the hedge surrounding the garden. The gate appeared in the middle of all the vegetation. It was ajar. He opened it all the way and stepped into the garden.

Out of the corner of his eye, off to the left, he saw a faint movement, and long before the pain hit him, he heard the dull pop of a gun with a silencer.

He threw his huge body full length onto the gravel path and pulled out his service weapon. Yet another shot whined right over his head.

Something was ignited in Gunnar Nyberg's eyes.

He got up and with a wild bellow ran like a crazed buffalo, firing one shot after another at the spot where he'd seen the movement a couple of seconds earlier.

A car started up a little farther down the road. He heard it approaching. He tossed aside his empty gun and, still bellowing, crashed like a bulldozer right through the thick hedge and came out onto the road just as the car came up.

Gunnar Nyberg tackled it like a professional hockey player.

He hurled his furious giant's body against the left side of the accelerating vehicle. It flung him off, and he landed with his face pressed to the asphalt.

The pain came. His field of vision was shrinking drastically, but he saw the car drive into a lamp post a dozen yards away.

Arto Söderstedt, with gun raised, rushed over to the car, yanked the driver out and pulled him over to the other side of the road. The last thing Nyberg saw before everything vanished in a sea of fire was Alexander Bryusov's bloody face being dragged across the asphalt.

Maybe it's my time to die, thought Gunnar Nyberg, and he was gone.

27

I miss the music.

That's the only thing he's thinking.

Here the sensitive fingers should have started on their cautious promenade.

He sits motionless for a while on the living-room sofa, imagining that he's listening.

Here's where the sax should come in.

The body performs no dance of death, as it lies there on the floor, without moving, with two holes in the head. It's a piece of dead meat; nothing more.

Yet another corpse.

Without joy, he mentally checks another name off the list.

Art has become a trade, and a mission has become an execution. All that's left is an inexorable, imperative list.

I miss the music, he thinks as he picks up the gun from the table and leaves via the terrace.

In the wall he leaves behind two slugs from Kazakhstan.

28

It's night and they're sitting in Hjelm's hotel room in central Växjö. Each of them is holding a photo of Göran Andersson; three pictures that they've brought along, given to them by Lena Lundberg.

Kerstin Holm is half-reclining on the bed. In her hands she's holding a group photo of the staff at the bank in Algotsmåla from the summer of 1992. They're posing outside the bank, all four of them smiling pleasantly. It's a PR shot. In the front stands Lisbet Heed and a young woman who is Mia Lindström; at the back are Albert Josephson and Göran Andersson. Andersson is tall, blue-eyed, blond, wearing a nice suit. He has one hand on Lisbet Heed's shoulder, and his wide smile shows very white teeth. The bridge in his mouth is apparently in place. There's nothing special about him. Just like hundreds of similar-looking Swedish bank tellers.

'He was always a model employee,' Lena Lundberg had said, speaking in the distinct, broad accent of Småland as she glanced up from her coffee cup for a moment. 'Almost a perfectionist, you might say. Never a day's absence, except after the accident. A real asset to the bank.'

On the wall behind her was a little framed embroidery that elegantly declared, MY HOME IS MY CASTLE.

Lena kept her hands clasped over her stomach, where a slight bulge had started to show.

'Would you say that he lived for his job?' asked Holm. 'That he had a personal investment in his work?'

'Yes, I think so. He lived for the bank. And for me,' she added hesitantly. 'And he would have lived for our child.'

'He can still do that,' Kerstin Holm had said without really believing it.

Jorge Chavez is sitting on the edge of the bed at Kerstin's feet. In his hand he has a photo of an utterly focused Göran, who holds a dart out in front of him and is just about to throw it. There is a tremendous, ice-cold purposefulness in his supremely attentive gaze. The date 3/12/1993 is printed faintly in pencil on the back of the photo.

On the wall directly across from the embroidery was a dartboard with three darts stuck in it. Chavez went over to the board and pulled out one of them. He studied with fascination the strange shape of the dart with its extraordinarily long point.

'Is this how darts usually look?' he asked.

Lena Lundberg stared at him with her sorrowful green eyes. It took a moment before she managed to shift gears: 'He special-ordered them from a company in Stockholm.

Bows & Arrows, I think it's called. In Gamla Stan. A dart can be as long as seven inches,' she told them. 'Half for the point and body, half for the flights. He experimented until he found a certain weight that suited him, and the ideal shape turned out to be that long point. But it does look rather strange.'

'Was he a member of any darts club?' Chavez weighed the dart in his hand to find the centre of gravity.

'The darts club in town. In Växjö, I mean. That was where he'd been on the night you were talking about, when somebody beat him up. He'd won some sort of record, and when the club closed, he wasn't ready to stop, so he went over to that restaurant and kept on practising. Otherwise he doesn't usually go out to pubs very often.'

'Did you play darts with him?' asked Chavez, throwing the dart at the board. It didn't stick, but instead fell down, puncturing the parquet floor. 'I'm sorry,' he said, pulling out the dart and looking at the annoying little hole in the wooden floorboard.

It seemed so irrelevant.

'Sometimes we used to play a game,' said Lena, without casting a glance at Chavez's dubious activities. 'Just for fun. Although it wasn't really much fun. He always gave me a head start, but he always caught up in the end. He hated to lose. You know, you go from five-o-one down to zero. You have to finish with the checkout, as it's called, hitting the double ring with the last dart you throw, so that you end up right at zero, no more, no less. The checkout and zero have to coincide exactly.'

Paul Hjelm is slouched in an armchair in the hotel room, staring at the third photograph. It's the most recent one of Göran Andersson, taken only a couple of weeks before the bank incident. He has his arm around Lena and is smiling broadly. They're standing outside in the snow in front of their house; they've made a snow lantern, with a little candle burning inside. His cheeks are rosy, and he looks happy and healthy. And yet there's a certain shyness in his clear blue eyes.

Hjelm recognises that look. It's the quiet shyness of a child.

'And he doesn't know that you're pregnant?' said Hjelm.

Lena looked down at her coffee cup again and murmured, 'I was just thinking of telling him. But he hadn't been himself after getting the pink slip. It arrived in the post in an ordinary brown envelope from Stockholm. Not even his boss at the bank, Albert Josephson, knew about it. I watched him open the envelope and saw how something died in his eyes. Maybe I knew even then that I'd lost him.'

'So you haven't had any contact with him since he disappeared?'

'On the morning of February the fifteenth . . .' said Lena, as if she were leafing through a calendar. 'No. Nothing. I don't know where he is or what he's doing.'

Suddenly she looked Hjelm straight in the eye. He had to look away. 'What exactly has he done?'

'Maybe nothing.' Hjelm lied, feeling ill at ease.

★ ★ ★

Jorge Chavez gets up from the bed, stretches and gathers the photographs. He hesitates for a moment. 'Maybe we should tell Hultin about this?'

'Let them spend one last night guarding the Lovisedal board members,' Hjelm says tersely. 'Nothing's going to happen there anyway.'

'Besides, we should probably wait for that sketch of our so-called colleague,' says Kerstin Holm, yawning.

'The guy who stopped the whole damned investigation,' says Chavez, and after a moment continues: 'No, listen. That's enough for today. A good day's work. Although with a rather bitter aftertaste.'

He places the photographs on Hjelm's nightstand and leaves the room in the midst of a huge yawn.

Kerstin is still lying on the bed, tired and incredibly . . . erotic, thinks Hjelm. He's still uncertain whether the previous hotel-room incident actually took place or not.

'Do you know anything about astrology?' he asks abruptly.

'Because I'm a woman?' she replies, just as abruptly.

He laughs. 'Presumably, yes.'

'The alternative way of thinking,' she says sarcastically, sitting up on the edge of the bed and tossing back her black hair. 'I know a little about it.'

'This morning – was it really this morning? – my daughter said that this . . . blemish on my cheek looked like the astrological sign for Pluto. What does that mean?'

'I've never thought about that,' she says, coming over

to touch his cheek. 'Maybe your daughter is right. Lately I've thought it looked like a hobo sign.'

'Have you really been thinking about my blemish?' He closes his eyes.

'Pluto.' She takes her hand away. 'It can signify a lot of different things. Willpower, for instance. But also a lack of consideration.'

'Hmm. Really?'

'Wait. I'm not done. The sign of Pluto also signifies an individual's ability to handle change. And catharsis, the final purification.'

'Well, I'll be damned.' Hjelm's eyes are still closed. 'But does it really look like the sign for Pluto? What do you think?'

Again he feels the light caress of her hand. He keeps his eyes shut.

'I think it looks like you have an erection,' she says lightly.

'I'm sorry,' he says without feeling sorry. 'And the blemish?'

'It's disappeared in the rest of the crimson on your face.'

He opens his eyes. She's now sitting on the edge of the bed a couple of yards away, looking at him with an inscrutable expression through the dim light.

'It's the only way to make it disappear.' He sits up. 'I have to ask you about the last time in Växjö. Did anything really happen?'

She laughs. 'The masculine need to demystify everything,' she says. 'You can't live with uncertainty, can you?'

'But believe me,' he says, 'the mist is still there.'

'I interpreted your wish,' she says. 'That question about Anna-Clara Hummelstrand's Gallic lover . . . I assumed you'd fantasised about me masturbating, that you had a certain preference for masturbating women.'

'Good Lord.' He'd hit the mark. 'But how did you get into my hotel room?'

'You know very well you left the door open.'

'So the whole thing was about fulfilling my wish? But what about you? You didn't look as if you were suffering.'

'One person's pleasure is shared by the other. As long as there's no coercion, no forcing the other person. It's all a matter of being viewed as a human being.'

A warmth spreads between them. Kerstin continues, her voice a bit hoarse: 'Have you interpreted my wish?'

He closes his eyes to think. Images of her fly past, phrases, words. He is feverishly searching for clues, hints, glances. He merely sees her with her feet propped up on the desk and her hand inside her panties.

He feels like a little boy. 'Give me a clue,' he squeaks.

'Take off your clothes,' she says curtly.

He takes them off. He stands there naked, confused. He's holding his hands in front of his genitals.

'Take your hands away and put them on top of your head,' she says. She's still lying on the bed, fully dressed, with her hands clasped behind her head.

He's standing there in front of her. His penis is sticking straight up, strutting with nowhere to go. Without ever getting there.

'Come here and stand next to the bed, near my feet.'

He walks over there, with his hands on top of his head. His penis sways back and forth as he moves. His knees are resting against the edge of the bed. His penis is sticking out over the bed. She comes closer. She studies it carefully without touching it.

'The scourge of woman,' she says without taking her eyes off his cock, 'and most of us have fallen victim to it in one way or another. Me, I was raped when I was fifteen, and then over and over again by my dear husband, the cop, although he had no idea about it afterwards, of course.'

Hjelm feels himself going limp, all at once.

'Come here and lie down,' she says.

He lies down next to her and closes his eyes. She lightly touches the blemish on his cheek. He lets everything happen.

'Can you forgive me?' she asks him softly. She sounds like a little girl.

He nods; his eyes are still closed. He hasn't stopped feeling like a little boy.

'Look,' she says in the same bright voice. 'Now the blemish looks like a tiny cross.'

He smiles and understands.

And yet understands nothing.

But it feels good.

29

They were eating breakfast in the hotel restaurant when Chavez's mobile phone rang. Jorge answered it, then didn't say a word, and his face turned noticeably pale. Hjelm recognised that kind of phone call. He could guess what it was about.

Another murder.

Had they committed a serious breach of duty by neglecting to report immediately the name of Göran Andersson and provide his picture?

If they had reported their suspicions at once, would Hultin have been able to redirect the surveillance from the members of the Lovisedal board to those on the Sydbanken board?

Hjelm looked at Kerstin and saw that she was thinking the same thing.

Had their determination to wait until they'd achieved complete clarity and put together a perfect resolution, with all the ends tied up, cost someone his life?

The thought made his head swim.

But that wasn't all.

'Gunnar Nyberg was seriously wounded last night,' said Chavez in a subdued tone as he ended the call. 'During the Lovisedal stake-out.'

The burden grew heavier.

'Goddamn it.' Kerstin Holm crushed her liverwurst sandwich in her hand.

'How seriously?' Hjelm was stunned.

'I couldn't really make that out. Hultin sounded so damned angry. Nyberg's injuries aren't life-threatening, in any case. It was apparently at the home of the chairman of the board, Jacob Lidner, in Lidingö. Nyberg was on his way in when he was shot. He got up and went totally berserk, crashed through a big fucking hedge and charged the gunman's speeding car with his own body.'

Hjelm couldn't suppress a slightly hysterical hoot of laughter. 'Sounds like Nyberg. It sure does.'

'Tackling the car did the trick too. The gunman drove right into a lamp post. Söderstedt pulled the guy out just before the car caught fire.'

'Do modern vehicles really catch fire?' said Hjelm, puzzled.

'You'll never guess who the gunman was,' said Chavez.

'Let's not play guessing games,' said Holm.

'The sole surviving Igor. Alexander Bryusov.'

'You've got to be kidding!' shouted Hjelm. 'What the hell was he doing there?'

'And there was another murder, wasn't there?' Holm said calmly.

Chavez nodded. 'In Göteborg. And he was a member of Sydbanken's board of directors, *anno* 1990. Ulf Axelsson was his name. A bigwig at Volvo.'

None of them said a word for a moment. Then Chavez went on. 'The worst possible scenario is that what happened to both Nyberg and Axelsson can be blamed on the fact that we didn't put in a call last night.'

Silence again.

'Although we'll never know for sure whether it would have helped,' he added.

Jonas Wrede looked a bit livelier today. He'd pulled himself together and helped to create a very clear and detailed sketch of the purported colleague from the NCP. The man who'd taken over back in February and buried the investigation surrounding the death of Valery Treplyov in the locked vault.

The face was staring up at the three officers from Wrede's desk. They all recognised him at once: fair-haired, powerful, hard-boiled.

The last time they'd seen him was in Nils-Emil Carlberger's kitchen in Djursholm.

It was Max Grahn.

From Säpo.

30

Jan-Olov Hultin strode with great determination through the corridors at police headquarters. He had two purposes in mind and no intention of mincing words. The two members of the A-Unit who were present, Söderstedt and Norlander, followed in his wake. Like the good, the bad and the ugly, they headed for the dried-out river bed of Bergsgatan with their hands resting on the butts of their revolvers while the rattle-snakes rattled in the background. It was impossible to tell which of them was the good, which was the bad and which was the ugly.

In a remote interrogation room sat Jacob Lidner, chairman of the board for the Lovisedal conglomerate. He sprang to his feet as soon as the heroic trio entered the room.

'What the hell is the meaning of this, detective inspector? Why have you brought me here against my will, interrupting my breakfast and throwing me into a damn prison cell? Do you know who I am?'

'Sit down and shut up,' Hultin said, his tone expressionless as he took a seat.

Jacob Lidner gasped. 'How dare you—' he managed to sputter.

'Sit down!' shouted Hultin. This was his territory.

Lidner sank down onto the chair. Hultin continued:

'When you stated that Lovisedal had resisted all pressure from the Russian mafia, that was a lie, wasn't it?'

'No, it wasn't. We haven't accepted any form of protection.' Lidner held his head high.

Hultin took a deep breath and controlled himself. 'What the hell was Alexander Bryusov, a member of the Russian mafia, doing outside your villa last night?'

'I don't know anything about that,' Lidner insisted.

'He shot one of my men!'

'I'm truly sorry about that, but it has nothing to do with me. I'm grateful for the police protection. It was probably me he was after. Now you have your mafia murderer.'

Hultin stared at Jacob Lidner, displaying a deep and sincere hatred. Söderstedt and Norlander exchanged surprised glances. Lidner, although a bit subdued, maintained his well-practised defensive posture.

'Let me tell you how this whole thing went down,' said Hultin between clenched teeth. 'You accepted our theory that the Lovisedal board might be in the danger zone, even though you knew that the Russian mafia was not to blame, for the simple reason that you're already closely connected to those crooks. But you didn't trust my men's ability to provide sufficient surveillance, so you brought in some extra life insurance, in the form of a mafia member to keep watch in the garden. Bryusov was also in your debt because you paid the superstar lawyer Reynold Rangsmyhr to defend him and then saw to it that Bryusov was able to disappear while still inside the courthouse. You posted him in the garden, with orders to shoot anything that was the least bit suspicious and then erase all traces. He knew that Söderstedt here was inside your house, so when another man, a giant of a guy not unlike Bryusov's former colleague Valery Treplyov, came into the garden, he opened fire, in accordance with his orders. Fortunately, if I can say such a thing, it was Gunnar Nyberg that he shot, and one shot wasn't enough to bring him down. The bullet passed right through his neck, but that didn't prevent Nyberg from stopping Bryusov. Do you understand what I'm saying? Your fucking illegal and amateurish attempt at surveillance almost cost one of my highly professional men his life!'

Lidner looked at him for a moment. Then he laughed right in Hultin's face.

He shouldn't have done that.

From their front-row seats, Norlander and Söderstedt witnessed something that would make Hjelm and Chavez jealous for the rest of their lives.

A genuine Hultin eyebrow-splitting headbutt.

He took aim at Jacob Lidner's bushy white eyebrows and slammed into him. The man's left eyebrow instantly split open.

Lidner stared in surprise at the blood dripping onto the table in front of him. 'Good God' was all he could say.

'Don't you realise that Alexander Bryusov has talked?' bellowed Hultin. 'Do you think I'm standing here bullshitting you for social reasons? So I can expand my "network"? The good Igor has told us everything about the close contacts that you and the Lovisedal conglomerate have established with the branch of the Russian-Estonian mafia headed by Viktor X. He's expecting to be the star witness, and he certainly will be. Your fucking tricks almost cost me one of Sweden's best police officers!'

Lidner was pressing his hand to the gush of blood from his eyebrow. He was now a different man.

'There weren't supposed to be two police officers,' he said quietly. 'There was always only one.'

Hultin stood up. 'You'll be remanded into custody immediately, of course,' he said as he opened the door. 'You'll be charged with the attempted murder of a police officer, but the later indictment will include much more. I'm sure I don't need to remind you to get yourself a lawyer.'

Out in the corridor Jan-Olov Hultin rubbed his hands together. Then the trio briskly continued to the most isolated section of police headquarters. Hultin had a card and a code that gave him access to these dimly lit passageways. He yanked open an office door.

There sat two solidly built gentlemen in their forties, wearing identical leather jackets. They looked up from their computers, and in only a second both men pulled out huge pistols and aimed them at Hultin, Söderstedt and Norlander.

'What a pleasant scene,' said Hultin calmly.

'This is a restricted area, Hultin. You have no right to be here,' said Gillis Döös harshly. 'Get out before we call the guard.'

'None of us is going anywhere until we find out what the hell happened with the investigation that Mr Max Grahn buried. The one where Valery Treplyov was found murdered and lying inside a locked bank vault in Algotsmåla, Småland.'

Döös and Grahn looked at each other.

'That's confidential,' said Döös, sounding slightly different.

'Since when do you have the right to pretend to be part of the NCP? And what the hell ever happened to the exchange of information? Do you realise how much you've delayed this case with your damned secrecy and your grotesque meddling? Do you realise how many of your precious businessmen have died unnecessarily? Murdered as a direct result of your actions?'

Max Grahn cleared his throat. Perhaps he turned a little pale.

'We had our sights on Igor and Igor long before they became relevant to this case. When that zealous inspector from Växjö called, we went down there at once; we realised that it was Treplyov that they'd found inside the vault. Igor and Igor were well established in that part of

Småland. We knew that a major Soviet infiltration was taking place in Sweden, and that it was as big as hell.'

'And you let us struggle our way through the whole damn Russian-mafia lead without giving us a single piece of information?'

'We've been working two lines the whole time,' said Döös, 'the Russian-mafia lead and the Somali lead. Both of these investigations are top secret, matters of national security.'

'What the hell is the Somali lead?' shouted Hultin.

'Sonya Shermarke, for God's sake!' exclaimed Döös. 'The cleaning woman that you've totally ignored. The one who "found", as she said, Director Carlberger's body. It turns out that she, along with a whole group of potential Somali terrorists, have been living in Sweden illegally. She pretended to be a cleaning woman and wangled her way into the homes of many influential families in Djursholm. We've been interrogating her and her cohorts for over a month now. And soon we'll have them.'

'Oh, now I remember,' said Hultin acidly. 'That's right! Seven Somali children, their five Somali parents and a pastor from Spånga. What an elite band! Sentenced to be deported, terrified and crammed into a little two-room apartment in Tensta, hidden by the local Swedish church. What a great coup. Seven children. Have you been interrogating them too for a month in your basement dungeon?'

'Do you know what a modern-day terrorist can use children for?' Döös said in all seriousness.

'For the sake of my incipient ulcer, let's drop the subject.' Hultin looked conciliatory. 'What have you managed to make of the blinded Treplyov in Algotsmåla?'

'Clearly a settling of accounts in the underworld,' said Grahn. 'Somebody wanted to take over Igor and Igor's territories. Mafia factions from the Soviet Union today are conducting a more or less open war for power in the Swedish underworld.'

'And the connection to the Power Murders?' said Hultin mildly.

'We're investigating the links between the Somalis and the Russians. We think it's a joint conspiracy based on old Communist values.'

Hultin stretched his back, still with a good-natured expression on his face. Söderstedt and Norlander feared the side effects of a well-aimed headbutt inside such a small space. Instead Hultin delivered a metaphorical headbutt.

'For over a month you've known that Igor and Igor were an important focus of our investigation,' he said gently. 'If nothing else, you must have seen the announcement of the manhunt published in the newspapers. You have wilfully and intentionally misled what the head of the NCP, as recently as yesterday on TV, has called the most important investigation in Sweden since the Palme case; in addition, you used the NCP for a highly irregular, highly illegal cover-up. All of these acts are not only a dereliction of duty, they are crimes. I'm going straight to the head of the NCP to inform him of your illegal activities, and I anticipate that both of you will be off the force by this afternoon, latest. You can start packing right now.'

'Are you threatening us?' Döös stood up.

'I prefer to think of it as a promise.' Hultin smiled politely.

31

Gunnar Nyberg was being fed through a tube. It protruded from the bandages that covered him almost entirely from the crown of his head to his neck, and large portions of soup were running through it. His eyes were the only things visible, and they were beaming with joy.

'As I've just told Nyberg,' the doctor explained to the three visitors, 'we've determined that, in spite of everything, his throat should heal completely. The bullet missed the carotid artery by half an inch; it missed the larynx by about the same distance, but it passed through the upper part of the oesophagus, just below the pharynx. He'll soon be able to sing again, but it will take a while before he can eat normally. In addition, his left zygomatic bone and left maxillary bone were shattered. He suffered a significant concussion and a number of bruises and burns on his face, and on the area from his shoulders up. He has four broken ribs, a fractured right arm and a wide assortment of minor cuts and burns over most of his body. But,' said the doctor, 'he seems to be in good spirits.' And then he left them alone.

Nyberg had obtained a little blackboard on which he could write messages in his wobbly left-handed script. '*Igor?*' he wrote.

Hjelm nodded. 'Alexander Bryusov. That idiotic tackle you made on his car uncovered the whole connection between Viktor X and Lovisedal, a very real connection. Bryusov is apparently going to be the star witness.'

Nyberg wrote, '*Not our man, right?*'

Hjelm had to ask Chavez and Holm for help in deciphering his scrawl.

'No,' said Chavez. 'Bryusov isn't our man. Our man is an ordinary Swedish bank teller by the name of Göran Andersson.'

The twitching under the wads of bandages could almost be interpreted as a laugh.

'We're conducting a nationwide manhunt for him now,' said Hjelm. 'But you may be back at work before he's arrested.'

Nyberg shook his bandages emphatically. The tubes that connected him to the surrounding machinery swayed alarmingly. One apparatus began beeping, as if in fear. He wrote, '*Damn it all, no, you'll get him in a couple of days.*' Then he erased the words and wrote a new message: '*Missa.*'

'Missa what?' said Hjelm.

'Is there something we've missed?' asked Chavez.

'Ah.' Kerstin Holm, who had been standing at Nyberg's

feet, walked over and sat down on the chair next to his bed. She took his hand, the only patch of skin visible in all that whiteness. She hummed a pure and clear note for ten seconds, then she began to sing. It was the lead alto part in Palestrina's *Missa papae Marcelli*.

Nyberg closed his eyes. Hjelm and Chavez just stood there, motionless.

When they returned to police headquarters, Hjelm found a fax lying on his desk. Since Hultin was waiting for them in Supreme Central Command, he cast only a quick glance at it as he headed out of the room. Not until he was out in the hallway did his brain register the name of the sender: Detective Superintendent Erik Bruun of the Huddinge police force. Hjelm went back to his desk.

'I thought it best that you hear this from me rather than in the media,' Bruun had written. 'Last night Dritëro Frakulla committed suicide in his cell at Hall Prison. At least now his family will be allowed to stay. Don't let this affect your work. You were just doing your job. Warm wishes, Bruun.'

Last night, thought Hjelm, holding the fax in his hand. What a strange night. Gunnar Nyberg was shot in Lidingö, Ulf Axelsson was murdered in Göteborg, Dritëro Frakulla killed himself in Norrköping and Göran Andersson was identified in Algotsmåla. And all of these events were vaguely connected.

What a small country Sweden is, he thought, realising

that he ought to be thinking about something else.

He was still holding the fax when he entered the room of Supreme Central Command. The other members of the A-Unit were already there. It was the first time he'd seen Hultin since they'd returned from Växjö.

'An outstanding job in Växjö.' Hultin gave him a searching look.

Excellent job, thought Hjelm, and for a moment he felt as if he was sinking into a pile of shit and had to stand on top of Dritëro Frakulla's body in order to keep his nose above the surface. He shook off the image, let go of the sweaty fax and sat down.

'Thank you,' he said.

'So outstanding that I'm even going to ignore the time between when you found out the perp's name and when you called in your report.'

Hultin's praise was seldom one-sided.

'Okay,' he continued calmly. 'The surveillance effort has been moved from the Lovisedal board members in 1991 to the Sydbanken board in 1990. Daggfeldt, Strand-Julén, Carlberger, Brandberg and Axelsson are all dead. Unfortunately, the board included an additional twelve individuals. Eight in Stockholm, two in Malmö, one in Örebro and one in Halmstad. The sole member from Göteborg has already been taken out. Of the twelve remaining members, we've located nine and set up surveillance for them. But one is out of the country, and two we still haven't found. Both happen to be Stockholmers: a Lars-Erik Hedman and an Alf Ruben

Winge. Finding them is our highest priority. An all-points bulletin was put out this morning for Göran Andersson's green Saab 900. It turns out that for almost a month it's been in the possession of the Nynäshamn police, without licence plates and with the VIN number filed off. The techs are going over it right now, but as is to be expected, the preliminary report says they haven't found any evidence. As for Andersson himself, we've put out a nationwide alert, and the most recent photo of him has been sent to all police districts and border stations. The question now under discussion at the highest level is whether to release his picture to the press and enlist the aid of that Big Detective, the public.'

'I think it would be a mistake,' said Söderstedt. 'As long as he doesn't know that we know about him, he's going to feel relatively secure about what he does.'

'Of course that's true,' said Hultin. 'It's just a matter of getting Mörner and the rest of the boys to understand that.'

'Do your best,' said Söderstedt. 'You do have a number of secret weapons.'

Hultin gave him a stern look. 'Our priorities are as follows,' he went on. 'One, locate Hedman and Winge. Two, check up on all potential Stockholm contacts that Andersson may have had, in order to find out where he's been living since February; we have that darts shop in Gamla Stan, but there must be more contacts, the darts association, or whatever else. Three, put some pressure on Lena Lundberg via that incident man in Växjö, Officer

Wrede. See what else she knows. Four, show Andersson's photograph around in the underworld.'

Hultin paused to consult his papers.

'This is how we're going to proceed. In Nyberg's absence, Chavez will go with the Stockholm criminal division to canvass the underworld; Holm will return to Växjö and accompany Wrede to check up on circles of friends and contacts that Andersson may have had in Stockholm; Norlander will check out the darts shop and the darts association, and afterwards, along with various foot soldiers, he'll check out hotels and apartment rental agencies for customers from around the fifteenth of February; and Hjelm and Söderstedt will locate Hedman and Winge. Keep in mind that you have access to the whole damned police force. And as usual, avoid all contact with the press and with Säpo. It's now twelve noon on the twenty-ninth of May. It's two months since Göran Andersson began his serial killings. Let's see to it that the number of victims stops at five, and that the case doesn't go on for another two months.'

Kerstin Holm went back to Växjö to 'accompany' Jonas Wrede, as Hultin had expressed it. He looked a bit jittery when she stepped into his office; he'd thought that he'd no longer have to be reminded of his sins of omission in the Treplyov case. But now he would have to spend yet another day in its shadow. Holm quickly discovered that Göran Andersson's circle of friends was largely limited to the darts club. Apparently he'd been the club's star, but even there no one made any real claim to have been his friend. And nobody knew anything about his possible contacts in Stockholm. She and Wrede went to see Lena Lundberg, but she didn't have the heart to 'put some pressure' on the woman. It was obvious to them that she knew nothing.

Jorge Chavez's excursions through Stockholm's under-world were not a success. No one recognised Göran Andersson's photo; he really didn't expect them to. Chavez thought he'd been given the shittiest assignment of all.

Viggo Norlander felt the same way. In the darts shop they had to look up Andersson in the computer files. The clerk behind the counter remembered the darts with the extra-long points, but nothing else. Andersson had always ordered his darts by post. At the darts association, no one knew anything at all about him, although they did find his name on a couple of local lists of results from Småland, always at the very top. Surprisingly, he never seemed to have competed outside Småland, even though several times he'd defeated national competitors.

Norlander finished off the day, with the assistance of a whole team from the NCP and the Stockholm police force, by going round to all the city's hotels and consulting the rental ads in the morning newspapers, as well as the free classified paper, for 15 February onwards. He got no bites at the hotels, but over the phone several people at rental agencies seemed to recognise the vague description of Göran Andersson. But when Norlander presented them with his actual photo, they all said they'd been mistaken. Norlander and his men stubbornly continued their search.

On direct orders from Hultin, the foot soldiers of the Stockholm police also went to the workplaces and residences of the Stockholm victims to show the photograph to colleagues, family members and neighbours. The Göteborg police did the same among the circles frequented by Ulf Axelsson. No one had seen Göran Andersson anywhere.

Söderstedt and Hjelm struggled to locate the other two members of the Sydbanken board of directors *anno* 1990.

Arto Söderstedt visited Alf Ruben Winge's company, UrboInvest, as well as his home in Östermalm. Nobody seemed especially concerned about his absence; apparently he would occasionally disappear from the surface of the earth for a few days at a time and then show up again as if nothing had happened. He had the pecuniary wherewithal to afford this type of luxury, as an astute employee expressed it. Söderstedt made a trip out to the archipelago, to Winge's impressive summer place on the island of Värmdö, but found the house closed up. And that was about as far as he got.

It had fallen to Paul Hjelm to track down the other missing former board member, Lars-Erik Hedman. *Fallen*, in a different sense of the word, was also what had happened to Hedman. He'd been the TCO union representative on the Sydbanken board from 1986 until 1990. At the time he was also a leading negotiator within TCO, with aspirations to become the union's president; he was married, with two children, and he owned an exquisite apartment in Vasastan. Now he lived alone in a two-room place in Bandhagen. He'd been thrown out of TCO and stripped of all board assignments. During a couple of years in the late Eighties he'd managed to combine a serious drinking problem with his work, convincing everyone to keep a lid on it. But after a number of bizarre performances in semi-public situations the union had lost patience, and Hedman was out in the cold.

Via the social-welfare office in Bandhagen, Hjelm traced Hedman to a park bench outside the state off-licence and roughly dragged him home to the man's filthy apartment. There he ushered in the police officers who had been given the dubious pleasure of protecting Lars-Erik Hedman's health – by definition, an impossible job.

Hjelm returned to police headquarters, certain that another fallow period in the case lay ahead. He hated the thought. Another dreary month. With the whole summer holiday frozen. And with an elusive Göran Andersson roaming the streets holding an aimed but invisible dart in his hand.

Hjelm was sitting in his office, staring blindly through the police building window at the other police building outside, when the phone rang.

'Hjelm,' he said into the phone.

'Finally,' said a quiet voice with an accent that made Hjelm instinctively switch on the phone tape recorder. The man was speaking a Småland dialect. 'It was hard to find you. A difficult switchboard staff. Paul Hjelm, the hero from Botkyrka. You've been given nearly as many labels as I have this spring.'

'Göran Andersson,' said Hjelm.

'Before you even think about trying to trace this call, I'll tell you the best way to avoid being tracked. Steal a mobile phone.'

'Forgive me for saying this,' Hjelm said a bit recklessly, 'but it goes against the picture we've formed of you that you'd call up to brag. It doesn't fit the psychological profile.'

'If you find somebody who does, let me know,' said Göran Andersson faintly. 'No, I'm not calling to brag. I'm calling to tell you to stay away from my fiancée. Otherwise I'll have to break even more with the psychological profile and take you out too.'

'You'd never be able to take me out,' Hjelm declared, contrary to all recommended psychological advice.

'Why not?' said Andersson, sounding genuinely interested.

'Helena Brandberg, Enar Brandberg's daughter. You could easily have shot her too and taken away the cassette, but instead you chose to flee and leave the tape in our hands.'

'Was it the tape that identified me?' Göran Andersson said in surprise. 'That couldn't have been easy.'

'No, it wasn't,' said Hjelm. 'How did you think we'd found you?'

'Because of the bank robber in the vault, of course. I was just waiting for that whole episode to come out and for you to start hunting me. But when nothing happened, I decided to proceed. Later he showed up in that police sketch in the newspapers, as if he were still alive. What was that all about?'

Why not tell him the truth? thought Hjelm.

'Säpo buried the investigation out of concern for national security.'

Göran Andersson laughed loudly. Hjelm was on the verge of doing the same. 'I guess their original intent kind of backfired,' Andersson said after a moment.

'Why don't you put a stop to all this and turn yourself in?' said Hjelm quietly. 'You've very clearly demonstrated your displeasure with the actions of the banks in the late Eighties and early Nineties. So why not stop? By now you know that we're watching every damned member of the board.'

'Not exactly . . . Besides, it's not a question of demonstrating anything; there have been so many coincidences that it's no longer a matter of chance. It's fate. There's a very fine line separating chance and fate, but once you've crossed that line, it's irrevocable.'

'What do you mean?'

'Don't you read the newspapers?' Göran Andersson said in surprise.

'Not very often,' Hjelm admitted.

ARNE DAHL

'I'm a folk hero, for God's sake! Haven't you read the letters to the editor? Getting a hangover without having had even a glimpse of the party is no fun. That's the mental state of Sweden today. Everybody who has the opportunity and authority to speak is telling us that we've participated in some sort of party, and now we have to pay the price. What party? So that's what I'm doing; this is the party, the people's retroactive party! Read the letters, listen to what people are talking about in the city! That's what I'm doing, and maybe you should too. But no, you're stuck in an enclosed space, and you think this case is playing out inside there. All the conversations going on in the city are about this. It's easy to see who's scared and who's cheering.'

'Don't try to tell me that this is some kind of political mission!'

'I've only been to one party during those giddy days,' said Andersson a bit more calmly. 'At the restaurant Hackat & Malet in Växjö on the twenty-third of March 1991. That's when I found out what the buying frenzy had done.'

'You're no people's revolutionary,' Hjelm insisted. 'This is all something you've invented after the fact.'

'Of course,' said Andersson soberly. 'Personally, I've always voted conservative.'

This is a very strange conversation, thought Hjelm. This was not the obsessed serial killer who sat and waited for hours in an empty living room, fired two shots through his victim's head and afterwards listened to jazz. The

380

mystery shattered into a thousand pieces, the myth crumbled away. *Misterioso*, he managed to think. Maybe the murders had somehow made him sane. On the other hand, maybe this was just the daytime version of Göran Andersson that he was having such a relatively normal conversation with; maybe the night-time version looked entirely different.

People, thought Hjelm, and then he said, 'Just one question, purely from a factual point of view. How did you get into the houses?'

'If you follow somebody long enough, sooner or later you'll have access to their keys,' said Andersson indifferently. 'Then all you have to do is make a quick impression on a lump of clay and grind your own key. It's no harder than grinding a dart point. And then you check out their habits and anticipate them.'

'Have you been following your next victim long enough?'

There was silence for a moment. Hjelm was afraid the man had hung up.

'Long enough,' said Andersson at last and went on: 'But we digress. I just called to tell you to stay away from my fiancée. Otherwise I'll be forced to kill you too.'

A question had been churning in Hjelm's mind the whole time. Would it be wise to ask? How would Göran Andersson react? He was even less sure after this weird conversation. Weird by virtue of its apparent normality.

Finally Hjelm decided to ask, possibly against his better judgement. 'If you've been in contact with Lena, then you must know that she's carrying your child. How does that child's future look now?'

Utter silence on the line.

After ten seconds he heard a faint click, and the conversation was over. Hjelm put down the phone, switched off the recorder, plucked out the tape and went to see Hultin.

'I've just talked to him,' said Hjelm.

Hultin looked up from his papers and stared at him through the half-moon lenses of his glasses. 'Talked to whom?'

'Göran Andersson.' Hjelm waved the tape.

Hultin pointed at his cassette player without changing expression.

They listened to the whole conversation. Once in a while Hjelm thought he might have been unnecessarily passive, and sometimes he'd been downright obtuse, but in general it was a lengthy and astonishing conversation between a serial killer and a police officer.

'I can understand your caution,' said Hultin when the tape was over. 'Although maybe you could have fought a little harder to get some leads. But in my opinion there are three clues here: One: even if we take that final silence to mean that he didn't know about his fiancée's pregnancy, he has apparently been in contact with her. She simply hadn't mentioned that particular detail to him. And with regard to the fact that he made contact with you so soon after you'd been there, it's likely that they've been in contact with each other before; it seems unlikely that their first contact after three and a half months would occur on the very day after you identified him. Holm is going to have to put the squeeze on Lena Lundberg down there in Algotsmåla. She knows more than she's telling us. Two: Andersson responds "Not exactly . . ." when you say that we're keeping watch on all of the board members. That may mean that Alf Ruben Winge is the target; he's the only one that we haven't yet located. We need to put every effort into finding him. Three: when you ask Andersson whether he'd followed his next victim long enough, he replies "Long enough". That could mean that he's ready to proceed tonight. Even though he was active in Göteborg as recently as last night. Okay, that's not much, but it gives us enough to go on. To summarise: we can probably find out from Lena Lundberg where Andersson has been staying in Stockholm; the next victim is most likely Alf Ruben Winge; and the murder is probably planned for tonight. I'll call Holm. You call Söderstedt about Winge. Use my mobile.'

Hjelm stood motionless for a moment; Hultin really was all fired up. He'd already picked up the receiver and called Kerstin in Växjö. He had almost finished talking by the time Hjelm grabbed Hultin's mobile from the desk and punched in Söderstedt's number.

'Arto. Winge is going to be the next one, maybe tonight. What have you found out? And where are you, by the way?'

'Here,' Söderstedt said dramatically, throwing open

the door. He switched off the mobile in his hand. 'I was in my office. What have you come up with?'

'Holm is going over to see Lena Lundberg,' Hultin said, seeming not to have noticed Söderstedt's grand entrance right away. Then he turned to Söderstedt. 'Who have you talked to about Winge?'

Söderstedt was quick to reply: 'His wife, Camilla, on Narvavägen; two secretaries, or rather office workers, at his company UrboInvest on Sturegatan, Lisa Hägerblad and Wilma Hammar; two of his colleagues at the firm, Johannes Lund and Vilgot Öfverman; plus a neighbour at the closed-up summer house on Värmdö, a Colonel Michel Sköld.'

'How hard did you pressure them?'

'Not particularly hard.'

'Is there any indication at all that anyone knew more than they were telling you? Think carefully.'

'A certain bitterness from his wife . . . Possibly a general sense of official secrecy at his company.'

'Okay. Do either of you know whether Chavez or Norlander has come back?'

'Both are still out,' said Söderstedt.

'Then we'll handle this ourselves.' Hultin stood up and put on his jacket. It's now . . . five-thirty. Someone may still be at the UrboInvest office; we'll call on our way over. If no one is there, then we'll have to look for them elsewhere. And we'll report all results, positive as well as negative, to each other via mobile phone. Avoid using the police radio. I'll try to get hold of Viggo and

Jorge and wait for Kerstin's call from Algotsmåla.
Everything clear?'

'No backup?' Söderstedt asked out in the hall.

'In due time,' said Hultin.

On the steps of police headquarters they ran into
Niklas Grundström from Internal Affairs, who glanced
at Hjelm. Hjelm automatically paused.

'Riding high on the hog now, Hjelm?' Grundström
said quietly.

'Or possibly wallowing in the mud with them,' Hjelm
said just as quietly.

'Go on up to see Döös and Grahn,' Hultin said to
Grundström. 'You'll find a couple of men who are really
in need of your services.'

Grundström watched them run down the stairs, each
headed for his own vehicle. Then he went inside and
fired the two Säpo agents.

They drove towards Östermalm, racing single file
through the rush-hour traffic.

'Vilgot Öfverman is still at the UrboInvest office,'
Hjelm reported on his mobile. 'He's expecting us. The
rest have gone home. I got an address for the office
worker, Wilma Hammar, on Artillerigatan. The other
two live outside the city. Shall I go and see her?'

'Yes,' said Hultin.

The three cars stayed in formation all the way to
Humlegården. Just before the intersection of Sturegatan
and Karlavägen, Hultin said, 'Kerstin reports that she's
over at Lena Lundberg's home now. She'll get back to

us soon. No contact with Jorge. Viggo is in Ösmo, of all places, checking out an apartment. He'll join us as soon as he can.'

Söderstedt and Hjelm turned right onto Karlavägen while Hultin continued for some distance along Sturegatan. After a few blocks Hjelm turned onto Artillerigatan, while Söderstedt headed towards Karlaplan and Narvavägen.

Hjelm rang the buzzer labelled 'Hammar' and was admitted by a polite male voice. The door on the fourth floor was opened by the owner of that voice, if a voice can really be said to have an owner. A pipe-smoking, solid-looking man, in what is usually called late middle age.

'Criminal Police,' said Hjelm, waving his ID. The man looked utterly confused. 'I'm looking for Wilma Hammar. It's urgent.'

'Come in,' said the man, then shouted, 'Wilma! The police!'

Wilma Hammar appeared from the kitchen regions, drying her hands on a tea towel. She was short and stocky and about fifty.

'I'm sorry for disturbing you,' said Hjelm hastily. 'I think you know what this is about. We believe your boss, Alf Ruben Winge, is in mortal danger, and we had the impression from our earlier visit that we hadn't heard the whole truth about his absence.'

Wilma Hammar shook her head, looking staunchly loyal at whatever the cost. 'He disappears for a couple of days every month or so, as I told the other officer. I'm not privy to what he does.'

'Periodic binges, if you ask me,' said her husband, sucking on his pipe.

'Rolf!' said Wilma.

'Do you know about the Power Murders—' Hjelm began just as his mobile phone rang.

'Okay,' said Söderstedt on the line. 'His wife openly confessed this time – she's quite drunk. He's got a mistress. I repeat, he's got a mistress. His wife doesn't know who she is, but she's expressed an interest in biting off the woman's nipples if we find her.'

'Thanks,' Hjelm said, ending the conversation.

'Do you mean that . . . Alf Ruben is going to be . . .' Wilma Hammar looked scared.

'The next victim. Yes,' Hjelm finished her sentence for her. 'Don't try to protect him out of some misplaced sense of loyalty. It might cost him his life. We know he has a mistress. Do you know who she is?'

Wilma Hammar pressed her hand to her forehead.

'I'm afraid that every second counts right now,' said Hjelm to prevent her from putting up any smokescreens.

'All right,' she said. 'But I don't know who she is. I've answered the phone a couple of times when she called. She has a Finnish accent. That's all I know. But Lisa would certainly know.'

'His secretary?'

She nodded. 'Lisa Hägerblad.'

'And she lives in . . . where was it? Råsunda? Do you have her address and phone number?'

Wilma Hammar looked them up in her phone book,

then wrote them down on a little yellow Post-it Note that Hjelm stuck on his mobile.

'Thanks,' he said and left. On his way down the stairs he punched in the number on the note. It rang ten times before he gave up.

Then Hultin called. 'I'm sitting here with the senior employee at UrboInvest, Vilgot Öfverman. After a little persuasion he's managed to come up with a first name and a description of the mistress. That's all he knows, I can guarantee it. She's short, has ash-blonde hair cut in a pageboy style and her name is Anja.'

'I can add that she's most likely Finnish or a Finland-Swede,' said Hjelm. He heard a beep.

'I've got another call,' said Hultin. 'Is there anything urgent?'

'The secretary in Råsunda. So far no answer.'

Hultin disappeared for a moment. Hjelm sat in his car, waiting in torment. Söderstedt came driving up in his Volvo and parked in front of him. Their mobiles rang. Both answered.

'Okay,' said Hultin. 'This is a conference call. I've got Kerstin on the line, as we used to say in the old days.'

'Hello,' said Kerstin from Algotsmåla. 'I've just had an intense conversation with Lena Lundberg. It's true that she's been in touch with Andersson every now and then over the past three months. She really fooled me. Andersson has told her only that he's involved in some-thing really important. As we suspected, she hasn't dared tell him about her pregnancy.'

'Get to the point,' Hultin said sternly.

'I'm going to have to be a bit long-winded to explain. Lena's brother lives in Stockholm, and the last time he was here to visit, which was only a week before the bank incident, he mentioned for some reason that one of his colleagues has a sister who's working in the United States, but can afford to allow her Swedish apartment to sit vacant. That was what Lena remembered, but she couldn't recall the name of the woman working in the States, even though her brother did mention the name when he was visiting. But the apartment is apparently somewhere in Fittja, and when she called her brother, she got the name: Anna Williamsson. The rest is up to you.'

'Good job,' said Hultin.

'How is Lena?' asked Hjelm.

'She's just beginning to realise the connection. She's not doing very well.'

'See you later,' he said.

'Don't go and get yourself shot,' she said, and was gone.

'Are the two of you ready?' asked Hultin. 'Hang up, and I'll find out the address.'

They waited, enveloped in the metal casing of their cars.

Hjelm's phone rang. But not Söderstedt's, as he noticed through the car window, so it probably wasn't Hultin.

'Finally,' Chavez said into his ear. 'My phone was stolen, believe it or not. I've just got it back from a junkie. What's going on?'

'We're hot on his trail,' said Hjelm. 'Where are you?'

'Sergels Torg. I've had a hell of a day. I didn't think Stockholm's underworld was so . . . big.'

'Hang up and I'll call you back in a few seconds. Hultin is checking an address. Göran Andersson's.'

'No shit,' Chavez said, and hung up.

Hjelm's mobile rang again. Söderstedt picked up his phone at the same time.

'Hello,' said Hultin. 'Anna Williamsson's apartment is at Fittjavägen eleven, fourth floor.'

Hjelm laughed loudly.

'What?' said Hultin, sounding annoyed.

'The hand of coincidence,' said Hjelm, starting up his car. 'It's right next door to my old police station.'

They drove in tandem over to Sergels Torg, where they picked up Chavez. He jumped into Hjelm's Mazda and was given a quick rundown.

'How did Andersson sound?' Jorge asked as they came out onto Essingeleden.

'Unpleasantly sane,' said Hjelm. 'As if he couldn't possibly be the killer.'

Hjelm was trying to make sense of the chronology of events. If the lead turned out to be a good one, then Göran Andersson had been living next door to the police station in Fittja while he was planning his crimes. He had gone in and out of the neighbouring door, and it was even possible that they'd bumped into each other several times in February and March. Hjelm wondered if he could have seen into the apartment from his old office. Then

Andersson had gone off to Danderyd to commit the first murder on the night before Hjelm, in turn, had gone into the immigration office to free the hostages. And while Hjelm was being grilled by Grundström and Mårtensson, Andersson had committed his second murder, on Strandvägen.

What was it he'd said? *'There have been so many coincidences that it's no longer a matter of chance. It's fate. There's a very fine line separating chance and fate, but once you've crossed that line, it's irrevocable.'*

Paul Hjelm thought he was close to crossing that line.

Even though they parked in the lot belonging to the Huddinge police force, it didn't occur to any of them to request backup from the station. They entered the building next door, went up four flights of stairs, and assembled outside the door labelled Williamsson. It was utterly quiet in the building.

Hultin rang the bell. No one opened the door. Not a sound came from inside. Hultin rang again. They waited a couple of minutes. Then Hjelm kicked in the door.

They rushed in with their weapons raised. The little two-room apartment was empty. In the bedroom they found a neatly made bed with a bunch of stuffed animals on the pillow. Posters typical of a girl's room hung on the walls. Chavez bent down and peered under the bed. He pulled out a rolled-up mattress, like a Swiss roll, with a blanket as the filling. Under the bed he also found a suitcase made in Russia. It was stuffed with bundles of 500-krona bills.

The living room looked just as unoccupied as the bedroom. The only thing out of place was that one of the shimmering pink posters was bulging out from the wall. It was hard to imagine that someone had been living here for over three months without disturbing anything. A clean saucepan stood on the stove. The inside was damp. A box was attached underneath the kitchen table. Hultin pulled it out.

The first thing that came into view was an assortment of keys, although all of them were blank, without notches or grooves, ready for grinding. Inside the box was another box, printed with Russian letters. Hultin put on a pair of latex gloves and opened it. There were the nine-millimetre cartridges from Kazakhstan, lined up in rows; not even half of them were missing.

Under the box of ammunition was a typed list of seventeen names. Hultin carefully picked it up and snorted an affirmative snort. Kuno Daggfeldt, tick, Bernhard Strand-Julén, tick, Nils-Emil Carlberger, tick, Enar Brandberg, tick, Ulf Axelsson, tick.

The last tick mark was next to the name of Alf Ruben Winge.

Hjelm went into the living room. He lifted off the poster that was hanging slightly crooked. Underneath was a dartboard. But there were no darts.

They searched the wardrobes and chests of drawers. There was no other sign that Göran Andersson had spent nearly three months living there. One rolled-up mattress, one Russian suitcase containing 500-krona bills, one damp saucepan, an assortment of blank keys, a box of bullets from Kazakhstan, a dartboard and a list of victims to be liquidated. Otherwise he hardly seemed to have been there at all.

Hjelm contacted his former colleagues at the police station next door and gave orders to cordon the place off, set up a night-time stake-out and have forensics do a sweep of the apartment. When they emerged into the early summer sunlight, a couple of cold gusts of wind reminded them that it was actually evening – in fact, it was almost eight o'clock. And they were going to have to start all over again.

Hjelm and Chavez called the secretary, Lisa Hägerblad, and this time she answered. She sounded resistant when Hjelm asked about Winge's absence. He didn't have time to tell her how important this was because she hung up. They sighed deeply and headed out to Råsunda to talk to her in person.

Hultin and Söderstedt drove to Stora Essingen, where Winge's younger colleague, Johannes Lund, lived in a villa with a view of Lake Mälaren. When they called him, all they got was his voicemail. They didn't leave a message after the beep.

Since Stora Essingen was located significantly closer than Råsunda, Hultin and Söderstedt arrived at their destination first. A man wearing overalls was walking up and down the steep front lawn, zealously fertilising the grass with a rolling apparatus that looked like a lawn-mower not very suited to the job. Visible in the opening

ARNE DAHL

of his overalls was a white shirt collar and the knot of a black tie. A mobile phone was sticking out of his pocket.

'Well, now,' the man said when he caught sight of Söderstedt. He stopped fertilising and leaned on the spreader. 'You weren't satisfied with what we told you?'

'Why didn't you answer your phone?' Hultin asked harshly.

'The landline is only for ordinary calls; they go straight to voicemail.' He patted his mobile phone. 'This is where I get the important calls.' He perceived their momentary silence as stupidity and clarified: 'The B-group of calls are recorded, and then my wife goes through them. The A-group come to me directly.'

And so does the A-Unit, thought Söderstedt. 'Look up at the sky.'

Johannes Lund looked up at the sky.

'It's now eight-thirty, and the sun is still up. In a couple of hours the sun will be gone. Then Alf Ruben Winge will also be gone. Do you understand? In a few hours your boss is going to be murdered by a serial killer who has already murdered five very prominent citizens much like yourself.'

Johannes Lund looked at them in surprise. 'The Power Murders?' he said. 'Oh shit. He's always struck me as a very *unimportant* person. This is going to give him a certain . . . status.'

'Tell us everything you know about these periods of absence,' said Hultin.

'As I said before, I don't know anything.' Lund cast a

pensive glance up at the Essingen sky. 'He's very suspicious of me. He knows that I do my job a damned sight better than he does and that I bring in much more money for him than he does himself. He needs me, but he hates me. That's it in a nutshell – hates me, but needs me. Whatever. He'd never think of sharing any personal confidences with me.'

'Does he have any close friends he would confide in?' asked Hultin.

Johannes Lund laughed. 'Good God! We're businessmen!'

'Have you ever met a short blonde Finn with a pageboy hairstyle who goes by the name of Anja?' asked Söderstedt.

'Never.' Lund looked him straight in the eye. 'I'm sorry.'

Hultin's mobile phone rang. It was Chavez. 'We're at Lisa Hägerblad's place on Råsundavägen. Do you have anything to tell us before we go in?'

'A complete washout here,' said Hultin. 'Unfortunately.'

'Okay.' Chavez ended the call and put his mobile in his jacket pocket.

They rang the doorbell. A lovely blonde in early middle age – *you might say, if it didn't sound so awful*, Hjelm thought fleetingly – opened the door, looking worried.

'The police, right?' said Lisa Hägerblad. 'I thought I already told you—'

'We don't have much time.' Hjelm pushed his way inside. He wasn't sure whether he actually apologised for skipping the normal courtesies.

Lisa Hägerblad's apartment was huge – three big

rooms with high ceilings. The furniture had been the highest fashion in the late Eighties: black and white, steel tubing, sharp angles, asymmetries, a slightly nouveau-riche chill. It was as if time had stood still in the apartment since the go-go years.

'You are Alf Ruben Winge's personal secretary,' said Chavez. 'It's as clear as hell that you know much more than you've told us. We can fully understand that you couldn't reveal anything in front of the others at the office. But now Director Winge's life is on the line; the threat is very real and very specific. He's going to be murdered within the next couple of hours.'

'Oi!' The secretary was evidently using her word for the ultimate shock. 'But the white-haired cop didn't say anything about that.'

'The white-haired cop didn't know about it at the time,' said Chavez. 'But the black-haired one does now. The situation has got darker,' he couldn't help adding.

'Come on now,' said Hjelm. 'She speaks with a Finnish accent, her name is Anja, she has a blonde pageboy hairstyle and Alf Ruben Winge disappears with her to a little love nest with sheets that get more and more stained a couple of days each month. Who is she?'

'I don't really know,' said Lisa Hägerblad. 'Everything you said is true. I often speak to her on the phone, but then I transfer her right over to Alf Ruben. I've never even arranged a meeting between them, and I'm the one who usually takes care of things like that. But have you talked to Johannes?'

'Johannes Lund in Essingen? He doesn't know anything,' said Chavez.

Lisa Hägerblad gave a short laugh. 'Sure,' she said. 'But since I prefer Alf Ruben to be my boss and not Johannes, I might as well tell you this: Alf Ruben Winge and Johannes Lund are like father and son. Alf Ruben has already chosen Johannes to be his successor and left him the company in his will. If Alf Ruben dies, Johannes will take over, and then we'll all probably be replaced by younger employees.'

'Do you know whether Lund has ever met Anja?'

'I'm positive that he has. They often have business dinners with their respective companions – meaning, not their respective *legal* companions.'

Chavez immediately called Hultin.

'Yes?' said Hultin.

'Where are you?' asked Chavez.

'We're going back to talk to his wife on Narvavägen to find out who his friends are. Right now we're in' – there was a crackling sound on the line – 'the tunnel under Fredhäll. Can you hear me?'

'Faintly. Turn round as quickly as you can and drive back to see Lund. He's going to inherit UrboInvest. I repeat: Johannes Lund will inherit UrboInvest if Alf Ruben Winge dies. He has every reason not to say a word about Anja. In all likelihood he knows who she is.'

'Okay,' Hultin's voice crackled. 'I've got the basics. We're heading back to Stora Essingen.'

Hultin hung up just as the car exited from the tunnel. He hailed Söderstedt, who was a couple of cars behind him, and they both turned round, re-entered the tunnel and drove across the bridge. A couple of daredevils were swimming down by the rocks of Fredhäll, where the setting sun was beginning to colour the waves red.

The beauty of Lake Mälaren made no impression on them. Even though they'd exited the tunnel a minute ago, it was as if the tunnel were still stretched out in front of them. At the end was the glimmer of a dark light by the name of Göran Andersson, but at the moment it was obscured by another dark light by the name of Johannes Lund. Söderstedt sat behind the wheel of his car, doing his best to keep up with the wildly speeding Hultin. He wondered, possibly with a certain anticipatory glee, whether Hultin was again going to make use of his rock-hard skull.

Lund was down by the water, smoking. The blue overalls were draped over the edge of the hammock. The hammock was swaying lightly, and the cloud of smoke, which kept gathering and then dispersing past the back of his robust neck, looked extremely pleased.

Hultin grabbed hold of the hammock as it swung towards him and gave it a yank. Johannes Lund toppled onto the lawn and got green stains on the elbows of his white shirt. When he saw the police officers, he didn't say a word, just quietly got to his feet. His expression was different now. He was ready to defend his inheritance, tooth and nail.

'Quick now,' said Hultin, his voice expressionless. 'Anja.'

'As I said before, I don't know anything—'

'If Winge dies, you'll be charged with being an accessory to murder. This is your absolute last chance to talk. If you don't, I'm going to arrest you and take you down to headquarters.'

'There's not a chance you can indict me,' said Lund calmly. He looked at his green elbows as he continued to puff on his cigarillo. 'I have no idea who this Anja is. And if at some time I actually happened to meet her, nobody ever formally introduced her to me.'

'Are you sure you want to do this the hard way?' asked Hultin quietly.

'Why not?' said Lund cockily. 'Go ahead and take me down to headquarters. I'll be released within an hour. And by then the esteemed Alf Ruben Winge will be dead. It has nothing to do with me.'

'You misunderstood me,' said Hultin as he butted open the man's right eyebrow. 'Going down to headquarters was the easy way. The hard way starts now.'

Johannes Lund stared in surprise at the blood on the hand he'd just rubbed across his forehead.

'Good Lord,' he said. 'My wife and kids can see us from the window.'

'And a fucking great show they're going to witness if you don't spit out Anja's name right this minute.'

'I thought police brutality was just something you read about in the papers,' said Lund, and got another taste of it.

Now he lay curled up on the ground, gasping for breath. Hultin leaned down, speaking calmly:

'There's a little too much at stake right now to be using the kid gloves. Within the next few hours we have the best possible chance of catching Sweden's worst serial killer in decades. After that he's going to slip out of our net. Today we happen to know who he's planning to kill. We're never going to know that again. And as you can tell, I'm not going to let your career plans save the killer. I realise that you see him as a tool that has suddenly appeared to allow you to take power at UrboInvest. I can even understand it. But if you don't spit out everything you know about Anja, you're going to end up seriously injured. It's as simple as that.'

'She has some kind of Finnish last name,' gasped Lund. 'Parkkila, Parikka, Parliika. Something like that. She lives in Söder. That's all I know.'

'Is her home their love nest?'

'I have no idea. I swear it!'

'No group sex orgies that you and some of your pals have taken part in?' Hultin said diabolically.

'For God's sake!' moaned Lund.

'Is she a prostitute? A call girl?'

'No. I don't think so. She doesn't seem like it. A completely different type. Very shy.'

'Thanks for your cooperation.' Hultin straightened up. 'If it turns out that you've been lying or withholding information, we'll be back to develop the essentials of this conversation a bit further. Is there anything you want to add or change?'

'I hope Cop Hell is big enough for the both of you.'

'I'm sure it's already very crowded,' said Hultin, and left him. 'Parkkila, Parikka, Parliika,' he said to Söderstedt as they walked back to their cars. 'Which is the most likely?'

'Parkkila and Parikka are both Finnish names,' said Söderstedt. 'Probably not Parliika.'

'Check up on Anja Parkkila and Anja Parikka in Södermalm,' said Hultin. 'And then all the other Parkkilas and Parikkas in the entire Stockholm area.'

Söderstedt called directory enquiries. There was an Anja Parikka on Bondegatan in Söder; no Anja Parkkila. There were six other Parikkas within a reasonable radius: three with the area code o8, two with o18, one with o175. Söderstedt scribbled feverishly in his notebook.

'What sort of area code is o175?' he asked.

'Hallstavik-Rimbo,' the operator said and gave him the address. That was the last of them.

'Thanks.' Söderstedt hung up and punched in the number for Anja Parikka on Bondegatan. No answer.

'Anja Parikka,' Söderstedt said to Hultin, who was waiting outside his car. 'Bondegatan fifty-three. No answer.'

'I'm going over there.' Hultin jumped into his car. 'How many others?' he shouted through the open window as he backed up from Johannes Lund's property.

'Six Parikkas. Three in the Stockholm area, two in Uppsala, one in Hallstavik-Rimbo.'

'Find out if the Stockholmers are relatives. Get Chavez and Hjelm to check out the rest. They're already on the north side.' Hultin drove off.

Söderstedt called Chavez. 'Her name is Anja Parikka, one *a*, one *r*, one *i*, two *k*s. Lives in Söder. Probably moved here from Finland. Hultin is on his way over to her place. Where are you?'

'Stuck outside the football stadium. Gnaget has just beaten Blåvit, strangely enough. Hundreds of hooligans are streaming past our car.'

Söderstedt gave them the 018 number and the 0175 number. 'Find out if they're relatives of this Anja. In the worst case, you'll have to go out there.'

'What's this 0175 number?'

'Rimbo,' said Söderstedt. 'I have the addresses. Call me back if they give you any trouble about telling you where they live.'

Söderstedt hung up and started checking out the three 08 numbers. Two in Skärholmen – fortunately, it was quite close; but one was in Hässelby.

The two in Skärholmen turned out to be brothers who had recently moved from Tampere, and they knew nothing about any Anja Parikka.

'Except for my father's aunt who lives in Österbotten,' said one of the brothers, speaking Finnish. 'She's ninety-three and deaf and blind, but still damned spry. Maybe she's the one you're looking for.'

Söderstedt cut him off and called the number in Hässelby. Irene Parikka in Hässelby Villastad was Anja's older sister.

'How old is she?' Söderstedt asked.

'Twenty,' said Irene Parikka. 'She's studying economics

at the university. Jesus, has something happened to her?'

Don't ask me, thought Söderstedt stupidly. 'Not yet, but there's a chance that something might. It's extremely important that we locate her. Do you know about an older lover that she might have?'

'There's a fifteen-year age difference between us. We don't have much contact with each other. I don't know anything about her love life, except that it's been rather chaotic at times.'

'And you don't know about any place where she might meet a lover?'

'Lover, lover! What the hell does that word really mean?'

'That's what this is about. So calm down and think.'

'The only place I know about is her one-room apartment in Söder.'

'Are there any other siblings, or are your parents still alive and living here in Sweden?'

'My older brother died right before Anja was born. Mama and Papa are still alive, although they're getting a bit senile. They live in Rimbo.'

Söderstedt gave her his mobile number and thanked her, as he saw the time slipping through his fingers. Rimbo was over thirty miles from Stockholm. He called Chavez. 'How's it going?'

'We've drawn a blank with regard to Uppsala. No answer at the first number; at the second we had a long and confused conversation with an elderly man named Arnor Parikka. An Icelandic emigrant to Finland who took a Finnish surname and then immigrated to Sweden. He kept claiming to be the father of Anja. But after a puzzling conversation it turned out that he'd been castrated by the Russians during the Finnish winter war. I was just going to call the number in Rimbo.'

'Do that. They're Anja's parents. You'll probably have to drive out there.'

'Shit,' swore Chavez. *Tempus fugit.*'

'And so should we,' replied Söderstedt.

He sat in his car in Stora Essingen, watching the final fading of the light – and with it any new ideas. He had nothing left to do. He sat there, utterly passive, with his hands on the steering wheel, feeling locked into a deep freeze. Time had flown, and he had absolutely no control over it.

It was past nine P.M. on the twenty-ninth of May, and in all likelihood Göran Andersson was already waiting somewhere for Alf Ruben Winge.

Söderstedt's mobile phone rang. He heard a clacking and crackling on the line, then Hultin. 'Anja's apartment on Bondegatan is empty. I picked the lock. Not a trace. The neighbours don't know anything. Viggo is here. We've found an address book. No mention of Winge in it, but plenty of names and addresses – seems like mostly friends at the university. We're starting to call them now. Do you know what's happening with Hjelm and Chavez?'

'No' was all Söderstedt managed to say. A terrible sense of impotence ran through him.

His mobile rang again. He made himself answer it

and heard Chavez's voice, which sounded strangely like his own: 'Couldn't get through to her parents in Rimbo.'

That was all. Göran Andersson was in the process of slipping through their net. The pace had been ratcheted up to maximum speed – and then stalled. The frustration was beyond comprehension.

When his mobile rang again, Söderstedt forced himself to answer.

'Hello,' said a woman's voice a bit shyly. 'It's Irene again. Irene Parikka. Anja's sister.'

'Yes?' Arto Söderstedt held his breath.

'I think I've thought of something,' Irene Parikka said hesitantly. 'Maybe it's nothing.'

Söderstedt waited.

'Mama and Papa have a little cottage in their allotment garden, and I think Anja sometimes uses it. Up on Tantolunden.'

'Do you have a specific address?' He started the car and wound his way towards Essingeleden.

'No, I'm sorry,' said Irene Parikka. 'I think the area is called Södra Tantolunden. That's all I know.'

Söderstedt thanked her sincerely – at least to him it sounded sincere – and called Hultin.

'I think we've got him,' he said calmly. 'A cottage in an allotment garden in Tanto. The area's called Södra Tantolunden. Belongs to the Parikka parents.'

Silence.

'Head for City Hall,' said Hultin at last.

Without having any idea why, Söderstedt drove towards

City Hall. Stockholm was almost deserted. When he reached the end of Hantverkargatan, Hultin was back on the line.

'Listen up, everybody!' he practically shouted. 'We've zeroed in on a cottage in Tanto. Rendezvous at the end of Lignagatan. We're going to handle this ourselves. Everyone head over there immediately. Except for Arto. I'll call you in a second.'

Hjelm stomped on the accelerator, and Chavez felt his torso thrust into the back seat.

They were the first to arrive. The place was desolate. Tanto was a rural black hole in the middle of the big city. Here and there a little light flickered in a few cottages up on the slope of the hill.

Somewhere up there was Göran Andersson.

They sat in the car in silence. Not a word, not a movement. Hjelm smoked a cigarette. Chavez didn't seem to notice.

A taxi glided up alongside the Mazda. For one brief, awful moment Paul Hjelm thought it was Andersson, come to 'take him out', as he'd said on the phone. But out of the taxi stepped Kerstin Holm. She jumped into the back seat.

'Straight from the airport,' she said quietly. 'Do you mind if I ask for an update?'

'Anja Parikka's parents have an allotment garden up there.' Hjelm felt Kerstin's hand touch his shoulder. Briefly, very briefly, he placed his hand on hers. Then they separated.

A Volvo Turbo came racing onto the truncated piece of road that was Lignagatan. Hultin and Norlander jumped out and got into the Mazda. It was starting to get crowded.

'Arto will be here soon with a map.' Hultin gave Kerstin a nod. 'And you're back. Good. I got hold of a guy in charge of the property records at City Hall. Arto is meeting him in the basement archives over there.'

'We're not bringing in any marksmen or anything like that?' Hjelm said hopefully.

'No,' said Hultin. And that *no* said a lot.

It took a while before Söderstedt's car came bumping along Lignagatan. He got out, brandishing a map. They all got out, and Hultin took the map and studied it.

'All right, people!' Hultin shouted. They gathered around. 'Here we have the cottage.' He pointed. 'Okay, can everybody see? It's on the other side of a small path at the very top of the hill. We can make our way up to this other cottage by the same path, if we're damned careful. It's the cottage right across, and also the one closest to our target cottage. The door is here, facing away from the Parikka cottage. That's our position one. One of you will go up there first and find out whether there's any movement inside the target cottage.

'There are a couple of other cottages nearby that look like possible sites for keeping watch, both on the other side of the target cottage; you'll need to make a round-about approach on the top side, here. One of the cottages is diagonal to it, on the opposite side; this one here, position two. And the other is right below, on the slope leading down to Hornstull Beach; here, position three.

'With these three positions we'll have the target cottage surrounded so that no one can go in or out undetected. Position one covers the entire front side of the target, facing the path. Position two covers the area above, as well as a good part of the back. Position three covers the area below and also part of the back. We'll put in our first man at position one. Then another will join him, since that's going to be our primary observation post. One officer at position two, and one at position three. Is that clear? We'll establish a rendezvous point at the very bottom of the hill and take care of liaison from there. That's where Norlander and I will be positioned, in charge of the operation.'

It was hard to tell whether Norlander was relieved or disappointed. Hultin ensured his goodwill by saying, 'Viggo's role is the most important of all. He's your closest immediate covering fire. Now, who's best at picking a lock quietly and quickly?'

The members of the A-Unit looked at one another. 'I can do it,' said Chavez.

'Okay,' said Hultin. 'You'll be the first man up there. Hjelm will follow you. When we reach the rendezvous point at the bottom of the hill, you'll head straight up the slope. It'll be a bit like mountain climbing at first; then it levels out. The first cottage you'll reach is visible from the rendezvous point. This one here.' Hultin pointed at the map and drew orange lines that glowed faintly in the night. 'Go past that cottage and three more; you can see them here. The path turns right, above position one; you should be able to see it after you've passed the fourth cottage. When you see the path, the position-one cottage will be right in front of you. All this applies to you too, Paul.'

'Question,' said Hjelm. 'Do we know that the three positions are all unoccupied?'

Hultin looked at him. 'No, but in all probability they are. Most people come out here only in the daytime to work in their gardens. But there *is* a chance that the positions could be occupied. If so, we'll have to make other plans.'

'Plus your route will take us across a whole bunch of allotment gardens. What if someone is home in one of the cottages and starts yelling because we're trampling their prize-winning tulips?'

'Cautious and silent pattern of movement applies, of course,' said Hultin, still looking at him. Could Hultin have overlooked all this? Hjelm wondered. 'Stay as far away from the cottages as possible. There's no question of launching an evacuation. Andersson would be sure to notice.

'All right, position two – Kerstin. Position three – Arto. You'll take off at the same time as Hjelm, after Jorge gives the all-clear from up at the first position, but you'll head left from the rendezvous point before making your way up the slope. You'll run into a small road, here, and follow it round. When the road intersects with the path, here, start counting: one, two, three, four, five, six, seven, eight, nine cottages. At the ninth, Kerstin will go straight ahead for three more cottages. The third one is position two. The door faces the top of the hill and should be completely hidden from the target cottage.

'Arto will continue along the road, past four more cottages, until the road starts climbing steeply. At the fourth cottage, after Kerstin has turned off, you'll head in too. Again it's the third cottage straight ahead. The location of the door is a little trickier and might be visible from the target cottage. Caution will be needed to force the lock in the dark without being heard or seen.'

Hultin paused, then nodded, and they all rushed down the grassy slope and into Tantolunden, which was remarkably pitch-black, an area of silent darkness in the middle of the noisy city's shimmer of lights.

'This will be the rendezvous point,' whispered Hultin, as he folded up the map and handed out small torches and walkie-talkies that he fished out of a shoulder bag. 'Use the earpieces. And keep your mobiles turned on, as backup, but for God's sake don't call each other unless it's a real emergency. The ringtone will be heard. And the torches are also only for emergencies. Do Jorge, Kerstin and Arto have adequate tools for picking the locks? If not, I've got some in our little emergency kit here.'

Each of them accepted their lock-pick tools.

'Okay, get going,' said Hultin.

Jorge began making his way up the slope and soon

disappeared from sight. They waited five long minutes.

Then they all heard Chavez's voice in their earpieces: 'Okay,' he whispered, out of breath. 'Position one has been taken. It's empty, thank God. Paul, the second cottage that you'll pass is occupied. A man is sitting on the terrace and looking out towards Årstaviken. You can pass him by going round behind. The other places are empty. As for the target cottage, here's what I can see: dark blinds pulled down in the windows. But there's definitely movement inside. It looks as if a light is on. Göran Andersson is here. I repeat, our man is here. Let's get going.'

'I'm sending in the rest of the troops now,' said Hultin. 'Don't do anything before everybody's in place. Over and out, for now.' Hultin's sign-off was surprisingly un-orthodox.

Holm and Söderstedt headed off to the left, while Hjelm followed in Chavez's footsteps. The man in the second cottage was no longer sitting on the terrace. He was poking about among his rose bushes in the middle of the night. Hjelm crouched down behind a shrub and waited for three minutes that seemed like hours. The man was a black silhouette against the darkness. He moved slowly, as if slightly drunk, among his precious roses. In his earpiece Hjelm heard Kerstin reach her position, then Arto. Their cottages were also empty. He heard them waiting tensely, but there was nothing he could do. Finally the man seemed to have had enough of his nightly wandering and went back to the terrace.

He belched loudly as Hjelm slipped past behind him and joined Chavez, who peered at him, wide-eyed, through the dark.

'What the hell happened?' he said.

'Your guy decided to fuss with his roses for a while. I was crouched down a couple of yards away. Is anything going on?' he asked, and then reported on his walkie-talkie that he was in position.

'No,' said Chavez.

Hultin's voice came over on the walkie-talkie: 'Good. Can anyone see an opening anywhere in the blinds?'

'Position one,' said Chavez. 'No opening from here.'

'Position two,' said Holm. 'None here, either. View of the target not as good as I'd hoped. Can only make out the top half of one window with a blind pulled down.'

'Position three,' said Söderstedt. 'I can see a slight gap with some light showing through on one side of the blind, but that's all. No movement visible in the gap. I'll let you know if I see anything.'

Hjelm turned to Chavez, who was nothing but a silhouette. 'How the hell can you tell that he's here?' he whispered.

'I could swear that I saw some sort of movement inside,' Chavez whispered in reply. 'And Arto can see a light. Oh yes, goddamn it. He's here all right.'

Seen from their angle, the little cottage on the other side of the path was dark. There was nothing to indicate anyone's presence.

The night was black and raw, the moon only a thin sliver that gave off almost no light. A few stars glimmered faintly in the background. It was like being way out in the country. *Göran Andersson's home territory*, thought Hjelm.

They were shivering in their darkened cottages.

They waited. Hultin was thinking on his feet down at the base of the hill. There was no real plan; that much was clear. The plan was taking shape as it went along.

'Should we make contact?' ventured Hjelm.

There was silence for a moment.

'It's most likely a hostage situation,' Hultin said pensively. 'He's probably sitting inside, holding Alf Ruben Winge and Anja Parikka. Making contact too abruptly could spell their death.'

'Why would he suddenly take hostages?'

'Because of what you mentioned in your conversation with him. Presumably Winge arrived with Anja. Andersson let Helena Brandberg live, even though it cost him the cassette tape. He doesn't want to kill Anja. He has his list, and he's going to follow it to the letter. Right now he's sitting in there with one person who's on the list and one person who's definitely not, and he's not really sure what to do about it.'

Silence again. A cold wind swept past the little cottage, blowing a few clumps of grass into the air, which tumbled about as if in slow motion.

'There's another option,' Hjelm said into the walkie-talkie.

'What's that?' said Hultin.

'He could be waiting.'

'For what?'

'For me,' said Paul Hjelm.

Absolute silence now. The small bursts of noise from the night-time traffic off in the distance slipped into the silence, becoming part of it. An owl hooted quietly. That too was part of the silence.

Chavez stirred. He'd pulled out his gun.

Time stood still.

Then a crackling in their earpieces.

'I saw it,' said Arto Söderstedt. 'I saw a gun in the gap next to the window blind. It moved past for a second. He's walking around inside.'

Time contracted. Long, muffled waves for each second that ticked by in their brains.

Hultin's silence.

The decision.

Still no sound from the little target cottage. But something had changed inside, not visible, but palpable.

Moving through the cottage was a presence, possibly several.

Then Hjelm's mobile phone rang.

A ringtone that was normally quite faint magnified itself in the silence to a mad peal of bells.

He answered as fast as he could.

'There, I heard the ringtone,' Göran Andersson said on the line. 'Very clearly. So you're in the cottage across the way. I've been waiting for you.'

For a good long moment Hjelm couldn't utter a sound.

Then he merely said, in an unrecognisable voice, 'Are they alive?'

'In the case of one of them, it's a matter of definition,' said Göran Andersson. 'The girl is scared, but alive. The other one already looked dead by the time he got here.'

Again silence. Chavez held his walkie-talkie close to the mobile phone. The conversation was being transmitted to the other cottages.

'What are you going to do?' said Hjelm.

'What am I going to do?' Andersson said sarcastically. 'What are *you* going to do?'

Hjelm took a deep breath. 'I'm coming in.'

Now it was Andersson's turn to be silent.

'All right,' he said then. 'But no gun stuck in the back of your waistband this time. And no walkie-talkie.' Andersson hung up.

'Jan-Olov?' Hjelm said into Chavez's walkie-talkie.

'You don't have to do this,' said Hultin.

'I know.' Hjelm handed his service revolver to Chavez, then put his jacket, walkie-talkie and mobile phone on the floor.

Jorge looked at him through the darkness, placed his hand on Hjelm's arm and whispered, 'Make some sort of noise for a few seconds when you go in, so I can get over to the left window. I'll keep watch outside.'

Hjelm nodded, and they stepped out into the night. Jorge stopped behind the cottage, while he continued on round the corner.

Wearing only a T-shirt and trousers, with his hands

raised, he crossed the little path between the cottages. Those few yards seemed endless. He thought he would freeze in the cold.

For a moment he thought he was running up the stairs to the immigration office in Hallunda.

The door opened slightly. No one was visible. Only the glare of a light.

He stepped onto the small terrace and slipped through the doorway. Seeing a little metal wind chime hanging from the doorpost, he purposely bumped his head against it. While it jangled, out of the corner of his eye he thought he saw Chavez crossing the path.

The light from the small ceiling lamp was actually quite weak, but it blinded him because his eyes had become accustomed to the dark. It took a moment before he could distinguish anything else.

On the floor in the far right corner were two figures, tied up, with tape over their mouths. Anja Parikka's pale-blue eyes were staring at him above the tape; Alf Ruben Winge's eyes were closed. She was sitting up; he was lying down, curled in a foetal position. Their bodies were not touching.

Along the wall on the left stood a small, unmade bed. *The love nest*, thought Hjelm without thinking.

On a chair just to the left of the door sat Göran Andersson. He looked exactly like the photographs and was smiling a bit shyly at Hjelm. In his hand he held Valery Treplyov's gun with the silencer attached. It was aimed straight at Hjelm's chest, six feet away.

'Close the door,' said Göran Andersson. 'And go over there and sit down on the bed.'

Hjelm did as he was told.

'All right then,' said Andersson, keeping the gun aimed at him. 'And the sharpshooters are swarming all over the Tanto cottages, am I right?'

Hjelm didn't answer. He didn't know what to say.

'Do you remember what I said I'd do if you kept pestering Lena?' Andersson said with a crooked smile. 'I just talked to her. From here. She's not doing very well.'

'That's hardly our fault, is it?' Hjelm said tentatively.

'My question was whether you remember what I said I'd do,' said Andersson, his tone a bit harsher.

'I remember.'

'And yet you still came in here?'

'You're not a murderer.'

Göran Andersson laughed loudly, but it sounded strained. 'A rather strange thing for a man to say with a gun pointed at him that's already killed five people.'

'Come on,' said Hjelm. 'I know you want to put a stop to this whole thing.'

'Is that right?' Andersson said calmly.

'I'm not really sure when that change happened. It's possible to pinpoint it to several different moments. Do you know?'

'No.'

'The first two murders were perfect crimes. You left not a single scrap of evidence. Carried them out with real thoroughness. Then all of a sudden, in Carlberger's living room, as you stood there wrapped in that marvellous music and pulling the slugs out of the wall with your tweezers, something happened. You left a bullet behind. Was that when you started to think about things?'

'Go on.' Göran Andersson's face was impassive.

'Then you took a long break, which made us draw a lot of erroneous conclusions. You could have stopped there and returned home to your pregnant wife.'

'Is that actually what you think?'

'Not really,' said Hjelm. 'No one who shoots another human being will ever be the same. Believe me, I know. But it's still possible to go on living. Put down your gun, and you'll get to see your child grow up.'

'Cut that out, and go on.'

'Okay. It took some time for you to plan the first three murders in such an elegant fashion. The victims had to come home late and alone, and within a reasonably tight time frame. It took two days in both cases. Then you had to plan the rest. Although I wonder whether you really needed a month and a half for the planning, from the early-morning hours of April the third until the early-morning hours of May the eighteenth. What were you doing all that time? Hesitating? Pondering?'

'Mostly I was listening. As I told you on the phone. I travelled around on public transportation back and forth, taking subways and buses and commuter trains. Everywhere people were talking, I sat and listened; listened to their theories and ideas and thoughts and feelings. Maybe you're right that I hesitated. But everyone's reactions made me go on.'

'One little question,' said Hjelm. 'Why the two shots to the head? Why such . . . symmetry?'

'You've been to Fittja,' Andersson said wearily. 'Didn't you count the bullets? Seventeen board members, thirty-four bullets. Everything fit together. Can you even understand how well everything fit? That ox in the bank gave me my weapon, the tape that was playing while I was getting beat up, and two bullets per board member. It was all so precise. And two shots to the head are the surest way to kill a victim if you only have two bullets at your disposal. It was as simple as that.'

'But then there was the cassette you left behind. Surely you could have grabbed it and taken it along, even without killing the daughter. But you left it. Why? It was your great source of inspiration. And then what happened? Was it unbearable without the music? Did it force you to look deep into your heart?

'And then the conversation with me, which you very deliberately sprinkled with the clues. And finally this. You knew all about Winge's habits, you knew that he'd be coming out here with Anja. And you knew that you wouldn't be able to kill Anja. You sat here as usual, waiting for your victim to arrive. Maybe they'd gone out for a walk, left their love nest and gone to a restaurant, and then you slipped inside. But this isn't the usual living room. You knew very well that Winge wouldn't be coming here alone. You set yourself up for this situation.

It's your own, possibly subconscious, but very intentional creation. You wanted to bring me in here. Why me? And why did you want this particular situation?'

Göran Andersson stared at him. Only now did Hjelm notice how tremendously tired the man looked. Tired of everything.

'There are so many reasons,' Andersson said. 'All the strange connections that have landed me here. Coincidences piling up that I thought were fate. Maybe that's what I still think. But without the music, the mystery disappeared. And you, you in particular, Paul Hjelm, were the final nail in the coffin. The empty apartment that I heard about turned out to be right next door to the police station in Fittja. Okay, that was to be expected; it was part of the overriding pattern. The fact that the hostage drama took place out there, at the very same time as my first murder, and that it stole all the media attention from me . . . that was also only natural. Everything was conspiring.

'But later, when it turned out that *you* had been out to my house in Algotsmåla and talked to Lena, that *you* were the one who was hunting me, then I realised that our fates were interlinked, yours and mine. I know that you were about to lose your job because of that hostage drama. I know that you, just like me a few months earlier, stood in your terraced house in Norsborg and looked at yourself in the mirror, but saw no reflection. I know that you felt the ground being ripped out from under your feet. I know that you were dangling in mid-air and wishing death on the police top brass because they didn't back you up, but just hovered somewhere high over your head. Maybe you even thought about killing the whole lot of them.

'Don't you understand how alike we are? We're just two ordinary Swedes that time has left behind. Nothing we believed in exists any more. Everything has changed, and we haven't been able to keep up, Paul. We signed up for a static world, the most Swedish of all characteristics. With our mother's milk we imbibed the idea that everything would always remain the same. We're the paper that people reuse because they think it's blank. And maybe it is. Completely blank.'

Göran Andersson stood up and went on.

'The next time you look at yourself in the mirror, it'll be me that you see, Paul. In you I will live on.'

Paul Hjelm sat mutely on the bed. There was nothing to say. There was nothing he could possibly say.

'If you'll excuse me,' said Göran Andersson, 'I've got a darts game to finish.'

He took out of his pocket a measuring tape and a dart. He placed the dart on the table in front of him, and with the gun still aimed at Hjelm, he eased over to the two figures in the corner. From Alf Ruben Winge's passive, corpulent body he measured a specific length, and then drew a mark on the floor a short distance from the chair. Then he sat down again, put the measuring tape on the table and picked up the dart, weighing it in his hand.

'You know how to play five-o-one,' he said. 'You count backwards from five-o-one down to zero. When I hit that bull's-eye in the bank in town, I only had the checkout left. I still do. And I've never left a game unfinished. Do you know what the checkout is?'

Hjelm didn't answer. He just stared.

Andersson held up the dart. 'You have to hit the right number inside the double ring in order to get down to zero. That's what I'm going to do now. But the game doesn't usually go on for four months.'

He stood up and went over to the mark on the floor.

'Ninety-three and three-quarter inches. The same distance that I measured in the living rooms.'

He raised the dart towards Hjelm. Hjelm merely watched. Anja Parikka stared wildly. Even Winge had opened his eyes. They were fixed on the dart.

'The same dart that I pulled out of the bull's-eye back home in Algotsmåla on February the fifteenth,' he said. 'It's time for the checkout.'

He raised the dart, aimed and hurled at the spare tyre that was Alf Ruben Winge's stomach. The dart stuck in his paunch. Winge's eyes opened wide. Not a sound slipped out from under the tape.

'The double ring,' said Göran Andersson. 'Checkout. The game is over. It was certainly a long one.'

He went over to Hjelm and crouched down a short distance from the bed. The gun was still aimed at Hjelm.

'When I play,' said Göran Andersson lightly, 'I'm a very focused person. When the game is over, I'm very ordinary. The tension is released. I can go back to daily life with renewed energy.'

Hjelm still couldn't get a sound across his lips.

'And daily life,' said Göran Andersson, 'daily life involves dying. I'd like you to grab my body when I fall.'

He stuck the silencer into his mouth. Hjelm couldn't move. *The hostage hero turned to stone*, he managed to think.

'Checkout,' Göran Andersson said thickly.

The shot was fired.

But the report was louder than it should have been.

Andersson fell forward. Hjelm caught his body. He thought the blood running over him was his own.

He looked up at the window above Anja and Winge. Shattered glass was everywhere. The blind had been pulverised. Jorge Chavez stuck his black head into the room.

'The shoulder,' he said.

'Ow!' said Göran Andersson.

32

Even Gunnar Nyberg was present. He was sitting in his usual place with his head wrapped in bandages and looking like the mummy in the old horror film. He really shouldn't have been there.

But there they all sat, ready to say goodbye to each other and return to the police stations in Huddinge, Sundsvall, Göteborg, Västerås, Stockholm and Nacka. It would be June in two days. Their summer was saved.

The mood was ambivalent. No one said a word.

Jan-Olov Hultin entered the room through his mysterious special door, this time leaving it open. They saw an ordinary cloakroom inside.

The mystery was gone, but the mist still remained.

Hultin plopped a thick file onto the table, sat down and set his reading glasses on his big nose.

'All right,' he said. 'A brief summary of last night is in order. Göran Andersson is being treated in hospital for his relatively minor shoulder wound. Alf Ruben Winge is being treated at the same hospital for an equally minor wound in his large intestine. Anja Parikka, not unexpectedly, was affected the most; she's in intensive care, suffering from severe shock. We can only hope she'll recover. What about you? Paul?'

Everyone exchanged glances, a bit surprised.

'I'm fine,' Hjelm said wearily. 'The hostage expert has recovered.'

'Good,' said Hultin. 'Tell us what happened, Jorge.'

'It was no big deal,' said Chavez. 'I made my way over to the window to the left of the door, as Paul and I had agreed. But I couldn't see a thing, so after a moment I slowly moved over to the window where Arto said he'd seen a gap. I got there just as Andersson went over to Hjelm. So, following a well-known example, I shot him in the shoulder.'

'Quite against the rules,' Hultin said. He went over to the whiteboard and drew the last arrows. It was a powerful diagram that he'd managed to create, a complex, asymmetrical pattern. Every name, every place, every event from the long and intensive investigation had been recorded.

Hultin stood there for a moment, studying his work.

'The beauty of the abstract,' he said, and came back to the table. 'And the filthiness of solid police work.'

He returned to what was solid.

'So,' he said, 'at least we achieved a final symmetry. Jorge's shot was fired before the stroke of twelve, so the case lasted for exactly two months.'

Söderstedt said in surprise, 'That means the case was

solved on the twenty-ninth of May, the anniversary of the Turks' invasion of Constantinople in 1453, which is the date of the start of the new era.'

They all looked at him so balefully that he shrugged apologetically.

'Thanks for that,' Hultin remarked. 'Well. One final question for those of you who live outside the city: are you ready to go home?'

No one replied.

'Do that, at any rate, and enjoy the summer. Then you'll all be coming back here. If you want to. As Mörner and the head of the NCP and no doubt many others who want to bask in your glory will tell you, the A-Unit is going to be made a permanent entity, although of course not under that ridiculous name.'

The former A-Unit members gaped foolishly at one another.

'The following applies,' said Hultin. Adjusting the position of his reading glasses, he silently read an official memo and shook his head. 'I was planning to read Mörner's memorandum to you, but I see that it's unreadable. I'll summarise instead. The A-Unit was, as you know, an experiment conducted by the NCP in order to avoid the idiocies that developed around the Palme murder case, with investigative groups that were too big, in constant flux and full of wasted resources. Instead, a small, compact core group was put together; officers who were prepared to work their arses off were invested with great authority to circumvent the standard procedures with entrepreneurial measures, so to speak, enabling them to focus all their attention on what was essential. The experiment was regarded as, and here I reluctantly quote, "at the present moment and in consideration of the contexts which as such, according to the aforementioned memorandum, expedited the ideal resolution of the present case, apparently satisfactory". In other words, Mörner is damned pleased. The A-Unit will become a permanent entity within the NCP and will focus exclusively on the hardest cases. At the moment that means it will be dealing with "violent crimes of an international character". What do you say to that?'

'Have you got a nice city-centre apartment for a wild Finn with five kids?' asked Söderstedt. 'I'm getting really tired of puttering around in my garden back home.'

'There probably won't be much time for puttering,' said Hultin. 'Am I to interpret that as a Söderstedt *yes*?'

'Of course I'll have to check with my family,' he added.

'Of course,' said Hultin. 'All of you will have a couple of free months to check with your families, and so on. We'll meet again on the fourth of August. Until then, you're on holiday, even though you'll have to be available for the prosecutor in the run-up to the Göran Andersson case. The fact that Jorge spared his life is going to cost the government millions.'

Chavez grimaced.

Hultin went on, 'Is there anyone here who wants to say right at the outset that they'd rather not continue with the NCP? You know what the wise man said: "Once you're in, you'll never get out. Except in an appropriate coffin." Stamped NCP.'

Nobody spoke up. Hjelm smiled.

'So be it.' Hultin stacked his papers. 'Have a wonderful summer. Provided that there's still some left.'

They stood up hesitantly and trooped out. Hjelm remained at the table, more or less incapable of moving.

Hultin picked up the cloth to transform his whiteboard masterpiece into a little spot on the fabric. He hesitated for a moment and said without turning round, 'Maybe you should memorise this outline and use it to replace the map of Sweden in your atlas.'

Hjelm studied the bewildering mishmash of arrows and squares and printed letters. There they all were. An insane and yet logical map of the mental fragments of a country. An unlikely constellation of connections among the various body parts, in the throes of death. A nervous system drugged out by money. An appalling diagram of spiritual decay and cultural veneer, he thought, laughing to himself.

Hultin frowned. 'Time has run away from us, Paul.'

'It's possible,' said Hjelm. 'But I'm not entirely sure.'

Neither of them spoke, allowing the pattern to settle like a screen over their retinas. When Hultin finally transformed it into a little blue spot on a cloth, it was still etched into their field of vision.

'Thanks for a great investigation.' Hjelm stretched out his hand.

Hultin shook it. 'You're a bit rough around the edges, Paul,' he said sternly. 'But you might turn out to be a decent officer some day.' Then he retired to his secret alcove. Hjelm watched him. Just before he shut the door, Hultin said mildly, 'Incontinence.'

Hjelm stared after him for a long time, thinking about football. A rock-hard wing back in nappies.

He went out to the hall, glancing inside each office as he passed, one by one. In each he saw a window streaked with rain. The summer had clearly been prematurely shelved. Maybe it was already over.

In the first office Söderstedt and Norlander chatted peacefully. The old antipathies, if not completely gone, were at least suppressed.

'I'm taking off now,' said Hjelm. 'Have a good summer.'

'Go in peace.' Viggo Norlander held up the palms of his hands with their stigmata.

'Come on out to Västerås this summer,' said Arto Söderstedt. 'We're in the phone book.'

'Maybe I will,' said Hjelm, with a wave.

Out of the next room came Gunnar Nyberg in his wheelchair, its arms forced grotesquely apart by the bulk of the giant mummy's body.

'You're allowed to laugh,' Nyberg said in his hissing mummy voice. Hjelm took him at his word. Nyberg continued to hiss as he rolled down the corridor. 'I've got my ride waiting downstairs.'

'Try to restrain yourself from tackling it!' shouted Hjelm after him.

Behind his back Nyberg gave him the finger, using his uninjured hand.

Hjelm went in to see Kerstin. She had just put down the phone. 'That was Lena Lundberg,' she said quietly. 'She wanted to know if she could come up here.'

'What'd you say?'

'That she could.' Holm shrugged. 'Maybe one of them will be able to give the other some sort of explanation. I can't.'

'Is she going to keep the child?'

'It sounds like it . . . But how would you tell your child that his or her father is a serial killer?'

'Maybe Andersson can do that himself.'

'If he lives that long,' said Kerstin, absent-mindedly emptying her desk drawers. 'Don't forget that he murdered a member of the Russian mafia.'

'Right,' said Hjelm. 'I won't forget that.'

He watched the aimless movement of her hands. He found it enchanting.

'What do we do now?' he asked at last.

She looked at him. He felt her marvellous dark eyes riveted on his. 'I don't know,' she said. 'What do you think?'

'I don't know, either. I've forgotten what daily life tastes like. Everything we've done has been in a sort of exalted state. How are things going to be between us when we come out of this little compartment? I don't know. It's a different world, and we're going to be different people. My life is in a rather unresolved state right now.'

She shifted her gaze away. 'Is that a no?' she asked.

He shrugged. 'It's a maybe. Maybe I'm going to need you terribly. It almost feels like that.'

'Okay,' she said. 'I've got to go back to Göteborg now, anyway, and take care of a bunch of things. I'll call you when I get back.'

'Call me before then,' he said.

They kissed. They were finding it hard to part.

'It could be,' Paul said as he left her office, 'that the pages in my dossier aren't blank after all. Even though they're being reused all the time.'

She shook her head and pointed to his cheek. 'Today the blemish actually looks like a heart.'

He went to his own office. He was met by the delicious smell of newly brewed, freshly ground Colombian coffee.

'Have time for one last cup?' asked Chavez.

'What do you mean, last?' said Hjelm, sitting down. 'I've bought myself a coffee grinder and a crate of beans.'

'Black-head coffee,' said Chavez.

'Yeah, well,' said Hjelm, 'I'm getting to be grey-haired myself.'

They laughed for a while. At everything and at nothing.

Hjelm still had a few things to take care of before he turned in his police vehicle. He drove out to Skog Cemetery and stood in the rain, peering through a pair of tree trunks at Dritëro Frakulla's grave. His wife was sobbing loudly and wildly, and Hjelm felt like a villain.

The little black-clad children clung to her black skirts. An entire colony of equally black-clad Kosovar Albanians followed Frakulla through the downpour to see him off on his last journey.

From his pathetic hiding place, Hjelm wondered how many people would come to his funeral. Maybe Cilla would manage to drag herself out of her personal crisis for a few minutes, he thought childishly.

Göran Andersson was alive; Dritëro Frakulla was dead.

He pondered the justice of it for a few seconds. Then he drove on to Märsta.

Roger Palmberg opened the door, using a remote-control mechanism. He was sitting in his wheelchair, looking like a pile of body parts amateurishly stuck together. Somewhere inside was the glimpse of a smile.

'Is it over now?' the electronic speech apparatus asked.

'It's over,' said Hjelm, then told him the whole story, from beginning to end. It took a couple of hours. Palmberg listened attentively, occasionally slipping in a clever follow-up question when he found a gap in the reasoning or a sloppily reported passage. There were many.

'Well, I'll be damned,' said the electronic voice when the whole story had been recounted. 'It almost sounds as if you've found yourself.'

'I've looked deep into my heart,' said Hjelm, and laughed.

Then they listened to Thelonious Monk for an hour, and Palmberg pointed out a number of nuances in 'Misterioso'.

Afterwards Hjelm drove back to police headquarters, turned in his vehicle and took the subway home to Norsborg. At the main subway station the headlines flashed at him from every news-stand: POWER MURDERER CAPTURED. IMMIGRATION POLICE HERO CAUGHT UP IN HOSTAGE DRAMA LAST NIGHT.

He laughed loudly, standing on the platform in the middle of the frenzied rush hour.

Role switch, he thought, and boarded the train.

He sat down near a group of people who seemed to be work colleagues; he wanted to hear if they were discussing the murders.

They mostly talked about their jobs at a small messenger company, about who had done what with the boss, about rises that had been given or not given and about people who had made fools of themselves in various situations. Only once did they mention the solving of the Power Murders case. They were disappointed. They had hoped for an international plot, and it turned out to be nothing more than a bank teller from Småland who had lost his mind. They were convinced that the police had made a mistake. Somewhere out there was the real conspiracy.

Maybe so, thought Paul Hjelm, and fell asleep.

33

It was late at night. Hjelm was staring out the window of his terraced house in Norsborg. The rain was still pouring down. Spring seemed to have vanished from the Swedish climate. It wasn't even June, yet it already felt like autumn.

Even so, the children were going out to the summer cabin on Dalarö for the weekend. To Cilla. While he had nowhere to go. Loneliness settled over him.

He was so unaccustomed to just being home. And being there without hearing Cilla's sounds in the house felt doubly strange. He'd been inside an enclosed space for two months and was finding it hard to come back. He wasn't sure he'd ever be able to do so a hundred per cent.

He missed Kerstin. And he missed Chavez.

He drank a can of strong beer and tried to imagine the long, long days ahead of him. Sometimes the holiday seemed more like a big, open pit instead. From total activity to total passivity in less than twenty-four hours. That was a difficult transition to make.

But maybe the holiday didn't have to be as passive as it had always been in the past. Maybe there were other things he could do. Besides, he was just starting to notice how abandoned he felt. And he needed room for that too.

He drained the beer can and went into the bathroom. He stood there, pissing into the pitch-darkness for a long time. As the stink of urine rose up from the toilet, the contours of the bathroom took shape around him. He saw himself in the mirror, a faint band of light around a darkness. *Like a helmet*, he thought. A protective helmet.

He waited as his face emerged from the dark. He was afraid of what he would see. But what he saw were not the Erinyes, and not Göran Andersson, but his own expressionless face, straight nose, narrow lips, dark blond hair cut short, a T-shirt. And a few grey hairs. Plus a red blemish on one cheek. The helmet was gone.

He ran his hand lightly over the blemish. In the past, as he stood in front of the mirror, he used to think, *No distinguishing marks, no marks at all*. Now he had one. For the first time he felt no hatred towards this facial defect, none at all. *A distinguishing mark*, he thought.

For a moment the blemish did look like a heart.

But at least it was himself that he saw, not Göran Andersson. And for a moment he actually liked what he saw.

He closed his eyes and saw instead the vast darkness.

Two months of accumulated fatigue washed over him. For the first time in two months he allowed himself to feel it.

He thought about Göran Andersson, about the fine line between them, and about how easy it was to cross it and never be able to go back. This thought of his came from deep inside that vast, all-encompassing darkness. But he himself was not in there. Not really.

The doorbell rang, one short ring, quite distinct. He knew at once who it would be.

When he opened the door, she was standing in the rain. Her expression was the same as that time in the kitchen. And that time on the pier. Abandoned. Infinitely lonely. But also so much stronger than his.

He let her in without a word. She didn't speak. She was shaking. He led her over to the sofa and poured her a glass of whisky. Her hand shook as she raised the glass to her lips.

He studied her powerful, small face in the faint light. The light flickered a bit, was about to disappear. That tiny, tiny flame of life. He made up a bed for her on the sofa and went upstairs to the bedroom. Everything could wait. There was finally a tomorrow.

He put his Walkman on the nightstand, slipped in the tape, crept into the unmade bed and thought of the millions of dust mites that he was cohabiting with. Every person a world, he thought sleepily, then put on the earphones and pressed the button to start the tape.

As the piano began its indolent strolling up and down, back and forth, she came into the room. She crawled in next to him, and he put his arm around her. They looked at each other. Their expressions were identical, their worlds so irretrievably separated. He felt her breath against his chest and heard the saxophone join the piano.

The mystery was gone, but the mist still remained. Misterioso.

The strolling duet had ended. The sax cut loose.

There's so much in this music, he thought as he fell into a deep slumber. A world had flown right past his nose. Maybe it was time to sniff it out.

The light went out.

He'd reached the zero mark.

Now only the checkout remained.